FORGETTING THE RULES

FORGETTING THE RULES

THE DATING PLAYBOOK, BOOK:5

MARIAH DIETZ

MD PUBLISHING, LLC.

FORGETTING THE RULES

For every woman brazen enough to be like Rose,
this one's for you.

1

ROSE

My phone rings three times before I manage to answer it. "Hello?" My voice is gravelly and deep with sleep.

"Wakey, Wakey! Time to get up! Beer. Breakfast. Let's do it. Get ready!" Chantay's voice is loud and boisterous.

I close my eyes. "When I invited you for breakfast and beer, there were also strippers," I remind her sarcastically. It was the end of a bachelorette party I attended for a yoga student of mine. I didn't know her very well, but she promised me a good time. By the time we got to the restaurant, many of the guests were too drunk to sit up after an entire night of dancing, drinking, and partying, so I called Chantay and invited her to meet me there since the restaurant had been privately rented out.

"I was up all night on a binger, and I need you, Rose. Plus, I told you I would get back at you for waking me up."

I lift my phone to see what time it is, and in the process, the romance novel Olivia lent me that I fell asleep reading tumbles to the floor with a soft *thump*. "It's not even six o'clock yet."

"It's close enough, and there are some good as fuck biscuits and gravy calling our name."

I rub my eyes. "I'll meet you in an hour."

"Nope. I'll be there in five to get you. Bonus points if you dress trashy, so they'll sit us in the back."

"You're the worst influence," I tell her.

"I learned from the best. I'm hanging up now."

I set my phone down, and for a moment, I consider staying in bed. It's Monday, the first day of our senior year of college, and I need to be at the school newspaper at ten, allowing prime sleeping time between now and then. But I have zero doubt that Chantay will make good on her word and be here soon.

I roll out of bed and rush to find a pair of jeans and a sweatshirt before brushing my teeth. I slip on flip-flops, grab my phone with my credit cards already shoved into the sleeve on the back, and quietly make my way across the small apartment to the front door. I glance around to ensure our cat, Juliet, isn't nearby, waiting to make a quick exit and slip out the door. I quietly lock it behind me and head toward the parking lot right in time to see Chantay drive up.

"You don't even look trashy," she objects as I climb into the front passenger seat.

"Looking like a hussy takes time, and you only gave me five minutes. Maybe next time, you'll give me a little more notice." I click my seat belt in place.

Chantay's cherry red lipstick is smeared, and she has heavy circles beneath her light blue eyes from her mascara. Her blond hair is a mess with leaves tangled in the strands, and her clothes are rumpled.

"Did you sleep with Bigfoot last night?" I ask, plucking a pine needle from her hair.

She smirks. "Don't be jealous."

"I'm trying not to, but your hair is making it kind of difficult not to be." I pull out two bits of broken leaves.

"I'm starving," she says, putting the car into reverse. "And trust me when I tell you I worked off *a lot* of calories last night." She speeds out of the parking lot and comes to an abrupt stop that jolts us both forward at the apartment complex entrance.

"I can't believe you didn't go out at all this weekend," Chantay continues, gripping the steering wheel and leaning forward to look both ways before gunning the engine and turning left through the red light. She whoops.

Five months ago, I might have laughed. But my addiction to adrenaline and the thrill fueled by parties and late-night romps have dissipated. I'm still trying to wrap my head around the change and understand if it's something I like or even want.

"I know," I tell her. "The real estate market's moving fast, and there was some new empty buildings downtown that I checked out with Gabriel."

Chantay cuts her eyes to me. "Ah yes, Gabriel, the infamous realtor. If he's got time to work on the weekend, he's got time to get laid on the weekend, which is what he should have been doing." She laughs. "I know you want to start your own company, but I can't believe you want to start *now*. We're seniors in college. This is our last opportunity to be lazy and unmotivated and sleep with any hot guy we choose."

"I'm pretty sure Lacy will always choose those things," I tell her, referring to our often third wheel when going out.

Chantay cackles.

"Speaking of Lacy, where is she this morning?"

The question wipes the smile off of Chantay's face. "She hooked up with Garett Feldon. Again."

"Again?"

"Three times now."

My eyebrows lift with shock. "Really?" Lacy has the same aversion to relationships that Chantay and I do, so anything more than a one-and-done comes as a surprise.

Chantay nods. "Two weeks, and they've been inseparable."

My thoughts slip to the memories I've been avoiding for the past couple of months that remind me of things I don't want to consider.

"Maybe she's not throwing in the towel. Maybe she's just hanging it up for a while." I shrug. "More power to her, right?"

Chantay shoots me a silencing stare. She and Lacy are best friends and often the devils on my shoulder—or maybe I was theirs? Fun is easy with them. Their privileged lives have given them little regard for structure, opinion, or even normality, which has often allowed an atmosphere perfect for excitement and fun.

"It won't last. We aren't girlfriend material. We were made for good times and better memories." She flashes a smile as she repeats her catchphrase.

"Don't give her too hard of a time," I say. "Maybe she just wants to try something else out for a while."

Another glare. "Who are you, and what have you done with my friend Rose Cartwright?"

I laugh maniacally. "It's still me, but some people are happier in relationships."

"You mean *Olivia*?" Chantay says her name with a note of disdain that makes the muscles in my shoulders constrict and my eyes narrow. Olivia is my best friend and roommate, and a topic that makes me feel like a starved and threatened honey badger. She and Chantay aren't enemies, but they're an ocean apart from being friends.

"Like Olivia and the rest of the world who are in relationships. Who are we to judge if it works for them and makes them happy? Everyone deserves happiness, whatever that looks like."

"You're such a hippy."

"My mom was the hippy. I'm a flower child. And you love it. Peace and acceptance to all." I lift both hands to flash peace symbols, then drop my pointer fingers on both hands, flipping her off.

Chantay tips her head back and giggles. "I've missed you, Rose."

"I've missed you too." I think.

"Also…" She turns in her seat so her full attention is on me, causing me to glance at the empty road as she continues to drive too fast. "I want to give you a heads up, girlfriend to girlfriend. Lacy isn't the only one looking to hang up her towel. Apparently, Isla is as well…." She pauses until I meet her powder-blue eyes. "This week-end, she was all over Ian Forrest."

The mention of his name has thoughts stacking like dominos in my head. I remain silent, knowing if one tips, they'll all fall.

Ian Forrest is the middle linebacker at Brighton University and

Roman God reincarnated. At six-foot-three, his broad shoulders make my tall frame feel small and borderline petite. His masculinity is softened by his messy dark hair and confirmed by his mesmerizing eyes—one a lighter shade of blue with gray accents and the other also blue but with hints of green—that are nearly as unique as the brief couple of months that we spent in an undefined relationship where truths and secrets were our intimacy. He managed to sneak into my life and routine. Then, summer came with news of him leaving for two months to visit his parents abroad. The announcement was shattering and relieving at the same time and led me to deliver a confusing mess of a non-breakup speech. I told him that I wanted him to have fun while in Italy, how important he had become to me—far more than I admitted to him or even myself—and how our relationship meant too much to potentially end or complicate with dating. In other words, it was a classy and eloquent friend-zone speech that I've regretted far more than I ever expected.

Isla Zimmerman is closest to Chantay. They met last year, and she joined our small circle, a willing participant in our craziest and dumbest ideas.

I work to look unaffected. Calm. Relaxed. Anything but how I actually feel, which is a confounding mess of jealousy and anger. "That's good," I tell her. "Ian's a good guy."

"He has this hot, broody thing going on, doesn't he?" Chantay asks.

At one time, I considered Ian to be broody as well, but last spring erased that term from all thoughts that pertain to him. He's quiet, intense, sexy, brilliant, driven, and the kind of alpha that most college guys aren't mature enough to embody because where they look to prove their strength and power with a punch, Ian does it with control. There's no bullshit with him—he's entirely and addictively honest and genuine.

"He's a really good guy," I say again.

"And you're okay with her dating him?"

I nearly wince at the term. "Yeah. Of course. Why wouldn't I?"

Chantay grins, slapping both hands on the steering wheel. "At least you're still sane. We may have lost two good soldiers, but we still have each other."

I suck in a breath and release it slowly to slow my racing heart as I think about last spring when my feelings for Ian were continuously questioned by my closest friends as well as myself.

Chantay and I park and are seated inside an old diner where the tables smell of bleach and sour milk, and the coffee is so weak I can see my spoon as I stir in the creamer, but they serve beer and the best biscuits and gravy in town, which leaves a lot of room for excuses about everything else.

When she drops me off at home, I find Olivia and her boyfriend, Arlo, on our couch.

"You're up early," Olivia says. "Is everything okay?"

I nod as I round the counter into our tiny kitchen, seeking fresh coffee. "I went to breakfast with Chantay."

"You went out for breakfast, and you're already getting more coffee?" Arlo asks.

"We had beer," I tell him, feeling a slight buzz from the alcohol. "I'm going to shower and get ready to head to the paper."

"Beer?" Olivia's surprise only slightly masks her disappointment. "For breakfast?"

"It's a long story." It's easier to say that than explain that I only drank half a glass and feel buzzed because I haven't drunk alcohol in months.

"Do you have anything this afternoon?" she asks, focusing on me now. "Do you want to hang out?"

"Yes! I recently read a review for a new Cantonese restaurant I want to try. We could do lunch or dinner since I only have the paper today.

"That sounds great. How about you go with us to the park cleanup, and I'll treat you to some dim sum."

I freeze with my coffee mug midair, still too far to drink. Arlo and Olivia have been trying to convince me to participate in the volunteering Arlo is obligated to do as part of Brighton's football team for weeks, but the idea of hanging out with a bunch of pre-teens and scrubbing at graffiti has had me doling out excuses. "How about we meet at seven, and I'll text you the name of the restaurant."

"Come on, Rose. We need you. We're short a volunteer, and it's just for a couple of hours." Olivia's voice is hopeful, laying on the first layer of guilt.

"I wish I could, but I can't. I'm allergic to kids," I tell her.

Olivia's expression falls, passing from disappointment to disgruntled, adding the second layer of guilt.

"I just had beer for breakfast, and I forget to feed myself some days. There's no way I should be allowed around kids. Especially not as a role model."

"She never said role model," Arlo says.

Olivia glares at him. "What he means is you're not giving yourself enough credit. You're a great role model. Your business goals and confidence are just two of your many traits that every girl should aspire toward."

"Exactly. And you'd be doing me a real solid," Arlo says. "Plus, Rae Rae and Poppy will be there," he says as though it matters, and surprisingly, it does. Raegan Lawson is dating Lincoln Beckett, AKA, The President, one of Arlo's teammates, and Poppy Anderson is her best friend. Over the summer, we developed a friendship that I appreciate far more than I expected.

Olivia's eyes lock onto mine. "Some of these kids don't have parents or any kind of support. You just have to help clean the park with them and hang out a little." She stares at me, looking right past my often salty exterior, and lays the final layer of guilt.

I take a sip of my coffee, burning my tongue. "I'm also ordering barbecue pork buns."

She smirks. "Deal." Her look of approval almost makes conceding worthwhile. Almost. Because I know Ian will be there.

I finish my coffee and hop into the shower, where the steam allows my past to sneak into the front recesses of my thoughts. Happiness and adventure have always been my true north. Some call me outgoing, others call me an extrovert, but everyone else probably thinks I'm too much. I've always danced to the beat of my own drum.

However, that drumbeat altered five years ago when my world came crashing to a halt. I went from attending parties every weekend and sneaking beer to becoming a gold medalist in worrying. Overnight, it felt like few knew me and less understood me.

That year and the one following, loneliness consumed me—day, night, it didn't matter. I was adrift at sea with no shore in sight. But two things saved me: words and my best friend, Olivia.

Words have always made sense to me. I grew up as a voracious reader, getting lost in the pages of stories that took me on grand adventures and epic romances that made me believe anything was possible. But I didn't want to be Lois Lane or Mary Jane Watson with wide eyes and a shock-filled expression as I waited to be saved. No, I wanted to wear the cape and the crown—I wanted to be the one who saved others.

I had it all planned out. I was going to graduate high school, take a year off before college, and join an organization where I could make a real difference. I wanted to get my hands dirty and see the impact of my hard work, not just attend fancy events for the latest trending charity and write checks like my dad.

I was going to be in the throngs, and I was ready.

Then, with one diagnosis, I wasn't.

It was the end of October during my senior year of high school. My biggest concerns were what costume to wear for Halloween and if my counselor would allow me to start classes after lunch since I'd already earned enough credits to graduate. My simple and easy life blew up with my mom's uterine cancer diagnosis. That's when my worrying began. Actually, if you ask my previous therapist, she'd tell you my anxiety started as a child, persisted through my teen years, and generally revolved around concerns about fitting in and doing as well as my older sister, Anna, who exceeds at everything.

While getting dressed and ready for my day, I recall the day my parents told me the news. It was one of the few times my mom refused to make eye contact with me. That night, my anxiety took form, closing in walls and darkening each possibility the future held. I dedicated my night to researching everything about my mom's diagnosis, determined to overcome my fears with facts and statistics. I even dared to go to the ugly and scary sites because I wanted to know our enemy so we could beat it.

The next day, I came out of my bedroom with my proverbial boxing gloves laced, ready with a long list of questions for my mom to ask her specialist and plans for what she'd need: rest, relaxation, healthy food, mint tea. I was prepared, and then my parents proved to me once again that I wasn't when they told me they were getting a divorce.

Cancer and divorce in neighboring days should never happen.

Yet, they did.

And everything else that shouldn't happen—that wasn't supposed to happen—did as well.

My mom moved into a condo the following week. It was newly remodeled and close to the hospital where she'd receive treatments. Over the next few months, all of the willpower and determination I had for beating her cancer became anger and resentment toward my father for carrying out the divorce and my mother's doctors, who told us there was little they could do except make her comfortable. What was left was distributed to my friends, who blissfully carried on with their lives, oblivious to how fast life can pull the rug out from under your feet.

We buried my mom on a cold, wet day in January. She didn't make it to see summer, her favorite season. She lost her battle, and so did I. I lost a lot that day, including my crown and cape, and any dreams of becoming a hero.

Two weeks later, while I was at one of my counseling sessions, which had begun shortly after my mom's diagnosis, my therapist insisted we start talking about my dad. It was a subject I aptly avoided and one I had no desire to explore. Her insistence led me to stop sessions within a couple of weeks with the realization that rules established boundaries which I clung to.

Arlo and Olivia are already gone by the time I leave the apartment, my thoughts still heavy with memories of that period in my life. As I head to my car, I think about how it was shortly after I stopped seeing my therapist that Olivia became an integral part of my life, though she deserves to be mentioned several chapters earlier in my life story. Unlike many who talk about meeting their best friend when they were in diapers, I met Olivia during our junior year of high school after she moved here to Seattle from Texas. She was my newest friend and one of the few who stuck around while I was quite possibly the worst version of myself. Somehow, she saw past my snark and scowls and loved me for who I was before I even realized who I'd become. She challenged me and provided me hope and friendship—two things I was desperately starved for.

I applied to Brighton University. It wasn't my first choice—which had included at least a couple of thousand miles between my dad and me—but it was where Olivia was going. Though I'd lost too much during my senior year, including a boyfriend, an intact family unit, and my mom, I'd gained a sister that year in Olivia and an entire set of rules so that if life served me another curveball, I'd be ready.

I began focusing my energies on goals that could be measured. Rather than being in the middle of the action and making changes, I decided I'd be on the sidelines, writing the large checks like my father so I wouldn't have to go through the messy red tape and failures that had already stripped me of my fight.

Meanwhile, my love for words spanned beyond books. I grew up reading the news, which sounds strange, but my dad wasn't fond of me bringing books to the breakfast table, so the next best thing was reading the many newspapers delivered to our house daily. When I began seeing my therapist, she suggested I stop reading the news because it "only fueled my anxiety," but by that point, I'd shelved my passion for fiction and focused on the realities of life. I preferred to consume news by reading it which felt more honest and informative than watching news anchors deliver stories about war, famine, and crime with a smile. My obsession for truth and reporting led me here to Brighton's college newspaper, *The Daily Dose of Brighton*.

"Hey, Rose!" Janet Chu greets me as I enter the newsroom. The familiarity of the space makes me smile and my dark thoughts clear. The desks and bulletin boards and the tiny office in the back where our editor will sit and yell, pretending like we're an actual newspaper staff—because that's how every editor we've had has acted in my three years at Brighton—allow me to breathe.

"Hey. How are you?" I ask Janet.

She smiles as she tucks her chin-length black hair behind one ear. "Good, but it sounds like there are going to be some changes this year." She scrunches her nose with distaste. "We're going to have assigned seats."

I don't tell her that this makes sense. Columnists and editors often rely on each other for insight and advice, and having them sit together, rather than yelling across the room like we always have, seems appropriate.

"Have they announced who the new editor is yet?" I glance toward Amita Patel, a fellow senior who will undoubtedly be making headlines after we graduate for the engaging and often thought-provoking stories she writes about uncomfortable issues.

Janet shakes her head. "Not yet."

The door behind us opens again, and Anthony Albright steps in with the same brown messenger bag over one shoulder and the same supercilious and arrogant smirk on his face. "Good afternoon. I know rumors are spreading about changes, and I want to take a few moments to clear things up with everyone."

Janet glances at me, her brows drawn low over her brown eyes reflecting the same warning bells that are ringing in my head.

"Yes, we *will* have seating assignments this year, and we're going to be moving up deadlines, so we don't have to fill any blank spots with fluff pieces that detract from the credibility of our newspaper. As you may have heard, I'm the editor this year and I'll be expecting more from you." He runs a hand over his sandy-colored hair as he moves his gaze to me, reminding me of how glad I am not to have slept with him sophomore year when I mistook his arrogance for intelligence.

Conversation explodes with shared confusion. Clearly, many of us expected to hear Amita named our editor, not this douche canoe.

He raises a hand to silence the room, but everyone ignores him for several minutes until he whistles. The sound makes my ears ring.

"Brighton doesn't fund the newspaper," he continues. "As I was saying, our operating budget comes from ad revenue. Local businesses buy ad space with the expectation that enough people will read what we write to see the ads, and cover their costs. Between the number of papers distributed and online traffic, we know readership is down. With only four publications each week, we're going to be working hard to make sure *The Daily Dose* remains relevant and grows in readers this year."

My frown likely reflects my disdain. Last year, Anthony was caught pilfering stories from his girlfriend, who attended another local college. He made his way onto my irredeemable list after bragging about the fact. Whoever voted for him to be our editor must have been drunk or coerced. Possibly both.

"Also, I've taken the liberty of assigning your columns. I'll post the manifest outside of my office. If you have any questions, you can request to schedule an appointment with me via the calendar, but it will likely be a few weeks since I have a lot of new implementations I'm working on."

"Implementations?" Janet mouths. "What a tool."

I bite my bottom lip to keep from laughing aloud.

"What about the seating chart?" another senior asks.

Anthony nods. "Already posted. You'll find a copy of it on the bulletin board that previously held article ideas and will now be a parking lot for updates. You're all responsible for checking there before you come to me with questions."

Snickers and murmurs meet his announcement, which has his eyes narrowing. Since my stint with therapy, I've been a bit obsessive when it comes to learning about psychology. The subject is right up there with local restaurant reviews, economics, and equality.

Last year, after working at the desk beside Anthony's for six months, I realized he checks every box for a narcissist, and he only confirms it now as he raises his chin and breezes past everyone's confused stares.

"Get moved into your desks. I'll be posting your sections in ten."

Teddy, another senior shakes his head. "That guy needs to get off his high horse before he falls, or someone knocks him off."

"Vile," Janet says before expelling a deep breath. "Let's see where we're seated."

I follow her to the bulletin board, skimming over the names until I spot mine—in the corner beside the printer. I stare at the sheet and then at the desk. It always sits empty, used as a catch-all for things people print and forget to collect. Apparently, Anthony doesn't think so highly of me, either.

"Where are you?" Teddy asks from over my shoulder.

I stab my name on the printout. "No man's land."

He chuckles. "Why did he put you over there? That makes no sense."

I shake my head. "He's trying to get in my head. It doesn't matter. I don't do most of my work here, anyway."

"And less now," Janet adds.

I nod. "Exactly."

"If he doesn't give me editing, so help me," Teddy says, eyeing Anthony's new office. "Did you sign up for entertainment again?" he asks Janet.

She nods. "It's my lifeblood. If Anthony messes with it, I'll help you spike his coffee with laxatives."

Teddy nods. "Deal."

Anthony opens his door as several students start arranging their desks, adding pens and sharpened pencils, and finding the right rhythm and balance to their workplaces. Without looking at anyone, he tapes a single sheet to the window outside his office and then quickly escapes back inside, closing the door behind him.

"I'm scared to look," Janet says.

I shake my head. "He's power-hungry, but he's not stupid. He wants the paper to succeed so he can take all the credit. He won't assign people columns where they're going to fail. His ego's too big for that."

Janet's brown gaze turns hopeful. "I pray you're right."

I nod confidently, leading her toward the list of assignments. "Janet Chu," I read her name. "Entertainment."

She releases an audible sigh. "Thank God."

"What in the ever-loving...." Teddy says, his gaze turning on me. "Since when did you want to write the sports section?"

"*What?*" I ask.

He taps the bottom of the sheet where my name sits beside my unwanted assignment. "I..." I shake my head, scanning over the rest of the names. "This is a mistake. It has to be."

"You didn't put it as a backup option?" he asks.

I swing my attention to him. "Do you think I'd forget if I had? I don't know a thing about rugby or football or soccer. I don't even know the terms or how they score or how much they score." Panic rises in my chest, pitching my voice.

"You have to talk to him," Janet says. "You know he's doing this because you refused to go out with him."

"What a pain in my ass," I mutter, marching toward his door. I wrench it open and take two steps inside.

Anthony sits behind his computer, his attention on his cell phone. "Rose?" he says, setting his phone down and looking at me obnoxiously calm. "Is there something I can help you with?"

I pull in a breath and count to three, trying to sound more diplomatic than I feel. "You made a mistake and assigned me the sports column."

He shakes his head. "I made the list myself. There are no errors."

"I've been covering international news since freshman year."

He nods.

"I don't understand. I've had multiple articles get picked up by local news stations. A couple have even trended on social media and made national news. I don't understand why you're assigning me sports when I won't be able to do it the justice we strive for here." I'm sucking up, and while it hurts and I'd rather be strangling Anthony, it aligns with his narcissistic personality.

Anthony leans back in his seat, and for a second, I see a flash of him twenty years in the future: his sandy-colored hair thinning and his face filled out and pudgy, making his eyes seem even beadier and more predatory than they are now. It's sad that he'll likely still be sitting behind a desk, holding far too much power and influence. There's no way he'll deserve it just as he doesn't deserve it now, but the way he exudes confidence makes people falsely believe him.

"Your roommate's dad is the head football coach," he says. "It makes sense. You have an inside connection that no one else here does. Use it."

"I have a tiny inside connection with football. That doesn't help me with water polo, cricket, soccer, or any other sports we have."

He shakes his head. "There's no cricket team at Brighton."

"You're proving my point," I tell him. "I have no idea what sports are here, and I know nothing about them. Someone else is certainly more qualified to write sports."

"If you want to stay on the paper, this is your assignment." He tilts his head and stares at me, silently challenging me.

I see more flickers of his arrogant future self, abusing his power over another unsuspecting victim who doesn't know how to counter his attack.

For a moment, I want to walk out and quit. After all, this extracurricular won't be a part of my future. I'm planning to build an empire centered around yoga and wellness, nothing near the realm of becoming a journalist.

I consider all the I've dedicated to the paper, my friends here, and how much I've learned, and my determination to argue with him wilts. He wants me to fight, I see it in his eyes.

"Fine."

His eyes flare with surprise as I turn on my heel and exit his office without another word. Hopefully, he's as clueless as I am about what I plan to do next.

"How'd it go?" Janet asks as she follows me to my desk.

"Apparently, I need to go home and start learning all about sports," I tell her.

She cringes. "I'm sorry."

I give a swift shake of my head. "I'm not. This is good—this is great. It will push me outside of my comfort zone and force me to learn about something new."

Janet's look of disbelief makes me want to admit how badly this will blow, but I'm determined to show Anthony up. "I'll see you tomorrow," I tell her as I grab my bag and head for the door, attempting to hold onto that ember of determination before it fades.

THE AFTERNOON SUN is round and brilliantly bright and warm. The maple trees on campus have the tiniest hints of yellow at the tips of their leaves, promising that autumn will be here soon.

I'm still staring at the endless blue sky, with a silent wish that summer will stay longer when my shoulder connects with someone else's, and my bag and my desire for an endless summer stumble to a stop as I come face to face with Ian Forrest. Seeing him causes my thoughts to blank and my heart to stutter in my chest as the dominos in my head teeter.

"I'm sorry," he says, bending to pick up my bag.

"No. I'm sorry. I wasn't paying attention."

He rights himself, a patient smile curving his full lips. "Neither was I. How are you?"

I take my bag and slide it onto my shoulder, trying to smother the hope that inflates in my chest as his eyes dance between mine as though he's trying to read more than just my expression.

"I'm well. How are you?"

He starts to nod, but a girl calls his name before he can reply.

I turn and see Isla Zimmerman speed walking toward us, her short floral skirt reveals her tanned legs, and her smile is so bright and flawless that I almost forget to feel jealous.

Ian's gaze cuts to me, his shock is evident as his gentle grin slips.

"Hey," Isla says, releasing a deep breath as she stands so close to Ian that their arms brush. "There you are." Her attention turns to me. "Hey, Rose. What are you doing?"

Seeing him with someone else stings more than I thought it would, and having it be Isla—a friend and one of the few people who knew that Ian meant something to me—makes it feel like a sucker punch. Still, I remind myself that this shouldn't be half this strange or uncomfortable. After all, things between Ian and me barely even began before they ended.

"I was just leaving the newspaper," I tell her.

"That's right. I forgot that you do that."

Likely, she didn't know. The four of us never talked much about school or our interests beyond boys and partying.

I force the biggest smile I can muster. "Well, I've got things to do, places to be. I'll see you guys later." I can't make myself look at either of them as I turn to leave.

My mom used to tell me that fake people are like pennies: two-faced and worthless. Too bad she hadn't told me how to identify them before they revealed their true colors.

2

IAN

My gaze strays to Rose as she walks away, immune to our first interaction in months. Meanwhile, my pulse races fast enough for both of us.

Being around Rose is similar to being stuck in a riptide. It's easy to confuse which direction is up and where the coast is. Instead, you get stuck riding the wave—until she tires of you.

Bitter? Disgruntled?

Marginally, but I'll proudly wear those titles because copping to anything more would be admitting that her easy brush-off after things seemed like they were headed to us being together, affected me more than I let on.

"Are you ready?" Isla asks, spinning to face me. She's the opposite of Rose in nearly every way, including her fair skin and blonde hair compared to Rose's olive skin and sleek chestnut-colored hair. Isla has a sweet and affable demeanor to Rose's cautious and often impatient disposition. Even their smiles are opposites: Isla's is fast and confident, whereas Rose's is often displayed in her gaze, making it harder to detect and somehow more rewarding.

Isla places a hand on my arm, her nails a Pepto-Bismol pink.

I shake my head. "Sorry. Did you not get my message?"

She lowers her eyebrows and reaches for her phone from her bag. "Sorry. No. I was in chemistry, and the professor's a tyrant about phones."

"We're doing a team-building slash volunteer event, so I won't be able to hang out today."

Isla's frown quickly becomes a grin. "Well, you can make it up to me later."

My initial reflex is to flirt back; with Isla, it would be effortless, yet I can't muster the energy even to crack a smile. I want to believe it's because everything is riding on this season. It's my senior year, and this is my last chance to get drafted, and I can't let anything or anyone distract me. I can't fuck this up. But there's an awareness in the corner of my mind that tells me this is only a fraction of the truth.

"I have to go. I'll see you later." I'm already moving backward as I say this.

I MAKE it to my truck and drive the short distance to Shady Grove Park. It looks like one of the many forgotten corners of our city with large overgrown trees, a broken swing set, slides covered in graffiti, and sparsely laid bark dust. The chain-link fence surrounding the park reaches my chest and is broken and cut in several spots. And to complete the dilapidated appearance, trash peppers the ground and follows the fence line.

Only half of the football team has arrived, but I find Luis Garcia and stop beside him. Luis and I have been friends since the fourth grade. While I'm close with several guys on the team, I'd spill blood for Luis.

He greets me with a smile. "Glad you made it," he says. "I think Coach Harris found the dirtiest park in the city for us to clean up. Watch where you step." He points. "That's like the tenth needle I've seen out here."

"Shit," I say, stepping over the uncapped syringe. "I thought this area was nice?"

"It is once you get about two blocks west," he says. "They just got a bunch of money in an attempt to regentrify the place. They've been working to clean this area up. Alexis grew up over here," he says, referring to his long-term girlfriend. "Her dad still lives nearby, so she follows what's going on. They just opened that strip mall with a bunch of fancy stores, and now they have a bus that runs for free to help people get to work, and they're building a new high school."

I didn't grow up rich, but I didn't grow up poor, either. My father worked as the attorney general, and my mom was an engineer at a small startup tech company that went public fifteen years later and made them overnight millionaires. Still, even the parks near where I grew up in a modest suburban neighborhood had play structures twice this size and more equipment. The most scandalous thing I ever found there was a used condom—fucking disgusting—but it pales in comparison to used syringes that kids could step on.

"Coach liked the attention we received from that beach cleanup last year. I'm sure that's what turned him on to this," Luis says.

It's true. Last year, Pax had us all participating in a cleanup spearheaded by the local aquarium and his sister, Raegan. Several news stations and newspapers showed up. We spent the first hour doing interviews and posing for pictures.

A news truck pulls up and parks on the opposite side of the fence. Another joins, and then another. I work to dispel the negative thoughts that make me wonder if we would be here if we weren't obligated.

"Welcome!" A woman with short, curly brown hair says. She's wearing a tie-dye shirt and has piercings lining both ears. "My name's Paige, and I work with Beacon Pointe. For those unfamiliar with our organization, Beacon Pointe is a place for kids of all ages to come and get help with homework and hang out. We're right across the street," she points to a large brick building. "this park hasn't been a safe place for the kids until recently. So we're excited to get this place thoroughly cleaned up so we can start using this space for games and activities. We want to thank you all for coming out and devoting your time.

"Today, you guys will be broken into four groups: trash cleanup, graffiti removal, debris removal, which will consist of leaves and fallen branches, and water cleanup. And to clarify, *no one* is allowed to get in the water. We're cleaning the bank and stream *only*."

Many of the kids have stopped talking and are listening to Paige with equal parts interest and intrigue.

"I just want to know if I'm allowed to tackle anyone who acts like an asshole punk," Luis whispers.

I glance at him. "That sounds like a winning headline."

Luis smirks and shakes his head. "Kids are assholes, man. Do you remember me at this age? Hell, if a bunch of college kids walked up to me and acted like they wanted to be my friend, I'd have been such a dick."

"You *are* a dick."

He flashes a quick grin, but in truth, Luis is far from an asshole. "Only when you keep cheating at poker."

I chuckle. "I wasn't even going to talk about what a sore loser you are."

He lays a hand across his chest as though I've maimed him. "Ten years of friendship, and you stab me in the back."

I pat his shoulder. "Let's see if one of these kids twists the knife."

"My money's on the kid with the red hat," Luis says, nodding to where a skinny kid is standing in jeans and a hoodie that are both too big for him.

"I'll take that bet. Twenty bucks."

Luis offers his hand. "Let's make it forty. I want to take Alexis out this Sunday."

I shake his hand.

"Volunteers, if you could please make your way over to Penny at the registration table, she'll get you a nametag and let you know what you'll be working on today," Paige continues, pointing both arms toward a table where a woman with purple hair is sitting.

Luis and I move toward her when long dark hair and the same sure gait I memorized last year catches my attention—Rose.

"Did I mention Rose has been hanging out with the team?" Luis asks, noticing my distraction.

"It must have slipped your mind."

He grins absently. "She's pretty cool, and it's senior year..." His voice trails off.

"Exactly. This is our last chance to be drafted. We have to focus this season."

"It might also be your last chance to hook up with her."

"I'm not going there," I tell him. "Not again. You remember what she told me?"

"No, because you never talked about it. Every other guy blasts his issues in the locker room. You take all your issues out on the field and run people over. That's how I know when you're pissed."

I rub a hand across the back of my neck. I prefer to keep to myself. Talking to the team about Rose or school or even my goals for this year aren't something I actively do. My younger sister, Cassie, calls me an introvert, and occasionally, someone who doesn't know me will call me arrogant. I don't really care what I'm labeled as long as they stay out of my business. "She wants to be friends," I tell him. "*Just* friends."

Luis squints with confusion. "Obviously, she's lying."

I can't stop myself from laughing. "Yeah, tell her that." I shake my head, hoping to dispel the conversation with a couple of carefully chosen words. "It's cool. I don't have time for a relationship this year anyway. Hell, I barely have time for classes as it is."

Luis nods. "I know. I hear you, man."

"Rose is a cool chick. There are no hard feelings. She did me a favor by eliminating all the drama that would have come out of dating."

"I'd probably call you a liar if I hadn't seen you giving Isla the brush off yesterday," Luis says as we join the rest of our team. "Alexis wants to set you up with her cousin. She sent me a photo to show you." He starts to reach for his phone.

"Tell her thanks, but no thanks."

"She's actually pretty hot. Don't tell Alexis I said that, but you know what I mean."

I chuckle. "I rarely know what you mean."

Luis laughs along, revealing his easy-going nature that has replaced most of his aggressive tendencies from childhood. He now reminds me of his dad, ready for a laugh and slow to the draw. "Alexis wants to double date."

I shake my head. "Not a chance. Do you remember when we did that group date to prom senior year? You ordered a fucking Caesar salad."

"That was years ago."

"You ordered it, knowing you were allergic to anchovies, and then itched your way through dinner and looked like a blowfish by the time we arrived at the dance."

He shakes his head, biting back his laughter. "Do you have to bring that up?"

"I swear I won't bring it up again if you don't mention double dating again."

"Deal." He shakes his head as his laugh recedes. "Your prom date was such a bitch. Do you remember how mad she was?"

"You blew chunks on her dress," I remind him.

"I had an allergic reaction."

"You spewed on somebody?" Lincoln Beckett, our wide receiver, turns around, his brow lowered. "Tell me you don't have the flu."

"Forrest is just reliving the past," Luis says.

Lincoln's gaze moves to mine. We have mutual respect for one another built on our devotion to the game and being two of the quieter guys on the team. Like me, Lincoln doesn't care if people like him because he's never trying to impress people. He's as authentic as they come, and that's the main factor in why I've become friends with his small circle, which includes our quarterback Paxton Lawson and one of our starting running backs, Arlo Kostas. Beside Lincoln is his girlfriend, Raegan, Paxton's little sister.

She glances at him. "Pax has a good story to share about throwing up. Want to tell them what happened to that old chair in our living room?"

Lincoln cracks a smile, but Paxton scowls, earning a laugh from Raegan.

"You skipped the bathroom and barfed on the furniture?" Luis asks him.

"Worse," Raegan says. "His girlfriend did."

"She'd probably shave your head if she heard you telling that story," Pax warns.

"She probably doesn't remember," Raegan counters.

"She'd still cut you," Pax says this with a grin like he knows he's hitting a button, only I can't tell if it's hers or Lincoln's that he's aiming for because Lincoln pulls in a breath and squares his shoulders, exposing his unease for the conversation.

"Hey, guys!" Olivia's Southern accent has us all turning as she, Rose, and Arlo join us in line.

"Hey!" Raegan's friendly tone only reiterates what Luis had told me, and then she confirms the fact as she wraps her arms around Rose. "Good to see you."

Rose smiles, but I see her nerves in the subtle differences as she avoids eye contact. She's uneasy around me, something she's never been before.

"I'm so glad Arlo was able to convince you both to come," Raegan continues, hugging Olivia. "I was worried since it's a four-week commitment that we'd only have five volunteers."

"Four-week commitment?" Rose swings her attention from Raegan to Olivia, accusations shining brightly in her eyes.

"It's a big park," Olivia tells her, earning another silent glare.

At this, Raegan chuckles. "Now that you're helping the team meet their quota think about what you can get in return. I'm sure you can convince one of these meatheads to give you an oil change, detail your car, get an invitation to an event...." She shrugs. "If you need someone to be thrown up on, we have two candidates."

Rose lowers her brow with equal parts confusion and revulsion. "I'll keep that in mind."

"I think this is a cool idea," Arlo says, peering around the vast, grassy space. "We get to be outdoors, helping some kids, and it's counting as our practice time."

Pax laughs. "Yeah, right. You know Coach will have us doing extra morning practices to make up for this."

"Don't ruin my mood," Arlo warns.

The easy flow of their conversation is infectious, and I find myself chuckling in response. While I tend to keep my friend group on the small side, these guys have all managed to get close.

"How was your summer, Ian?" Olivia asks. The others turn their gazes on me, but Rose stalls a few moments before looking my way. When she finally does, trepidation greets me before aloofness settles in.

"It was great," I tell Olivia.

Luis looks at me with round eyes and a silent *'now's your chance'* expression that is more lost on me than Rose's reaction. Before anyone can change the subject, Luis clears his throat. "I've got to say I was jealous. Beautiful city, beautiful beaches, beautiful women, this dude spent the summer living in paradise and rubbing it in with all the selfies he sent me."

I look at him, confused and annoyed because I didn't send dick-face a single damn selfie.

Paxton nods. "Color me jaded. I would have spent a summer in Italy."

The woman at the table with purple hair greets us by asking for our names and licenses, halting our conversation as we shuffle for our wallets. Rose is the first to hand hers over, and the woman wearing a nametag that reminds me her name is Penny begins filling out a form as we all turn over our licenses.

"You've got to make her jealous," Luis murmurs under his breath.

I close my eyes and try to swallow the plethora of curse words that pop into my head. I don't know why he can't get a fucking clue, and understand I don't want to make Rose jealous or play any other type of game.

"Rose, you're going to be on garbage duty. You can grab some gloves, a red vest, and an empty garbage bag over there by that tree and set to work wherever you'd like." Penny hands Rose her license back, and then for the second time today, Rose walks away without looking back.

"This might take more than dim sum and barbecue pork buns," Olivia says as Penny registers Paxton.

Arlo shakes his head, a wide grin forming on his face. "Like food could save you."

Olivia elbows him, and Arlo smirks. "I'm serious. It's Rose," Arlo says with a shrug. "She makes the best out of every situation. You're overthinking this."

Olivia frowns. "She had a bad day. Maybe I can get on trash and go around with her?"

I hate that I'm listening so intently, and even more, I hate that I'm considering what made her day so bad.

"Paxton and Arlo, you're going to be on water. Lincoln, you're on graffiti with Luis and Poppy. Raegan, you and Olivia are on debris, and Ian, you're also on trash pickup," Penny says before directing us to the different stations, but I don't hear what she's saying because I'm staring across the park where Rose is shoving something in her bag, her thoughts clearly elsewhere.

Fan-fucking-tastic.

"Where am I picking up trash?" I ask.

Penny shakes her head. "Anywhere you want. This park is ten acres and leads to the forest, but you aren't permitted to cross the river, as Paige told you all."

Ten acres. That gives me a little room to breathe.

Luis looks at me and then at Paxton as we step away from the table to allow more to get signed in. "I preferred your beach cleanup. This is too organized."

Raegan laughs.

Olivia looks at me with a smile. "At least you're with Rose. The two of you can catch up. I know you haven't seen much of each other since you left for Italy." Her words remind me that others besides Luis were aware of my interest in Rose.

Arlo reaches forward and pats me on the shoulder. "Fate's giving you a gentle shove."

I shake my head. "Don't even start with fate and curses and all of that bullshit. Not again." Arlo spent the first half of the year convinced he'd been cursed. It's what brought him and Olivia together.

Arlo grins.

"He does have a point. All the other couples were separated, but you and Rose are on the same team. You know what that means?" Luis asks.

Lincoln doesn't work to hide his smirk as Paxton yells out like he's just scored a winning touchdown.

Arlo grins. "Good thing red is your color." He winks before saluting me and turning to Olivia.

"You guys are assholes," I tell the group collectively.

They chuckle in response as we go our separate ways.

Forty minutes later, I'm cleaning along the fence line with a small group of kids nearby who have been slinging questions about football at me. Most of them have grown bored of the subject and are now focused on finding the most disgusting piece of trash to throw away.

"Do you have to practice every day?" I look beside me at the kid Luis bet me was going to be a pain in our ass and see from his nametag that his name is Logan.

"Mostly."

"Does that part suck?" Logan grabs a stray shoe mostly buried under a pile of leaves, and shakes his head before tossing it away in his garbage sack.

"It sucks the most at the beginning of the season. Coaches push the hardest then as a warning for what will come. Or if someone on your team breaks your team rules, that always blows."

"My mom worries that if I play, I'll get hurt," he says.

"It's a fair concern."

Logan swings his gaze to me, shock and betrayal shining in his eyes.

I shrug off his reaction and move down the fence. Logan follows me, waiting for some sort of explanation. "My buddy had knee surgery last year after blowing out his ACL, and we played against a team where a guy broke his back and can't walk anymore. This sport is full contact, and it can be brutal. My mom worries about concussions, just like I'm sure yours does. They worry because the concerns are all plausible."

"Does it scare you that you might get hurt?"

"Not while I'm playing. When you get scared, that's when you make mistakes, and that's when you get hurt."

"How'd your mom get over it?"

"She didn't."

Logan follows me farther along the fence, helping me collect the mass number of plastic bags that have gotten tangled around the fencing. "My coach thinks I'm good enough to play in high school."

My knee-jerk reaction is to crack a joke because most high schools here don't cut students from their teams, but I can tell Logan has taken this compliment to heart. "That's awesome—if it's what you want to do."

"I kind of like basketball, too," he says.

"Yeah? What about video games?"

He kicks a rock that's sticking up out of the ground. "They're okay."

"You don't have a favorite?"

Logan shrugs again.

In the distance, Rose frowns as she shoves what appears to be an old diaper into her trash bag.

"You know her?" Logan asks.

"What twelve-year-old doesn't like video games?" I counter.

"She's hot," he returns.

"She's too old for you."

He scoffs. "In ten years, she won't be."

I bite out a laugh that makes Logan scowl.

"What? Age is just a number. Unless ... you *do* like her...."

"What position do you play in football? Offense? Defense?"

"You really don't want to talk about her, do you?"

Maybe Luis was right. Maybe I'm going to lose forty bucks. "I thought we were talking football?"

"Is she your ex?"

"When you get a little older, you'll realize girls are far more complicated than you ever thought."

Logan drops his trash and rubs his palms together. "Lay it on me. I'm great at this. I have two older sisters."

I shake my head. "I'm not looking for advice."

"You've looked at her a thousand times since we've been out here."

His estimation probably isn't far off. "She doesn't want a boyfriend." I don't know why I tell him this. I haven't even laid out all of the facts with Luis, and here I am, spilling it all to a twelve-year-old stranger.

"She's lying," he says automatically.

I blow out a laugh. "She doesn't date."

"What happened?"

I shrug. "What makes you think something happened? Maybe she just doesn't like to date."

"Well, you should probably find out." He gives me a look as though I'm dense and shoves a lost glove into his trash bag. "Something obviously happened. My sister once dated a guy who beat her. We didn't know for months, but after she finally got out of the relationship, she didn't want to date anymore because she had some serious trust issues."

My gaze cuts to Rose, my thoughts spiraling as Logan's story replays in my head.

There's no way someone laid a finger on Rose.

Right?

I clear my throat. "I have too much on my plate this year. Even if I wanted to date someone, I wouldn't have the time."

Logan twists his face like he's tasted something bitter. "I hope you do a better job lying to her when you say that."

A dozen excuses sit on my tongue like missiles, but before I can decide which one to deploy first, my teammate, Tyler Banks, approaches with a garbage sack and a frown. "Ian," he says with a nod.

"Hey, Banks, meet Logan."

Tyler offers his hand. "Nice to meet you."

"Ah, man. I bet you don't even have to try," Logan says.

Tyler looks from Logan to me and then back at Logan. "Try what?"

"Impressing the ladies. All you've got to do is talk, and they probably line up," he says, referring to Tyler's British accent.

Tyler shakes his head. "Only one girl for me." He turns, glancing across the park.

"The blonde?" Logan asks.

Tyler turns back to him and nods. "That's the one."

"*He* makes time," Logan says dismissively as he grabs his sack and moves farther down the fence line to gather more trash.

Tyler looks at me with his brows raised.

I shake my head. "You drew trash."

Tyler winces. "Ten bloody acres." He glances across the park again, stopping at Chloe.

"Everything okay?" I ask.

He nods. "Chloe just had a shit day."

His obvious distress only confirms what I've been saying—dating someone is a distraction I don't have time for.

Rose

Trash.

Of the four groups, trash was my last pick. No one wants to be outside in the Northwest picking up garbage that's been stewing for all four seasons and is now infected with mold, mildew, and bugs.

Fall dances in the breeze, leaving a cool trail along my bare arms and the back of my neck as I stuff another cigarette butt in my half-filled garbage sack. I wish I'd brought a sweatshirt, but I hadn't given the situation enough thought, hence my nice top and new jeans.

My brain is frazzled today. Maybe it's because the day started with Chantay and beer, which led to too many thoughts about the differences between summer to last year, or perhaps it's because my mom has been on my mind so much today, something that brings comfort along with a dumpster of regrets and wishes. Or maybe it's the freshness of the school year paired with new professors, classes, and a horrible editor.

I expel a deep breath and glance around to see if anyone else from our group was unlucky enough to draw trash. I need a distraction. Desperately. I would happily be willing to talk with Raegan about her love of the ocean and dolphins or to Olivia about the children's book she's been writing. Hell, I'll even dissect Paxton's relationship with his crazy-ass girlfriend, Candace—anything to get out of my thoughts and onto safer grounds.

"Can you believe how many people smoke?" a girl asks, drawing my attention. She looks maybe twelve, with short, wavy, wild brown hair that desperately needs a straightener and some product. Her hair momentarily distracts me from her gangly frame, all arms, legs, and knobby knees.

A kid is not the distraction I had in mind.

"Did you know cigarettes cost around fifty cents each? I've probably picked up a hundred dollars worth of cigarette butts already," she continues, either shockingly bad at math or disturbingly accurate.

The obligation to reply sits heavily on my shoulders as I reach for a single, lost mitten. "I guess we all have our vices, right?"

She stares at me, two giant brown eyes that are too big for her face.

I stare back.

She was talking to me, right?

"Couldn't people choose a vice that doesn't stink, pollute, and kill everyone around them?"

Logic. Adults think kids have endless imaginations, which prevents them from being logical when, in reality, I'm convinced that their imaginations allow them to see logic in the clearest form.

"I have an uncle who used to smoke. He dropped a cigarette butt in our living room, and it burnt through the carpet. My mom was furious." She cracks a smile that brings joy to her features. She's beautiful in an innocent and sincere way that reminds me of weekend mornings with Olivia when our hair is a mess, and we wear pajamas and Friday's makeup, and neither of us cares or judges the other. "I'm Bree, by the way," she adds, pointing to the nametag on her shirt.

"Rose," I tell her.

She gives another brief smile and then puts her head down and works to gather the rest of the pile of cigarette butts she happened upon.

I look up, ready to move on to another area, realizing I'd prefer to be alone with my thoughts, when I spot Ian. He's beside Tyler and a kid wearing a red sweatshirt and red hat, talking and laughing like they're old friends.

That's my role.

I'm the friendly, outgoing one who doesn't know the definition of a stranger.

Ian's the quiet introvert.

But this is all an afterthought to the painful reality that he's on trash cleanup and chose to avoid me.

I turn back to Bree. "What grade are you in?"

Her eyes are suspicious under her lowered brow. "Seventh."

I try to think back to when I was in the seventh grade and what held my interest.

Boys.

Boys.

And more boys.

I tasted my first cigarette in an attempt to look cool for a boy—an eighth-grader who I had a crush on. He'd invited me into the woods after school with two of his buddies, a can of warm Pabst beer, and a half-filled pack of cigarettes he stole from his mom. Looking back, I realize I was a prime example of why adults don't think kids can apply logic. I was distracted by how to impress this older boy and utterly oblivious to the idiocy of hanging out with three boys alone, in the woods, without anyone knowing where I was. Combine that with alcohol and hormones, and I was the poster child for bad decisions.

"Do you like school?" I ask.

She shrugs and picks up an empty chip bag. "It's okay."

I wonder where Olivia is and which of the four groups she was assigned. Maybe I can trade someone.

"You don't really want to be here, do you?" Bree asks, her eye trained on me again.

I shake my head. "Not really. I mean, this is great, don't get me wrong, but I'm not exactly mentor-ship material."

She smirks. "All you're doing is cleaning up a park. Are you qualified to pick up trash? You look like you are."

I raise a brow. Did she just insult me?

Bree grins. "Are you in college?"

I nod. "I'm a senior."

"What do you want to do when you graduate?"

"I want to open a yoga studio."

I can tell that my answer surprises her because she pulls her head back and blinks. "You're going to college to open a yoga studio?"

"I want to start an empire."

"What's an empire?"

"I want to own several studios and open a line of products and at-home programs."

Bree doesn't look impressed, a confused look lingering on her face. "Why?"

"Why not?"

She shrugs. "I can't get into the whole yoga thing."

I want to tell her this is because she's twelve, but refrain from doing so.

"I mean, drinking kale and wearing skin-tight pants and listening to that boring music." Her face pinches. "No thanks."

"What do you want to be when you grow up?" I ask.

She shrugs. "A mom."

"A mom?"

Bree nods. "And the president."

"I don't know if that's a big enough goal. You should probably aim higher."

She laughs. "I want to help people. I want to make the world a better place."

And without even meaning to, Bree cuts a hole directly into my past, reminding me of the days when I thought I could wear the cape and crown and make a difference in a more meaningful way.

"You should," I tell her.

Her brown eyes focus on me, confidence radiating in her straight shoulders and raised chin. "I will."

3

IAN

I t's only Wednesday, and it feels like an entire month has passed. The beginning of the season is always long, but the first week of classes makes it seem endless.

"Hey!" I stop, hearing Pax's voice. He jogs toward me. "Are you on your way to the offices?"

I nod. "I'm meeting with Danielson before practice."

"Yeah. The President and I are heading over to meet with Craig and Harris now." He blows out a belated breath. "This year feels different."

"I think it's because the team's so young."

His eyebrows draw up as he nods. "They are young. I'm already sick and tired of their bullshit. So much arrogance." He wipes the back of his wrist across his brow like we're on the field. "That and it feels like regardless of how many wins we have, it won't be enough because we've already been the undefeated team. How do you top that?"

"By doing it twice."

He laughs. "Dance, monkey, dance." Something pulls his attention to the side for a moment as we continue through the parking lot, and when he looks back at me, a note of seriousness has washed away his humor. "Dude, I'm not trying to pry, but I know Arlo can be dense as a brick, so I just want you to know that if you're not comfortable having Rose come to the barbecue this Saturday or other parties, I can talk to him. She doesn't have to be there."

I'd forgotten about the barbecue he, Arlo, and Lincoln had planned for our first home game. "It's whatever. I'm completely neutral when it comes to Rose."

His eyes pinch with doubt.

"How about we move the party from your place to mine? Celebrate our first home game win without worrying about overcrowding," I suggest.

"I don't know if that solves your Rose problem. Arlo will keep inviting her along."

I shake my head. "There is no Rose problem. If she wants to come, I'm okay with it." I shrug the thought off, knowing the chances of Rose attending will be slim. Luis told me she spent a decent amount of time with them all over the summer, but I'm confident he was elaborating for dramatic effect and to get in my head.

"Are you sure? Saturday's in three days."

"No sweat." Three years ago, Cassie moved away for college, and shortly after, my parents moved to Italy, leaving me to live in the massive house they purchased after they came into money. "I'll see you at practice."

Pax nods before bumping his fist against mine and then patting my shoulder. "See you, man."

MY THOUGHTS ARE CIRCLING Rose as I make my way to Coach Danielson's office, recalling the surprise in her jade-colored eyes when she looked at me on Monday and the instant retraction that followed. How she diligently kept her distance from me during the entire park cleanup.

It feels like summer all over again. I spent the month of June trying to forget her, and then right when I was on the brink of accomplishing the difficult task, it was as though she sensed it, and she called me.

I almost didn't answer.

But that undeniable pull she has on me had me accepting her call before I could talk myself out of it.

It was late in Rome, the nine-hour time difference between us something I'd become familiar with since my parents had moved abroad. She spent the first hour of the call asking me about my trip and telling me everything about everyone but herself. Exhausted from trying to break through the same brick wall I'd already scaled on more than one occasion, I was ready to hang up and call it a night when she surprised me by talking about her older sister, Anna. Another piece of the puzzle that makes up Rose Cartwright. I listened as she confided about feeling inferior to her sister, who was moving back home to Seattle after years of being on campaign trails for presidential candidates.

We spent hours on the phone that night, trading stories of our lives, and as always, Rose picked up on the most minute of details, commenting on what I least expected and showing me that she still cared.

The next day, I told my dad about Rose as we toured the Roman Forum. My dad and I have always been close, but trying to explain Rose to him was surprisingly difficult. I was exhausted from trying to read between the lines or pick up on vague hints. Whenever I knocked through a wall, four new ones seemingly appeared. I needed a sounding board, someone to simplify the situation and make sense of it all because I'd never been so unsure of anyone's intentions in my life. And while Dad didn't magically have the answer to the mystery that was Rose, he did point out that I was getting distracted from the goals I'd set more than six years ago.

My thoughts of that afternoon with Dad drift away as Coach Danielson waves me in. "Glad you could fit this meeting in," he says, patting one of the seats across from his desk before he rounds it and sits down. "We have a big year ahead of us and several new players. How do you feel about our team? What are your thoughts on the new guys? Desantos is strong at breaking through tackles, but I'm worried about his pursuit. He runs straight every single time."

"He's fast but doesn't seem to get the angles. He needs to learn how to read the play better and adjust on the fly," I say. Coach nods for me to continue. "His speed made up for that deficiency in high school, and he did okay last year as a Freshman at Wisconsin, but he wasn't going against teams like San Diego and Utah. Desantos can't rely on being the fastest anymore because he's not, and he needs to work on what he's lacking."

"Glad you studied up over the summer," he replies with a smirk.

"We should put him on the field and run some plays with The President or Paulson. Pres is quick and always sees the fields and openings, and Paulson would give him a hard run for his money at being the fastest."

"Paulson couldn't find an angle if it blew him," Coach says, shaking his head. "Thankfully, he's Craig's issue, not mine. But, you think Desantos has potential?"

I nod. "He's smart and fast, but as I said, he doesn't read the field very well, and he's stubborn about it. He wants to be a leader, which I think he can become."

Coach nods, flipping his bright red Brighton U baseball hat backward before grabbing his water bottle and leaning back in his chair. The action brings forth an uncanny resemblance to my childhood best friend, Isaiah Templeton. It silences my thoughts for a solid moment as I realize how close I am to accomplishing my goal of being drafted into the NFL. I've worked tirelessly for this, dropping classes, forgoing relationships and parties, and almost everything else that didn't fit into my practice routine.

"I think you're right, but he needs to earn that leadership by learning all of our plays, improving, and paying his dues," Coach Danielson says.

"I like Wilson, too. He seems to get along well with the team. And he takes direction well. Plus, he's a tackling machine. Nothing gets past him."

Coach grins. "Yes. I noticed him at practice yesterday, and he knows how to drop that shoulder and use his legs."

"Torres is good, too. He understands the cut. I think he could actually pressure Pres if he's up for the challenge," I add.

"I don't know," he says, crossing his arms. "With it being his senior year, Harris won't want to take many risks with Beckett. He's too valuable. Plus, at least three NFL teams are already courting that kid. If the draft were tomorrow, he'd likely be a first-round pick, but we'll see what this season brings."

Pride has my chest inflating while jealousy pricks at the base of my shoulders, constricting my muscles and making it difficult to focus on Coach's following words. Lincoln is one hell of a player, but more than that, he's one of my closest friends. Our team has built a brotherhood as we've pushed ourselves physically and mentally toward the same goal. Of course, there are a couple of dumb fucks on the team who I'd happily cut if I had the power and say, but thankfully they're outliers rather than the norm. Still, Coach Danielson's words serve as a stiff reminder that even if we manage to pull off another undefeated season, it won't guarantee that he, I, or anyone else who has worked their asses off will get drafted to the NFL.

"We need to show up Saturday and shut Montana down."

Coach Danielson nods. "We'll definitely win, but it would be nice to shut them out. Our offense is fucking amazing, but our defense is pretty incredible as well." A wistful expression fades from his features. The offense gets us wins, but the defense keeps us from losing. I don't mind not being in the spotlight. Just the idea of people recognizing me in public like they do Paxton and Lincoln, and even Arlo after he went viral last year, makes me itch. The thrill of breaking through an offense and sacking the quarterback is all the notoriety I need and want. "We have to focus on the three main keys of defense: tackle, turnover, and pursuit."

I lean forward, my elbows on my knees. Aside from playing, talking shop is my next favorite thing.

We devise a plan for practices this week and our game against

Montana on Saturday, discussing how we'll utilize our strengths against their speed until it's time to head to practice.

The field is where all of my thoughts fade. As I slide my helmet into place, my adrenaline spikes, ready to lose myself in something that makes sense.

"ELBOWS IN!" Coach Danielson bellows. "Shed that blocker, or you'll never get to the damn ball, Hoyt! You guys are better than how you played last week against New Mexico," he reminds us, pacing along where we're lined up, working on hitting drills.

My muscles are fatigued from a full practice, and my shoulders and hands ache. Sweat drips down the back of my practice jersey, making my neck itch.

Coach Danielson's stare stops on me, and with his tightened jaw and nod, I know he's telling me that he's reminding me to push my teammates and remind them what we're working toward. Few realize the toll we put on our bodies and how rest and being mentally strong are as important as knowing our handbook. I nod my understanding.

With a final tight jerk, he dismisses us to the locker room.

"Fuck me, that was brutal," Desantos says, wiping his face with his forearm. "I get that we weren't running on all cylinders last week, but we still won by over twenty points."

"It should have been closer to fifty," I tell him.

Desantos shakes his head in short bursts. "What about the offense? It wasn't us—the defense—who kept our offense from scoring." He shakes his head. "It has to go both ways."

"You're right." I shrug, too tired for this conversation but still straightening my shoulders because division is the last thing our team can tolerate. "But, we're two halves. They have to take care of their shit, and we have to deal with ours. New Mexico shouldn't have scored as much as they did, and we need to make sure Montana doesn't do the same. We have to shut them down and stop them from getting on the board. That's our job. If the offense is losing our games, I'll go to Pax, but we can't point fingers when we had too many of our faults last week. We were weak, and it showed."

We weren't weak—we were lazy—but mentioning weakness makes our team rally, while laziness only makes them defensive.

Desantos furrows his brow, his top lip rolling back with a sneer. "Way to stand up for your team, Captain."

I grab his practice jersey in my fist. "My job isn't to wipe your ass. We didn't play a game worth being proud of. Period."

He shrugs me off. "I'm sick of taking all of the blame."

I nod once, knowing that Coach Danielson is the biggest hardass on the coaching staff. The other coaches can turn off their anger and annoyance, yet Danielson is either angry or livid once we hit the field. Even when we're winning, the man is relentless. Desantos isn't the first or only one to be tense by the constant state of Coach's disapproval.

"Don't listen to his tirade," I tell him before patting my chest. "Listen to me. We could have done better. We *are* better. We have three more practices, and then we get to prove that we're the best fucking defensive line, not just in our division but the entire fucking league."

Desantos releases a long breath, his shoulders sinking. "We hold them to thirteen," he says.

I nod. "Thirteen."

He pats my shoulder, his jaw tight as he debates whether to trust me. His hunger and determination for our team to go undefeated for a second year is a shadow compared to the skyscraper I'm holding onto since he wasn't with us last year.

"And then we're going to celebrate our win at my house Saturday night." I pat his shoulder pads again.

"Your rules against drinking paired with a curfew don't spell party, Cap."

I shrug. "It's part of the role."

He smirks. He's likely seen or heard that some of the guys drink during the season—Paxton is one of them. But rather than defend Pax's actions, I prefer to play ignorant and focus on the defensive team, which is my responsibility. "My tolerance is small. I wouldn't waste it on drinking. Especially at my house."

He releases a sigh, and I sense his resolve. Sometimes, it's a matter of realizing how far you can push a person to know where the limits are. He's been testing mine since the season began, and I've held steady. I'm not about to let his ego hinder my future. I give him a nod and move past him.

The locker room is filled with happy tones. A jeer is thrown, followed by laughter and a rebut that makes everyone laugh even harder.

"Hey," Arlo says from his locker beside mine. Kostas is one of those guys I know I will be talking to in forty years, bullshitting each other and ensuring we have one another's backs. "Rough practice?"

"You could say that. How's the knee?"

He looks down at his knee, covered in a thick black brace. At the end of last season, Arlo tore his ACL, which could have potentially ended his days of playing altogether.

"It's feeling good," he says. "Not too much longer before I'm cleared to play."

"You're the Terminator."

He laughs.

"How has school been?"

Arlo shakes his head. "The beginning of the year sucks ass. I don't know how you do it. You should have chosen an easier degree. Just the words computer science makes my brain hurt."

I scoff. "Too many syllables?"

He belts out a laugh. "Did I hear right? The party has been moved to your house?"

I nod. "As long as I'm not stepping on anyone's toes. I figured it would make it easier since you guys have neighbors."

He laughs. "And a little less space." More laughter. "Works for me, man. Do you want to place bets on who tries breaking the drinking rule first? I'll put twenty bucks on Hoyt."

"He better not. Pax will bench his ass. His tolerance seems especially low lately toward Hoyt."

Arlo nods as his eyes grow wide. "It is toward everyone."

I glance toward Pax's locker, but he's absent. "Is he getting clean?"

"Trying to."

"Girl troubles, still?" I ask, knowing if anyone knows about our quarterback's personal life, it will be Arlo, who is roommates with him.

Arlo bobbles his head with a no and then a yes. "He always has girlfriend trouble. Candace should have come with a warning label. But I think he's feeling the weight of the world on his shoulders right now."

"Tell him I'll be blocking the team, so they won't be able to order drinks. Even him. This year we can't afford to cut corners. We've got to be at one hundred percent with every game." I close my locker. "You'll get the word out about the party?"

He grins. "Who would want to miss the stuffed mushrooms?"

"I'd advise against it."

Arlo slams his locker shut and grins. "Me too. Liv and I will be there. I'll talk to Rose."

I wince at the mention of her name, which has seemed like a constant over this past week. I can tell he notices based on the double look he gives me. "I know it's none of my business, but I thought you two were hitting it off?"

To anyone else, I'd likely shrug off the question and say something colorful or rude, but Arlo's friends with Rose and his loyalty to her is as strong as a teammate—potentially stronger—since she helped him and Olivia get together.

I release a sigh, but my lungs still feel weighted. "So did I, but you know Rose." I shrug, working to regain my indifference. "It's cool, though. With everything riding on this year, I don't have time to date." The words are beginning to feel like a mantra.

His eyebrows rise, and I hear the silent '*bullshit*' that never crosses his lips. "I'm glad you're both being cool about it."

I nod.

More thoughts ghost across his face, ones of doubt and disbelief and confusion.

"I'll see you later, Kostas." I grab my duffel and skip the showers. The scrutiny of his questions—even the silent ones—follow me to the parking lot.

"Wait up!" I pause, catching sight of Luis jogging toward me with his duffel slung over one shoulder. "I thought we were watching tape tonight?"

I nod. "We are."

His gaze crosses over my sweat-dampened hair and the tee I'd put on in place of my practice jersey and pads. "Smelling like ass. Why didn't you shower? I know your mom taught you basic hygiene."

"You're such a dick."

His eyes become bright with humor. "Is there a reason you're running out of the locker room like you've got a quickie waiting for you?" His brows lower. "Wait. You don't have a quickie waiting on you, right? Tell me you didn't double-book me."

Before I can tell him to relax, Hoyt catches up with us.

"Did I hear Kostas mention Rose? Rose Cartwright?" His eyebrows are raised, his smile crooked with insinuation. "Did you guys make a deal to hook up?"

Luis's eyebrows arch, looking at me for a quick reply.

I shake my head. "You need to stop spying on people in the locker room, perv," I tell Hoyt.

He laughs heartily. "C'mon, I hear her name, and I can't help but listen. That girl is hot, and I've heard she's got a rule that she only sleeps with guys once. Talk about a win-win."

Luis winces as he turns away. The guy can't mask his thoughts to save his life, much less my back.

"You should ask her. I don't know anything. We hung out a couple of times because Arlo dates her roommate."

Hoyt's grin returns. "I know. She came and hung out this summer. We went tubing down the river and did some bonfires and went to the beach—"

"Why are we talking about this? Shouldn't we be discussing how you failed to strip a single tackle last week?"

Hoyt takes a step back, rubbing his hand over his short-cropped hair. As one of the most easy-going and excitable team members, regret attaches to my words and shoves me dangerously close to apologizing. But before I can consider it, he nods. "You're right. We've got to stay focused on the game. It's more important."

"You keep trying to hit down, and you've got to hit up, pop that ball out. We'll work on it tomorrow at practice."

Hoyt extends his fist, and I knock my knuckles against his. "See you later, Captain," he says before heading toward the parking lot.

"She's still under your skin, huh?" Luis asks.

I shake my head. "Nope."

"I get it, man."

Luis has been dating Alexis for three years. The two are basically stitched at the hip. He doesn't understand a damn thing.

"Trust me—it's over."

"Let's go watch some tape and get some food. God, I'm missing pizza. I'm eating some Sunday night. No regrets."

"Stevie made something with salmon for tonight."

"Oh. I can go for salmon, especially if it's got that soy-ginger sauce he made last time. You can tell him to expect me for dinner every night."

"He says you insulted his cooking."

"I grabbed the salt one damn time."

My laughter is interrupted by my phone ringing with multiple alerts. I reach for it, reading through the train of texts.

"Everything okay?" he asks.

"My parents are moving back next week," I tell him, scrolling through the lengthy number of messages from my dad. "My dad's going to run for governor."

4

ROSE

Our professor stalks to the front of the class, her back straight, shoulders pulled back. Professor Krayzer is fierce and whip-smart. She garners attention by choosing engaging topics, which makes her class far more enjoyable than a traditional lecture. This morning, we've been picking apart our first reading assignment. She manages the discussion thoughtfully and provocatively that doesn't tarnish the author but the ideas mentioned from the early nineties when it was published. I kind of want to be Professor Krayzer in twenty years, sans the teaching.

It's Thursday, our first class, and already I know that Labor Economics will be my favorite course of the semester—with the giant exception that Ian is in the class. I'm still nursing the wound he inflicted when he came in, swept his gaze across the room, and chose the seat farthest away from me.

I glance in Ian's direction again and consider the article I need to write for *The Daily Dose*. I'm supposed to cover their home game against Montana. He stares straight ahead, allotting me a brief moment to trace over the planes of his jaw that are chiseled and perfect, leading to his chin, which has the slightest dimple. I can't see from this angle. He leans back and twists in his seat like he feels my stare. I casually turn my attention from him to my laptop, where my notes for the piece are currently open. After the shock and disappointment of my new assignment for the paper had settled and determination fueled me, I reached out to Dean Putney. He previously wrote the sports column but quit last year, disgruntled about cutting a day of publication due to budget constraints. His hard truth was I had to focus my writing on football because football was proven to drive readership. Thus, Arlo's been teaching me about football every night for the past three days, like it's my new part-time job.

"In conclusion," Professor Krayzer says, catching my attention. "Tournament Theory—is there a place for it in society, and should we continue to allow it?" She looks across the class.

"Yes," a boy with dark, curly hair and a scraggly mustache answers from where he sits near the back of the class.

"Why?" the professor asks.

"Because winners should be compensated. They work hard to be the best, and we should reward them for it. Plus, it encourages others to work harder."

I scoff, drawing the attention of Professor Krayzer, whose lips are tipped with an amused grin. "What are your thoughts, Miss...?"

"Cartwright," I tell her. "The movie *Wonder Woman* made over eight-hundred million dollars, and Gal Gadot, Wonder Woman herself, made a measly three-hundred grand. Compare that to movies in the same genre that have been far less successful, with actors earning millions more. Not to mention you're completely discounting chance and skill from your consensus and how to prevent people from cheating to earn those top spots."

Professor Krayzer turns her attention from me to the guy who needs to be introduced to a razor. "Any response?"

He sits taller in his seat, his dark eyes flashing in my direction for a second with a challenging sneer. Maybe a rusted razor is what he deserves. "Tournament Theory incentivizes and reduces shock in markets. I think the only ones who are going to complain about it are those who want to try and twist it to find disadvantages."

"Twist it?" I ask, my mouth puckering like the words are sour.

"The facts are simple. If you create a model where the winners benefit most, employees will never share valuable and efficient processes or knowledge. In addition, you increase your chances of unethical behavior, cheating, and division among employees, which won't help most business models grow or even survive. The simple way of looking at this would be gladiators: the winner won his life, and the loser lost his. How we can call that barbaric and not this when it's the same concept but with monetary gifts only proves how slow some are on the evolutionary path." I give the scraggly bearded guy a sideways glance.

"But if I'm in the NFL and driving ticket sales up, and television stations are getting increased viewers and therefore making more profit from advertisers, shouldn't I receive a piece of that pie?" The deep voice has me turning to look at Ian. From this far away, I can't see his eyes and the different hues of blue that are fringed with sooty lashes, but I note the shadow of a beard that deserves applause, and his broad shoulders make my heart race defiantly.

"That depends. Why are you driving viewership? Is it because you're the best player or because you're throwing tantrums, and people find it entertaining?"

Amusement twists his lips, but rather than revealing the smile I'm expecting, he turns his attention to Professor Krayzer and kicks his feet out. He folds one ankle over the other. "Would it matter?"

"If you were the best player, it would," I tell him. "If someone is gaining attention and therefore driving costs for being theatrical, those working tirelessly to be the best would certainly be annoyed. Look at Hollywood and those who create the most drama. Many of them are driving costs up because people are constantly shocked at what is being said or done rather than caring about their music or acting performance. Not to negate that women purchase eighty percent of products, thereby giving a massive advantage to guys with a pretty face and a tight ass."

His grin widens into a smile that isn't for me but for the entire class. "I'll take that as a compliment."

He should, though I'm not about to admit it because the very last thing someone as attractive and confident as Ian needs is either a compliment or assurance. The class laughs, and so do I as I shake my head. He's not entirely wrong, which keeps me from saying anything more. That and the fact class is over, and I need to get to the yoga studio for an aerial class.

"I like the dialogue, class," Professor Krayzer says. "Don't forget to check your reading schedule. Next week, we'll discuss job security, which should segue nicely after today's discussion." She glances across the room again, her light brown hair tied back in a bun that gives me new inspiration. "I'll see you next week."

I close my laptop and kick myself for glancing toward Ian a final time. He slips out of the door, making my chest and hopes fall.

"Keep challenging them," Professor Krayzer says from her desk behind me.

I right my bookbag and turn to face her. "I'm not entirely opposed to Tournament Theory," I admit. "Smugness just irritates me."

Professor Krayzer laughs. "Are you majoring in economics for law school?"

I shake my head. "I'm going to start an empire and become the fortieth female CEO of Fortune 500's."

"Fortieth? I'm pretty sure there are less than that now."

I nod. "I'm hoping a couple more are elected before I hit the mainstream."

My explanation makes Professor Krayzer smile again, but unlike the tired grin that is always accompanied by an eye roll when I tell this to my dad or older sister, Anna, hers seems genuine and intrigued.

"You should consider law school. It could help your ventures in starting a business."

"Empire," I correct her.

"Empire," she repeats with a nod. "Few can see the other side, much less argue it." She gives me a knowing look. "I'll see you next week."

Her words ring in my thoughts as I make my way down the long, mostly bare hall, trying to leave the traces of disappointment that often follow conversations about my future and leaving my family's history of law and politics behind.

I reach for my phone to call Olivia. Sometimes my thoughts are too loud and too consuming, and Olivia often manages to silence them or, at the very least, soothe them. When we met, I had pegged Olivia as a loner. She avoided parties and afterschool functions and was seemingly allergic to all extracurriculars, whereas I thrived. However, during our senior year, after months of navigating unexpected circumstances, I found more comfort and refuge with Olivia than with the same friends who had once voted me as homecoming queen.

I underwent a transformation of sorts that began with me feeling the most alive and happy around others—their energy, laughter, and excitement feeding and nourishing me. I liked being the center of attention, needed it—wanted it— to suddenly feeling isolated and alone when surrounded by the very same crowds. Our conversations about fashion and drama that filled the hallways of Pinehurst High made me feel like a stranger.

Maybe I was more of an introvert than I'd realized. Perhaps tragedy reveals who your real friends are.

Olivia became the yin to my yang, the salt to pepper, and the jelly to my peanut butter.

After moving in together, we developed a routine made with care and patience. Our friendship grew into a sisterhood that extended beyond binge-watching our favorite shows while ordering Pad Thai from every takeout restaurant in the city to find the very best. I dragged her to yoga dates with me and my dad's for brunch once a month. In turn, she made me go to her family dinners with her dad, stepmom, Whitney, and two devil-spawns she calls stepbrothers and to used bookstores around the city because the only thing my best friend loves more than a good Netflix binge is a great romance book —our one great difference. While I love reading, my enjoyment of romance novels ended when my mom got sick. Olivia believes in happily ever afters, while I believe in happily and ever afters—note they're not co-dependent.

We were two peas in a pod. A happy pod, and then Olivia met Arlo, and everything changed.

Arlo brought out sides of Olivia I didn't know were dormant—smiles, enthusiasm toward simple things, a love for Seattle, and overall happiness. My friend had never been dull, but it was hard not to see how he brought the rest of her to life.

Our duo became a trio.

This is where many expect me to say my friendship with Olivia changed. I grew jealous. She grew distant. Arlo became her priority.

That wasn't what happened.

Not even close.

Instead, Arlo's presence added humor and variety to our routine. And seeing them together made me reconsider what I thought I knew and wanted. Watching my best friend fall in love and witnessing what a healthy relationship consists of and how both people work to bring the other up, and themselves made me question wanting to remain single.

"Hey!" Olivia greets me on the second ring.

"Is it June yet?" I ask her.

She laughs in return. "I hear we're going to look back and miss these days."

I release a long sigh. "People also claim to miss the seventies, and that decade was filled with terrible fashion and economic struggle. They have to say it."

She laughs again like she always does when I turn too many shades of negative. "I have two classes and then work, but I should be home around six. Do you want to grab something to eat or try that new series on Netflix?"

"Take out and Netflix."

"I'm in. Also, we were invited to a party on Saturday after the game. We don't have to go, though."

"No. We should go. It will be good for us to get out and have fun. I'm beginning to resemble an old spinster."

"It's at Ian's," she tells me.

Hearing his name makes me flinch. It's like the shadow of him is following me everywhere this week.

"That's okay," I say, nearly choking on the words. "Totally fine." My voice is clearer this time, more confident. "He throws great parties. We should go."

"We don't have to," she says again.

"It's okay. We said we were going to be friends."

"You mentioned that he acted kind of weird the other day. Maybe you should talk to him?"

"I don't think that's a good idea. He was with Isla."

"Isla? Do I know Isla?" Olivia asks.

"Probably not. But he does."

"I'm sorry," her voice is sincere and sorrowful. We've discussed Ian more than we should. "I still think you should talk to him. Maybe tell him you got scared and were worried about him being gone so long."

I shake my head and pull in a deep breath through my nose. "No. It's good. I'm good. You know me, I'm not the dating type."

"Rule one, I know," she says.

"Actually, rule one is always have coffee within ten minutes of waking up."

Her laughter tickles my ears and lips, lightening the weight in my chest that arrived with the mention of Ian's name. "Maybe we make a backup plan for Saturday? Just in case the party's lame," she suggests.

"That isn't the worst idea you've ever had."

Olivia laughs. "Where are you?"

The sun shines down on me, warm and inviting against my bare arms. "Heading to yoga. I'm teaching an aerial class this afternoon."

"Is that the one with the hammocks where you twist your legs in the fabric and hang upside down?"

A smile breaks across my face. "That's one way to describe it."

Then, just as quickly as my smile and calmness had appeared, they both abandon me as Anthony makes a beeline toward me, his eyes bright and his smile cruel. A warning bell sounds in my ears, a premonition of sorts that tells me I'm not going to want to hear what he has to say.

"Your story for Monday just got more interesting," Anthony tells me.

"I'm on the phone," I tell him.

He shakes his head and continues, his voice louder. "Not anymore. Trust me—you need to see this. It's going to make headline news and help our sales."

"I'm only listening if you tell me I can run with the food security article." I pitched it to him yesterday, offering to write both pieces.

Olivia chuckles in my ear. "Call me when you're done with baby T-rex."

I keep my phone to my ear, refusing to let go of the escape route.

Anthony shakes his head. "No one cares about that, Rose."

"I know, but we can change that. We *should* change that."

He sighs heavily. "Then you're going to sound preachy. No one wants to hear about starving people in foreign countries. They want to hear things that make them happy. And do you know what else they want?"

"I realize people like happy news. *I* like happy news. But people also want to be informed, and as a society, we like to help each other. That's why people give up their Thanksgiving dinners to volunteer at a soup kitchen. Come on. I will make the story relatable and edgy and explain how everyone can help. One in nine people is going hungry in the world, and as journalists, it's our responsibility to inform people—"

"Are you out of excuses yet?" He gives me a pointed look that's directed at my chest, where I have my cell phone pressed after waving it around because I'm nothing, if not slightly theatrical.

"No! And I was talking to someone and not an imaginary some-one. They let me go because they heard you being an ankle biter." I release another sigh. "I'm already doing one assignment that I don't want. I'm not doing another."

I consider myself a pretty good judge of character, but Anthony's

Grinch-like smile reminds me that generalities can leave large enough gaps to allow for massive regrets.

"Well, consider yourself hitting a two-in-one." He holds up his phone, revealing a picture of Hoyt naked, his groin barely covered with a couple of heart emojis.

I blink back my surprise. "Why are you showing me this? Why do you even have it?"

"Someone sent it to me anonymously."

"Anonymously or *anonymously*?" There's a massive difference between someone asking not to be named and a truly anonymous source.

"*Anonymously*." His grin widens. "They said they have more pictures from everyone on the team and plan to start sharing them daily. This one is going out Saturday."

He flashes another picture of Hoyt fully naked except for a small caption covering his penis.

"Unless what?"

Anthony stops, his brow furrowing. "What are you talking about?"

"What's stopping them from releasing them all at once? Why prolong the process unless they're trying to get something?"

"Maybe they're trying to build their audience?"

I shake my head. "I call bullshit. This person probably photo-shopped the picture."

"They sent me proof with more pictures they plan to share." He shrugs. "They look legit, and if I think they look legit as the editor of a newspaper, you damn well know others will too." He offers his phone.

I take it and scroll to see a picture of Lincoln and Raegan making out at a party, his hand creeping up her shirt—another of Paxton Lawson appearing drunk as he poses with two beers in his hands. I stop on a picture of Ian, shirtless, his hands palming a faceless girl's ass. "Did they say what they want? Aside from Hoyt's picture, these aren't very provocative," I point out to him.

Anthony smiles, and it's purely evil. "They said they have secrets."

"Secrets? What kind of secrets?"

"They didn't share."

I shake my head. "I don't like this. Why would someone go to the work of going after the football team?"

He gives a quick shake of his head. "That's what you're going to find out."

"We're a college paper. There's no way the University will allow us to publish about the site."

"I'm the editor. I'll worry about what we publish. You stick to the facts."

5

IAN

"Fuck me, it's cold out tonight," Luis says as we jog to the sideline to start warmups. It's Saturday, our first home game of the season. The energy in the stadium is palpable.

"Look at this—you can see my nipples." Luis stares at his chest. "Hoyt, why are your nipples so goddamn small?"

"One day, a girl will let you touch their nipples so you don't have to stare at mine," Hoyt returns.

I shouldn't laugh, but the pre-game adrenaline is coursing through my veins, and the memes of Hoyt naked have been circulating campus the past two days, becoming the highlight of my week. He's been in good spirits, prideful even about the photo.

I turn to Luis. "I tried to get you to come work shoulders and chest yesterday so you can tone up."

"Tone up." Luis Scoffs as he flips me off. "I could flatten a fucking beer can between my pecs." He pounds on his chest.

"I'll give you a thousand bucks to do it," I offer.

His stoic expression fades, replaced with a smile. "You know I can't. Could you imagine? My pecs would have to stick out like four inches to have any grip." He starts to move his hands like he's placing an imaginary can to his chest when Assistant Coach Foley and Coach

Danielson start heading toward us. We fall silent, knowing they don't feel the same rush of energy before a game. Instead, they become so uptight they could crush beer cans with their asses.

"Let's get warmed up," I yell. "Make sure your eyes and hands are up." Our linebacker team forms two lines as Foley claps his hands to get us started.

I stretch forward, resting my fingers against the turf. The chalk lines are sharp and bright white, painted fresh this morning.

The whistle blows, and I lift my hands and face, pretending there's an opponent in front of me as I jog forward. Unlike practice, we don't push ourselves during warmups. It's strictly to get loose and get focused. It's the calmest time out on the field and one of my favorites when a thousand memories saturate my thoughts—all of them positive.

"Forrest," Coach Harris, our head coach, calls my attention to where he's standing at the fifty-yard line.

I jog toward him, a nerve of trepidation coiling around my spine. "Hey, Coach."

He chews a giant wad of gum and wears what he does to every game: jeans, a red Brighton sweatshirt, and a baseball hat pulled low. "Remember how we were talking about how you come off a bit..." He winces and chews his gum for a moment as though considering the right word. "Hell, I'll give it to you straight. You come off like a pompous asshole. You don't smile or apply any effort to make small talk. People outside of your circle think you're rude, and it works for you because you're a defensive linebacker. You're supposed to be tough. But it's going to be a handicap with your career. You have to improve your interviewing skills. I've taken the liberty of making you our lead liaison for the team with the school paper. So, head on into the locker room. One of their reporters is waiting on you."

I inwardly groan, but Coach Harris looks at me as though he can hear my displeasure and grins. "Try not to swear."

"The press wants to twist everything we say."

He pats my shoulder again. "The school paper won't. They want to make us look good and sell ad space, which requires readership.

And you need to be thinking about your long game. With your skills, the media will want to talk to you once you're in the NFL. This is a good opportunity for you to get your feet wet with someone who will be wearing kid gloves. It's probably the same kid from last year. He knows football, and he's probably just going to ask you for some quotes. It will be a cakewalk."

When I was a sophomore in high school, my parents talked about my younger sister and me taking courses with private speaking coaches because our dad had been talking about running for governor then. His ambitions were seemingly abandoned after they came into money, and we went from ordering Italian takeout to traveling to Italy to eat fresh Italian food.

I head into the locker room, already missing the field and the pregame energy, when the sight of Rose makes me come to an abrupt stop. Her green eyes flare with surprise as she uncrosses her legs and stands. "For the record, I didn't ask for anyone by name. I emailed Coach Harris and asked to interview a few members of the team. I assumed he'd send Paxton or Arlo. I didn't... I mean, I wasn't...."

I stare at Rose, listening to her ramble—something I've never witnessed from her. I should probably tell her I know she didn't request me and that this was entirely Coach's decision, but call me a masochist because there's something perversely satisfying about seeing her borderline embarrassed.

Rose clears her throat and waves in the direction of the bench she was sitting on. "Would you like to take a seat? I'm supposed to have a photographer with me, but she's late." She twists her wrist to look at the white watch on her slender wrist with the shadow of a scowl.

"Coach described you as a guy."

Her delicate eyebrows inch toward her hairline, but then she smiles dismissively, quickly regaining her composure and finding the confidence that follows her like a shadow. "Olivia always said he skims emails. I probably should have sent it from my personal email rather than the paper's."

"I had no idea you were such a sports enthusiast."

She lifts her chin and tucks her dark hair behind an ear, revealing one of the tiny tattoos that cover much of her skin like a treasure map. This particular pattern of ink makes up the silhouette of a small, detailed bird. "There's a lot you don't know about me." Her smile is a challenge, reminding me of the many brick walls Rose has built around her that are nearly impossible to see or even sense because everything about her feels warm, inviting, and accessible.

Bitterness tangles with the annoyance I feel over missing the time and energy of the warm-up.

Rose doesn't sense it, or if she does, she doesn't address it as she sits and scans over her notes. "I hope you don't mind, but I'm going to record our interview. It's only to help move our conversation along. Otherwise, you'll be waiting for me to take notes after every question. She sets her phone between us and taps the screen. "How do you feel about this upcoming season?" she asks. "Is starting with a previously undefeated season intimidating, or do you think it helps define the year?"

I shrug. "I think everyone on the team would answer that question differently."

She traces the seam of her lips with her tongue and then smiles. "What about you?"

I stretch my neck. I've had a knot sitting between my shoulder and neck for weeks, refusing to submit to all the Epson salt, massage therapy, and stretching that the team trainer insists will help. "I think last year proved we have what it takes to be the best team in the league."

Rose's smile is like a secret, visible only in her green eyes. "Do you think that will change this year with so many new players on the team? More than half of the guys on your defense are freshmen this year. That's a lot of change."

I shake my head. "We have a strong leadership team, and though we lost some great players, we're ready for this year's challenges."

"As the captain of the defense, is there a lot of pressure riding on your shoulders?"

I shake my head, annoyed because each question feels more personal and foreboding.

Rose tilts her head, reading my annoyance. "How do you prepare for a game? Do you have any rituals or superstitions?"

I glance toward the tunnel that leads back out to the field. "Yeah. I like to focus on my team and lead warmups. I find the fewer distractions before a game, the better." I pointedly glance back at her, but she's staring at a list of notes and misses it entirely.

"Which game do you think will be your greatest challenge this year?"

"All of them."

She blinks slowly before gently shaking her head. "There's not a particular game or team you guys are preparing for above the rest?"

"Every game is a new challenge, and we have to prepare for all of them."

"How does it feel to be a senior? Are you ready for what comes after college football?"

My thoughts race as her question plays on a loop in my head. This year is the definition of bittersweet, yet, admitting that seems as ridiculous as it does juvenile.

"We're great at plugging backers. This season is ours, and we're going to take it."

She seems to understand this is my attempt to end the interview, but I take things one step further and stand up.

"It was nice seeing you, Rose."

"Ian," she calls my name after I've gained only a yard. "Off the record, I want to give you a heads up about something my editor received."

My interest is ice cold. My parents hammered being smart into me. I don't send nude photos or ask for them. I don't even send scandalous texts or emails, knowing my words will forever live in cyberspace where some asshole could access them. I don't pay for someone to do my assignments. I don't do steroids—hell, I barely take Aspirin. If her editor has anything, it's going to be laughable. Still, I wait as she walks toward me, flipping through her phone until she stops. A crease is between her furrowed brow, and her eyes are filled with questions as she passes her phone to me.

It's the picture of Hoyt, butt-ass naked. "I don't know if you missed it, but this picture is everywhere," I tell her. "Hell, look up Hoyt's pages, and you'll see he's sharing and liking every post made." I return her phone.

"But, whoever shared it has more pictures, and they're not just of Hoyt."

The shock has me pulling my head back. "What are you talking about?"

"They said they have something on every player on the team, and they plan to drop one every day along with a secret."

I take her phone again, but this time, I see there's a slideshow of pictures and thumb through them. "A secret?" I scoff. "Everyone knows Hoyt's a player. That's not a secret." I stop on the last picture. It's of me. Anger builds in my chest. I hate feeling like I need to explain myself when I shouldn't have to. Rose made it clear she wanted to be nothing more than friends, and yet, seeing the image of me touching and kissing another girl makes the excuses pile up faster than my concerns about others seeing it. "Rose, this—"

"It's bullshit," she says, interrupting me. "And I have no idea if anyone has or will see these images, but they've clearly invested a lot of time into it."

"Who sent them?"

She shakes her head. "I was hoping you might know. They sent these to my editor anonymously earlier this week."

"You knew Hoyt's picture would come out, and you didn't say anything?" Accusation sharpens my voice.

"We haven't exactly been on speaking terms," she points out. "Besides, I had no idea if it was real or what they would do with them or even when."

"And now you want to write a story about it?"

She shakes her head again, eyebrows drawn low. "This is off the record. Anthony wants a story because he's desperate for readership, but I have no interest in being a tabloid columnist."

I consider why and *how* anyone could have these photos. The team is coveted and respected. The only one who would stand to gain something is someone looking to profit from a scandal. And if her editor knew about this and had these photos, is he involved? Is Rose?

Rose draws her face back like she can read my thoughts. It's not only unnerving, but it's annoying as fuck because she reveals so little in her own expressions and less with her words. "I had nothing to do with this. I don't know who sent them or why. I just thought you'd like to know since one of the pictures sent was of you."

"Did you share this with anyone?"

Her eyes turn cold. "No. I'm giving you a heads-up. Thanks for your time, Mr. Forrest, and good luck tonight." She moves to step around me.

"Mr. Forrest?" is all I can manage to get out. When the fuck did I become Mr. Fucking Forrest?

She pauses and faces me. "You clearly have no interest in doing the interview, so rather than wasting both of our time, you can get back out to your team, and I'll finagle my way into the press room to hear the interviews after the game." She gives me a final sweep with her eyes and then continues toward the tunnel.

"You're going the wrong way," I tell her. "The door to the stands is back that way." I point to the right.

"I know exactly where I'm going. Thanks," she says without looking back.

I follow Rose out onto the field, where she finds Coach Harris and greets him with a smile and a hug.

My thoughts comb over the information she just shared with me. *How* would someone have gotten these photos? *Why* would someone have these photos? And potentially the most important question: what's their end game?

6

ROSE

"Do you want to leave?" Olivia asks as we tread deeper into the lion's den. "We can go home and binge-watch *The Marvelous Mrs. Maisel* and order pizza."

I'm tempted to say 'yes,' but instead, I shake my head. "No. We're here. It's the beginning of our senior year, and we're going to have fun tonight." I make the pledge to myself because, after three years of carefully crafted plans to have fun and make the most of my time at Brighton, things have been different—off—for the past several months.

Olivia grips my hand in hers and sears me with an intense gaze. "If you want to leave at any point, just say the words, and we'll go."

I hate that she senses my unease nearly as much as I hate the unease itself. "I'm not going to combust spontaneously. I promise," I promise her. Brighton just dominated with their first home game, and I know Arlo wants Olivia here to celebrate the victory just as much as she wants to be here.

Her smirk says she knows how much I hate life right now, but her grip on my hand tightens as she leads me farther into Ian's house. The living room has been transformed into a dance floor, and people are already grinding against each other. We keep going and see two ping pong tables in the dining room where a dozen of our peers are playing beer pong.

Of course, Ian is the main reason being here has me feeling so unsettled—which feels amplified after our interaction before tonight's game. Obscenely wealthy, he lives in this giant house alone and has become notorious for his house parties, which are increasingly over the top with catered food, a staffed bar to ensure no one messes with the drinks and the hottest and most exclusive DJs. But as appealing as those things are, many still attend the parties just to catch sight of Ian, with his perpetually messy dark hair, piercing eyes, and crooked smile that makes his six-foot-three frame seem almost approachable. I hate admitting that I'm now one of his admirers as I take a quick glance around the room, looking for his squared jaw and enormously broad shoulders. I sometimes attribute his interest in me last spring to pure fascination—as if he was convinced he could change my outlook and rules about relationships. Or maybe he had been genuine in his attempt at getting to know me. Who knows. Regardless, the picture I saw of him on Anthony's damned phone revealed he had no problem getting over me this summer.

The problem is this feeling is foreign to me. Before Ian, a boy hasn't managed to hold this much real estate in my thoughts, but like too many things, he's the exception. Last year, I began caring what he thought. I cared about his past and future. I knew what he ordered at the coffee cart on campus and that he liked when I wore blue, and I'd started to care more about him and less about my rules.

This shocking realization quickly faded when he shared the news with me that he was going to spend the summer abroad. Maybe I was terrified that he'd get bored of whatever we shared, or maybe my reaction was pure cowardice that had me defining our relationship as a friendship. Whatever the case, his complete lack of communication paired with these photos has me realizing that it was the right decision.

On our way here, I was prepared to find a rebound stat. I wanted to forget about feelings and memories that have me recalling his favorite brand and type of cookie while grocery shopping and comparing him to every guy I meet. Moreover, I felt annoyed and jaded from him being so short with me when I interviewed him tonight, treating me like a stranger—a stranger he didn't like. I came ready to return to last-year-me and embrace the single title that I'd neglected over the summer because those weeks with Ian bled into months with Olivia and Arlo and becoming friends with the team and many of their girlfriends. I spent the summer avoiding anything that resembled flirting. Instead, I focused on my new job as a yoga instructor at Zen Fitness and finding the best mocha in Seattle—a feat considering we have a coffee shop on nearly every corner in this city I've called home for the past twenty-one years.

"Incoming," Olivia warns.

I glance up to see Ian making his way through the crowd like he's parting the Red Sea. Crooked smile. Sexy mussed hair. And a dark stare that's pinned on me.

Shit.

I swallow my nerves and lift my chin with a false sense of bravado that I cling to like the ledge of a mountain.

He stops in front of us. "What's up, Liv?"

Only Arlo calls Olivia Liv.

She pastes a smile on her face. My best friend is proficient at lying with that very smile. It's a forgery that her sweet, Southern accent only accentuates when she says, "Hey, Ian. Nice game tonight."

Ian still doesn't look at me as he nods. "Glad you're here." He pats her shoulder once and then moves around her and past us.

Olivia slowly turns to look at me, brow furled. "That was weird."

Everything about Ian has been weird this week.

Everything about *me* has been weird since him.

I glance at where he's talking to a few girls wearing short dresses and heavy makeup. He props one hand on the wall and lowers his face with a stance that assures he's flirting. The girls giggle and lean closer.

Bitterness sits heavily on my shoulders, but I attempt to shake it off as I turn my attention back to Olivia.

"Do you want to go?" she asks.

I shake my head. "This is for the best."

"Liv!" Arlo's voice carries over the crowd. He's smiling his Olivia smile—the one that consumes his features. He makes his way toward us with Paxton and Lincoln at his sides.

"There's my girl," he says, sliding his fingers into Olivia's hair. The lust emanating from him is so intense I turn my attention to Paxton and Lincoln.

"Hey, Rose," Paxton says as Lincoln scans over the partygoers, likely looking for Rae.

"Hey. This place is pretty crazy tonight."

Pax grins lazily and nods. He's confident, but I know it's a carefully constructed shell. Last year, his dad had an affair that went public and created a media frenzy for his family, and since, I've heard his coping methods include binge drinking, pot, and his crazy girlfriend, Candace. "It's the beginning of the year. Parties are always craziest the first month of school."

He's right. Previously, I basked during these weeks because everything was so simple, less homework, fewer social obligations, and fewer family obligations, with the holidays still several weeks in the future. "Are Raegan and Poppy here?" I ask, knowing the two girls are the same brand of best friends as Olivia and me.

Lincoln's gaze cuts to me. "Not yet, but they should be soon."

"Ian just came by," Olivia says. "He acted really strange."

Arlo nods. "He's been channeling Coach Danielson and acting like an asshole all night." He shrugs. "He has a lot of freshmen on the team. I'm sure he's sick and tired of acting as their babysitter."

Paxton nods. "He'll get over it. They wanted to hold Montana to thirteen, and they did."

I hate that I'm listening so closely. And loathe that I'm hoping Isla isn't here tonight.

"Hey." The change in Lincoln's voice reveals that Raegan and Poppy have arrived. The girls are sophomores, but it's a detail I often forget when we spend time together because both are grounded, intelligent, and easy to like.

Poppy smiles at me, and it takes me only a second to decode the third-wheel ally grin she's giving me and = a second more to grimace internally. I don't know Poppy's background, and we're still at that stage where conversation can occasionally feel awkward or forced, so asking why she's single hasn't come up yet. Relationship advice has never been my strength, right up there with forming relationships, calculus, and not yelling for Olivia when I find a spider in our apartment.

Raegan ties her arms around Lincoln's waist and smiles in greeting.

"Hey! Hey!" More of their teammates approach, loud and already laughing.

Hoyt shoves a glass into my hand before reaching forward like a cobra and grabbing Ian's arm.

Ian meets my gaze for a second and then looks past me.

"I thought we discussed putting a hot tub in the living room?" Hoyt asks him.

Ian's shoulders are still rigid, but his face relaxes as he laughs. "There were zero deals that included a hot tub. In fact, this is the last party here for a while. My parents are moving back next week."

Hoyt's eyes grow wide with mock horror. "Tell me it isn't so. Can't they afford another mansion?"

Ian scoffs before laughing. "I'm moving out to the pool house. So do it up well tonight."

"When is Banks going to start hosting house parties?" Hoyt looks across his teammates. "Where the fuck is that wanker?"

A cup lifts, followed by the bright blue eyes of Tyler Banks. He's handsome in a way that makes you forget your name, and when he speaks with his deep voice and smooth British accent, your heart fails to function. "Never," he says before dipping his lips to the blond beside him.

"Who's that?" I whisper to Olivia, signaling with my eyes to the girl his arm is wrapped around.

"Chloe Robinson. It seems pretty serious. They moved in together."

My eyes grow wide with surprise. "That violates *all* of the rules."

Olivia grins. "I like her. She's sharp and clever. She reminds me a little of you because she hates bullshit."

"Who actually *likes* bullshit?"

Olivia grimaces. "*Way* too many people."

Ian clears his throat.

I glance at him, attempting to read his expression as his eyes dance over the room beyond us. It's silly and useless because I don't know Ian well enough to understand or know his expressions, regardless of how long I stare and try to.

His gaze lowers to mine, and for a second, I feel that same pull and connection I fought tirelessly against last spring. The same ones that made my palms sweaty and my lungs shallow because it felt like we were somehow in a different dimension, in another place where it was only him and me and us together. Where our pasts and mistakes didn't define us, and we understood one another without a single word because things were so simple and honest. "Do you have a minute?" he asks.

I want to say no and hold onto my determination to abide by my rules and find sanity again, but before I can respond, he nods toward the hallway, and my body marches to an order I'm not issuing.

I follow Ian through the dimly lit crowds and down the hall, where he stops at the doorway to a dark room. My traitorous and confused heart pounds obnoxiously in my chest as the lights flash on, and my thoughts dash from self-preservation to books—*so* many books. The room is circular and two stories high, with maple bookshelves built along each wall that stretch from floor to ceiling, filled with hundreds of books. The spines range in shape and color, beautiful. I glance at the second story, where a slender rail wraps around the opened space leading to a high ceiling where a skylight has darkness bleeding into the room. My feet sink into the plush area rug covering much of the floor as I follow him farther into the room. It's a sight I've never seen except in my imagination.

"I've been thinking about that email you showed me. Did you guys respond to whoever sent you those photos?" he asks, interrupting my appreciation for the room.

I turn my attention from the ornate stained-glass lamp with water lilies to Ian and shake my head. "I didn't receive the email." Annoyance is cast into my words because he knows this—at least, he should.

"Do you think Anthony would have done it? Last year, you mentioned that the budget for the paper was down, and you guys were going to have to cut back on the number of days you'd be printing."

Looking at Ian, I wonder if this is how my parents felt after their divorce. That edge of regret for having shared information because it can be thrown back and used as an accusation or, in this case, serves as a reminder of a time when feelings were reciprocated.

I shake my head to clear my thoughts. "You're giving Anthony too much credit. He's not this creative."

"Did the sender say anything else? Ask for anything?" Desperation or possibly annoyance has his eyes dancing between mine, his question again brief and direct.

I shake my head. "Anthony said they sent him the photos with a brief description of what they planned to do and told us to watch."

His brow knits. "So you guys *are* taking this as a story?"

"No," I tell him instantly. "This isn't newsworthy. This is garbage and a complete abuse of freedom of the press. No reputable journalist would accept this story."

His gaze softens as his shoulders fall from the rigid stacks of muscles they'd been in, reminding me of when he's on the field. I can smell his cologne standing this close—sweet, spicy, and delicious. It's not fair that he smells this good, and my body should absolutely not be responding to him.

I need to find a distraction or rebound. I don't care what the label or price is, but I know I need to leave before I consider kissing Ian.

"What does Anthony want you to do with the information?"

Ian's concern has the pictures in question percolating in my thoughts. More specifically, the image of him with his hands on a half-naked girl. How long ago was the photo taken? Who was she? What did she mean to him? And then, I quickly realize that his reaction has nothing to do with my feelings and everything to do with his reputation.

"You have nothing to worry about," I finally respond, lifting my pointer finger with its black matte nail polish. "Because one, aside from the fact I have no interest in writing about who the football team wants to screw, you're forgetting my best friend is dating one of yours, and I would never do anything to hurt her. Two," I add, lifting a second finger, "If this comes out, it won't do anything but bring you positive attention, proven with Hoyt's recent stardom. Guys can get away with this sort of thing. Three." My ring finger pops up. "They're not showing anything shocking. Nudity is only scandalous to talk about, not to see. And finally." I turn my wrist and drop all but my middle finger. "If you want to know who's digging up dirt, you should be looking at your teammates. One of them likely knows what's going on and why."

Ian stares at me. I see the divide he builds between us before he takes a step back. "No one on the team would know about this and not say anything," he spits out icily.

I shrug, wanting to call him an amateur for trusting so many, especially when he barely knows the freshmen.

"Have a nice time at the party," he says.

Is he dismissing me?

Before I can wrap my head around the possibility, he walks out of the library, leaving me.

Did he just leave for another girl?

Should it matter?

God, why does this hurt?

I need to get out of my head. One of the hardest things about spending time with people is realizing there are no equal measures of giving and taking. Sometimes you forget to stop someone at the foyer, and the next thing you know, they're in your closet and have seen too much—know too much. Meanwhile, they haven't even opened their front door for you. I let Ian in, and knowing he clearly didn't like what he saw stings. I hate that sting. And I hate that I allowed him close enough for this to hurt so badly.

Moving toward the door, I separate this gorgeous room and Ian as two entities and glance around. The wooden ladder on rails catches my attention, sparking memories from when I was little and still believed in fairy tales and taming beasts rather than trying to forget feelings for one.

I make my way back out to the living room so I can find Olivia.

"I tried calling you four times," she says quietly. Arlo and a few of his teammates have crowded around, laughing. Two years ago, these guys would be doing stupid stunts like sledding off the roof into the pool or something equally dangerous. Now, they're nursing glasses of pop and talking about classes.

"Sorry," I tell her. "I didn't hear it ring."

Her gaze turns quizzical. "What happened?"

I sigh as I look around the room, trying to avoid an audience.

Olivia reads my thoughts instantly. "We're going to get something to drink," she says to Arlo before linking her arm with mine and turning us to face the kitchen.

Within five steps, I'm feeling better. Stronger. Braver. I pull in a deep breath, and when a cute guy follows me with his eyes, I even find myself smiling.

We're silent as we wait to order drinks. Olivia's giving me a moment to be with my thoughts—another reminder of how well she knows me. Most friends would be sharing a million opinions and asking a million questions, and making a million assumptions, but Olivia knows that would only overwhelm me and cause me to panic.

"Hi," she greets the bartender with a kind smile. "Do you have any Coke or Pepsi?"

He smiles at her, a twinkle in his eye that says he appreciates more than her patience. "I have both."

"Two Pepsi's, please," she says.

He nods. "Would you like ice?"

"Oh, that's okay. We'll just take the cans."

He gives another curt nod, turns to the fridge behind him, and withdraws two cans of Pepsi that he opens before handing them to us. "Anything else?"

"No. Thank you so much." She places a tip in the jar in front of him, and we turn away as the people behind us start ordering a slew of drinks with little patience and fewer manners.

I grip the can, allowing the coldness to soak from my fingertips up through my arm, a welcomed distraction. "I didn't realize this was going to be so awkward," I tell Olivia.

She shakes her head. "I can tell Ian still cares about you. He looks at you like you're the only thing he sees."

I grimace. "Trust me; it has nothing to do with me. I told him about the email Anothony received, and he had a mini freak out."

Olivia's brows jump. "At least he's concerned. Arlo just laughed and thought it was a joke."

I shrug. "I'm still not convinced it's not."

Olivia releases a breath, her gaze cast on Ian. "I think you make him nervous."

I shake my head. "He just wanted to ask more questions about the website and who sent the email." I switch hands with my pop, placing my chilled fingers on my exposed collarbone. "I don't know what to say or how to act around him. It's awkward. This is why I don't date—*almost dating* is too complicated. I can't imagine what the real deal is like."

Olivia smirks.

"Rose!" Lacy calls my name before Olivia and I can dissect the situation further. She wraps her arms tightly around me. "How are you? How was your summer?"

Behind her are Isla and Chantay. I was Isla for a long time in their trio, and this summer, when I began canceling more and going out less, they began spending more time with Isla. It was my decision, yet envy and betrayal dance with regret as they start sharing stories from their night.

"Have you guys seen Paxton Lawson tonight?" Chantay asks as she fans herself with one hand. "Totally hot," she says, peering around as though she might spot him.

Olivia takes another sip of her drink. She's never liked hanging out with them. They're loud, have short attention spans, and rarely care to discuss anything but a great party and a hot guy—the polar opposite of Olivia.

"It's senior year," Lacy adds. "Time to put all the cards on the table."

I shake my head as I force out a laugh. It sounds fake, but the noise of the party hides the fact.

"You've been stuck in neutral for a while," Lacy says. "Maybe this has to do with a certain someone with dark hair, blue eyes, and killer tackle...." She gives me a pointed look, and for a second, it feels like she's trying to offer me the opportunity to tell her—to tell myself—that I have feelings for Ian.

Chantay's eyes shine with excitement. "Maybe you should date a professor!"

Genuine laughter hits my ears, shocking me because it's mine. "No," I tell her with a conviction that stills my focus. "Absolutely not."

Lacy's smile is patient and kind, verging on sad for a second, almost like she feels sorry for me.

I shake off the feeling with another quick drink of my pop.

"Oh, God, there he is." Chantay turns, deliberately staring at several guys on the football team who are gathered together. "Could you introduce us?" she asks, turning to Olivia. "Aren't you like *friends* or something with one of them?"

"She's dating Arlo," I remind her with a warning glare.

"That's right," Isla says. "Arlo was fuck buddies with Jade-what's-her-name and got injured at the end of the year," she tells Chantay.

Olivia's gaze turns icy as she lowers her can of pop.

"He's been *dating* Olivia since *last spring*," I enunciate and punctuate the important words.

"Way to go, Olivia. He's sexy. He has that smile and those muscles. Oh, and he was all over social media last year!" Lacey says, turning to Chantay. "Remember? He was the guy who beat up like ten dudes. *Boom. Boom. Boom.* Knocked them all out." She punches the air.

"There were five of them, and he only hit three of them, and it was because they were bothering two girls," Olivia says, anger bristling her shoulders. That fight nearly cost Arlo his future and place on the team.

Chantay raises her eyebrows at Olivia's tone and looks at me. They're here looking for a good time—a few drinks, dancing, and the hope of ending the night with a hot guy. We're ruining their buzz by fact-checking them.

Before anyone can stir the pot or ease the tension, Lacy's phone rings.

"Tell me that's not Garett," Chantay says.

Lacy looks guilty for a second before grinning. "He's here." She winks at me.

"So is the football team," Chantay challenges. "And the basketball team, and the soccer team...."

"You've already slept with the entire basketball team," Lacy tells her.

Chantay grins mischeviously. "So can you."

Lacy laughs.

"Stick around for a little while. Make Garett at least work for it," Chantay says bitterly.

I intentionally avoid looking at Lacy. I don't want to see her decision because either way, I know I'll feel conflicted. "She can go. We'll introduce you and Isla to the football team," I offer Chantay.

Pure, undulated joy fills her blue eyes. "Isla's all about Ian this year." Though she warned me, and I saw Isla flirt with him, hearing the news declared so openly makes my breath catch, and my lungs burn as though I've just inhaled a cloud of bleach.

"I told her she had to check with you before pursuing him, though, because I know something was going on between you two at the end of last year," Lacy adds.

I feel Olivia's gaze on me as I shake my head and look at Isla. "No. He's free game."

Chantay laughs joyfully. "I knew you'd say that. We all know your rules. Sleep with him once, and it's over. Smartest lesson I've learned during my time at Brighton."

I shake my head. "No. Ian and I just hung out for a while. Friends. Nothing ever happened between us."

Isla laughs. "Is that how we say rejected now?"

Indignance snaps my spine straight. "I wasn't rejected."

"You were pretty into him," Chantay says, her eyebrows and voice raised with doubt.

Her words settle on my skin like the old, red wool sweater my mom used to insist I wear that my aunt had knitted for me: itchy and uncomfortable. It was several sizes too big, which led to my mom insisting I wear it for several years when fall arrived and the temperatures began to cool. Hearing that others knew I had feelings toward Ian is even more uncomfortable.

"I'm pretty sure *he* was into her," Lacy says.

Chantay snaps. "He was borderline stalking her. Last year, he waited outside her classes and would show up at the coffee cart." She wrinkles her nose. "I knew it wouldn't last."

Pride wants me to jump on this train and ride it into safer territory where the attraction was one-sided, but instead, I find myself feeling sympathetic and even defensive as my thoughts tangle with her accusations.

Chantay turns her attention back to Isla. "But, I guess that means it's your lucky night."

Olivia exchanges a look with me, her confusion and weariness evident as she turns and scans the crowd. I want to assure her that they have no interest in hanging out and talking with Arlo or the rest of the team, for that matter.

"I'm going to meet Garett. You guys have fun and be safe," Lacy says. She blows me a kiss and waves at the others before disappearing into the crowd.

"I can't believe she's choosing Garett Feldon over the football team," Chantay says.

I spot Paxton and start moving toward him with Olivia at my side, grateful that Lincoln is beside him. He has the lowest tolerance for bullshit.

My heart skips as Ian joins them. He turns his head a few degrees, and our eyes meet. And though there's more space and people between us than before, it feels more personal, like these obstacles allow us the excuse and ease to stare. Or it might just be Ian, who has never been anything but confident and assured.

"This is a terrible idea," Olivia whispers as we stop in front of them.

"Hey," Arlo says.

My attention bounces from Arlo back to Ian. He's watching me with a hint of curiosity, and a note of humor, recognizing my discomfort.

The muscles in my shoulders and neck grow tight as I wonder if it's more uncomfortable to know what he's thinking or to have him see past my smile and confidence.

I clear my throat. "Guys, these are my friends, Chantay and Isla. They're looking for some volunteers to play drinking Jenga," I say, motioning to them like a game show hostess announcing a prize.

Hoyt whistles. "I'm in," he says, turning to Bobby, who nods.

"Pres?" Hoyt asks.

Lincoln shakes his head and tightens his grip around Raegan. "I'm going to be calling it a night pretty soon here. So should you guys."

"What?" Bobby asks. "We're supposed to be celebrating. We won."

"Doesn't change curfew," Paxton says.

Chantay grins. "We can be done by eleven. You want to play, Pax?"

Beside him, I catch the grimace that crosses Raegan's features before she wipes the look clear with a smile. I wonder if it's because it's Chantay or because it's her brother.

I imagine what it would have been like to see my older sister, Anna, date guys who attracted trouble. Instead, she dated one guy and married him a year after they graduated from law school. It was perfect and boring and so damn predictable it hurt.

Paxton smiles. I'm not surprised that Chantay likes him. He's not only incredibly attractive, but he has this tortured soul/bad boy vibe playing for him mixed with a small-town charm and sweetness that has nearly every girl on campus vying for his attention. "Sure," he says.

"Midnight," Lincoln says quietly, like a warning.

"Ian?" Isla asks. "You want to join us?"

I hold my breath, waiting for his answer. I hate that I can't seem to look away from him.

His gaze dances to mine and then to hers. "Yeah. Let's do it."

That sting returns with a vengeance as Isla meets my gaze and smiles.

I take another drink of my pop, wishing it was straight alcohol so I could stop looking at Ian or at least stop caring that I keep looking at him.

7

IAN

"Hey! You finally stopped ghosting me!" my little sister, Cassie, says as I answer my phone.

"I would've, but I fat thumbed it while trying to see who was calling."

"Harsh!" she cries. "What happened to sibling love?"

"It's a myth," I tell her, abandoning the stack of books I've been putting away. I glance at the stove to see what time it is. It's Sunday, which is supposed to be my rest day, but I've carved out time for a meeting with my Dad's campaign advisor, and then I need to study the tape of last night's game.

"I saw you on some *sportsy* news show yesterday," Cassie continues. "You know it wouldn't kill you to smile occasionally, right?"

"It might."

She snickers. "I'm serious. You come across so ... intense."

Asshole was the term Coach Harris used when he texted me this morning with some additional tips.

"Dad's PR people will probably tell you to avoid the media at all costs."

I run a hand through my hair. "It wasn't that bad."

"It was," she says. "It *really* was. I'm not going to tell you that my roommate thought you were super hot because that would be gross and wrong on so many levels, but just in case you ever want to get back out onto the *other* field, you'll need to smile. Girls like that."

I want to tell her that she's full of shit. I've seen plenty of girls throw themselves at Lincoln, and he's often misconstrued as the biggest asshole on the team. "Are you really calling to offer me dating advice?"

"More to see how you're doing with Mom and Dad moving back and the anniversary of Isaiah coming up."

Cassie would remember. She does each year. As much as I like to give her a hard time, my sister's heart is pure gold. I swallow the rest of my two-word replies that make others consider me gruff and take a seat on the couch to focus on our conversation. "Football has been so busy I've barely seen Mom and Dad. I moved out to the pool house and am getting things settled."

"I'm a little jealous you decided to move out there. I can't believe I didn't think about moving out there while in high school."

"You would have freaked yourself out being out here alone."

"Shut up," she says.

I chuckle. We both know I'm right. "How's California treating you?"

"Gloriously. I'm on my way to brunch, and this afternoon I'm going to play beach volleyball with some friends. I don't know why you decided to stay up in Seattle."

"Yeah, you do." Brighton was my first choice.

"Beach volleyball!" she repeats. "Need I say more?"

She's trying to make me laugh, and I oblige this time, regretting my short-tempered introduction. "How are classes going?"

"As one of the only females in a predominantly male field, it can get a little stodgy at times. I've had to put a couple of guys in their place, but aside from that, it's good. What about you?"

I rub my eye with the heel of my hand. The truth is, school is a fucking nightmare during football season. I have no idea how Banks is taking the class load he is and manages to be on both feet every day. We're currently investing forty to fifty hours per week toward football, leaving little time for classes or anything else. "Mondays are pretty brutal. My first class is at six am."

"You aren't human. I don't know why you have so many early classes."

"Football," I tell her.

"Yeah, yeah," she deadpans. "I bet it will be an adjustment to have Mom and Dad back, but hopefully, you can reap the benefits of all the cooking classes Mom took while living in Itlay."

"She used to burn frozen pizzas," I remind her.

Cassie breaks into laughter. "How many times did she forget to remove the cardboard piece on the bottom?"

"I'm sure the old neighborhood could tell you because of how often the smoke alarms went off."

Her laughter turns into giggles that slowly fade. "Gosh, some of the excuses Isaiah would make so he didn't have to eat dinner with us used to crack me up."

I glance at the framed photo of my childhood best friend sitting on the bookshelf I'd been putting old comic books and other favorite novels on. "That's because his mom was such a *good* cook."

"Have you seen Mrs. Templeton lately?"

I shake my head, and though she can't see my reply, she seems to assume it as the silence stretches. Isaiah passed away during my sophomore year of high school, an accident that never should have happened that left a loss too significant for words. "They're doing the annual road cleanup in his honor," I tell her.

"I know this is always a tough time for you," she says. "If you need to reach out and talk or *not* talk, I'm here."

We both know I won't, but the sentiment is still appreciated. "Thanks, Cass."

"Anytime. Now, let's just focus on you smiling a little more, scowling a little less, and don't forget my birthday month is coming up!" she exclaims, retreating from the topic of Isaiah.

"You're too old to have a birthday month."

"Blasphemy!" she cries. "I can, and I will. I'll send you my Amazon Wish list."

I shake my head. "Eat some pancakes for me. I've got to head into a meeting for Dad here shortly."

"Ian," she says, her voice calm yet tentative. "Don't forget to have some fun this year. It's your last year of college."

"Already happening," I tell her. "I threw the biggest party in history last weekend. People are still talking about it."

"Good! It's all about balance. I'll talk to you later."

"Love you, Cass."

"I love you, too. Say hi to the parental units for me and let them know I'll call them tomorrow." Cassie has always been good at keeping in touch, something I fail miserably at.

"Will do."

She hangs up as my phone starts vibrating with a handful of messages.

> **Luis:** Did you see this? Who the fuck took this picture? I'm ready to beat someone.

Dread has my heart accelerating as I click on the attached link. It's a picture of Luis and his girlfriend, Alexis, her breasts mostly exposed from where he's lifting her bathing suit top so that his hands only cover her nipples. They're outside, likely at the beach or a lake.

"*Rumor has it that Luis Garcia refused to sign with Brighton unless his girlfriend received a scholarship.*" The picture says.

The picture is nearly as offensive as the claim.

> **Me:** Shit, dude. How's Alexis taking it?

It's been eight days since Hoyt's picture was published and my interview with Rose, and I haven't heard a thing. I'd hoped everyone chose to ignore the site like me.

> **Luis:** She's fucking pissed.

> **Me:** Rightfully so.

Alexis is whip-smart and works her ass off, not to mention they didn't meet until freshman year at Brighton.

A knock on the door stops me from responding to Luis. Mom is at the patio door, her hands folded in front of her. It's awkward, yet I appreciate the privacy.

"Hey, Mom."

She grins. "Mind if I come in?"

"Of course."

She steps past me, wearing a blue dress that sweeps the floor. "Do you think I look all right?" She stands nervously in the small living room. "Never mind. That's not a question you want to answer. I'm nervous," she admits.

"Mom, you look great. There's no reason to be nervous. You don't have to impress these people. You're paying them, remember?"

She laughs. "It's politics, honey. You have to impress everyone." She spins, looking around at the space. "This place looks...." Her voice trails off as she turns her head around to look at the rest of the pool house. "Like a hotel."

I shake my head. "It's ten times the size of any dorm room."

"You're sure you want to be out here?"

"This way, I won't bother you and Dad when I get home late or have to leave early for practice. Besides, with classes and football, I'm not home much. I basically need this place to sleep and do laundry."

"Don't tell me I'm going to see you less while living across the pool than I did on the opposite side of the globe." She tilts her head with a silent warning.

I shake my head, but can't make many promises. Between my practice schedule and classes, I barely have time to sleep.

A smile spreads across Mom's features as she sweeps her dark hair over one shoulder. "We should have this place redone. Make it a little homier. At least hang some of your art pieces in here."

I shrug. "Don't worry about it. It works fine."

She smiles again before pressing her fingers to her temple. "I'm telling you, jet lag is so much worse when you're old."

"You're not old," I tell her. "But you should take a nap."

She shakes her head. "I don't have time for a nap. Your father's campaign adviser is supposed to be here in ten minutes. Besides, if I nap now, I'll sleep for eight hours and be up all night."

The reminder of the meeting nearly has me grimacing. "Are you sure I need to be there for this meeting?"

"Your dad said they requested to meet you. Sadly, they'll probably want to parade you around a little since you're our household celebrity."

"Everyone loves a winner," I chide.

She wrinkles her nose. "We don't want you to feel like we're using you. If you don't want to be a part of this, we can draw a hard line, and you don't have to."

I shake my head. "I want to help. I know this means a lot to Dad, and if my smiling and standing next to him will help his chances of being elected, then that's the least I can do."

"We'll see how it goes. If it becomes too much, just say the word."

"Coach thinks it will help me prepare for interviews. He's starting to put me in front of the press."

Mom's eyes shine with the same level of pride as they did when I brought home pictures of stick figures and cereal glued onto paper when I was in elementary school. "I'm sure you'll do great. You're always poised and humble." She uses the same adjectives others use to describe people who are uptight assholes.

"Will you have enough room in here for your easels?" Mom looks at the space again.

"I barely have time to paint," I tell her.

She blinks back her surprise. "Maybe you should try making some time for it."

"We should get inside," I say, changing the subject. "It's almost time to find out how our lives are going to change."

A heavy sigh breaks through her lips. I doubt she would tell me whether she wants Dad to run for office. My parents have always been a unified front, making it oftentimes difficult to know whose dream is being chased. However, Mom loved living in Rome. She worked hard to learn Italian, made friends, and built a routine she enjoyed. Then again, it could have been stepping away from a job where she worked twelve-hour days that made her so blissfully happy. "You're right. Let's go meet the advisors and see if they can teach us how to take a proper selfie."

We make our way across the backyard, and though I won't voice the thought to her, it feels strange to have them home again. If I've learned anything in my life, it's that few things ever remain constant. Things, people, and relationships are like the weather and constantly change.

"There they are," Dad says as we step through the french doors that lead into the living room, where a small team of people are gathered in the formal living room, all in varying shades of blue and black suits.

"This is my wonderful wife, Michelle, and my son, Ian." Dad moves to stand beside us. "Guys, this is Anna Pollard and her team."

"You have a beautiful family, Mr. Forrest," Anna says. "We're looking forward to working with all of you and getting to know you better." She introduces the swarm of people behind her, addressing them each with titles that mean little to me before suggesting we take our seats.

MOM HAD ASKED if I could clear my afternoon for this meeting. At the time, it didn't seem like the worst idea, but sitting here now and listening as they start to address my Dad's history and dissect our lives, my attention keeps jumping to the one thing I've been actively avoiding: Rose.

Regret has been stitching its way into my thoughts since the pregame interview with her last Saturday. In our shared Labor Economics class, she spent the duration of class on the opposite side of the room, ignoring me.

I've considered texting or calling her, but neither seems appropriate nor genuine, which will only worsen the situation. Rose is everything I swore I'd never like in a woman: impulsive, stubborn, and guarded. I don't want someone obedient and silent, but the women I'm usually interested in are bubbly, warm, and friendly—three words that fit Rose and yet don't at all. We first met in January of last year during a study group. She'd been sitting alone, highlighting her textbook and scribbling notes. I remember because she didn't look up or participate with anyone in the group though she continued to show up every week.

Four weeks later, she showed up after me for the first time, and I saw her entire face for the first time. She was stunning—the kind of beautiful that demands and holds your attention.

I memorized every detail about her, from her straight nose to the unique green shade of her eyes, to her perfectly full lips, and imagined burying my hands in her long, dark hair and deciphering her elegant tattoos with my tongue.

The study group had grown, and there were only two open spots, and she chose the chair next to me. It was then that I realized she wasn't even studying the same subject. We were meeting for Statistics, and she was reviewing macroeconomics. But she sat down, opened her textbook, and began studying.

The hint of her perfume distracted me the entire night, along with the elegant scripted tattoo around her forearm and black nails. The distractions didn't end there. Every time she quietly sighed, sipped her coffee, or chewed a pen cap, I lost focus.

I don't know if it was luck or a curse that she chose the seat beside me because, since that day, Rose Cartwright has been impossible for me to ignore.

The following week, she was already in her seat when I arrived, and I decided to sit beside her. In my quest to be smooth, I knocked over her coffee and a stack of her notecards.

"Shit," I'd said. "I'm sorry."

She grabbed a stash of napkins from the front of her backpack and quickly mopped up the mess.

"I'll get you a new one," I'd offered.

She smiled, then. And if I hadn't already been intrigued by this girl, I would have been then. Flawless lips, high cheekbones, and eyes that shone with humor confirmed she was perfect. She pushed her dark glossy hair back and shook her head. "Don't worry about it. I've had it since this morning. You probably saved me from food poisoning."

"You're clearly doing college wrong if you can hold onto a coffee for eight hours."

Rather than smiling again, she cocked one eyebrow. "Normally, I'd agree. But this coffee was gross."

I glanced at the generic cup. "Bad coffee stand?"

"Bad order," she admitted. "I was trying to be less cliché and order something dark, bold, and sophisticated, and it was just bitter and gross. Say what you might, but I'm content being a cliché coffee drinker, and I'll take my cute boots and plaid shirts as well—zero shame." She shrugged but then winced. "Well, maybe a little shame. The group leader is a coffee snob, so don't mention it to her because I need this study group." Her smile turned playful.

"You know this is a Statistics study group, right?" I asked, nodding to her opened textbook.

Her eyes grew wide. "What? I had no idea." Her voice was entirely even, and her face gave nothing away. For a moment, I couldn't tell if she was pulling my leg or clueless.

She leaned closer. "Is this the part where I smile, and you check out my boobs, and we go on our merry little way?" she asked.

"Why are you here when you're studying macroeconomics?"

She gave me a warning look. "Because," she whispered. "This is the best study group I've found on campus. The moderator hates when people talk and leads with fear like a dictator. It's glorious for studying purposes."

I unzipped my bag and withdrew my coursebook. "Your secret's safe with me. The coffee and the macroeconomics."

She grinned. "That's good. Otherwise, you might have become my new archenemy, and I don't have time to plan revenge plots." She turned her attention back to her opened book.

"By the way, you're hanging out with the wrong crowd if you're exchanging smiles for boob stares," I told her.

Rose glanced up at me but didn't say a word.

I was distracted for the next two hours, wondering what that single glance meant.

A throat clears, drawing my attention to the present. Anna is looking at me. "You should know that people might try to dig up things from your past. It's ridiculous stuff they try to spin most of the time, but occasionally, something can make it out that you don't want to be public. It would help us if you could tell us about any of those things beforehand. It doesn't have to be now, but if you can make a list and get it to me, we can get ahead of things and put the correct connotation on the situation." Anna looks between my parents and then me. "Sadly, this could impact you, as well. Most politicians don't go after kids, but the rules of politics have changed a lot, and it seems there are few things left untouched."

Dad shakes his head. "Ian's way smarter than I was at his age."

I think of the picture of me playing grab-ass with a girl the summer before last and feel myself cringe.

I hope he's right.

8

ROSE

"Secrets are being spilled like beans over on a brand-new site that is giving us a whole new look at our football team," I reread the headline.

"No," I whisper, staring at where my article should be in *The Daily Dose of Brighton,* and continue reading. 'Drawing attention and intrigue, the players' deepest secrets are being revealed one player at a time, and if you saw Saturday, you know my pun was intended.'

My jaw drops. "No!" I repeat. "No! No! No!" I finish reading the butchered article and crinkle it in my fists, and head toward the newspaper room.

I push the door open so hard it hits the door stopper. The classroom is mostly empty, so I head to the back, where Anthony's tiny office is, and hammer on the door with my fist. "Anthony!" I yell.

When he doesn't reply, I try opening that door, but it's locked. "Don't you hide from me, you weasel." I pull out my phone to call him.

He doesn't answer.

He wouldn't.

He's probably hiding.

"I don't know why you assigned me sports and then hijacked my article!" I say to his voicemail, then grind my teeth to prevent calling him a dozen expletives. "I spent my entire weekend writing and researching this piece, and instead, you printed this bullshit and butchered my name and journalistic integrity, not to mention you lowered *The Daily Dose* to tabloid status! Thanks for signing my name to your disaster. Much unappreciated. Call me, you coward." I hang up and release a long breath.

I wonder if he's hiding from me or CJ, the lineman who was featured on the rumor website today and in my article—which was definitely not my article.

I want to go home and hide under my bed until this all blows over. I want to call my dad and cancel our plans for Sunday. I want to find a familiar show on Netflix and the most comfortable pair of pajamas in my closet and hang out with our cat, Juliet, all day.

"Is everything okay?" Amita asks from her desk, where she's blowing on her steaming cup of coffee.

"Have you seen Anthony?"

She shakes her head. "It's just been me in here this morning."

I'm not surprised. Amita is dedicated to the paper and has been since freshman year.

I release a quiet sigh. "I'm sorry you didn't get editor," I tell her. "I voted for you. I assumed everyone voted for you. You deserve it so much more."

Amita shrugs. "I appreciate it, but it's okay. This gives me more time to focus on other opportunities."

"Oh yeah?" My response is an instant reaction rather than genuine interest, my gaze still directed at Anthony's closed door in the back corner. Is he just pretending not to be here?

"I've begun writing a column as an independent contractor for a blog that's trying to target younger generations and educate them on world issues." She pushes her large, white-framed glasses higher on her nose.

I think of the article I wrote and submitted to Anthony last week about food security that he refused to print. "That sounds amazing," I tell her. "I told Anthony that people want to be informed and help make a difference. This is why *you* would have made an awesome editor, and I'm currently trying to hunt our *crappy* editor down so I can strangle him."

Amita smiles and leans back in her chair. "What did he do?"

"He rewrote my article," I tell her. "Not only did he rewrite it, but he butchered it into a tabloid piece and made me out to be a complete liar because I promised someone we wouldn't write anything about the story."

"Oh, is this about that website?" she asks.

"Yes." I release another sigh. "Apparently, Anthony knew it would be released, and he wanted me to do a pseudo-investigative piece to find out why and help make this a juicy, exciting story to get more reads because all he cares about is ad sales." I throw both my hands up. "And he left my name on the article, which really pisses me off. I don't want to be associated with this crap. Did you read it?"

She nods. "It was pretty awful."

I groan. "It's beyond awful. And how is it newsworthy? We should be publishing content that opposes this website, not giving it a platform. We've just poured gasoline on a tiny ember."

"Did you see today's photo?" she asks.

I splay my hand across my face to cover my wince. "Yes." The photo was of CJ, a freshman lineman I don't know. He was nude except for a pair of cowboy boots. Emojis of beakers covered his nether regions, and the caption rumored that he slept with his high school science teacher.

"Do you think the rumor is true?" she asks.

I shake my head. "I have no idea, but I don't think it's our job to be the jury when we have no facts. A claim like that could ruin his teacher's life if it's not true."

Amita nods. "I know. Could you imagine?"

"I don't think it will spread that far. I doubt anyone in Alabama or wherever he's from cares about Brighton's football team, but still, this is ridiculous."

"I can't believe people think it's attractive," she says.

Behind me, the door opens. I turn in hopes of finding Anthony, but instead, Janet slips in. "Hey," she calls. "I read your article."

"It wasn't my article," I tell her.

"Who do you think is sharing these pictures?" she asks, ignoring my clarification. "I hope they have some of Paxton Lawson. He is so freaking hot. I saw him last week and didn't realize how big his hands were." She lifts her hand to model the size of his. "Like *huge*. And you know what they say about guys with big hands..." She wriggles her eyebrows.

Amita scoffs, a smile spreading across her lips. "Am I broken? I don't think these pictures are hot."

Janet exchanges a look with me and then looks at Amita. "Like at all?"

Amita shakes her head. "No. It makes them all seem like players."

"Luis dates Alexis," I point out.

"Yeah, but he was pictured pulling her bathing suit off in public," Amita says. "Super respectful." She scoffs.

"I'd let him pull my bathing suit down in public," Janet says.

Amita laughs. "No, you wouldn't."

Janet shrugs. "Probably not. And I get it. I mean, some of them are kind of players."

"But is that a bad thing?" I ask. "I mean, as long as they're upfront and honest about it, should we or anyone else care about how many sexual partners they have?"

Amita turns her gaze to me.

I shrug. "I don't date, but I like sex."

Janet smirks. She knows my rules.

"So, you sleep with like a fuck buddy?" Amita asks.

I shake my head. "No, that leads to confusion and feelings. There's no way to be casual fuck buddies. I don't sleep with the same person twice."

"Ever?" Amita asks.

I shake my head. "Nope."

"So you've had like a hundred sex partners?"

I laugh. "How do you take me saying I don't sleep with the same person twice and translate that to me having a hundred sex partners?"

"Well, if you're having sex very often, you must have slept with quite a few guys."

"I don't keep track," I tell her. "But I don't sleep with everyone who has a penis."

"I'm shook," Amita says. "I need more details."

"There aren't that many details," I tell her. "I'm not looking for a serious relationship, but I like sex. I lay out clear rules that nothing will transpire, and if they're interested, we go from there."

"Aren't you terrified of catching an STD?" Amita asks.

"Oh, I have rules for that as well. I am all about safe sex."

Amita's eyes are three times their natural size as she stares at me. "But, there's still a risk. I mean, condoms don't protect against syphilis, herpes, or genital warts...."

"Absolutely, which is why if I'm interested in having sex with someone, we go get tested together and share our results. And trust me, there is nothing more awkward than learning hot boy's got chlamydia right along with him."

Amita looks at Janet. "I feel like such a prude right now. But rock on for making the guy go and get tested with you. I mean, it seems like it would be awkward as hell to me, but it's kind of brilliant."

I nod. "Sex isn't something to be embarrassed or ashamed about. It's normal. Natural. STDs and accidental pregnancies rise when people *don't* discuss sex."

Janet grins at me. "I want to be you when I grow up."

I laugh. "You should feel empowered. And if you aren't comfortable asking someone to get tested, I can refer you to some great battery-operated boyfriends."

Janet shrieks with laughter while Amita covers her face with both hands. "I can't believe we're having this conversation in the newsroom."

"It's a good conversation to have anywhere," I tell her. "Also, if you're interested, I have a ton of notes and an article about food security that Anthony refused to print. You can have it and maybe find some inspiration for that blog you're working for. It might be a better audience."

Amita grins. "Really? That sounds amazing."

"Yeah. Here." I reach for my phone and scroll through my email. "I'll send it to you now. Also, if either of you sees Anthony before I do, text me his location. I may or may not be plotting to throat punch him."

"Deal," Janet says.

"I'll see you guys later." I head outside, searching for the rays of sunshine on the sidewalk. It's windy today, and I should have brought a sweater, but I'm still in denial that summer is ending.

I am considering blowing off volunteering today for the millionth time. Last week consisted of more cleanup and more of Bree. She told me about a report she was writing on Franklin D Roosevelt, who inspired her, not because he was in office longer than any sitting president, or because he created the New Deal or any of the other random facts I was taught in school, but because he appointed Frances Perkins, the first woman to hold a cabinet position in a U.S. Presidential Administration.

I enjoyed the conversation and the difference we were making at Shady Grove Park from the hours of cleaning. However, facing the team after today's article has me feeling like the biggest traitor and idiot in the history of idiots.

"Hey..." Olivia approaches with a look of apprehension that I feel in my soul. Beside her is Chloe Robinson, which couldn't be any more uncomfortable considering she's another football player's girlfriend, and I look like an enemy of the state thanks to Anthony.

"You saw it?" I ask.

Olivia winces as she nods. "What happened?"

I throw my hands over my face. "I don't know. You saw my article. My *real* article."

"I read it three times," she says.

I press my palms against my eyes as I pull in a deep breath. I right myself and drop my hands before facing Chloe. "I promise I didn't write that article about the team. I would never...."

Chloe shakes her head. "It's okay," she says, but a chilling note of indifference and calculation in her eyes defies her words.

"Honestly," I continue. "I still have a copy of my article. It talked about the victory of the game. Some stats about Lincoln beating the record of yards run at Brighton, and some interview questions from Ian, Paxton, and Coach Harris...." The words rush out too fast and jumbled.

Olivia glances from me to Chloe. I can tell how badly she wants to say something, likely more assurances to plead my case because that's the kind of friend Olivia is. "I read it, and so did Arlo. There was no mention of the website or the scandal."

Chloe releases a short breath. "Honestly, the team doesn't seem that bothered by the rumors," she says. "I don't think half of them are even following the site. I asked Ty if this would be different since it's accusing CJ of sleeping with a teacher, and he didn't know."

I nod. "I feel sick over it."

Olivia shakes her head. "Anthony screwed you over."

"I hoped this stupid site would flounder and die, and now I'm right in the middle of it."

"I don't like it," Chloe says. "There's something strange about what's going on. Plus, I feel paranoid after seeing that picture of Luis and Alexis."

I cringe. "That was so off-limits. Do you guys think many people are looking at the site, though? I mean, Arlo went viral overnight last year when that fight happened. The videos were everywhere, but I haven't seen much chatter about this except for the first day when Hoyt was sharing his junk everywhere."

Olivia shakes her head. "Same."

Chloe scoffs and shakes her head. "I couldn't believe he took so much pride in that picture."

Olivia nods. "Arlo says Hoyt's phone is still blowing up. It made him more popular. So many girls want him."

"In my opinion, the team has two choices: ignore it or own it and let the rumors slide off their backs," I say.

Olivia glances at her phone. "We need to get going. We have to be at the park in fifteen minutes."

"I can't go," I tell her. "There's no way I can show my face to the team after that article was published. I sounded like a teeny-bopper."

"Yes, you can," Olivia says. "I'll be there with you. I'll trade someone so we can be on the same committee. We'll tell them what happened."

"Ian's going to be pissed," I tell her. "I swore to him I wouldn't mention the stupid website."

"I'm sure Arlo's already told him that it wasn't you," Olivia assures me.

I desperately want to believe her.

"It will be better if you come," Chloe says. "That way, we can address the article and get it over with. Otherwise, it leaves room for rumors and misinterpretations, and there are enough of those right now."

Olivia nods. "She's right."

My shoulders slump with defeat. Both options are as appealing as having a second set of wisdom teeth pulled sans anesthesia.

"By the way," Olivia says, "Chloe, this is my best friend, Rose Cartwright. Rose, this is Chloe Robinson. We're giving her a ride to the park because her sister, Vanessa, left early to pick up some bagels."

I offer my hand. "It's nice to meet you. Sorry, this first impression is such a shitty one."

Chloe grins. "You're making a great first impression. I'd be worried if you didn't care or thought this was funny."

Olivia smiles. "Rose is the best. We'll rip off the Band-Aid, and everything will be fine."

"Famous last words," I say.

Olivia links her arm with mine and directs us toward the parking lot. I had offered to drive Olivia to the park because Arlo's Tahoe is having engine problems, and he had to borrow her car. Now, I wish I hadn't because my dread heightens with every mile that brings us closer to the park.

"Arlo told me you're studying to be an astronomer. Is that right?" Olivia asks, turning to look at Chloe.

"Yeah, I'm kind of a space geek," she says from the backseat. "What about you both? What are you studying?"

"Well, I'm studying technomathematics, which is basically engineering mathematics, but I've decided to take some creative writing and English courses this year because I think I want to write children's books and never graduate college."

Chloe laughs. "I also plan never to graduate, so I fully support your decision."

Olivia looks across at me, a broad smile spread across her face. I can tell she likes Chloe and is giddy over the fact. When we met Candace, Paxton's girlfriend, over the summer, Olivia was terrified the other girlfriends would all be dramatic and snobby like her.

"What about you, Rose?" Chloe asks.

"Business management with my bachelor's degree in economics."

"Economics? You two will have to meet my sister, Nessie. She's a math whiz," Chloe says.

"Rose is in the process of opening a yoga studio," Olivia tells her.

"Really?" Chloe leans back in her seat, her gaze on me. "I've never done yoga. Coordination and I aren't exactly besties. What made you choose yoga?"

My thoughts shift from my butchered article to my past with her simple question. "My mom was a huge fan," I tell her. "She always wanted to own her own studio but was always busy with a thousand things for my sister and me, so she kept putting it off."

"Are you guys doing this together?"

I pull in a breath. Many things about my mom's loss have become more routine—pragmatic. It doesn't make her loss any easier, but applying logic and reasoning allows me to remember the best things about her and work to avoid how much I miss her, which makes answering questions mildly easier. "She, unfortunately, passed away a few years ago after a short battle with cancer."

Olivia reaches across the middle console and gives my hand a gentle squeeze filled with compassion and strength.

"Rose..." Chloe says. "I'm so sorry."

"Me too," I tell her. "She was an amazing woman and a yoga superstar, so this is kind of my way of honoring her."

"That's amazing," Chloe says.

"Not to sound gossipy," I say, ready to spin the conversation as it edges closer to that place where emotions take over and it becomes impossible to think of anything else but pain and loss. "We need some details about you and Tyler." I glance at her green eyes in my rear-view mirror. "Not to write about them, I swear."

Chloe laughs. It's a sweet and effortless sound. "That's good because your readers would be bored to tears. There's nothing juicy or exciting to share. We've known each other since freshman year. He's really good friends with my best friend, Cooper, so we've hung out off and on for a couple of years, and this past summer, we made a road trip across the country to return to Brighton, and things just kind of happened between us."

"Friends to lovers are always my favorite stories," Olivia says.

Chloe belts out a laugh. "Oh no. We were more enemies than friends."

My curiosity is piqued as I take another fleeting glance at her. "Enemies?"

"Not *enemies*, enemies," she says. "I didn't mastermind ways to torment him or anything like that, I just avoided him, and he avoided me. He would act like a tough asshole, and I would ignore him and avoid him even more."

"What changed?" Olivia asks.

"Well, not to brag, but I'm pretty cool," Chloe says as she blows on her fingernails and shines them on her shirt.

Olivia turns to me, a smile tugging on her lips.

"I'm totally kidding," Chloe cries from the backseat.

Olivia and I break into laughter that settles slowly, my cheeks remaining stretched. I like her, too.

"We had something between us for a few years that we both fought. He was this rich, mouthy, tough guy, and I loved studying space and science and exploring. We seemed too different, but the road trip changed that. Being with him every day, seeing some amazing places, and just sitting in the car and talking forced us to acknowledge our feelings for each other, and we realized they were much bigger and more important than our egos."

"Maybe that's what we need to do," Olivia says. "Lock you and Ian up in a car for a few weeks."

"*Ian?*" Chloe asks.

"She's joking," I say automatically, glaring at Olivia.

Olivia glares back at me. "He and Rose had a thing, but Rose has rules about not being in a relationship."

"Really?"

Olivia nods. "I've been telling her it's time to forget the rules."

9

IAN

"Three days, three pictures," Paxton says where he, Banks, Hoyt, Arlo, and I are huddled, waiting for the rest of the team to arrive before we commence park cleanup for the third week.

"You wouldn't believe how many girls have been calling me," Hoyt says. "Seriously. I've never gotten so many titty pics. They all want me. You've got to see this one...." He reaches for his phone.

Arlo takes a step back. "It's a good thing we're working outside. Your ego's getting so big you won't be able to fit through a doorway soon."

Hoyt cups himself. "Because I've been getting so much action."

"We don't want to see it," I tell him.

Pax shakes his head. "Watch your asses and keep your noses clean," he warns before turning his attention to Arlo and me. "I need a word."

Banks gives Hoyt a condescending look and peels away, heading toward Cooper Sutton, a fellow teammate and Tyler's closest friend on the team who arrived with his girlfriend, Vanessa Robinson, and several dozen bagels.

"Are we worried?" Paxton asks, pivoting to make our huddle smaller.

Arlo shakes his head. "No."

Pax looks at me, and I shrug. "I wouldn't even fucking know about the site if Hoyt and Luis hadn't messaged me. I hate social media."

Pax pulls in a leveled breath. "Did you see the school paper today? Rose wrote an article telling people to follow the website."

Arlo's smile falls. "Rose didn't write that shit."

Pax nods. "Her name was on it."

Arlo shakes his head. "Trust me. I went over formations and positions with her twenty thousand times this weekend because she insisted it be perfect. She didn't write shit about the website and these damn rumors."

Paxton's eyes pinch with doubt.

"Dude, do you really think I'd cover for her if I thought she was trying to stab us in the back?" Arlo asks.

Pax shrugs. "No offense, but I think you'd do almost anything for Olivia."

Arlo pulls back. "I would. But I'd do anything for you, too. You guys are my family, and there's no way I'd knowingly allow someone to post this shit and keep it from you. That article wasn't Rose's. I know because few things piss Rose off more than slut-shaming and because Olivia texted, saying Rose is freaking the fuck out. She thinks everyone's going to be pissed off because of the damn article."

I watch their conversation volley back and forth, recognizing Paxton's resolve before he wipes his brow. "It's not a big deal. At this point, it's only gaining us more attention, and these assholes are eating it up." He gestures to Hoyt. "The fucker was basically getting a hand job outside of the science building."

"What in the hell were you doing by the science buildings?" Arlo asks.

Paxton flips him off. "My point is, it's not a big deal *yet*, but if we find out who's doing this, I want to know."

Arlo shrugs. "I say we set our concerns on San Francisco and beating the shit out of them this weekend." He reaches for his phone, checking through a series of messages. "Liv's here. She wants to make sure everyone's cool." He glances between us.

Pax nods. "Yeah."

Arlo nods and heads for the parking lot.

Pax clamps his hand around my biceps. "You all right?"

"Yeah. I just wish I understood why this was happening. We just came off an undefeated season. Who in the hell would want to try dragging us down?"

He shakes his head. "It's probably a joke. Right now, there's no harm, no foul. I'm probably overreacting."

Denial and doubt keep me from agreeing with him.

"How are things going with your parents being back?" he asks.

I run a hand over that same pinched spot in the muscle behind my shoulder that's been nagging at me for weeks. "My dad's running for governor next year, so I have a feeling they'll be pretty busy."

"Governor? Shit. Is that good or bad?"

Something caught between a laugh and a scoff leaves my lips. "I don't know."

Paxton pats my shoulder, laughing.

"What about you?" I ask. "How are things going? I didn't see Candace at the party on Saturday."

His demeanor darkens as he rolls his shoulders. "That's because she hates me."

"Past or present tense?"

He shakes his head. "With her, who knows. I'm telling you, I'm about to follow your vow of celibacy for the year. Forget girls, forget drama, forget expectations for the time I don't have and dates I can't afford."

Candace and Paxton have been dating since we became friends. She's hot, but it took only five minutes to realize she was a special brand of crazy that has me avoiding him anytime they were together. She craves drama, and she creates her own when there isn't enough.

"Meanwhile, Hoyt said he's hooked up with ten women this week."

I shake my head. "Let's hope he's double wrapping it, so there aren't any surprises in nine months."

Pax laughs as he nods. "That rumor probably wouldn't bring him the attention he's swimming in." His laughter fades as CJ approaches us, annoyance lowering his brow.

"Hey," Pax says.

CJ releases a long breath. "What's up, Captain." His southern accent is a drawl, slower than Olivia's.

"I take it you saw the rumor website today?" Pax asks solemnly.

CJ blows out a breath and scrubs his cheek with his fingernails. "It's been a really strange day. Chicks are blowing up my phone, and guys are asking me for details...." He shakes his head. "I just hope my mom doesn't see it."

"It's not true, right?" I ask.

"Well, not entirely."

I stand straighter, panic stirring in my chest, praying this won't cause an issue for the team or our season. "What the fuck does that mean?"

"Shit." Pax rubs a hand across his brow. "Only the teacher gets in trouble in these cases, right?" He looks at me.

CJ Shakes his head. "It's not like that. She was a student-teacher, and I graduated before we got together."

"How would anyone know?" I ask.

CJ shrugs. "Beats the hell out of me. You don't think this will impact my place on the team, do you?"

Paxton pats CJ on the shoulder. "No. It would be consensual if you had graduated and were over eighteen," But as Pax reassures him, I can hear the dread in his voice—because this time, the rumor is bordering on truth.

Paige, the director of Beacon Pointe, claps her hands. "Thank you all for coming back out. We made a lot of progress in these past two weeks. We removed most of the graffiti, and a local arborist volunteered his time and cleaned up all the trees and bushes."

I look around as she says this, noting how much work still needs to be done compared to the triumphs she's listing.

"We still have a lot of trash to pick up, and today we're going to be working on repairing the fence. We also have some volunteers here who will install footers so we can build a bridge across the stream."

Luis jogs over. "What'd I miss?"

I shake my head. "There's more trash to clean up."

Luis nods. "All right. We've got this. Do we have to check in again?"

I shrug. "She hasn't made it that far."

Luis starts to say something in response as Paige continues with instructions, but my attention shifts to Rose. She's standing at the edge of the group beside Olivia and Chloe. Rose is always at the center of every group setting, drawing attention, whether wanted or not. Seeing her on the outskirts, her gaze unsure as she peers around reminds me of when I told her she was in the wrong study group.

Luis elbows me. "Ready?"

I nod, and we head to the check-in table to get our assignments. My thoughts are at war with each other. I want so badly to hold on to my resentment toward Rose for being so damn insecure about us and calling things off between us as soon as I got too close, but her unease has me ready to stand beside her.

"You're going to be picking up debris and garbage near the woods," Penny, the purple-haired woman, tells me. She points at the map taped to the table. "You'll need a red vest, gloves, and a bag. They're all over there." She points toward a tree.

I head toward the station and gather my things. When I turn around, Arlo waves at me from where he's in line with Chloe, Tyler, Cooper, Vanessa, Olivia, and Rose. Agitation climbs my spine like a ladder. I need ten minutes to myself in a closed room with my paint-brush and canvas or on the field where I can tackle any damn son of a bitch who dares to get close to me.

I stop in front of them, intentionally standing next to Tyler because he's the furthest from Rose.

"Trash again?" Arlo asks. "I'm going to have jokes all year about this."

"I wouldn't expect anything less. I'll see you guys out there." I turn and make it a hundred feet before someone calls my name.

Not just anyone.

"Ian!" Rose calls my name again, but I don't stop or turn around. I know all of my words will be scathing because, despite reason and logic, I want to be mad at her—need to be upset with her.

"Ian!" She jogs to catch up. "Can we please talk? Just five minutes."

I stop and pivot to face her. She nearly runs into me. She takes a measured step back and raises her chin.

"Two," I tell her.

"I want to explain. I know I promised I wouldn't write about the site, and I didn't. That crap about the site was not mine."

I want to believe her—the scary thing is, I do believe her—yet I still feel like she drove a stake into my back. It just has nothing to do with the rumors.

"I'm sorry that it happened. If I'd known, I would have tried to stop it or, at the very least, given you a heads up," Rose continues.

"It doesn't matter," I tell her.

She blinks and then sighs. "From what I understand, the rumors are going to be more damming. Maybe you guys can get ahead of this and take Hoyt's approach. Own up to the images and spin the narrative."

"No one cares. No one's even paying attention."

Surprise has her brows arching. "Whoever's behind this is clearly trying to do something more than just post scandalous pictures."

"It doesn't matter," I repeat.

"No one has to know if the secrets are true or not. If you guys—"

"I'm done," I say, interrupting her. "I don't want to play these games. I don't give one fuck about some asshole behind a keyboard." I point in the direction of the line at the check-in table. "Girls are blowing up their phones and social media accounts. If this person thinks they're fucking us over, they're wrong."

Rose stares at me, her green eyes scanning over my face. For once, she's silent, and fuck me if it doesn't annoy me. I want her to argue and pick a fight because I have so much anger rippling through my veins and thoughts that need an outlet.

"That's good. You shouldn't care," she says.

We stare at each other for several seconds, her eyes expressive and bright though she says nothing more.

"Why do you care?" I ask. "What are you telling me this? Why are you even here? And why in the hell are you apologizing for the article if you weren't involved?"

Her mouth falls open, but she doesn't say anything.

"What is this, Rose? Why do you show up at my house and follow me with your eyes? Why do you care about these damn pictures or the stupid goddamn site?"

She takes another step backward, her green eyes shifting between mine as a dozen unspoken words remain locked behind her lips.

I take a step closer, anger vibrating in my chest. "Dammit, Rose. Would you just tell me for once what you're thinking?"

She moves in one fluid step, so fast, I don't have a chance to respond. She twines her arms around my neck, and I barely register that her hair smells like summer, fresh and new, before her lips collide with mine. It's a challenge and a punishment rolled into one demanding kiss that is all pressure and intention.

I drop the supplies and grasp her waist, skating my fingers beneath the hem of her shirt, finding her warm, silky flesh. I dig my fingers into her skin and pull her closer to me, feeling her warmth invade me, dancing on the flames of my anger and somehow making them grow and wither at the same time.

I contest the feeling, sweeping my tongue along the seam of her lips.

She responds with a gentle moan that makes me instantly aroused. But more than that, it triggers the same feeling I experience when on the field, the one that has me feeling like I'm more than a man—more than my future. I want to allow the feeling to consume me and ignore the doubt and trepidation that has prevented me from kissing Rose prior, knowing it would change everything—unfavorably—because I know her rules.

Annoyance and betrayal blow on the flames in my chest as I claim her mouth, tasting the spearmint on her tongue as it slides against mine with an equal level of defiance and determination.

Her grip around my neck tightens, pulling our bodies closer. I slant my head and oblige, kissing her deeper as her hands rake through my hair with the same lack of control as her lips. Our tongues battle as our grips become tighter. I don't know if it's lust or fury controlling me at this point as I devour her, taking and giving until I can't remember if she's the one who's angry or I am.

Rose pulls away, but her fingers remain locked in my hair. Her chest rises and falls with heavy gasps against mine, her cheeks are flushed, and her pupils dilated. Then, with one final sweep of her gaze, she withdraws entirely from me, turns, and walks away.

Rose

With every step, my resolution weakens. There's a warmth in my belly and desire between my legs that feels like a second pulse. I want to turn around, peel off Ian's shirt, and study every inch of his chest with my eyes, hands, and mouth. I want to feel his bare skin against mine. I want to hear his deep, perfect voice call out my name as he climaxes.

The woods are mere feet away, and I can't force myself to care how difficult it would be to get far enough away from everyone else and find a spot where we can carry out this fantasy playing out in my thoughts. Hell, we could slip away to my car in a few minutes or my apartment, which is just fifteen minutes away.

I realize I've stopped walking as these thoughts manifest into plausible realities.

If I turn around right now, what would happen?

If I return to where I left him standing, would I see something more than betrayal and anger shining in his blue eyes?

"Hey, Rose." Luis interrupts my thoughts as he approaches me wearing the same red vest Ian had been carrying. The memory of

Ian's hands digging into my skin hits me with another blow of desire. I want to feel his hands on me again—*everywhere*.

"Are you on trash pickup again?" he asks.

I shake my head, struggling to find words or thoughts that aren't of Ian naked. I swallow thickly. "No, I just wanted to apologize to Ian," I tell him honestly. That had been my intention. Initially, at least. I don't know what led me to kiss him. Was it because he implied my feelings were fake or because I was afraid I might never get the chance since things between us continue to feel increasingly strained?

God, why did I kiss him?

Why did I just make things more awkward between us?

Why am I risking hurting him?

"You want my red vest?" Luis asks. "I won't tell anyone."

I know what he's offering me: the chance to turn around and go back to Ian.

I shake my head. "I need to go check in and find Olivia."

A mocking smile rests on his lips. He knows I'm full of shit.

"You act different," Luis says as I take a step.

"I'm sorry?" I pause, my gaze daring to wander past Luis and over to where Ian is watching us.

"When Ian's around, you act differently."

I shake my head. "I don't know what you're talking about."

"Yeah, you do."

He's wrong. I know he's wrong because everyone's been commenting on the fact that I've been acting differently for months now, and I've barely been around Ian.

"He likes you," Luis tags on. "But you already know that, too."

I stare at him, hearing his words replay in my head, delivering a shocking amount of relief, fear, and doubt. It feels like another lie. Last year, I was confident Ian liked me, but this year, the adoration and kindness that softened Ian's expression are gone.

"You're both so damn stubborn," Luis says before he shakes his head and continues past me down to the water.

My heart beats erratically as I make my way back to the remainder of the line to check-in.

"Did you find him?" Olivia asks as she approaches me from the side, righting the red vest she's pulling on.

I nod.

"Good. Arlo said they knew you didn't do it."

I smooth my hair and nod because I don't know what to say.

"You look a little pale. Are you feeling okay?" Olivia asks.

"Yeah. I'm just tired."

"You were out late last night," she says.

"I think I finally found a study group that I like."

Olivia chuckles. "Things are looking up for the year."

"Except I still need to hunt down Anthony. Maybe I should quit the paper," I say as I approach the check-in table as the last person in line. I hand Penny my ID.

"You can't give Anthony that satisfaction."

"I can't let him publish more shit with my name on it, either. And if I'm able to get the yoga studio opened, I won't have time to be a part of the paper, anyway."

"Thank you, Rose. We have you on the trusses today," Penny tells me as she hands me my driver's license. "You're going to need one of the blue vests and a pair of gloves, and you'll meet down at the river."

I look at Olivia. "It's like they're working to keep us apart."

Her smile is instant and wide. "Never. Someone left coupons on my windshield today for cheesy garlic bread at the new pizza restaurant that opened a few blocks from us. We'll load ourselves up with breadsticks and pizza and devise a diabolical plan to get back at Anthony."

"Arlo leaves again this weekend," I remind her.

"I know."

"I don't want you to miss seeing him."

Her smile turns thoughtful. "Dating Arlo doesn't change us."

It has, but mentioning this seems hurtful, especially when she's trying to make a point to be there for me. "I'll see you at five."

She blows me a kiss before turning toward the play structure.

I'm trying to ignore how each of my breaths feels more uneven than the last as I head back down toward the river when a familiar head of messy brown hair pops up beside me. "Hey. I didn't know if you were coming today or not," Bree says.

"Hey, yourself. We're not done yet, so I'm here."

A grin slowly spreads across her lips. "Good. I was worried you might not after last week."

"You mean because I was picking up old dirty diapers out of the mud?"

She laughs. "That was pretty gross."

"Indeed. Well, future Madame President, you got stuck with me again." I point at her blue vest. "Blue's your color."

She smiles shyly. "That's what my dad says."

"Wise man with a sense of style. Sounds like a keeper."

Bree gives a tight-lipped smile but doesn't say anything more as we slowly descend to the bank of the stream. "Do you have any brothers or sisters?" I ask.

"Two older sisters."

"Ouch," I say. "I have one, and that's rough."

This earns me a full-on belly laugh in reply. "Tell me about it. All my sisters care about are boys and clothes."

"Those aren't horrible things to care about, are they?" I ask, realizing she's Anna and I'm her sisters.

"It is when that's *all* they want to talk about."

I smile. "I'm sure it's a phase."

"A *never-ending* phase," she says with a scowl.

Over her shoulder, Ian and Luis are carrying what appears to be an old washing machine that is rusted and dripping water up the embankment.

Bree stares at me.

"What?" I ask.

"Do you like one of them?" It's barely a question, more of an accusation.

"We're friends."

She quirks her eyebrows, delivering a look so cool and bold that I nearly high-five her. "You aren't interested in any boys? Or girls?" I tag on.

"I like boys. I just don't *live* for boys."

"That's fair."

She goes quiet again, but her gaze creeps back to me like she wants to say something more. I'd likely pretend I didn't notice if this were a year ago. "Are you okay?"

Bree swallows. "Are you close with your mom?"

The question catches me off guard. Two mentions of my mom in a mere hour have my chest aching. "I was," I tell her. "But, she passed away."

Bree stops. "I'm sorry."

"It's okay," I tell her, realizing she's apologizing for the question more than my loss.

"My mom's gone, too," she tells me, her eyes on the uneven path that leads down to the stream that is mostly mud rather than grass. "She left with her new boyfriend four years ago and never came back."

Statistics start to bubble in my thoughts as memories of my limited days in therapy remind me of terms like abandonment and trust issues. I wonder if Bree has ever heard of the potential impacts or if she exhibits them. If so, does she fight against them as I did?

"I'm sorry," I tell her sincerely, though my thoughts are still chaotic, trying to make sense of her situation and compare it to mine. We've both lost our mothers, and I would bet my life savings that she thinks about her mom as much as I do mine, possibly even more since she's still a kid, and her list of what-ifs is likely endless, whereas mine often gets tangled around the same pattern.

"He smoked," she says, her voice soft.

The random fact seems incredibly displaced, but the sight of our trash bags has me recalling our first week and her comments about cigarettes.

We stop at the bank, and Bree uncomfortably shifts her brown gaze to meet mine. I'm pretty sure this is where I'm supposed to say something prolific—something comforting and kind, hopeful and meaningful. I think of all the books and stories I've read and the words that have given me that glimmer of optimism and courage, and yet, as quickly as they form, they're replaced with memories of me drinking beer for breakfast with Chantay and skipping classes throughout high school, and kissing boys because it helped me forget how much I hurt. "I suck at this," I admit, shaking my head. "I'm sorry."

A grin tugs at her lips. "I prefer it that way," she says. "Everyone else always wants to tell me how it's her who's missing out and her who will regret this time like that should mean I don't care or can't be mad or upset." She shrugs. "I've learned there are no words for pain and loss. There's only patience."

Her words settle in my thoughts, reminding me of Olivia and how our friendship didn't happen overnight or because she said or did any one thing. It was built slowly and carefully with mistakes, setbacks, and time, and she's the best friend I've ever had.

"Patience and *lots* of pizza," I tell her.

Her grin widens into a smile, and then her gaze drops to my clothes. "Who did you make mad?"

"What are you talking about?"

She glances at my white shirt and new jeans. "Didn't you hear that this is one of the messiest weeks? We're going to be digging in the mud."

I frown.

Trash and now mud.

10

ROSE

"Is this good?" Anna asks, giving the container of sour cream she pulled from my fridge a hesitant sniff. My sister is stunning, like our mom. Her dark hair is short and blunt, her nose is narrow, her eyes are large and round, and her mouth is a perfect bow.

"What's the expiration date?" I ask.

She shakes her head. "I don't know. I can't read it because it's all rubbed off."

"I'm sure it's fine."

"Ingesting expired dairy could make us horribly sick."

"Eating enchiladas without sour cream would make me *horribly* sad," I counter, taking it from her. "There's no mold."

Her nose crinkles. "Please tell me that's not how you judge whether food is safe to eat or not."

"I read an article that said most expiration dates are bogus."

"Food poisoning is not bogus," she says. "I got food poisoning, and I was...."

"Sick for two weeks and had to be hospitalized," I say along with her.

Anna furrows her brow. "Why are you mocking me?"

"I'm not. I was there. It was terrible. You're right."

She still looks offended but doesn't say anything more on the subject. "How are classes going?"

I nod because a delayed response would make her suspicious, but my thoughts are spinning. It's difficult to recall anything aside from the fact that it's been two days since I kissed Ian.

Two days that I've been avoiding him.

Yesterday was easy. I had an early class and spent my afternoon at the yoga studio, where I taught two classes, then spent the evening with my realtor, Gabriel, looking at several properties.

Today has been harder to avoid the itch to call or text him. I feel like a jerk for asking my sister to get lunch because I desperately needed a distraction, but it was a good excuse since we've barely seen each other since she moved home. "Good, except for the newspaper. I'm considering quitting."

Anna leans back in her chair with both hands spread as though I've just told her the earth is flat. "*What?* Since when? Why would you quit?"

"Because I hate the editor," I tell her as I add a healthy dollop of sour cream to my cheese and onion enchiladas.

"You can't quit because you hate the editor."

"Oh, but I can."

"You're going to be the next Barbara Walters."

"If you said that on campus, I bet half the student body wouldn't know who you were talking about."

"Another reason that you need to be the next Barbara Walters."

"Barbara Walters is an American Broadcaster, not a journalist."

"You could be both! You're good at writing, and people think you're pretty."

I place both hands under my chin to pose before making myself go cross-eyed.

Anna belts out a laugh and then throws a taco chip at me, hitting me squarely in the nose. "Tell me you invited me over to convince you to stick with journalism. You still have time to change your major.

And in ten years, you can credit me when you receive the Pulitzer Prize."

I shake my head. "Gabriel's putting in an offer for a yoga studio as we speak."

She throws another handful of chips at me.

I manage to deflect half of them.

"What's going on with your stupid editor?" she asks.

"You just said it—he's stupid."

Anna scoffs.

"He assigned me the sports column."

She winces but quickly turns impassive. "That could be a good challenge for you. Pushing yourself outside your comfort zone is always good."

"He rewrote my last article."

Anna's eyes flash from her lunch to me. "Like he changed your prose?"

"He made me look like a trash writer and a liar."

She blinks quickly, likely because my tone and words express more of my frustration than intended. "What happened?"

I sigh and stand up to retrieve a copy of the paper with the article he butchered.

Anna is smelling her taco salad with a puckered face when I return. "Does this smell strange to you?" she asks.

I ignore her question and pass her the paper. "I highlighted the parts that were mine."

She sets her fork down and accepts the paper. Her eyebrows cinch higher with each condemning word. "Someone is posting pictures of the football team in compromising positions?"

"And this article makes it sound like I'm encouraging people to follow the site!"

Anna reaches for her phone and double-checks the site twice before punching it in. Her lips curl into an "O." "Did you see this?" she asks.

"I've been avoiding it," I admit.

"These are college guys?"

I peer over her shoulder at the picture of receiver Marcus Williams. "You mean Kurt didn't look like that in college?" I ask, knowing full well her husband has never looked like that.

"Are they on steroids?" she asks. "No way can anyone have that big of muscles at that age."

I grin. "I think that's what happens when you spend forty hours a week working out."

"Forty hours?" she screeches. "How are they getting a good education if they practice that much?"

"That's not what you're wondering when you look at that picture," I tell her. "And he's only a sophomore."

Anna nearly drops her phone. "Guys did not look like this when I was in college."

"They did. You just didn't see them because you spent all your time in the library and with Kurt," I tell her.

She flips her phone over to look at the picture one last time before turning it off. "Did he do it?"

"Do what?"

"Oh, and I'm the one who couldn't see past his muscles?"

I ignore her poke and take her phone. In the bottom corner of the picture of Marcus standing in a pair of boxer briefs, it reads, *"Rumor has it that Marcus Williams keeps a girlfriend in both Montana and Washington."*

That niggling feeling returns. "I have no idea," I tell Anna. "I don't know Marcus or his girlfriend."

"If it *is* true, it's probably a good thing he's being called out. He's acting like Christopher."

My rebuttal freezes on my tongue as I consider her words. What if I had been told my ex-boyfriend was cheating on me this publicly? Would it have been more embarrassing? Would it have been easier because everyone would see what a snake he was?

I shake my head, separating the two situations. "We don't know if it's true," I point out.

"Why else would they post it?"

"People lie all the time."

Anna tips her head to one side, a silent warning that she's about to be patronizing. "People lie about how much money they have and about plans when they don't want to go out. They don't lie about someone cheating."

"A mountain of tabloids would contest that."

Anna shakes her head. "Why are you defending this guy? Do you even know him?"

"Why are you condemning him? First of all, this is none of our business. And even if it were, we shouldn't pass any judgment unless we know all the facts. This could have come from a bitter ex looking for revenge or trying to break up his current relationship to weasel her way back in. We need his side of the story before making any assumptions."

"You know what he'd say. Some bullshit like Christopher did about how he was coerced and tricked."

I shake my head. "Can we stop talking about Christopher?"

"No, because he's relevant. Imagine if you guys had laid out both sides of your story for the internet to cast votes on. What do you think he would have said? Do you think he would have owned up to being a cheating bastard? He didn't own up to it even after you confronted him."

"All I'm saying is this site is wrong, regardless. Whoever's behind it is grossly invading these guys' lives by posting pictures and comments that are sexually exploiting them in an attempt to condemn them publicly."

Anna's expression turns smug. "Did I mention you should become a journalist?"

"Eat your taco salad," I say, pushing her lunch closer to her.

"It smells funny," she says.

I lean forward to sniff it. "It smells like a taco salad."

"Do you know how many bacteria live on iceberg lettuce?"

"Why'd you order it if you're afraid to eat it?"

"Because carbs make it so I can't fit into my pants."

"Carbs aren't your enemy. Your crazy delusions are." I swap her takeout container with my own. "You need to eat something."

"This is all gluten and cheese."

"And deliciousness," I tell her.

"I can't eat this. My skin will break out, and I'll gain ten pounds."

"But you won't have E-coli." I stab my fork into her salad and take a giant bite.

Anna huffs out a loud sigh but slowly picks up her fork. My sister is six years older than me and started college when she was just fifteen. She's a genius, but sometimes her brilliance is detrimental to her sanity because she worries about everything, a characteristic that went into overdrive after our mom passed away.

"How's work going?" I ask.

"Busy," she says. "Everything seems so trivial now."

"Really? I figured it would have been the opposite." She recently decided to work with local politicians at the federal level because the next item on her checklist is to have kids—two, a girl and then a boy.

Anna shakes her head. "After running a presidential campaign, everything seems so ... simple."

"You could do local politics."

Anna rolls her eyes. "I don't want to advise on mayoral elections."

"You always say local elections are the most important."

She releases a long breath and finally cuts into an enchilada.

"Delicious, right?" I ask.

"I can taste the calories," she says, making me laugh out loud.

"And they taste delicious." I pour the additional salad dressing she requested on the side before taking another bite. "Though, I'm not hating your salad. It's actually pretty good. It needs more cheese." I scoot my chair back. "But, what it really needs, is some hot sauce." I pull open the fridge.

"You and hot sauce," she says as I pick through our shelf devoted to hot sauces.

"You should try it on the enchiladas," I tell her.

She waves me away. "We'll see how this role goes, and then I'll decide what I want to do."

"That's right. You started with a new client."

Anna nods. "Dad referred him to me."

"Is that a good thing?"

She lifts her brow as though trying to decide for herself. "Yeah, Dad likes him. They went to Brighton together. He's running for governor. In fact, I think...." Anna reaches for her phone and flips from the site to what I'm assuming are details on her new job, her mouth ajar. "His son plays on the football team," she says.

Dread tangles in my stomach.

"Ian. Ian Forrest. Oh, god," she says, looking at me. "You're cringing. Why are you cringing?"

"I'm not cringing."

"You looked like you were having a stroke, you were cringing so bad. What do I need to know? Is he terrible? Tell me he doesn't kill and torture small animals."

"He doesn't kill and torture small animals."

"*Roooooossseee.*"

"He's a good guy, and he hasn't been on the website ... yet."

Anna winces before taking another bite of enchilada. "Okay, I need to know the details of this website. Tell me what you know."

"It's not a lot," I warn her.

"That's how all scandals start."

I lay out the minimal facts for her, showing her the email that Anthony had received. We go back to the website, catching up on yesterday's rumor victim, Damien Cooke, a junior running back accused of cheating on his midterm paper.

Anna has demolished both enchiladas by the time we finish reviewing details a second time. "Whoever's doing this doesn't have a big following," she says. "It's not trending on any social media platforms." Her heavy sigh contradicts her words. "But, they've clearly spent a lot of time and energy on this, and they paid to hide their domain, which is a little concerning. I can't believe I went from discussing homeland security policies to investigating college cheating scandals—in all its forms."

I grin. "Nice pun."

"Did you really put in an offer for a yoga studio?"

"I did, and I met this awesome duo trying to break into the

fashion industry with activewear. We're meeting to discuss some mockups next week."

"Is this really what you're passionate about? I get that you love yoga as a hobby, but do you want to make it your whole life?"

"Why not? Life is filled with so much stress. Why not do something that I love?"

"What if you do it on the side?"

"Anna, I'm happy with my decision and direction."

"But you're so smart."

"Why does smart have to equate to an office job and a six-figure salary?"

"I just worry about you. I don't want you to pour your heart and all the money you got from Mom's life insurance policy and invest in a business model that flops in a year."

"Life is short, you have to take risks, and I'm lucky enough to be able to afford some."

"Sure, but why not use some of that money to buy a house or a nice condo? You're putting all your eggs into one basket."

"I'm not. I have my degree to fall back on if necessary. I don't know why you care so much."

"Because you were meant to change the world, Rose." It's the same sentiment my mother used to tell me whenever inspiration struck and I did something that others would often find crazy or strange.

"It's not my place to change the world. I'm simply making my own place *in* this world."

She stares at me for a moment. Her eyes are the same shape as our mom's, but Anna lacks the same patience and insight.

I reach across the table and shovel some of her rice and bean mixture into the guacamole and sour cream she pushed to the side.

"We do not share," Anna protests.

"We just did. You now have all of my cooties."

She shivers. "You know I hate when you do that."

I grin because I do.

We spend the rest of the afternoon discussing her husband, Kurt, and his recent promotion at his law firm, her frustrations with their neighborhood's HOA, and how they're not enforcing screens for garbage cans. I let her vent and then distract her with one of the few things we both love: travel. Anna and I have been creating individual travel bucket lists for as long as I can remember. They started with us tearing the pages out of our mom's magazines. Over time, the lists grew, and we began researching the locations, cuisines, and cultures.

"I need to get going. I'm ovulating," Anna says as the afternoon begins to fade.

"That sounds romantic."

She glowers at me before picking up her phone. She does a double-take before flashing me the picture of Marcus. "Is he *really* a sophomore in college?"

I smirk. "He really is. And if you want to use him as inspiration for … *ovulation night*, I won't tell Kurt."

She throws Juliet's cat toy at me. "I hate you."

I'm still laughing too hard to respond as I follow her to the door, where I straighten and look for Juliet as Anna pulls on her shoes. "Don't forget, we're doing brunch with Dad next weekend."

"You've already reminded me five times this week, and it's only Wednesday."

Another glower. "Some might say I know you too well."

"I'm very punctual."

"You also make excuses and cancel plans. *Often.*"

I roll my eyes. "I'll be there."

"I don't know why you can't just talk to him and clear things up?"

"Because it's not a misunderstanding, Anna."

"You can't be mad at him forever. Mom wanted the divorce."

We've had this conversation a dozen times, and still, it doesn't get any less infuriating. "She was sick!"

"It was their relationship, though. You can't allow that to interfere with your relationship with him."

"What relationship? Do you realize that Dad lived in the White House longer than he lived in the same house as me? If I were asked twenty questions about him, I'd fail every single one, and he'd fail them about us."

Anna tips her head with another patronizing warning. "He was working for the entire country, Rose. Can't you see that? He worked directly with the President. He got to help influence our country's laws and affairs and, therefore, the entire world. How can you not see how amazing that is?"

"Likely because I was eight, and all I knew was my dad was never home."

She pulls in a deep breath through her nose and counts to three.

"I hope you do that tonight before having sex."

Anna scowls. "Why can't you just be an adult? You're nearly twenty-two. You need to grow up. Don't blame Dad for Christopher and every guy who you think is an asshole—"

"Are you serious?" I thread my fingers into my hair, struggling to hold in my growing frustration. "I don't blame Dad for Christopher. I blame Christopher for Christopher, and just because I'm not living my life how you want me to doesn't mean I'm doing a bad job." I pull in a deep breath and release it with a sigh. "Listen, lunch was great. Let's not leave this on a bad note."

"I'm not asking you to be besties with him. I just want you to accept him as a part of our lives."

"I do. I go to brunch every month."

Anna slips her fingers over my hair, smoothing it like our mom used to. "Bank holidays and monthly brunch dates aren't exactly what I'm talking about, and you know that."

"Drive safely. I love you. Don't let my cat out."

She releases another long breath. "I love you, too. I'll call you soon. Thanks for the additional homework with this website mess."

"Don't lie. You're going to enjoy staring at that *homework*."

She flips me off and slips out the front door, leaving me with more unwanted thoughts than when she'd arrived.

11

IAN

"What's up, asshole?" Luis calls as I arrive at the gym. I lift my chin in acknowledgment, but rather than join him and Paxton to talk shop or lift weights, I slip in my earbuds and move to the treadmill. It's Thursday morning, chest day. We're flying to San Francisco tomorrow, and I need to run and get the excess thoughts out of my head.

This week's game is our first real trial. San Francisco has a strong defense and an even stronger offense, and as hard as I try to recall their sets and how we're going to meet each one, I can't get Rose out of my mind.

I smell her. Taste her. Feel her. It's like she left a piece of herself with me, and it's been following me around since Monday, taunting me and daring me to try and ignore her and our damn kiss.

I finish four miles before Luis waves his hand in front of my face. "You're going to wear yourself out and not be able to practice tonight," he warns.

He's using this as an excuse to talk. Last year, he and Alexis broke up after multiple fights that revolved around football and how much time he had—or didn't have. I knew he was upset and going through a lot, but our relationship was built on sports, stats, food, and working out with the occasional childhood crush. We've never spent much time in the weeds with each other's thoughts or feelings, which is probably why our friendship has lasted as long as it has.

I slow the treadmill to a fast walk to cool down.

Luis raises a brow. "Got something on your mind."

"Just how fast San Fran's offense is. I run a hand over my sweat-dampened hair. "We'll have to cover them and rattle their QB."

Paxton blows out a breath from where he's doing bench presses. "They have a wide receiver that runs a four-forty and does a great job at reading plays. That's who you need to pay attention to," he says, tipping his head to make sure I understand. "Arlo's been studying their tape. You should track him down. The dude's turned insightful since his accident."

"Is he excited to play this weekend?" Luis asks.

Pax shrugs. "I don't think it's really hit him yet, you know? He's probably going to be jumping around the field once he gets out there and the lights are on. Dude's got so much pent-up energy that he'd give a Border Collie a run for its money." He racks his weights and wipes his forehead with the back of his forearm. "Have you guys been following the stupid rumor website?"

Guilt trickles to the front of my thoughts, recalling the image of Paxton wasted with a joint between his teeth that was posted first thing this morning with the rumor that he was a functioning alcoholic.

"I'm getting worried," Pax says.

Luis laughs. "I just want to know if Marcus has a girlfriend in both states, and if so, did they find out?"

Pax narrows his eyes. Like me, I can tell he's worried about how damning these images will be and what they might do to our team. "Maybe we ask Cooper to look into it. He's supposed to be a computer whiz. Maybe he can hack into the site and take it down?"

Luis nods. "And find out who's behind it all. But, I guess the real question is, do we want them to stop?"

I use my towel to wipe my forehead and temples. "Why would we want them to continue?"

Luis shrugs. "Most of the guys don't seem to care. Hell, they're happy about it. Girls are filling up their inboxes, and most of the shit probably isn't true, anyway. I mean, hell, you could say that picture today was photoshopped if anyone tries to say you broke any rules." He looks at Paxton. "I don't think it's worth our time or effort when it's not doing anything negative."

"What if they get worse? We have no idea what else they have."

Paxton looks at me and gives a quick nod. "They sure as hell are being persistent."

"Why don't we just keep our hand on the button? We'll see what happens, and if shit starts to go in the wrong direction or problems start, we'll go to Cooper." Luis looks at both of us.

I consider what Rose said after the first game when I confronted her about the page in my parent's library. "Do you think anyone on the team knows who's doing it?"

Paxton and Luis look at me and then at each other.

"No way," Luis says, shaking his head.

Paxton slowly shrugs. "It's possible. I mean, fucking Derek Paulson is always looking for a new angle to get ahead. Maybe he's doing this in an attempt to transfer since he isn't getting the attention he wants here. It would give him an easy excuse to wash his hands of Brighton."

Pax is salty over Derek for numerous reasons, most of them legitimate, but regardless, it's a reminder that there are cracks in our team.

Luis shrugs. "Yeah, but other universities won't love the rumor posted about him." Derek was featured early on the rumor site, while I still avoided it, hoping it would disappear.

"We have a shit ton of freshmen," I say. "They all seem cool, but everyone's an asshole when they're a freshman. They all think they're gods because they've been recruited, and girls are finally interested in sleeping with them."

Luis laughs. "Not me. Girls have lined up to have sex with me since I was fourteen."

I turn to Luis. "I knew you when you were fourteen, asshole, and they weren't."

Pax smirks and then straightens. "You're right. Having so many new guys on the team means there's a lot of baggage we don't know."

"They could have slept with someone's girlfriend or blew off a girl or...." I shake my head as my words trail off. There are endless possibilities.

Paxton rubs his temples. "Let me call Coop and see what he says. Maybe we should get ahead of this and at least see if we can find out who's doing this."

Luis nods. "If you guys kibosh the site, let the team assume that the administration did it. They're loving the attention."

Paxton nods. "I've received a shit ton of messages from girls today."

Luis points at him. "See?"

"Candace is ready to cut someone," Pax says. "It's a good thing we have an away game this week. Otherwise, she'd probably go nuclear."

"How are things between you two?" I ask.

"We're trying. I'm reading a book about communication and trying to understand how to prevent so many fallouts. I don't know if I can have another year like last year, with the constant fighting."

"Make-up sex is pretty great, though," Luis says.

Paxton scoffs as he moves to the cable crossover station. "She threw my laptop in the dumpster this summer because she thought I was talking to other girls."

"Were you?" Luis asks.

"I was emailing my sister in Africa."

Luis's laughter echoes through the gym. "Shit, dude. That's borderline psycho."

I take a seat at the pec deck, their conversation drifting into the background as I put a single earbud in. Rose and I have a class together this afternoon, and I have no idea if I should talk to her or allow her more space.

My phone vibrates against my thigh, interrupting my music. I pull it out to see a message from my mom.

> **Mom:** Hey, honey. Sorry, I meant to catch you before you left this morning. What time do you get home on Sunday? I'm going to give Stevie the weekend off. But, I'd like to have dinner together, just the three of us, no politics or advisors. I can make lasagna like my neighbor in Rome taught me.

> **Me:** Sounds good. We should be home around noon.

> **Mom:** Perfect. If I don't see you tonight, have a safe trip! We'll be cheering for you.

"Is that Rose?" Luis asks.

I flip him off and turn my music back on.

He snickers. "Nope."

Rose

"It was a kiss," I tell myself as I check my reflection in my rearview mirror and apply some tinted lip gloss before smoothing my hair. "No big deal."

My heart pounds in my chest, calling me a liar. "Shit," I say, wiping off my freshly applied lip gloss with a spare napkin because it feels like I'm trying too hard. "What am I doing?"

I lean my head back and take a deep breath. Maybe it wouldn't be a terrible idea to talk to Ian? Maybe we could pick up things where they left off at the beginning of summer?

I glance at the clock on my dash, realizing if I don't get moving, I'm going to be late for class, and then I won't have a choice about where I sit.

I slide out of my car, appreciating the warm day as I grab my bag from the backseat and lock my doors. I start reciting a pep talk that would likely be so much better if it were coming from Olivia, but I haven't had the *cojones* to tell her I kissed Ian. Not because I'm embarrassed but because I know that if I tell her, there will be questions, and I haven't been ready to answer them or even hear them. And though Olivia wouldn't pressure me to answer any of said questions, I have no doubt she'd get that wistful look in her eye that happens whenever Arlo's name is mentioned. She'd tell me that my rules don't have to apply because I made them and, therefore, can change them, which would segue into how great and wonderful Ian is and how she knows we had a special connection. Then, I'd likely believe her because I see her and Arlo and how much they care about each other, which has created fractures in my rules and thoughts. Occurrences like this morning, when I ran into Arlo while he quietly made his way into our apartment with a bag of pastries and a coffee from Olivia's favorite spot, are wreaking havoc on my convictions.

I wonder what type of a guy Ian would be like to date. Would he send me flowers when he's out of town? Would he call me for no reason except to hear my voice? Would he be the kind of guy who wants to hang out at home with a pizza and a movie or go out to eat at a new restaurant?

My phone ringing interrupts my myriad of thoughts. It's an unknown number, but I accept the call since I still have an offer out on a yoga studio.

"Hi, this is Rose," I answer.

"Rose Cartwright?" a woman asks.

"Yes."

"This is Sandy with Something You Boutique over on Crown Hill. We have your little sister here. We caught her trying to shoplift."

"*Little sister?*"

"Bree."

Recognition dawns. Bree. Bree from the park, who I gave my number to out of obligation after she told me she'd like to learn more about yoga.

I wince. "What was she trying to steal?"

"A pair of pants. She said you were her emergency contact."

I have no idea how a situation like this works. "Did she give them back?"

There's a pause, and I wonder if that was the world's dumbest question. "She's wearing them. She won't talk to us. She wrote down your name and number when we asked her for an emergency contact."

I rub a hand over my brow. Labor Economics isn't just my window for seeing Ian—it's also a class that has seventy percent of my grade tied simply to attendance.

"Can I just pay you for the pants? I can give you my credit card information." I cringe at my words, hoping beyond hope that this is a feasible possibility.

"Ma'am, if you don't come, we're going to call the police. She should be in school."

I barely know Bree. We've spent a few afternoons together, and sure, I've told her more about my mom and yoga than most, but having her list me as an emergency contact exceeds every guideline for our roughly defined friendship. *"You've never been very good at coloring within the lines."* I hear my mom's voice in my head as my shoulders roll forward. "I'll be there in fifteen minutes," I tell the woman.

I'm distracted, considering if I should go and tell my professor I have to miss class for a family emergency that I almost collide with a poor, unsuspecting stranger.

"I'm so sorry," I say, reaching out to help him.

Kind brown eyes meet mine, paired with a gentle smile. "You nearly ran me over," he says. "Is there a fire?"

I shake my head. "Sorry. Apparently, this is becoming a habit of mine. Are you okay?"

He shakes his head. "I'd be okay with you making it a habit of running into me every day. I'm Noah," he says, offering his hand.

"Rose."

He grins. "I know. We're in Labor Economics together, which is...." He points over my shoulder. "This way."

"Yeah, I know. I had something come up," I explain as I grab a fallen notebook and return it to him when something catches my attention. I realize it wasn't something but *someone* as I focus on Ian. He's standing on the pathway that leads to Scott's Theater, Isla at his side. She's laughing at something he's said, her body swaying closer to his. Her adoration for him is apparent, even from here. She drops something, her phone, I think, based on the size, and Ian moves to pick it up. As he stands to return it to her, Isla goes up on her toes and plants a kiss on his mouth. It's like one of those meet-cute moments I've been reading about for weeks in the romance books Olivia has pedaled to me—the complete opposite of the demanding punishment of a kiss we shared just a few days ago.

"Are you okay?" Noah asks.

My skin is clammy, and my chest feels tight as I nod and force a smile. "Yeah." My voice is hesitant and uncertain. "Yes," I repeat. "Sorry again for running into you. I'll see you next week."

He opens his mouth like he's going to object, but before he can say anything, I hurry toward the sidewalk, wishing the parking lot wasn't a few blocks away.

My strides are so fast that I'm nearly running as I weave through groups and individuals, their faces blurred in my haste. I tell myself I'm rushing to reach Bree so they don't call the cops and nothing to do with watching Ian kiss another girl.

I release a weighted breath and try to focus on the situation. Why would Bree have stolen something?

Why isn't she in school?

Why would she tell someone that I'm her sister?

The questions float through my thoughts like safe spots to land in a videogame as I reach the parking lot. It's crowded, the spaces all too narrow like many of the tiny lots on campus. I slide into my car, set my bag beside me, and catch sight of my reflection. My eyes are red, and tears cling to my lashes.

The sight of Isla kissing Ian replays like a scene out of a horror film, sudden and unwanted. My chest tightens as I close my eyes.

This shouldn't hurt so much.

I don't know Isla that well, but I've wanted so badly to vilify her the past couple of weeks, and as the image of their kiss plays through my mind again, I realize with painstaking clarity that it's because this is what I've feared since Chantay told me that Isla was interested in him.

I pull in a broken breath and start my car.

Bree. I need to focus on Bree.

I arrive at Something You Boutique thirteen minutes later, though the drive felt like it took a year as my thoughts danced around every subject I've tried to avoid for the past several months.

Bells chime as I open the door. It smells like leather and men's cologne. "Welcome. Is there something I can help you find?" A woman with dark hair that nearly reaches her waist greets me.

"My name's Rose Cartwright. I'm here to pick up Bree."

The woman's expression changes from an interest in my attire and how much commission she might earn from me to my black nails and the tattoo encircling my wrist. When her eyes meet mine again, judgment is all I see. "She's back here with our manager." She extends a hand. "After you." Her words are curt, her gaze watchful.

Offense grates at me, but I remind myself Bree was caught shoplifting, and they're likely assuming I'm cut from the same cloth.

The woman knocks on a black door. "The girl's sister is here," she yells.

The door opens, and a heavyset woman with dyed orange hair and bright red lips stares at me, her disinterest and mistrust even more apparent than her employee's. Behind her, Bree is sitting on a chair, eyes puffy and red, nose running.

I still don't know what to say. "Was anything ruined?" I ask.

The manager sneers. "She tried to steal a pair of pants that retail for a hundred-and-thirty dollars."

Bree shudders, refusing to meet my gaze.

"I'm sorry for the trouble. I'll make sure this doesn't happen again."

"She ripped the pants trying to remove the tags," the manager continues.

"I'll pay for them," I tell her again, reaching for my purse.

The manager narrows her eyes, untrusting.

"I'm sorry for the trouble. If I can pay you for the pants, we'll get going. She's late for school, and I have class...."

The manager turns to Bree. "You're not welcome in my store again, young lady."

Bree doesn't say anything as she stands and slowly moves toward the door. She follows me to the cash register, where the manager scans a set of tags to ring up the pants. I can't believe I'm spending hundred-and-thirty bucks for a pair of pants that aren't even mine. But I can tell by Bree's expression that she's already paid severely for her mistake.

I don't say anything as I swipe my credit card and sign my name.

The manager asks to see my license and credit card, her distrust still high. She studies them both for several seconds before returning them and handing me a bag. "Here are *her* pants."

I glance at Bree, realizing she's still wearing the stolen pants. They're a pair of gray joggers with what appears like bleach stains across the front that ride too low on her narrow hips. I just paid hundred-and-thirty bucks plus tax for the ugliest pair of sweatpants in the history of sweatpants. It's a tough pill to swallow.

I accept the bag and tags—she doesn't hand me the receipt—and we leave, both of us still silent.

Outside, the skies are overcast as a fine mist falls on us, dampening my skin and mood.

"I'm this one," I say, unlocking my car.

Bree looks at me and slowly moves to the passenger door, and climbs inside.

"Well, sister Bree, what the heck?" I ask, passing her the bag with her pants.

She's silent.

"Can you be the president with a police record?" I ask.

Bree places both hands on her face and bends forward. Her cries fill the small space, shocking me and making me feel like the queen of jerks.

I warily rest my hand on her shoulder. "What happened?" My voice is soft and apologetic.

Her cries grow louder.

I am so in over my head. I should call Anna or Olivia's stepmom, Whitney; surely one of them knows what to do or say.

Is this supposed to be a tough love, no compassion, no bullshit speech? Do I know how to deliver that message? Are her tears an act?

I pull in a deep breath, trying to rid my thoughts that are searching for all the ways she might be using me or lying to me, realizing that though I don't know her very well, I know I have to stop looking at everyone as trying to screw me over. I've been trying to work on this for a couple of months now—I just didn't realize it until this moment.

"Bree," I say her name softly. "What happened?" I ask again.

She wipes her hands down her tear-stained cheeks. "I'm so sorry. I'll pay you back. I swear."

"I'm not worried about the money. I'm worried about why you were shoplifting. Shoplifting *hideous* pants."

"They were the cheapest ones in the store," she tells me, wiping the space under her right eye.

"I can see why."

She wipes at the same spot on her face with the back of her hand as fresh tears quickly replace those she cleared, her breaths still uneven and ragged.

"Why'd you steal them?"

"Because my period started. I bled through my pants, and my dad's at work."

My shoulders slump forward with a combination of relief and compassion that has tears burning my eyes. "Bree," I say. "You should have called me. I would have come. You didn't have to steal these."

"I was going to pay them for them ... eventually. This is just the first stop on the city bus, and I have a math quiz I can't miss." More tears slip from the corners of her eyes. "I didn't realize they were so expensive."

"Don't worry," I tell her. "Don't worry about the money or the pants or this place. Most of their stuff was ugly and overpriced."

She sniffs as she wipes at the fresh tears.

I reach into my backseat, where there's a box of tissues, something

I always keep in my car just like Anna does, just like our mom always did. I pass them to her. "Do you have tampons or pads with you?"

She shakes her head. "I used a bunch of toilet paper."

"Oh man, I've been there, done that. If only every girl didn't have to earn that awful badge of honor." I fasten my seat belt. "Put on your seat belt. Let's go get you some underwear, pads, and a pair of pants that won't make this day even worse."

She shakes her head. "I only have a couple of bucks."

"I'm not expecting you to pay for them."

"You just bought me pants. I can't ask for more."

"You're not asking—I'm insisting."

Bree's cries grow louder again, her face puckering.

I reach across and rub a hand over her shoulders. "I know how hard it can be to accept help," I tell her. "But I want to do this. I want to help you, and one day, you'll do something for someone else who's having a bad day, month, or year. It's the cycle of karma."

She leans her head against the seat, eyes still closed. "This is so embarrassing."

"Asking for help is scary," I say. "I get it. I *totally* get it. Accepting help can be even scarier because then you question if there's a price, or if it's genuine, or if they're simply there out of obligation. I'm helping because I want to help. Because you're *worthy* of receiving help. Everyone is."

Bree slowly opens her eyes. "I'm sorry I gave them your number."

"I'm not."

Without warning, she leans forward, rests her head on my shoulder, and cries even harder.

I unbuckle my seat belt and wrap my arms around her. My vision turns blurry with more tears that I struggle to hold back.

I don't rush her. My class suddenly feels far less significant, and even the expensive joggers feel meaningless, but there's a niggling feeling in the back of my thoughts that refuses to be ignored. It's the realization that Ian tried so hard to show and give me kindness and a relationship built on more than attraction and rules last spring, and I'm realizing it too late.

12

ROSE

"I should give up on finding the best mocha in Seattle and focus on finding the best ramen," I tell Olivia, smelling the savory aroma of our takeout. It's Saturday night and another girl's night due to Arlo being in San Francisco for their game.

"We should do both," she says, popping the top off her drink. She's on cloud nine after Arlo's return to football without injury or problem and the accompanying victory. "Whitney and I had some delicious teriyaki last week. She said Seattle is known for it. How did I not know this?"

I grin at the mention of her stepmom. The two had a cordial and polite relationship before last year. "Because until last spring, you didn't want to stay in Seattle."

Her smile falters, and her gaze dips.

"Everything okay?" I reach for my chopsticks.

Evelyn nods as she glances at me. "Arlo mentioned the draft this week. He was talking about how he thinks his chances are the highest with Colorado and Illinois, and now I can't stop focusing on how he might get drafted to another state. He already trains and studies football for forty-plus hours every week. What will happen if he gets drafted? How will we find time together?" Her gaze falls again, this time followed by a sigh. "And he already has so many girls interested in him. Can you imagine the attention he'll receive once he's pro?"

"Do you need me to give you the guacamole speech again?" I ask. "Because I'm ready. Arlo is the real deal. He's not with you because of how you look or because your dad's the coach—trust me, you're a little surly in the mornings, and he still loves you. It's about how you make each other feel—your connection. If he gets drafted, you'll go with him. It's that easy. After all, you're going to be writing books and changing the world."

Olivia breaks apart her chopsticks and goes after one-half of the hardboiled egg in her bowl. "But you're here, and my family's here."

"Arlo will be rolling in the money. You guys can have a house here and a house there. Split your time."

She scoffs. "He didn't talk about me going with him."

"Of course, he didn't. It's Arlo. He already assumes you're going with him, so he didn't feel the need to clarify."

A smile starts in the corners of her lips. "Now that I've spilled my beans, it's your turn."

I take a bite of the seasoned pork and quietly hum. "This is so good. I don't want to ruin good food with a discussion of work or school."

"Oh, good. I don't, either. I want to talk about boy drama."

"I don't have any boy drama," I remind her. "One of the perks of not dating."

Her eyes narrow on me as she chews. "Arlo said they had a team meeting yesterday led by Pax and Ian. He said they couldn't figure out how to take down the site or who is even posting it and asked everyone if they had any information."

"Did anyone?"

Olivia shakes her head. "Nope. Though, at this point, I'm not sure anyone would admit to knowing anything, even if they did. That picture yesterday accusing Rockway of sleeping with a sixteen-year-old...." She winces. "It was bad, and it's starting to gain attention. An investigation has been opened."

I scrub a hand over my face, my appetite shrinking. "Do they know if it's true?"

She shakes her head. "Arlo says some of the rumors hold partial truth."

I raise a brow.

"You remember that freshman accused of sleeping with his teacher?"

I nod.

"Apparently, it was true but stretched. He had graduated, and she was a student teacher."

I mull over these details. "I can still see the moral discrepancy, but that headline was meant to leave the impression that he slept with her while she was his teacher."

She nods. "For sure."

I sigh. "Thankfully, Anthony got his hand slapped pretty hard by the faculty for rewriting my article, and he still seems afraid of me after I finally tracked him down."

"He deserved to be punched."

"Do you think Ian assumes I know more than I do?"

Olivia tries to hide her grin as she shakes her head. I've changed the subject every time she's mentioned him this week. "I don't think so, but you should talk to him."

"I can't."

"You can't avoid him forever."

"I kissed him," I blurt out the words.

Olivia drops her chopsticks. "When?"

I cover my face with both hands so I don't have to see her reaction. "It's not a big deal. It was just a kiss."

"Not a big deal? This is huge! When did this happen? Where was I? Was there tongue?"

I slide my hands down my face. "Monday, at Shady Grove Park."

"When you went to talk to him?"

I nod. "He was frustrated and asking me all these questions, and I just ... kissed him."

"*And?*"

I shake my head. "Nothing. I didn't know what to say, so I left."

Olivia's shoulders fall with the anticlimactic ending. "You need to talk to him. Ask him out on a date or to get coffee."

I shake my head to catch up with her train of thought. "I haven't heard from him all week."

Olivia picks up her chopsticks and gives me an unnervingly calm look. "I think my dating Arlo has changed our perspectives."

I take a deep breath, recognizing that she's baiting me. "Okay, I'll play. How? What perspective?"

"I previously believed you only fall for one guy ever, and after you fall, you'll only ever be thinking of that person, and I think you did, too."

"We aren't talking about Christopher," I warn her, setting my chopsticks down. "I had this conversation with Anna, and I refuse to have it again."

"Oh, we're talking about Christopher." Her tone is factual.

"I didn't stop dating because of Christopher," I tell her. Not entirely. "He inspired the idea of setting rules and boundaries."

"I know. Because you're a strong and independent woman, and you wouldn't let some sniveling, two-timing excuse of a guy change your entire mindset."

"Are you trying to reverse-psychology me?"

Olivia's eyes grow wide with innocence. "*Me?*"

"Christopher and I broke up four years ago," I remind her.

"I know." She takes a bite of her dinner and chews slowly. Then, she takes a drink and sets her glass bottle down. All the while, her gaze is on me. "But I also know pain doesn't follow a specific timeline. We both know that." She smiles weakly. "I know that Christopher cheating on you pales in comparison to everything else you experienced that year, but it certainly didn't help build your confidence or trust in relationships or men in general."

I don't respond, taking too long to eat several bites of food as her words invite years' worth of memories and thoughts into my brain.

"Anyway," Olivia says, "I saw Ian yesterday before the guys boarded their plane." She stares at me but doesn't continue.

"You know I won't beg for the details, right?"

Olivia giggles, knowing I'm mostly hot air at this point. "He told me about his parents moving back home. Did you know that his dad is running for governor next year?"

I hate that it hurts to hear this for the second time from a third party rather than Ian, but per my usual, I disguise this with humor. "No, we mostly only discussed me all of the time. *My* dreams, *my* aspirations." I shrug.

This time her laugh is a cackle.

"I saw him kissing Isla," I say, dropping the second truth bomb on her.

Olivia sobers instantly. "*What?*"

I nod. "Exactly."

"When? Where?"

"Thursday, before class."

She shakes her head as though trying to make sense of the news. "Are you sure it was Ian?"

I laugh in response. "I gave Isla the green light to pursue him."

Olivia reaches forward, resting her hand on mine. "I know how scary it is to like someone. Trust me when I say that it only gets scarier. But it's worth it, Rose. I know Ian likes you. There has to be an explanation for what you saw."

13

IAN

"Whoa," Arlo says as I stop at my locker. "Who pissed in your Wheaties?"

My scowl deepens.

Paxton and Cooper stop beside us before I can respond, their faces somber. "How's Wickizer?" Pax asks.

Dusty Wickizer was today's victim on that fucking site. They posted a picture of him kissing another guy this morning—a personal detail he had kept exactly that, personal.

"I'm ready to kick someone's ass," I tell them.

"We have to find a way to stop this," Pax says. "I don't know who's doing this or where they're getting these pictures from, but it's bullshit."

"Has anyone heard from or seen Wickizer?" Cooper asks.

I shake my head. "He didn't answer any of my calls. I blew off my class this morning to stop by his place, but if he was home, he didn't answer."

Pax rubs his hands down his face. "I'll talk to Coach. Maybe I can skip practice and head over there. This week's game is going to be a gimme."

I don't share his confidence. While we managed to defeat San

Francisco, the game was closer than I would have preferred. Our defense still lacks the harmony we possessed last year with a more seasoned team, and our offense is becoming predictable to defenders.

Pax looks at me. "Lincoln can lead the offense, and Jacob can get some playing time."

"You can't see who's doing this?" I ask Cooper.

He shakes his head. "They're paying a server, so their name isn't on it. They're smart. I've tried hacking into it twice, and both times, they retaliated by doubling the pictures and rumors the next day."

I close my eyes. "Let me talk to my dad. He's working with a team of PR people. Maybe one of them knows something or someone who can help us."

Pax pulls in a breath, looking hopeful. This afternoon, we were pulled into a meeting with all the coaches and some of Brighton's faculty to discuss the rumor website. Many of the rumors have begun to sprout legs and are starting to circulate, additional questions are being asked, and more answers are being demanded. Investigations are beginning to dive into our lives, and our reputations are unraveling, along with my sanity.

"There's another angle we can take," I tell them. "Rose suggested that we could get ahead of this and control the narrative."

"What do you mean?" Paxton asks. "Like, post our own pictures."

"Exactly," I say.

Pax shakes his head. "People are eating this shit up because it looks and sounds like a scandal."

"I can try some more … illicit ways to take down the site," Cooper says.

"How illicit?" I ask.

Cooper shrugs. "We could try a DOS attack. Or we could try flooding the search engines with reports on the website. The site would remain online, but it would be harder to find. People would need a direct URL."

"Do you think either of them would do anything?" Pax asks.

Cooper shrugs again. "I don't know how people are finding the site. Are they searching for the rumors? Or do they have the website saved?"

Paxton looks annoyed and bored by the details. "What would you suggest?"

"Depends how bad you want it to disappear," Cooper says.

"Stick to the legal route. We don't need to add more shit to this fire," I say. "Do you have time to put something like this together?" I ask.

Cooper does a noncommittal nod. "Not entirely, but I know people who can help us."

"Music to my ears," says Arlo. "I know somebody who knows somebody." He uses his native Jersey accent.

"Let us know what the cost is," I tell him. "I'll reimburse you if they can bury this shit fast."

He nods. "Buy me ten minutes."

"I'll give you twenty," I tell him.

"This is good," Pax says. "I'm sick of lying around waiting to see what pops up next."

"We could try both. Redirect the narrative and bury them. You know who could help us?" Arlo asks, his gaze turning on me. "Rose. She's still pissed that her editor hijacked her article and would probably write anything we ask."

Pax shakes his head. "That last article was pretty damning. It had links and reminders about how often to check back on the site and how to follow it...."

"Hoyt fucking blasted the site everywhere," Arlo points out. "Others have too."

"But it was theirs to share," I say.

Pax points at me. "Bingo."

"Does it matter?" Cooper asks. "If the school paper has some reach and our objective is to touch that same audience, it makes sense to go back and have them redirect readers' attentions."

I wince. "If we do this, we need Rose to write the articles with the message *we* want to share."

Arlo nods.

I turn to Pax.

He shakes his head. "It's your call, man."

I release a shallow breath and turn back to Arlo. "Talk to her. See if she's on board."

Paxton nods. "I'm going to check in with Coach and see if I can find Wickizer. I'll be at the gym later." He grabs his bag and heads down the hall toward the offices.

"I'll get a site up and running. We'll need photos," Cooper says, making a list on his phone.

Arlo stares at me, his accusations silent, yet I understand them clearly.

"What?" I say when he doesn't relent.

"You're going to need to talk to her," he says.

I shake my head. "This is all you."

"I don't know if you've noticed, but Rose hasn't written a football piece since that article. Her editor is about to cut her from the paper and trust me when I say it's not because she doesn't understand the fucking game."

"She'll write it for you. Rose likes and respects you. You're friends."

"Have you met Rose? Queen of stubbornness and crusader of injustice. She doesn't give two shits about these rumors. Have you seen her articles? She's been attacking the inferiority of female sports all week."

"She's made it clear she doesn't want to talk to me."

He shakes his head. "Call her tonight or have her meet you Saturday morning before the game."

"Knowing Rose, she won't be available for either of those times. She probably has a hookup already planned."

"Rose?" he asks, surprise drawing his brows toward his hairline. He smirks. "It's great to be on the other side this year, watching how idiotic it looks from the outside looking in."

"What's that supposed to mean?"

"Rose hasn't had any dates or hookups since early last spring. She stopped going out to parties and hanging out with other friends. She's focused on work, school, and her fucking yoga studio."

I stare at him, waiting for something aside from relief to hit me.

Arlo reaches forward and pats my shoulder. "Trust me. It's so much simpler on the other side. Getting there takes some work, but you've got this."

"I hate you," I tell him.

He laughs. "Let's go take that anger out on the field."

The thing is, I don't have much anger about the situation—I have confusion. A lot of fucking confusion as well as reluctance and a desire to maintain this distance she's put between us because my will to stay away from her was demolished after she kissed me. Yet, she's seemingly strengthening her defenses because I haven't seen Rose since last Monday. She skipped our shared class last week, and yesterday's volunteering date at Shady Grove Park was canceled due to inclement weather.

Arlo's right. I need to fix this not only for the team but to regain my sanity.

Rose

"Rose." My heart thrums in my chest. I hate how Ian's voice has a way of silencing everything else around me.

I turn to face him, ready with a pair of solid excuses to leave.

He holds a copy of the student newspaper in his hand. "A punishing loss for Oregon," he reads my words back to me.

I stare at him. If he thinks I'm going to be flattered because he read my column—an article about our women's soccer team—he clearly doesn't know me as well as I sometimes fear.

"I like how you made the players relatable and mentioned their lives off the field. Sometimes, it feels like we're looked at as little more than athletes."

Okay ... *maybe* he can flatter me a *little* with my own words.

"Do you have a few minutes?"

I glance at my watch, primed with my first and easiest excuse: Olivia. "I'm on my way to meet Olivia."

The ghost of a smile teases his features. "I won't keep you for long. I have an exclusive to offer you that might get you on your editor's good side."

"What makes you think I'm not already?"

He raises his brows knowingly. "Call it a hunch."

"My editor likes to stare at my boobs. We're fine."

His humor vanishes, replaced by a clenched jaw that only enunciates the strength and power he emanates. He pulls in a long, slow breath through his nose and slowly opens his eyes. In the sun, the different colors of his irises are starker and more distracting, making me forget about my need to keep my distance and our rather tumultuous relationship status. "I need a favor," he says.

We stare at one another for a solid minute, and I wonder if multiple expressions are apparent on my face, like his, as I read the trepidation, nostalgia, and plea. And just like that, my defenses slip. "I can give you twenty minutes. There's a new coffee shop just past the arboretum."

He nods. "Let's check it out."

There's a chill in the air today—another reminder of autumn. Still, the sun is out, and the skies are clear, which keeps me from complaining about the cooler weather. Many students are outside, milling around on the brick pathways.

"How'd you know where to find me?" I ask. After all, running into someone on campus, unless you have a shared class or similar crossroads, is rare.

"Olivia told me where to find you," he says, not working to hide his grin that tells me he knew I was lying. "I saw her and Arlo before they left for the beach."

"Can you blame me?" I ask, skipping over apologies.

He grins. "No. I'm sorry for acting like a dick."

"Like a bent dick."

Ian chuckles, his eyes finding mine once again. I've missed this: the silent conversations that often have more weight and honesty than most verbal ones. It's uncomfortable and leaves me feeling exposed, yet in the same vein, it is immensely comforting.

"I deserve that," he says as we stop at the crosswalk.

I pull in a deep breath knowing this is where I should accept his apology and offer my own and some kind of explanation for kissing him. Maybe it would smooth things over? But then again, I've never been the best at accepting apologies. Words are so simple, so easy, so recycled. And too often, people say the right words when it stands to benefit themselves, and Ian's already forewarned me that he's looking for a favor.

"Find a good study group yet?" he asks.

I cut my gaze to him again, liking the whisper of his smile more than I should. "I'm still heartbroken Leah graduated. No one ran a study group like her."

His smile brightens. "I was thinking about that yesterday."

"About Statistics?"

"About meeting you there though you weren't taking the class. You wouldn't tell me your name for two months."

"You didn't ask," I say.

Ian flashes a full smile, one that makes him tilt his head back and close his eyes. "I still don't understand why you thought you needed a study group to focus. You understand economics better than anyone I know."

"Don't tell my dad that."

He grins but doesn't tack on a question or retort. He knows my dad is one of my least favorite topics of discussion.

"It can be hard for me to focus sometimes," I admit.

Ian nods. "I know what you mean. I concentrate best when there are no distractions, and it's silent."

"That's the hardest time for me to focus."

He raises his brow with a silent question, and for whatever reason, I continue down this path of honesty we've begun to construct. "When it's quiet, and I'm alone, my thoughts can be deafening. Distracting."

"Maybe it's because there's something you're trying to avoid," his brow quirks upward.

There's a meaning behind his stare, yet without asking or prying, I know it has nothing to do with him. I'm sure he's assuming it's due to my mom's passing or my struggling relationship with my father—most do. "Pretty sure it's just my OCD," I tell him.

The crosswalk icon turns from red to green, and without wasting another second, I make my way across the street with Ian at my side. I don't wait for him to open the door to the small, white brick coffee shop door. Inside, the aroma of freshly ground coffee beans greets me like a warm hug.

"Welcome," a man with a bald head calls from behind the counter. Behind him is a chalkboard filled with eclectic designs that remind me of an adult coloring book.

"I have a feeling I'll know where to find you every Wednesday," Ian says as he stands beside me, letting me soak up the rich scent of coffee and the subtle lights that twinkle over our heads in small glass jars against a black painted ceiling.

"They might have terrible coffee," I whisper. "Looks can be deceiving."

His eyes dance between mine again, a similar uncertainty to what I often feel around him. Neither of us seems to know when the other is talking about each other or something else entirely, and both of us are too smart—or stubborn—to believe it's the former, which leaves a lot of missed opportunities for flirting and innuendos.

Ian saunters up to the counter, hands tucked into the pockets of his gray sweatpants. It's a beautiful view. His shoulders are broad, stacked with defined muscles even under his red Brighton T-shirt. There's something incredibly sexy and masculine about not only his shoulders and chiseled back and the way he carries himself. Even now, he greets the barista with kindness and respect. Yet, there's a noticeable difference in him compared to most guys, and it lies in being confident in himself and not caring if the male barista knows he could likely bench press his weight.

"Could we have a chocolate mocha and a drip coffee with skim milk, please?" Ian orders.

The barista nods. "Anything else for you?"

Ian looks at the small glass case at his side and then back at me. "They have sour cream doughnuts."

"I shouldn't."

"We'll take two," he says, taking out his wallet.

I'm the only weirdo who doesn't care much for doughnuts, but sour cream doughnuts are in a separate league and my weakness.

I shake my head and turn toward the wall of windows at the front of the small shop. A dark green couch is facing the window with two mustard yellow pillows at either corner and a gold floor lamp on one side with fuchsia-colored flowers on the lampshade. I love funky fashion, and this place is filled with it. I really hope their coffee doesn't suck.

I skip past the couch, the setting too intimate. I need a physical barrier between Ian and me, so I sit at one of the tables set for two. It's painted a glossy black with high-back chairs that make me feel short and petite even though I'm tall. I pull out my phone and skim over my schedule. Between classes, the paper, yoga, and a couple of associations I've recently joined for aspiring professionals, nearly every minute of my day seems booked.

Ian places a cup of coffee and a doughnut on the table in front of me. Real dishes. It's a charming detail I appreciate because it makes me want to forget about should-dos and need-to-dos and just stay here sipping on refills for the rest of the day.

"I've gone up a pant size since June," I tell him, pushing the doughnut away.

He slides the plate back toward me. "You've never looked better. Eat the doughnut. I'm around guys counting their calories and carbs all fucking day."

His phone buzzes.

"Arlo doesn't," I tell him as I ruthlessly attempt to ignore his compliment. "He eats everything in sight. He's like a human garbage disposal."

Ian chuckles. "I knew I liked that guy for a reason."

"Do you have to pay close attention to what you eat?"

He takes a sip of his coffee, but his gaze jumps to mine. With the muted light, his eyes appear gunmetal gray. "We have nutritionists who tell us how much protein and carbs and how many cups of vegetables to eat daily."

"Cups. Of. Vegetables? Does that translate to like half a bag of tater tots?"

His phone buzzes again.

He laughs. "Mostly spinach. But cauliflower, broccoli, Brussels sprouts, kale..."

I wrinkle my nose. "Maybe that's why I was never an athlete. My body knew it couldn't stomach eating the worst vegetables."

"You like broccoli."

I shake my head. "Only in Chinese food."

He laughs again. "I won't tell you about the caffeine restrictions."

"There are restrictions? You might as well just call football torture."

He takes another sip of his coffee.

I want to ask him more questions and prolong this easy banter, but I don't have time, even if I want to. I have a yoga class to teach in an hour.

"So, what's this favor you need?" I ask, bringing my cup of coffee to my lips. It's too hot, but the whipped cream pattern on top is sweet and velvety smooth.

"I'd like your help. I'd like you to write another article and draw attention to a new website that we're making."

I shake my head in confusion. "What?"

"We're going to change the narrative—as you suggested. We'll include some of the old photos from the rumor site and post some new ones as well. Better pictures that don't look like they were taken from a dark corner."

My mind instantly recalls his anger when I showed him the site and the accusation during our follow-up discussion. "I don't understand."

"Cooper tried hacking the site to see who's behind it and to see what else they have, but they caught him and doubled the number of rumors posted."

Ian doesn't mention the one of him with the girl I'd seen with the rumor that he paid her off to get out of his life after she told her friends about him. Considering how private he is, I could imagine it being feasible.

"Since we can't figure out who it is, we've decided we're just going to beat them at their own game and make it go viral."

"Why not just take the rumor site down?" I ask. "Cooper's a master hacker. Chloe told me he hacked into dating sites last year to get revenge on some guy. If he can do that, I'd imagine he can bury this thing."

"We're going to try that, too."

"What narrative are you going to share?" I'm flustered, annoyed because I know what he's about to ask of me, though he's barely given me an explanation.

"Whatever bullshit necessary to distract everyone. The article needs to redirect people's focus to the next shiny thing."

I consider his comments about my women's soccer article and how the compliment feels almost backhanded. "Send your request to Anthony. I'm sure he'd be interested in your pitch."

"What? Are you really not going to help me with this? You suggested we change the narrative."

"I don't write fluff pieces."

"Some of these guys could lose their futures. They're starting to investigate these claims. You know what they have on Pax—that shit shouldn't get him kicked off the team, not after he's worked as hard as he has." His admission stops me.

"People are following this site because it's scandalous," I tell him. "People love a winner, but what they love even more is watching a winner burn."

He pulls in a deep breath through his nose, his muscular chest somehow becoming more sculpted. "We'll offer them something better then."

"What's that?"

"The truth."

I shake my head. "It can't be what you're studying in school or records you've broken. You guys will have to share stuff that people want to know about–stuff you don't want them to know about."

Ian nods.

"We'll need to do more than a single print. It will need to be a series of articles, and it will need to include something either shocking or fascinating with lots of pictures. Headlines and a couple of misleading quotes will be able to catch interest, but there will need to be *substance*." I say, reiterating that this will be uncomfortable, possibly more than the current site, because truths can hurt more than lies.

He tips his chin to one side, his lips curving upward but only fractionally. "So you'll help?"

"Yes, but I don't know that it will garner much attention. Even if we do a series, you're still competing with a site that has already piqued the curiosity of campus."

"Which is why Cooper is going to work on making it so our new website is what gets turned up on searches."

"Is this worth it to trade fake secrets for real ones? I mean, overall, the interest is mostly positive. People aren't mad or disgusted. They're curious and enthralled."

"If it were just the fans, I wouldn't give a shit, but as I said, the university is opening investigations, and it could fuck up our season and our futures. We don't stand a chance if we lose Paxton as our QB."

I feel myself frowning.

"I know," he says. "It's a shitty situation. I wish whoever had this would turn it over and allow the University to investigate the claims fairly. If one of us did something that hurt someone or caused significant harm, it should be addressed, but this is a shit show. Wickizer had his sexuality blasted on the site—that wasn't fair, and posting claims like Alexis didn't earn her spot at Brighton—it's bullshit."

"Are you guys prepared if the rumor site has more photos? *Worse photos?*"

Ian swallows. "This is where we're putting a lot of faith in Coop and trying to engage people elsewhere."

"What about filing an injunction?"

"It could take too long. Plus, each time we fuck with this person, they retaliate."

His phone buzzes again. It's gone off at least a dozen times since we've sat down. "Do you need to get that?"

He scoffs, his thickly fringed eyelashes falling shut for a moment as humor dances across his features and relaxes his shoulders. "No."

"Are you avoiding someone?" Hope makes my heart beat a faster rhythm.

He spins his phone around to face me and taps the screen to illuminate it.

"Two hundred missed calls?" I read.

"They published all my contact information," he says, like I missed seeing the photo of him.

His phone vibrates again with a text from an unknown number. "You can look," he says, recognizing my curiosity. "I'm not going to respond to any of them."

I slowly lift his phone, wondering if I'll see something from Isla. My curiosity should serve as a warning. I should decline and set it down, knowing that it will only torture me for days to come if I do find something.

I don't heed my own warning.

His texts are filled with messages from unknown numbers: sexual requests, innuendos, naked pictures, and a zillion compliments.

"I have to go change my number," he says.

"We can make the articles be an exposé. You guys will need to decide if you want to include the original rumors or avoid them altogether."

Ian nods. "I'm an open book."

"I'll also need to meet with some of your other teammates.

Lincoln, Pax, and Tyler are getting a lot of attention this year. Maybe Hoyt?"

"You can talk to anyone on the team. Anyone but Hoyt."

I pause, waiting for a joke or something more, but instead, Ian clenches his jaw once again, creating those sinfully hard planes along his jaw.

I grab my doughnut to distract myself from wanting to lean across the table and draw my tongue across those lines. The doughnut is sweet with that hint of tartness that makes me love them, but it's dry and slightly stale. I take a sip of the coffee. "I'll need to interview Hoyt. The first rumor was of him."

Ian saws his jaw, watching me as he does. It's not in the same way he sometimes does when he hears more words than I'm actually saying. No, this is a look I don't recognize and has me debating if I should laugh or think of something sarcastic to say. "You can talk to him under one condition."

My surprise has me sitting back several inches. "Now, there are conditions?"

"Just one."

"What?"

"I have to be there."

I lean against the cold, hardback of the chair. "You think I need a babysitter?"

He saws his jaw again. "Take it or leave it."

I laugh. "You know what happens when you tell someone not to do something, right? They usually end up doing it out of curiosity. Though, it would likely be defiance *and* curiosity for me."

His eyes narrow on mine. "Can't you just take my word?"

"You aren't giving me your word, you're giving me an ultimatum, and I'm pretty sure I'm doing this as a favor to you...."

"I don't trust him. Not with you." His words are two sentences—or maybe one. I can't tell because my stupid and unruly heart is thumping as though I've just read a scorching scene in the recent romance novel I've been reading.

"Does it matter?" It's a blanket question cast far and wide beyond what we've set regarding labels and descriptions for our once friendship that was verging on more and then came to an abrupt stop.

He holds my stare. "We leave Friday at five, but we'll be back on Sunday afternoon and can all be at your disposal."

"Deflection isn't attractive on you, Ian Forrest."

"Yeah, well, I doubt jealousy would look much better."

The thought of him kissing Isla makes my coffee taste more bitter than it is. "I need to get going, but I'll email you. We'll figure something out."

"I'll see you in class tomorrow?" he asks.

I nod. "Yup."

14

ROSE

There are three reasons to hate the first Sunday of the month.

1. Monday follows
2. I have to see my dad
3. I have to see my dad at *his* house

Only this month, our brunch date was moved to today, the fourth Sunday of the month. October is just around the corner, and my article for the paper is taking too many of my thoughts. I'm still trying to figure out the right angle to twist this series to add something with more substance than their favorite color and idea of a dream date.

Additionally, Olivia, who usually accompanies me on these dates, has caught a nasty cold and has quarantined herself in her room since Friday.

I roll over and release a long sigh, curling in my overstuffed duvet. Juliet is asleep beside me, her legs stretched out like the mini queen she's become.

"You want to come with me?" I ask her.

She purrs in response.

"You say that now, but you have no idea what you'd be getting yourself into."

Juliet stretches her front paws further, encouraging me to scratch her belly. "Think you can handle holding down the place and watching over your other human for a few hours? Olivia might need some extra snuggles today." I bury a kiss on Juliet's head and roll out of bed. "Save a spot for me. I'm hoping to be back in record time today."

My phone rings as I move to my closet, causing me to detour back to my bedside table. Anna's name is on my screen with a video call.

I answer, coughing into my elbow.

"You aren't trying that again, are you?" Anna asks.

"Trying what?" I use a hoarse and broken voice and frown for added dramatic effect.

"I can tell you're faking it."

"Can your husband?"

"*Rose!*" She wears a scowl like a uniform. She always has before noon. I can't say that I hate it. I have my own version of resting bitch face, plus, the expectation for women to appear friendly and smiling at all times is nauseating.

I shrug. "Just wondering."

"I'm on my way over."

"Over to where?"

She looks at me like I've just sprouted a third eye in the middle of my forehead. "Your apartment."

"I have not caffeinated yet. Can we flip the bitch switch down to medium until I shower and have some coffee?"

"Why are you always late?" Anna isn't trying to wear the crown of bitchiness this morning. She just lacks a filter.

"I'm not late. I just wasn't going to be early."

"We're not going to Dad's."

It has never been anywhere else in the three-plus years that we've been having these brunches. "Why?"

"He tried to reschedule to a weekday, and you said you couldn't. Maybe this will teach you to be more flexible. Now, shower, put on some casual clothes, and get some coffee so you can hold a full conversation." She hangs up.

I look at Juliet. "How did we grow up in the same house? Is she even human?"

Juliet doesn't move.

I take a quick shower, get the coffee started, and then stand in front of my closet for too long, trying to consider Anna's definition of casual. I opt for jeans and a gray sweater before blow-drying my long hair. Next, I turn to my makeup. Cosmetics remind me of my mom. I loved watching her put on makeup when I was little, and I still remember the first time she allowed me to put some on.

I still love makeup, though I have mad respect for those who opt not to wear it. I always feel better and more confident with some foundation, blush, and a thick sweep of eyeliner.

Knowing Anna will be here any moment, I race across the apartment and silently peek into Olivia's room.

She's on her side, watching TV with a wad of tissues in her hand.

"How are you feeling?"

"I hate the start of school. I hate germs," she murmurs, her words distorted from being so congested.

"Can I get you anything? Some water? Sprite? Soup?"

She shakes her head. "Sorry to bail on you."

I wave a hand dismissively. "Don't worry. I'm a big girl. You should drink some tea. The lemon and honey will help, and so will the steam."

She shakes her head. "Not yet. I just took some more of that decongestant stuff you bought. When I took it yesterday, I slept for eight hours."

"I'm just going to get you some in case you change your mind, and I'll have my phone on me the entire time. I will be here if you need anything from water to food to snuggles."

Olivia smiles weakly. "You're not allowed in here. I'm in quarantine. Whitney said she would come by this afternoon with some soup, but I told her she was only allowed in the kitchen. I don't want to pass this gunk on to the rest of you." Though Whitney is Olivia's stepmom, she's far less like the evil stepmother in Cinderella and much more like the fairy godmother.

"Good," I tell her. "But my offer still stands."

"I hope the crepes are amazing for you," Olivia says. "Drive carefully, and if Anna starts talking about politics, you can always fake my cold."

"I already tried."

Olivia starts to laugh, but it turns into a coughing fit.

"It will be okay. We're going to breakfast, which might be the best idea yet. It will force us to leave and break up the chit-chat."

Olivia gives a final cough. "Keep me posted. Love you, Rose."

"Love you, too." I blow her a kiss and close the door behind me. As though on cue, there's a knock at the front door.

I pull it open, startling Anna. "I asked you to call me," I tell her.

"No, you didn't."

"I texted you."

"I don't read my texts while driving."

"What about after you park?"

"Why'd you want me to call?" She peers over my shoulder like she's expecting to see something scandalous.

"The orgy is over," I tell her. "We have a great cleaning guy who comes and gets everything picked up. He's crazy fast and affordable, but the only catch is that he likes to clean in the nude." I lift my shoulders. "Not the worst problem if you like a little eye candy."

"Are you finished?" Anna asks.

"Am I ever?"

She releases a long breath as she shakes her head. "Is Olivia coming?"

I grab a pair of tennis shoes from beside the door. "No, she's sick."

Anna frowns, showing her humanity. "I've heard it's going around. She needs to have some ginger. It will help boost her immune system."

"Already on it," I tell her as I move around the kitchen to grab some things for Olivia. I drop them off in her room and leave the door cracked so Juliet can come and go.

I grab my purse. "Where's Kurt?

"He had to work this morning."

I frown. Losing half of our party and distractions is guaranteed to spell trouble. "Where are we going?"

Anna gives me what can only be described as the stink eye. "That client I told you about, Barrett Forrest, Dad's joining the team to offer advice, and he thinks volunteering is a good idea."

'The client' translates to Ian's father.

"Okay.... What does that mean?"

"Well, since you couldn't reschedule, you get to join us."

"Aren't you extra Grinchy today."

"I know...." Anna grumbles. "I'm just...." She releases a long sigh. "My period started, and I really thought we were going to be pregnant this month." Her shoulders fall. "And now Dad's helping on my first campaign at the state level, and I get it, they're friends, and Dad has a ton of connections and knowledge, but I just feel like I'm taking the back seat. And to top it all off, I really want some steak and eggs with béarnaise sauce, and I know that is super first-world whiny, but considering I've worked the last fourteen days straight, all I want to do is sit and eat and be selfish."

I wrap my arms around Anna. My sister can sometimes come across as unfriendly and high-strung, but under her rough edges is a heart that is three sizes too big that she often conceals out of necessity and exhaustion ... and a bit of snobbery that likely exists from a combination of exclusive private schools and constantly being told she was a genius from the age of six.

"I'm sorry. When it happens, you're going to be the best mom. I'll tell you what, if you have time, I'll take you out for a late lunch after we volunteer. We can get Dick's."

Anna's eyes narrow. "Did you not hear me? I said steak, eggs, and béarnaise sauce."

"I know, but the next best thing is a nice, greasy, and delicious cheeseburger from Dick's."

"Do you see my skin?" She points at her face. "I can't eat burgers and maintain this skin."

I laugh. "How would you know if you're not eating them?"

She rolls her eyes. "Don't believe me. Just wait until you reach the age where just looking at fried food makes you gain weight and break out."

"Never. Now, where are we going? Are we planting trees? Cleaning a park? Is it just the governor-elect?" I ask, my chest holding equal parts of hopefulness and dread. "Is that what he's called? Governor-elect?"

"He's just a candidate. Elect is after he wins and before he takes office. And I think it's just him."

I'm relieved.

I'm disappointed.

I'm still really confused.

Since we met Wednesday to discuss *The Daily Dose's* articles, I haven't seen Ian. Avoiding him makes it easier for me to rationalize my feelings and sort things out so I can review the articles objectively. I'm doing this for friends and because, regardless of my personal thoughts on many of the rumors, too many revolve around sex shaming and lack facts and ethics—the backbone of good journalism.

"And I don't know where we're going. Dad said it was at a sanctuary but then mentioned having to go through background checks."

"Background checks?"

Anna shoots me a look of impatience. "I don't know."

"What happened to 'I'll share the deets when I get there?'"

"I have the address."

"Deets is plural. Address is singular."

"I don't understand how you learned to be such a smartass."

I laugh. "So many reasons, so little time."

Anna and I head outside in time to catch our neighbor leaving his apartment. He's lived here longer than we have and has a young daughter who periodically stays with him. Olivia thinks he's nice. I'm still not ready to remove him from creeper status.

"Morning, Rose." He lifts his commuter cup in greeting.

I offer a small wave but don't say anything. I've learned that most men have easily stimulated egos, and talking to or even smiling at them only makes them grow.

"He looks creepy," Anna says, mirroring my thoughts.

"I think so too. You should tell Olivia next time you see her."

Anna's brown eyes grow round. "She doesn't see it?"

"She's nicer than us."

Anna bursts out laughing and then links her arm with mine. "How's school going?"

"Good."

She gives me a cross look. "*Well*," she corrects my grammar. "When you say good, it makes you sound like you attended public school."

"Just when you start to be likable, you say something like that," I tell her, following her to where she's parked.

She rolls her eyes. "I have Starbucks for you if you get in the car and listen to me whine about my new assistant."

"Reduced to bribing?"

"She's awful, and I need to word vomit to someone I trust."

"Isn't this why you're married? Kurt's supposed to listen to your word vomit."

"He thinks my expectations are too high."

I slide into my seat and rub my hands together at the sight of a venti iced coffee with whipped cream. "You do love me," I say, reaching for it.

She grins. "A little less today because I'm not getting my steak and eggs."

"With béarnaise sauce, yeah, yeah."

"Okay, so my new assistant is late every single day."

"*Late* late or Anna late?"

She glares at me. "I'm the one talking. You're supposed to be drinking."

I grin. "Does Kurt get tired of you always being on top?"

"Why do you make everything sexual?"

"That was my first joke."

She gives me the side-eye. "I'm serious. You talk like you're a fourteen-year-old boy."

"How many fourteen-year-old boys do you spend time with?"

"One. You." She puts her car into drive and heads out onto the main road.

"I don't understand why talking about sex is so taboo. Why is it okay to talk about a great sale or some disgusting medical tale, but we can't discuss what brought a toe-curling orgasm?" I take a quick drink of my coffee. "People don't even feel comfortable talking about sex with their partners. I don't get it. Sex is everywhere. It's on TV, in books, and on billboards, and practically everyone we know is doing the dirty, and yet, if you mention it, people all get squeamish and embarrassed."

"Because it's awkward. I don't want to picture my business partners on their knees, humping their wives."

"I'm not saying you should talk to your business partners about what sexual positions they prefer. I'm talking about me." I point at my chest.

"No."

"No, what?"

"I'm not talking to you about sex."

"Why not?" I ask.

"Because it's *weird*."

"It's only weird if you make it weird."

Anna shakes her head. "You've already made it weird."

"I like sex."

"Oh my God," Anna says, dropping her head back.

"I like saying that, too."

She glares at me.

"You set me up for that one—that's on you. But really, Anna. You're married and trying to conceive. You're supposed to be having sex. I'm twenty-one and healthy—I should be having sex. Why is this embarrassing?"

"I'll stop and buy you sushi if you shut up."

"I'd rather have this conversation."

Anna sighs. "Are you going on about this because you want to tell me about something you did?"

"No. I just don't understand why talking about sex is so uncomfortable."

Another heavy sigh greets my words. "Because it makes people feel vulnerable and uncomfortable."

"But *why*?"

"For many reasons. Some people aren't comfortable with their body image, and some are uncomfortable with not knowing things about their body or why or how things work."

"Do you feel vulnerable while having sex?"

Anna wipes a hand across her forehead. "Sometimes. Kind of. Yeah."

"I feel empowered."

She belts out a laugh. "You would."

"I'm serious. I didn't rely on a guy to teach me about my body or how to have an orgasm, so I know exactly what I want and what I like."

"You're an anomaly," Anna says, looking at me as she turns on her blinker.

"If we talked about sex more, maybe there wouldn't be two-hundred-million girls and women who had their clit surgically removed."

"I don't think making sex a household topic will stop female genital mutilation."

"But it might. We've stigmatized sex so that it's only acceptable for guys to have as many sexual partners as they want and to be seen as sexy for being experienced, and it's disgusting if women aren't virgins. Like that thin layer of skin in our vaginas somehow equates to a price or worth."

Anna looks at me. "I'm glad you were born in this generation."

I grin. "Also, you shouldn't open your birthday present in front of Dad, but you should open it in front of Kurt."

"Rose! Don't tell me you bought me a book about sex."

"I didn't."

She glances at me. "What is it then?"

"A vibrator."

"I hate you."

"After you use it, you'll love me."

Her cheeks redden. "How are you my sister?"

"You're welcome."

"On the way home, you can't say two words. It's my turn to talk," she says as we pull to a stop.

"Then I should probably say now that I agree with Kurt, and your expectations are a little too high."

Anna scowls at me. "The death of accountability is the problem with our world."

"Really? I'd have guessed famine or disease or maybe corruption."

"Out!" she screeches, pointing at the car door.

My smile slips as I face the building we're parked in front of. I haven't been here in years, and only ever with my mom. After all, she had fitted me with my idea of a crown and cape and told me that we had the opportunity to change the world—I'd just always interpreted that to mean saving the world.

Memories rush through me, stealing my breath and stinging my eyes. I want to tell Anna to take me home because being here infringes on our monthly deal.

"God, we're out in the middle of nowhere," Anna says, rubbing her arms.

We are out in the middle of nowhere, which makes being here even less appealing. When it comes to spending time with my dad, I rely heavily on routine and expectations. Our brunches consist of a thirty-minute pre-brunch drink on the patio when it's nice and in the living room when it's not. During that time, we make small talk which is generally taken up by Dad asking me about classes and Anna grilling me on professors and theories. I spend this time finding ways to include Kurt in the conversation—for my benefit, not his. He often looks like a deer caught in the headlights as he stumbles over his sentences. Eight years later, Kurt still looks at our father like a celebrity. Once brunch is ready, I usually deflect the conversation by asking Anna about her work, and on the few occasions that doesn't work, Olivia fills the gaps with small talk—something I can't seem to manage with my father.

This place changes everything, creating a new game board and pieces that don't make any sense.

"Why are you pouting?" Anna asks.

I turn my attention to her, and for a second, I see our mom. Anna has always looked so much like her, more so as she gets older. The greatest difference these days is their hair, which Anna insists on wearing short, whereas Mom always wore hers past her shoulders. "I don't understand why we're here," I tell her.

She shrugs. "Me either. But let's just get it over with."

I trail behind her through the single glass door that still has a broken spring. Inside, a woman is behind a counter wearing a hunter-green top.

Anna goes straight to her while I hang back, trying to recall if I recognize her. "Hi, we're here—"

"Anna!" Dad peeks his head out from behind the doorway leading to the back, where some of the animals are kept. "These are my girls," Dad tells the woman in the green polo.

The woman behind the counter lights up. "Of course. I can see the resemblance. Go on back."

I glance at Anna to share a look of bewilderment—a look I know Olivia would be exchanging with me right now if she were here—but Anna is already moving toward Dad with a smile plastered across her face, reminding me that some of our differences span far and wide.

"Girls, I'm so glad our monthly brunch date didn't work out. This is such a great opportunity for us. Rose, it's my pleasure to introduce you to our future governor, Barrett Forrest, and his lovely wife, Michelle, and their son, Ian."

15

IAN

I don't hear the rest of Bill's introduction. I'm too distracted by Rose's silent reaction and the few details of her past sliding into place before my eyes.

I met her dad only an hour ago, introduced to me as Bill, my dad's buddy from college and previous White House Deputy Chief of Staff. This translated to me as a man with connections and talents who my dad was convinced he needed at his side to win the election for state governor.

The similarities between Bill and Rose are nearly imperceptible, except they have the same full smile they can turn on in a second. Next, my attention turns to Rose's sister, Anna. Her hair and eyes are darker than Rose's, but it's easy to tell they're related. With her last name being Pollard rather than Cartwright, I hadn't connected the dots until just now.

Rose refuses to look at me. It's as though I can hear her thoughts telling me this isn't a part of her life she wants me included in. I know because the few times we discussed her father, she'd give answers laden with sarcasm and regret before quickly changing the subject.

"It's so nice to meet you, Rose. We've really enjoyed working with

Anna," Mom says as she takes a step forward and shakes Rose's hand. "What a small world that you go to school with Ian."

"We have a class together," I say. "Rose is also the sports columnist for the paper at Brighton. She's actually going to be breaking the story with the new website."

"Oh," Mom blinks several times, "I didn't realize you guys had decided to go forward with that idea...." She rolls her hands, her discomfort apparent.

Dad looks at me, shock making him blink rapidly in response as he pieces together his own puzzle of recognition, realizing this is the same Rose we discussed in Italy over the summer.

Bill clears his throat. "Are you sure you want to post the new site?" He looks at Anna. "I know your PR team is advising you to come out with this new approach, but I would bury it. Hammer through a dozen injunctions and get it buried and forgotten."

Upon meeting Bill, I liked him. He's personable and well-spoken. However, now that I know he's Rose's father, it's hard to look at him the same way. Rose has never openly shared why she doesn't get along with her father, only that she doesn't.

"I would hate for you to roll it out there and for it not to go right." Bill's uncertainty is apparent on his wrinkled brow and audible in his light tone.

"That's why we need the home-court advantage," I say.

Dad nods. "I hate that it's out there, too, Bill, but we've gone over this, and we believe this is the best way to control the situation, so it doesn't blow up in our faces."

Bill nods. "Understood. I'm glad you have Rose writing the piece. She and Anna will be able to work together." He turns to Rose. "I liked your piece that came out yesterday on the women's volleyball team. You did an exceptional job of shedding light on the proportionality aspect. Readers will be thinking about that article for a while." His compliment seems genuine, but the fact he tells her this here and now reminds me of how little she sees him.

Rose's smile dims, her teeth disappearing as she presses her lips together with a tight smile that looks both foreign and uncomfortable on her.

Before our conversation can continue, the woman who introduced herself as Debra when we arrived returns. "Are we ready?" she asks. Her attention stops, and she tilts her head with curiosity. "Rose?"

"Hey, Deb," Rose says. She pulls in a breath through her nose and then swallows thickly.

I stare at Rose, sensing her unease and myriad of emotions and finding myself utterly confused like most interactions involving her.

Bill looks at his daughter and then the other woman, curiosity clear on his beveled brow. "You know each other?"

Debra nods. "Rose volunteered here for years."

"With Mom," Anna says, her tone filled with realization.

Rose forces another smile. "It's nice to see you." She turns her attention to her dad. "How'd you find this place?"

Bill sobers. "The environment's high on Mr. Forrest's list of agenda items to protect here in Washington. He wanted to come and learn what's plaguing the wildlife in our area."

"Of course." Rose lifts her chin.

Behind us, a bird screeches.

I turn to see a medium-sized owl flap its wings and screech again from where it's perched on a mounted branch. Unlike the other birds that are all in enclosures, this bird is roaming freely.

Debra smiles. "That's just Harry. He's all bark and no bite. He's been here with us for seven years now—refuses to leave."

Rose looks at the bird, a flash of something dark and sad crossing her features. This isn't the first time I've found myself wanting to ask her a dozen clarifying questions for a single expression, but this is undoubtedly the closest I've been to some of the shadows of her past that she often evades with humor.

"Many owls are brought here during the spring months," Debra says. "Mostly owlets: baby owls that have fallen from their nests due to logging or people cutting dead trees. We're a full rehab center, so if an owl is hurt or just malnourished, we get them strong enough, and then our goal is always to get them back out into the wild."

"Why does he stay?" Mom asks Debra, giving a nervous glance at the owl she called Harry, who is now resting quietly, observing us.

Debra smiles. "We've tried multiple times, but he's determined to stay. At least, for now." She rubs her hands together. "Many owls stay with us for a short period. Owlets grow into adults in just sixteen weeks, so we need to get them back into their natural environment as quickly as possible so we don't interfere with their natural instincts.

"We also have adult birds brought in, like this little lady." She points at a large metal cage where a sleek owl with a round white face sits. "This is a barn owl. She was brought in last week after being caught in a fishing wire and nearly drowning. She broke her wing trying to get free and lost a lot of feathers. It left a nasty scratch on her head, too. Adults tend to stay longer because their injuries are often more extensive. She'll probably be with us for eight to twelve weeks." Debra points into the distance. "We take care of other wild birds in the area, but we specialize in owls. They're brought here from all over the state and surrounding areas like Montana, Idaho, and Oregon. We even had an owl come all the way from Colorado this summer. He'd been hit by a car and had to undergo a pretty substantial surgery. But you'll see hawks, crows, ravens, ducks, seagulls, ospreys...." She shrugs. "Basically, all the wild birds in the area."

"They all get along?" Anna asks.

Debra grins. "No. Owls are very independent creatures." She walks a few paces and stops. "Today, I thought I'd show you around and talk to you about available volunteering opportunities. People sometimes think that volunteering means they get to pet the birds and play with them, so I've realized it's crucial to be upfront and let everyone know you can't interact with the birds. I know it sounds cruel, but we don't want them to return to the wild and seek out humans. It wouldn't be safe for them, and it wouldn't be safe for volunteers, either. Owls are raptors with incredibly sharp talons and beaks meant for hunting. That said, many volunteering opportunities will still have you in contact with the birds if that's something you're interested in.

"Some of the opportunities include cleaning the animal's cages, prepping the animal's food, assisting with calls, and we do monthly field visits where we teach schools and others in the community about the birds and what we do here. This can be a great photo op situation," she says, turning to my dad.

"There are also opportunities to work out in the field. We're currently looking for volunteers to help build safe structures for burrowing owls. We also have fundraising opportunities which involve making cold calls, stuffing envelopes, that kind of thing." She sweeps her gaze across us, hands poised on her hips, almost as though she's waiting for us to tell her, don't call us, we'll call you.

Hell, that's what I want to tell her. When Dad asked me to meet him here when I got off the plane from the Bay area, I was ready to give him a dozen excuses why I couldn't make it—only a couple would have been lies. Between needing to study, preparing for tomorrow's practice, catching up with my laundry, and getting some decent sleep, I had no interest or patience in meeting someone else from the campaign. But Anna had asked that I be present to finalize details about the new website.

I'm not as concerned as my mom about the new site or the potential backlash. I have faith in Cooper and Rose to believe we will at least present a fight.

Mom was horrified when she saw me on the rumor site. Truthfully, I wasn't worried about how people perceived the rumor about me. I've spent little time in my life giving a fuck about what others think, but I've been trying to find the right time and place to explain it to Rose since it was published.

"When you said to dress casually, I didn't realize you meant to prepare to climb a pine tree casual," Anna says, looking at her dad.

Mom laughs kindly, likely feeling the same way.

Debra flashes a knowing smirk.

"Since we're here, we'd love to help out however we can, and then we can decide how to proceed later," Dad says, ever the diplomat.

"Great idea. Maybe we can even bounce some ideas around regarding the article and the new website," Mom says. I know she's not trying to be rude or even offensive. There are few things she wouldn't do to help Cassie or me, and this website fiasco has visibly irked her.

"Mom, it's fine. I've met with Dad's PR team, and they've given us a library of suggestions and advice," I tell her.

Hesitation hangs on her furrowed brow. "Bill's right. I don't want you to live with this rumor for the rest of your life. I mean, that picture was two years old."

Rose turns to look at me, light finally flickering in her green eyes, but before I can study her expression, Anna turns to Rose and quietly says something.

"Our neighbor in Italy hated birds. She said they're bad luck," Mom says beside me. She cranes her neck to look at Harry, who's still perched nearby, but his eyes are closed now.

I glance at the owl that drew my attention the moment we stepped back here. It's large, covered in pristine white feathers peppered with gray. It's majestic, reminding me of every fantasy novel I was too embarrassed to read in public as a kid when all my friends preferred comic books and horror movies. "I think they're pretty awesome," I tell her.

"Do you remember that time you and Isaiah found that injured owl out by the fishing hole?" Dad asks. "This was the sanctuary I contacted. They're who came and got it." The memory sparks to life, recalling how Isaiah and I had cut through the woods to avoid our old eccentric neighbor and found the owl on the ground.

"Cassie wanted to keep that owl," Mom says.

"Owls are amazing and essential birds, but they make lousy pets unless you work at a bird sanctuary," Debra says as she returns with a box of disposable gloves. "You guys are going to want these. Owls are solitary creatures, so they need to be kept alone. But since our vet is here today, she'll do some checkups, allowing you to clean out their enclosures while I prepare their food."

Debra leads us outside, where larger enclosures are arranged. She tells us the steps for cleaning them and then gives us a handout with all the same instructions. After a few clarifying questions, she takes the first owl out to be seen by the vet, leaving us to get to work.

"Dad, these jeans are four hundred dollars," Anna says. "I had no idea this was what you had in mind when discussing a nice community outreach program."

"Four hundred dollars?" Bill asks. "For pants? Do they wash and fold themselves?"

"No," Anna says thoughtfully, "but they also weren't made in a factory where a child made five cents for making them."

"*Touché,*" Bill replies. "I'll tell you what, why don't you take some pictures for us. Maybe we can get a couple of good ones to use for Barrett's social media campaign."

I stretch my back. Everything aches today. Sundays are the one day a week our team doesn't practice because after hitting it hard on the field where we don't leave an ounce of our strength and effort back, we're all fatigued and aching. I typically spend my Sundays wrapped in ice packs, drinking a dozen sports drinks, and trying to catch up on my homework.

"I think those are the things we're supposed to be preserving," Mom says, pointing at something that can only be described as looking like something you'd find in a litter box. Mom's cheeks balloon as she works to hold back her disgust, remaining by the door. The enclosure is big enough for several of us to fit inside.

Rose pulls on her gloves. "It's easier to stomach if you remind yourself it's not droppings, more like a giant hairball."

Anna covers her mouth as Rose reaches around the space and collects the owl pellets they save for schools to dissect. "I think I just threw up a little in my mouth."

Rose grins. "Pull up your sleeves, Anna. Things have only just begun!" It's her playful side, which I've only seen in short glimpses since last spring. I forget my exhaustion and obligations and bask in her smile.

"I have so many questions to ask you girls," Mom says as she seals the container with the owl pellets and moves them out of sight. "Anna, I know you've worked on presidential campaigns, so this probably isn't nearly as big of a deal for you anymore, but since your dad worked in the White House for eight years, did you get to meet the President? And were you able to go into the White House?"

My curiosity is piqued. When Rose told me that her dad worked in politics, I had no idea she'd meant he worked as the White House's Deputy Chief of Staff, and while it seems noteworthy, I can understand why she kept the details to herself. I know what it's like with my mother having come from what is now a tech giant. The first questions people always ask are who she knows and how much she's worth.

Anna nods. "We did meet the President," Anna says. "And we were allowed to see quite a lot of the White House. My mom and I loved the parties hosted by the White House."

Mom's eyes grow round with interest. "Did you get to meet many celebrities? What was the food like? I bet the gowns were gorgeous."

The two fall into conversation, each detail and fact pulling them further from our current task. Rose, however, maintains her focus on gathering the food and water dishes.

"Deputy Chief of Staff," I say, grabbing the hose.

Rose looks at me with a silencing stare.

"I wasn't going to ask if you've met Oprah."

The hint of a smile slips across her lips. "Most people have no idea what that job title means."

"When you said he traveled a lot for work, I didn't realize he lived on the opposite side of the country."

"We moved over there for a year," she says. "But he worked like fourteen-hour days, sometimes longer, so we barely saw him anyway, and Anna had been accepted into private school, and our mom wanted to be close to her."

"What about you?"

She turns to look at me, confusion creating a thin line between her brows. "What about me?"

"Did you like living in DC?"

She closes her mouth and then shakes her head. "I was only eight."

"And knowing you, you had an opinion, even at eight."

Her eyes brighten with another flash of humor. "I'm pretty sure I'm supposed to be interviewing you, Mr. Forrest."

"This isn't an interview. It's a conversation."

Rose rubs her lips together as though deciding her next move. "I enjoyed the bustle of the city and experiencing so many new things. But my mom missed Seattle and our house and the quiet here, and the more she talked about it, the more I was convinced I missed those things, too." She tilts her head to the side with the slightest of shrugs, and I can't determine if it's meant for herself or me as she shares this detail with me.

"Was it hard to have your dad gone all the time?"

"At first, it was," she says. "And then it became normal, and having him home was sometimes hard because he didn't fit into the routine we created. Sometimes stupid stuff, like we found a new favorite pizza place, and he'd come home for a week and order pizza at the old place we used to like but had stopped going to. And sometimes bigger things like we got a dog and the dog didn't know him and growled and barked at him all the time. He didn't know what time I went to school or got out or that Mom and I liked to drink our coffee outside when it wasn't raining." She grins again. "My mom was the ultimate hippy." Rose glances toward my mom and her sister and then returns those brazen green eyes to me. "You're probably experiencing what I did with my dad firsthand since your parents just moved back. Is it kind of weird?"

"It probably will come spring when I'm home."

"By then, they'll probably be busy with campaign stuff. Granted, I don't know much about local elections." She scrunches her face. "My dad was gone for a full year before the inauguration, but I'm sure your dad will have to do quite a bit of stuff, even for the state level."

"Likely."

A gentle laugh slips through her lips.

"What?" I ask.

She shakes her head. "Sometimes, you're a man of few words."

I laugh in turn. "You probably know more about this than I do. All I know is what I've been told, which is not to comment unless I feel comfortable or want to."

"Solid advice," she says.

We continue to work through cleaning multiple enclosures, creating a system. First, Rose and I clear out the owl pellets and dishes, then I spray them down, our dads scrub them, and then I go back and rinse them.

"We're almost done," Rose says as she comes out of one of the enclosures, this one smaller, only allowing one of us in at a time, and even then, we have to bend over.

Questions about her mom and her history here have been building over the past few hours. Still, our conversations have revolved around the articles she plans to write, stories about her cat, and how she recently made an offer on a studio space that she thinks she'll lose.

I glance toward our parents and Anna, gathered at the edge of the garage that leads outside. "I think they're done."

Rose laughs as she blows at a few strands of her dark hair that have settled across her face. "They were slowing us down, anyway."

I peel off my glove and reach forward, grazing my fingers across her cheek to brush the strands behind her ear.

Rose freezes, her green eyes focusing on mine as her lips part.

I lean forward, a reaction I'm not certain is by choice but by instinct and desire.

"Rose!" Anna calls.

Rose takes a step back, her gaze filled with questions and a hint of anger.

"I'm emailing you some ideas that Michelle and I discussed— topics and questions that will generate some intrigue without being too personal," Anna tells her.

Rose nods. "Works for me. I'm going to see if Deb needs any help with the food." She doesn't look at me before disappearing inside.

I can't help but wonder if this is a consequence of our kiss. She's been ignoring me for months, but never this blatantly.

My annoyance fuels me to finish cleaning the rest of the enclosure alone.

Rose wanders back outside as I'm rinsing the dishes. "They didn't help?" she asks, still avoiding my gaze.

"Are things going to be weird between us going forward?"

"Define weird." Sarcasm curls her lips.

"You know what I'm talking about. We've barely spoken except when I asked for your help with the articles."

Her gaze drops to my jeans. "Speaking of that, I haven't heard your phone blowing up. Did you turn it off? Bury it? Drop it into the Pacific?"

She's the queen of deflection, but my dad is heading this way, and I know this isn't the time or place to push her. "Actually, I need to give you my new number."

"This is looking great," Dad says. "Debra said she doesn't have any more projects for us today." He rubs his hands together. "Why don't we get some lunch?"

Rose smiles. "It was wonderful meeting you, but unfortunately, I have a prior engagement."

Jealousy burns in my chest, despite Arlo's assurance that she hasn't been out with a guy since last year.

Dad looks from me to Rose. "That's too bad. It was nice meeting you, Rose."

"I should probably get going as well," I say.

Dad slowly looks between us again before nodding. "Sure. Sure. You've met your time allotment with your old man. I get it."

"I told you I'll see you come February when the season's over," I remind him.

He laughs. "That's right." He turns his attention back to Rose. "Drive safe. Rose, I hope we'll get to spend time together again, next time without the manual labor."

She shakes his hand. "This place was a great choice. Hopefully, it will give you both some positive press."

Dad smiles. "I appreciate that."

She smiles and turns away without looking at me or saying another word.

Dad releases a whoosh of breath. "That's her, huh?"

I follow her with my gaze. "That's her."

"I had no idea it was Bill's daughter when you told me."

"Would it have changed anything?"

He shrugs. "I'm not sure. She's beautiful."

"That she is." I shift my gaze to where Rose is talking to her dad.

"Bill and I haven't been close since college, but I know his wife passed a few years back. There were whispers of a scandal involved, but I never heard the details—I didn't want to hear them because it seemed cruel and unfair when he was losing so much. Knowing the two of them, I can't imagine it was true, but you know how rumors can be. Anyway, I know you mentioned Rose is hard to get close to. That kind of loss can build walls."

Rose turns toward the building to leave, and I set my hand on my dad's shoulder. "I'll see you later, Dad. Have a good lunch."

He grins. "I thought so."

I pass through the building and step outside to find Rose wandering through the parking lot with her phone raised above her head. "What are you doing?"

She looks at me and then at her phone. "I'm looking for a signal. Anna drove me, and she needs to be at that lunch so my dad doesn't railroad her plans."

I tip my head toward my truck, though she's not looking at me. "Come on. I'll give you a ride."

She slowly lowers her phone and looks at me.

"You're on my way home."

Reluctance keeps her frozen in place.

I move to my truck and open the passenger door, daring her to object.

Her chest swells with a silent breath, and then she moves closer, climbing into the seat and reaching for her seat belt as I close the door.

"This feels like a small world moment," Rose says as I close my door.

"That our dads went to school together, or that your sister is leading his campaign?"

Rose releases a laugh and shakes her head. "All of it." She clears her throat. "Thanks for giving me a ride. I blame my lack of caffeine for not thinking about it earlier." She crosses her arms and sets her hands on her knees, which are pressed together.

"Why are you nervous?"

Green eyes flash to me. "I'm not."

"No?"

Her response is to turn and look out the windshield.

"What do you have going on this afternoon?" I ask her.

"I have a yoga class, and then I'm meeting someone."

"Someone from the team?"

"No. I'm interviewing Tyler tomorrow. He'll be the first story." She lowers her brow with confusion. "You were on the email chain."

I nod. "I saw that Hoyt asked you to meet today."

"What's with you and Hoyt?"

"You said you would allow Pax or me to be there for all the interviews so we're not blindsided again."

"And you will," she says. "I sent invitations to you and Paxton for every interview." Her voice is curt, her patience stretched.

Unfortunately, the feeling is mutual. I hate this uneven ground we're on where our admissions are told through long stares and skipped words. "What happened last week?"

"I need a little more context. Are we referring to what happened in Syria? Or in a particular class? Or are we talking about something else entirely?"

"You ditched Labor Economics."

"I needed to meet someone."

"Right," I say, feeling anger and resentment crawl across my skin, creating that same urge to be on the field and hit someone so I can release a fraction of this overwhelming betrayal I feel at the thought of her with another guy.

I start my truck and drive across town in silence.

As I turn into her apartment complex, my knuckles are white from gripping the steering wheel so damn tight.

Rose remains silent.

"We have a target on our backs. If you're meeting Hoyt to have sex, do it behind closed doors." I regret the words as soon as they leave my mouth.

Her eyes snap to mine, and she rears her head back. Then her brow lowers with accusation and betrayal, and her green gaze turns icy.

Before I can apologize, she pushes the door open and hops out of my truck.

"Rose," I call her name, but she doesn't turn around. "Rose." Thank fuck she has to fish for her keys, slowing her down.

"You're not invited inside."

"I wasn't trying to insinuate anything."

She turns to me with narrowed eyes. "Yes, you were. You don't want me to spend time with Hoyt because you think I want to have sex with him, which, quite frankly, is none of your goddamn business. Goodbye, Ian." She sticks her key in the door and twists it open before slipping inside.

In a prouder moment, being a better version of myself—the version I wish I could be around her—I'd knock and ask her to have this conversation again, but her lack of denial toward the claim has anger drilling a hole into my chest. I head for my truck before I can say or do anything else I'll regret.

Rose

I take a deep breath and then another, working to slow my heart which currently aches as Ian's accusation replays in my head.

I kick off my shoes and am halfway to Olivia's door before Juliet sashays out of the room, her tail curling around the doorjamb.

"Hi, Jules," I whisper. "How's our patient?"

She threads herself through my legs, meowing softly. I pet her black fur. "You were right," I tell her. "I should have stayed home." I give her a final pet and eek inside Olivia's room. She's on her side, huddled under a mass of blankets.

"How are you feeling?" I ask, eyeing her glass of water and the untouched crackers.

"Freezing."

"Want me to turn up the furnace?"

"I don't want you to be miserable."

I shake my head. "I'll turn it up. I'll be right back."

We haven't had the furnace on all summer, causing it to smell like something's burning as it kicks on. I go to my room and find a pair of warm socks before returning to Olivia. I dangle the socks in front of me as a warning before I flip up the blankets and find her feet freezing and curled. I slip the socks on her and rub her feet between my hands for several minutes.

"How was brunch?" she asks.

"Anna and my dad are working for Ian's dad's campaign."

Olivia's eyes stretch with surprise. "I need details."

I shake my head. "Those *are* the details," I lie. It's not because I don't trust Olivia with my thoughts or even my battered feelings, but while she's sick, I only want her focused on feeling better and resting. My drama can wait. I place my hand on her forehead. "You still have a fever." As hard of a time as I sometimes give Anna for her hypochondriac tendencies, I feel the same fears prickle my thoughts when someone I care for doesn't feel well.

The front door opens, and a few seconds later, Arlo appears, carrying two bags of groceries and his team duffel bag.

"You need to stay away," Olivia warns. "You can't get sick. You just started to play again."

He kicks off his shoes. "Try and stop me." He walks to the bed and gently brushes Olivia's hair back. "I brought you some sports drinks. Those orange ones you like. And my mom said you need some zinc, so I picked some of that up, too." He empties the contents of one bag on her nightstand. "How are you feeling?"

"Like a bus hit me, backed up, and ran me over again."

I smile, flipping the blankets to cover her feet again.

"Rose has been taking good care of me."

Arlo looks at me, softness in his soft brown eyes. "I know. She's been texting me with updates. Sorry, it took me so long to get here. The trainer wanted to test my knee and make sure it was okay before he let me go, and I needed to pick up some clothes at my place, and then my mom called and told me to get the zinc."

"She's been sleeping a lot and is currently on a water strike, so good call on the sports drinks. I have a yoga class and am going to pick up Bree first, but then I'll stop by the store and get some more of those mashed potatoes you liked. If you guys need anything else, just let me know."

Olivia shakes her head. "Don't worry about going to the store."

"I'm not worried about it," I tell her. "I was worried about leaving you alone."

Arlo is already climbing under the blankets beside her.

"Drive safe," Olivia says. "Text me when you get there."

"I will. Get some rest."

"Thanks, Rose," Arlo says.

I nod once and head back out to the living room. For months, watching Arlo and Olivia's love has influenced my thoughts and judgments about relationships. While I'm incredibly grateful he's here, for the first time that I can recall, it leaves a stinging sensation that reaches my eyes.

I don't try and understand why. I don't want to take a closer look at my emotions when I feel so fragile and vulnerable after today.

TWENTY MINUTES LATER, I pull into the driveway of a small ranch-style house. It's blue with a lighter blue trim. The paint is peeling, the bushes around the house are overgrown, and the grass is too long. The numbers on the house are bulbous and appear like they're from the seventies.

As I get out of the car, I step on a pile of dried pine needles that crunch under my feet.

The front door of the house opens, and Bree appears on the cement stoop. "Hey, Rose!" She waves, and behind her, a man I estimate to be in his forties with a high widow's peak and the same narrow frame as Bree steps out. "This is my dad, Greg. He's insisting on meeting you even though I told him you volunteer with Beacon Pointe." She rolls her eyes.

I chuckle. "He should," I tell her, stepping forward to meet him. "It's nice to meet you." I offer my hand, and he shakes it with an amiable grin.

"You, too. Bree mentioned she was going to attend a yoga class?"

"Yeah. I'm an instructor, and I want to start offering some classes for teens and kids, and Bree offered to help me out. I hope that's okay. I'll be with her the whole time."

He looks at Bree. "No causing trouble, okay?"

"You're telling this to the wrong kid," she chides.

He smirks. "Keep me posted."

"I'll have her home around five. Is that okay?"

He nods as he reaches forward and musses her hair. "Smell you later."

She hits him with a glare. "*Bye,* Dad."

I work to hide my smile as I climb back into the driver's seat. Due to the new playground equipment and bridge being delayed, they canceled our park cleanup for the next couple of weeks, freeing up my Monday afternoons. I'm surprisingly disappointed by the change. As much as I didn't want to participate, I've enjoyed the long afternoons outside and hanging out with Bree and the others.

"How has your weekend been?" I ask her as I wait for her to get situated and put her seat belt on.

She nods. "I got an A on my history test, so my dad let me play two extra hours of video games."

I smile. "Nice job on the test."

Bree's eyes pinch. "Are you okay?"

"Yeah, why?"

Her inquisitive brown eyes remain on me as I drive back to the main road. "I don't know. You just ... you look sad."

I shake my head. "It's because I don't wear makeup to yoga. Without makeup, this is how I look. Stay young, kid."

She doesn't react to my attempt at a joke, but she also doesn't inquire any further, and I'm grateful because I'm still not sure what branch I've climbed out on with her. I have no intention of leading any teen or kid yoga classes, and inviting her has cost me more money because I bought her a yoga mat and some clothes and gear, but she offered her advice as a way to repay me for the joggers she'd stolen, and I wanted to ease her guilt and clear the slate. Plus, as weird as it is, there's something refreshing about spending time with her and not worrying about boys, school, or parties. Instead, the world seems vaster, as do my thoughts and our conversations.

16

ROSE

"Are you wearing lipstick?" Olivia draws her head back from where she's seated on the couch to look at me. It's Friday night, and the first time she's been out of her room for more than a shower all week. Her face is pale, and her eyes are heavily shadowed with exhaustion.

"Hey, you can finally pronounce the letter 'R' again. Congratulations, you're finally beating the cold from hell."

Olivia tucks some of her dark hair behind one ear. "Whatever this bug was, it was terrible. I can still only breathe out of one nostril at any given time."

"You should lead with that fact when Arlo gets here."

"I will," she says.

"You want me to heat some soup for you?"

Olivia shakes her head. "I'm not hungry."

"You should still eat."

"I will. But first, I need to know what's going on. My best friend has only worn lipstick on a handful of occasions, which means something has happened. I need details."

"I'm going out with Chantay tonight."

Olivia does a terrible job of hiding her surprise and judgment. "You are?"

I nod. "I haven't gone out in months."

"Where are you guys going?"

"I don't know, but I'll keep you posted." I open my wallet to make sure I have some cash on me. "What are you and Arlo doing tonight?"

"An exciting night out to the living room," she jokes. "But he's picking up some potstickers and pizza on his way over. You're welcome to join us."

" I love you for that, but you guys should have some fun tonight now that you're feeling better. Besides, I need to get out. This week has been a doozy. I had two interviews with the team and had to write four articles plus two more for people who were out sick."

"Speaking of which, did you see who was posted today on the rumor site?"

I shake my head. "I haven't been watching it."

"It was Paxton again," she says. "Not the one you received originally, but still a damning picture. He's naked and playing cards. The tagline was a rumor accusing him of having a gambling issue and selling himself for payment."

"*Selling himself for payment?* Whoever's running this site must be getting desperate. Their claims are becoming ridiculously stupid."

"I know, but the crazy part is, people believe it. It's like because this person has hit on the truth—or near it—a couple of times, everyone now believes everything posted as fact."

"That makes my head hurt. Everyone who reads and believes this site should be stamped with a gullible sticker so I can follow up and sell them an alpaca farm."

"You'd be rich," she says.

I nod. "Hopefully, the picture blows over. I know Ian was worried about Paxton."

"Yeah, Arlo's worried about him, too. Also, next Friday, the guys are throwing a carb-loading barbecue. Be there or be square."

"Can I be called a diamond instead?"

Olivia pulls the blanket spread over her lap up to her chin. "Only if you attend the party with me. I told them we'd bring a dessert."

"Potluck? That has me feeling a little too close to middle-aged."

Behind me, Juliet trots out of my bedroom, meowing.

"Hey, lazy girl," I say. "Nice of you to finally join us." I squat to pet her sleek, black fur. "I have to get going," I tell Olivia. "Apparently, I don't know how to say no to people anymore, so I'm volunteering at the bird sanctuary again with Anna tomorrow."

"Bird sanctuary?"

"Yeah, instead of brunch, that's what we did last weekend. It's something my mom and I used to do. Maybe once you're feeling better, you can come with us. It could be a good inspiration for another book in your series. They specialize in helping owls, and many owls are on the endangered species list."

"Owls? I had no idea."

I nod. "My mom loved owls," I tell her. "She always said they were a sign of good luck. But their numbers have been shrinking with deforestation and farms getting larger."

"Do you think anyone will want to read these books?" she asks. "How will I put a positive spin on animals being killed for us to have the food we like at prices we want?"

"This is the same argument I had with Anthony regarding food security. People want to help, and I believe that if they know they can make a difference, they will choose to do so. It's not a political issue— it's about being a decent human being. People have no idea that they should avoid foods with palm oil to help save orangutans. They can't make an educated decision unless they know."

"You can put a blanket trust over all of humanity, but not a boyfriend?"

I point at her. "Low blow." I move to the fridge to fill a glass with water. "You know me. Dating just isn't my thing. I like being single and independent. It's my jam. Plus, we both know you're the only person on this Earth who could tolerate living with me. I'm messy, I stay up too late, I take up every inch of my closet and bathroom, and I hate movie previews."

Olivia gasps. "You hate movie previews? How have we lasted this long?"

"When did you get so sarcastic? I thought that was my role?"

She bows. "The teacher is now the student."

I wave a hand at her. "That's all Arlo. I take zero credit for pop culture references."

Olivia's nose scrunches as her smile shows all of her teeth. "I asked Arlo about Isla and Ian."

Panic hits me in the chest, knocking the air out of me. "Tell me you didn't."

"He said he hasn't seen her around at all. Are you *positive* she was with Ian?"

"Of course, I'm positive."

"You should talk to him."

I rub a hand across my temple that instantly begins to ache at the subject of Ian. "There's nothing to say. I'm not going to get involved and become a home wrecker."

"They're not married. They're not even dating."

"According to Arlo, who didn't recognize you had a crush on him until I hit him over the head with the fact."

Olivia shakes her head. "You'd be clearing the air."

"With the wrong motivation."

She growls, making Juliet scamper from the couch and halfway across the room.

"I know you, and I know Ian terrifies you because you like him, regardless of how hard you try not to. You have feelings for him and it has you rattled. Talk to him Rose. Tell him you like him. Let him choose."

"I have no idea why this interest in Ian won't go away, but I'll be honest, it might be as shallow as knowing he's unattainable or because he's just freaking hot. Regardless, we both know if I pursue this and get bored, or restless, or tired of the monotony, that I'll hurt him."

"Or *he* might hurt *you*."

My lips fall shut.

Olivia swallows. Her gaze is unwavering and unforgiving.

"It doesn't matter. I know what I saw, and there's no way I'm going to interfere with whatever's going on when I know she likes him."

Her shoulders slump with defeat. "Call me if you need anything."

"I will." I head outside, enjoying the snap of cold air that hits my flushed face and nerves.

I push my shoulders back, trying to find confidence or at least lose the guilt that's shadowing me as I make my way to my car.

> Me: Hey! What's the address I'm meeting you at?

Chantay replies nearly instantly, and before I lose my gumption, I enter the address into my car and go.

ONCE PARKED, I double-check the address to ensure it's the right house because I've passed four parties in just a few blocks. I text Olivia the address before shoving my purse under my seat and zipping my key fob into my jacket pocket. My black skinny jeans and low-cut white top have me feeling overdressed and underdressed at the same time. I pull my black leather jacket tighter as the wind blows through my hair.

> Me: I'm here.

> Chantay: Bitch, yes!!! Kitchen! Body shots! Let's go!

Body shots have never been my thing, but right now, I really *want* to like them. I want to feel sexy, strong, and confident, and more than anything, I want to feel attraction and desire toward someone else.

The door is wide open, and tendrils of fog crawl out onto the porch, along with the strange acrid scent that fake fog makes. Inside, a half-circle of guys are shotgunning beers with a small crowd of girls in crop tops cheering them on. Behind the girls is a giant ice sculpture that looks like a small mountain where people pour drinks down while others slurp the alcohol from the homemade track.

"Rose?" The guy I'd run into before going to get Bree two weeks ago when she had her period mishap takes a step closer to me.

"Hey," I say, forgetting his name.

He grins. His dark hair sticks out from his backward baseball hat in a boyish and endearing way, and the plain white tee and simple jeans he's wearing add to his appeal. "You forgot my name again, didn't you?"

I wince. "It's nothing personal," I tell him. "I'm terrible with names."

"Noah," he tells me.

"Noah," I repeat.

He nods. "It's nice to see you outside of class. You want something to drink?"

"I'm meeting a friend."

Noah instantly retracts at the word friend. He assumes it's a guy— a date.

"*She* said she'd be in the kitchen."

His face brightens. "Let's see if we can find her."

I nod, plastering on a wide smile.

"You look nice," Noah says as we pass girls that are dancing on a kitchen table. I'll bet the table's broken before I leave.

"Thanks," I tell him, my attention dancing across the crowds of people all having a good time. I yearn to channel this feeling and stop caring about inconsequential things. I want to have fun and let loose.

I try to recall what made it easier last year to do this or the year before, but my focus stops on Paxton Lawson. He's standing next to a girl with purple hair with one hand on her waist. His smile is so broad I know he's drunk.

I scan the living room, searching for another player from the football team, but it's stranger after stranger.

Shit.

"I'll meet you in the kitchen in just a second," I tell Noah. "I see a friend, and I want to say hi really fast. Five minutes tops."

Noah grins. "Let me see your phone," he says, already reaching for it before his words fully hit my ears over the noises of the party. He looks at the lock screen, another broken grin, before he turns it toward me. "Unlock it, and I'll add my number. It's getting pretty busy in here."

I oblige, taking another discreet look at Paxton so as not to draw any more attention than he already has. Noah enters his number and then gives me a parting smile.

I wait until he's several feet ahead before changing direction and heading over to Paxton. He's making out with the girl with the purple hair now. Before I get much closer, I see Hoyt holding two Solo cups. I have no idea if this is good news or worse news. Hoyt doesn't exactly seem like the responsible friend who will tell someone when they've reached their limit. I consider texting Arlo or Raegan, knowing Lincoln would undoubtedly be able to handle the situation.

Paxton pulls back, and his eyes meet mine. I take it as an invitation to move closer.

"Hey, Paxton," I say, looking from him to the purple-haired girl. She's wearing a lace top and a killer pair of jeans. I smile at her, but her response is a sneer. I turn back to Paxton. "Are the guys here?"

"Hoyt, Bobby, and me." His words are evenly paced and clear, and his eyes are as well. Maybe he's not as drunk as I'd assumed.

"I'm here with my friend Chantay. If you guys need anything—a ride—or whatever, just let me know."

He grins. "I'm okay. Thanks, Rose."

I nod. "See you later."

He hooks a hand around the girl's waist again and says something in her ear that makes her giggle.

I feel compassion for him, but it's more than that—I feel understanding. I have the same desperate desire to get someone out of my head and knowing about the reckless and unhealthy relationship he's been in with Candace, I have no doubt that's where he is right now.

I make a mental note to check on him in a few and head into the kitchen. I spot Chantay instantly. Her blond hair is pulled back with one hand as she dances with a guy at her back and a girl at her front.

I'm too sober, and seeing Paxton drinking after he was featured on the rumor site today has me struggling to find that zone of fun and bliss I'm seeking.

Someone waves, drawing my attention. It's Noah, standing beside the keg. I head over to him, enjoying his smile and warm regard more than I should. "You want some beer?"

"Please."

Noah grins and fills a cup that he hands to me before filling a second. "Did you find your friend?"

I nod, pointing at Chantay.

Noah laughs as he cheers. "If you want me to hold your beer so you can join, I'm here for it."

"I bet you are."

He laughs again, and before I can stop myself, I'm comparing the sound to Ian's laugh, and it's like a domino begins to wobble in my thoughts. I take a drink of my beer to rid the thought, and when that doesn't dull it, I take another and another, working to drown the memories.

"Rose!" Chantay cries my name and peels away from those she was dancing with. "I knew you'd come. This is what I love about you. You don't care about stupid Garett Feldons. You know that being single is so much better!" Unlike Paxton, her words are slurred. She takes my half-filled beer and swallows it in one drink.

Noah raises a curious brow, and I shake my head, not about to crack into that can of worms.

"Let's dance," Chantay grabs my hand and pulls me with her out to where a group of people are dancing near another fog machine.

It's loud, my ears ringing with protest, and for some ridiculous reason, I'm thinking of advice I want to give Bree for when she attends her first college party, specifically noting she should avoid parties with fog machines as I choke on the scent.

Chantay giggles and a cute guy with a piercing gaze and addictive smile rests a hand on my waist. I try to force everything out of my thoughts and be present. Have fun and seek that attraction and desire I came for.

. . .

MAYBE IT'S the bad music, the damn fog machine, or the fact I'm hot, and my jacket and pants are sticking to me, but as time ticks by, my mood begins to spiral.

I pull off my jacket, and turn to find Chantay making out with Noah.

I should care.

I *want* to care.

Yet, I can't find it in me to care one bit—instead, relief dances along my spine.

I leave the dance floor and am halfway to the front door before remembering Paxton is here. I turn to where he'd been when I arrived, but he's gone.

"Shit. Shit. Shit," I chant. I should not have left him.

I spin, looking for Hoyt, Bobby, or Paxton, but the house is packed, making it difficult to see anyone. I thread my way through the crowds, searching each face. A loud cheer has me working my way into a sunken room, where Paxton is shirtless, shotgunning a beer.

"Oh boy," I mutter, weaving through the crowd of people who all seem to have their phones out, taking pictures and videos of this damming moment.

"Paxton," I call his name. "Paxton!"

His blue gaze drops to mine, a lazy smile on his face. "Hey, Rose. How's it going?"

"I could use your help. Would you mind coming outside a minute?"

"Do we need to tap another keg?" He looks in the direction of the kitchen. "The last asshole had no idea what he was doing, and he—"

"I actually need my car jumped."

He shakes his head. "Sorry. I didn't drive."

Thank God for that.

He starts to turn toward the same girl with purple hair from earlier, but before they can engage in a second act, I grab his wrist. "Paxton."

Liquid hits my face and drenches my shirt before I see the cup flying at me.

Cheers ring out, and then someone starts chanting, "Girl. Fight. Girl. Fight!"

I wipe my eyes and pull my hair out of my face. Beer. I'm soaked with beer.

Awesome.

Paxton looks at me, his jaw hanging open. "What happened?"

"We need to go," I tell him. "Come on." I tug him forward, and thankfully he doesn't fight me.

We're nearing the door when Hoyt appears. "Rose!"

"Where's Bobby?" I ask him.

He shrugs, looking from me to Paxton. "I thought he was with you?"

I point at the front door. "Outside. Let's go."

"Rose!" Chantay yells. "Where are you going?"

"I'll be back," I tell her.

She looks from me to Paxton, and her lips curve into a smile that makes dread reach all the way to my shoulders.

"He's not feeling well," I say. "Food poisoning."

Her brow draws low with doubt, then her forehead smooths. "I could take him upstairs and find a place for him to lie down." Her gaze is filled with suggestions that have Paxton taking a step toward her.

I yank him back by the wrist. "His ride's here."

Disappointment puckers her lips. "I could always drive him home later."

"Why don't I get him outside, and we can find the basketball team?" I suggest.

Chantay gives a final gaze at Paxton and likely recognizes he would have a severe case of beer dick tonight and wouldn't be worth her time or energy. Her powder blue eyes meet mine. "Deal."

"I'll be back," I tell her, shoving Hoyt and Paxton toward the door.

They oblige, stumbling when I make them cut through the shrubs so we can take a shortcut to reach my car.

I unlock my car doors and turn to look at the two of them. "I need your phone so I can call Bobby."

"Did you say *boobie*?" Hoyt asks.

Paxton snickers.

"I *swear*, I heard boobie," Hoyt continues.

My anger spikes. "Phones!" I stick my hand out.

Paxton shakes his head. "I broke mine."

Hoyt starts to laugh again. "He was pissed. He needed to blow off some steam." He starts to giggle again. "He threw his phone at the wall, and it made a hole, but his phone was fine, so he grabbed a hammer and beat the shit out of it."

I blow out a long breath and grab my phone, thinking of the long list of people I'd like to call and yell at right now, starting with my dad and Anna for being so perfect, then Olivia and Arlo for modeling a relationship so great that it makes me want it. Bree is on my list for making me care about her, and because since meeting her, this ridiculous voice of reasoning continues to grow louder. My short list ends with Ian, who I stop on and call.

He answers on the fourth ring.

"Your teammates are drunk, and I can't find one of them."

"What?" he says.

"You guys came to me, asking me to write some stupid article to change the narrative, and they're feeding into the persona that's being cast. Paxton's making out with strangers, and Hoyt can't walk straight, and I can't find Bobby. I'm not a goddamn babysitter. These are *not* my strengths."

"Where are you?"

"Never mind that. How do I find Bobby? I need his phone number, and I knew if I texted and asked for it, you'd assume I wanted to have sex with him, so I'm *calling* so I can give you the entire damn roadmap."

"Rose, where are you?"

"I don't want your help. I just need his damn phone number so I can call him and tell him to get his ass outside."

"If Bobby's drunk, you won't be able to get him outside. Tell me where you are so I can come kick his ass."

"I get first dibs. I'll text you the address." I hang up and forward the address from Chantay to him.

I turn back to the other two, my anger making me too warm. Hoyt's singing, and Paxton is looking greener by the second as he wraps his arms around his bare torso.

"Tell me you're not the vomiting type of drunk."

Hoyt stops singing and starts laughing again. "Captain gets sick before every game. He's totally going to blow chunks."

I cringe. "Okay. Paxton, sit down in the grass, head down. Start counting or something. I think I have some water in my trunk and maybe a blanket. What happened to your shirt?"

Paxton looks down and seems surprised to find his shirt missing. Hoyt laughs and begins singing even louder.

I hate my life.

"Hoyt, I need you to shut up. If you keep singing, someone's going to hear and pull out their phone, and then we're all going to be on the damn rumor site. *Again.*"

Hoyt stumbles, nearly falling before his butt connects with the backseat of my car. I'm pretty sure he hits his head or maybe his elbow, but before I can check, he closes the door and locks it, then starts singing even louder than he was.

I blow out a long breath and go around to my trunk. I have four bottles of water and a blanket. I grab it all and move to sit beside Paxton. I crack open one of the water bottles. "Here. Drink this."

He takes it and gets only a couple of drinks in before he leans over and throws up.

Fucking feelings.

Fucking emotions.

Fucking attachments.

17

IAN

My headlights hit Rose's car, and I pull to a stop, not giving a single fuck that I'm double-parked. I hop out of my truck as Rose stands. She looks tired, annoyed, and a bit relieved. My gaze drops to her soaked white shirt, which is now see-through, exposing a black bra. She dusts off her backside but remains standing beside the blanket that's next to her, covering someone.

"Is he okay?" I ask before I even ask which asshole it is.

"I think so. He threw up, which is probably for the best." She pushes some of her dark hair behind one ear. "I tried to wake him up to make him get in my car, but he's dead weight at the moment."

I nod as I go to peer under the blanket and see Pax.

Fuck.

"You said Hoyt's here, too?"

Rose quirks a brow and takes a few steps toward her car, where she taps on the back window with a single knuckle. Broken lyrics are belted out off-key. "He's not in a very helpful state."

I move beside her, catching a strong whiff of beer. On the short drive here, questions were plaguing my mind. Why were they here?

Why were they here with Rose? Why didn't she call me sooner? Why didn't they?

Shit has been blowing up in our faces, and they're loading the damn ammunition by being here.

I try to open the back door, but it's locked.

"Yeah, he..." she points and then drops her hand and shakes her head.

I lean down. "Hoyt, unlock the fucking door."

Hoyt hits the button, and I open the door while still leaning down so I'm face-to-face with him. He stops singing instantly, blinking as the light overhead makes him wince. "What's up, Cap?"

"I need you to sober the fuck up and help me get Pax into the car."

He grunts and slowly scoots forward and stands. I reach forward to brace him. "We might have overdone it," he says.

"You think?" I ask. "Can you lift his legs without face diving onto the cement?"

"He puked," Hoyt announces. "Don't step in it."

I rub the back of my neck, seeing the evidence. "We should get him into my truck. That way, if he pukes again...."

Hoyt starts to nod, but he stumbles and narrowly manages to catch himself on the hood of Rose's car.

"I can help you get Paxton in my car, but I won't be able to lift him into your truck," Rose says.

My eyes cut to her. "I'll have your car detailed if he throws up again."

"Pretty sure that show's over," she says, moving to pull the blanket off Pax. He's on his side, arms folded over his bare chest.

I bend down and shake him. His only response is a soft grunt.

"If you can grab his legs, I'll get his shoulders."

Rose nods and bends to grab his legs, her shirt dipping, revealing a clear shot of her cleavage. She rights herself and tries to smooth the fabric, but with its weight from being damp, it's useless, and she gives up. "Paxton's date threw a beer on me," she says. "Apparently, he only knows how to date Candaces."

I wince, but my apologies are still behind a boulder of questions.

"Boobies!" Hoyt yells.

Rose rolls her eyes but doesn't comment as we carry Paxton to the side of her car. She repositions him, supporting both of his legs with one of her arms as she opens the front passenger door.

"You've got some muscles," I say.

"Yoga," she says, glancing from Paxton to the car.

"You can set him down. I've got him," I tell her. She was right. He's dead weight at this point, all two-hundred-and-thirty-five pounds of him. I heft him into the seat and nearly regret I didn't hit his head on the top of the car because I have a feeling my back will remember this tomorrow, and it only seems fair his head should as well.

"What are we going to do with them?" Rose asks.

"I'll call Lincoln and make sure he's home. He's going to kick their asses."

"Bobby's still inside," she reminds me as she folds up the blanket and sets it in her trunk. She looks at me when I don't respond.

"I don't like my current options," I tell her.

"You don't have many options," she tells me. "You need to go find him."

"Leaving these two assholes could lead to Hoyt wandering. And I really don't like the idea of...."

"Will you get over thinking I want to have sex with Hoyt?" Her green eyes meet mine, fueled with anger and what I think is hurt.

"I'm not worried about you wanting to have sex with him. I'm worried *he* wants to have sex with *you*."

Her brows pinch, and then she looks over her shoulder at Hoyt, who's still lying across the hood of her car. She looks back at me. "I have a better chance of being barfed on than hit on. Help me get Hoyt into the backseat, and I'll babysit these morons while you go find Bobby." She turns to Hoyt before I can respond.

"Tell me you can walk," she says.

"I can walk," Hoyt responds, his voice muffled. He doesn't attempt to move.

"Come on, asshole," I say, grabbing his shoulder and pulling him to his feet. "Is Bobby still here?"

"Hot blonde asked him to be her first." He stumbles toward me.

I open the back door, and he slumps into the backseat. I have to physically lift his feet into the car before closing the door. I'm about to suggest to Rose that she lock the car and go inside with me, but her phone rings before I can.

"Hey." She pauses. "Yeah, I just need some air." She pulls her hair back with her fingers and nods. "I know. It's hot in there." She nods a few more times. "I'm glad you guys hit it off." Another pause. "No, I'm not mad at all. I don't know him." Another pause. "I have to be up early, so I'm probably going to head out soon. I'll come and say good-bye." She hangs up and turns to face me, releasing her hair in one wave that falls sinfully over her face.

I reach forward and brush the strands aside. It isn't a thought, just a need to touch her. But Rose takes a wide step back and slowly shakes her head.

"Don't you get it?" she asks. "This is hard enough. I'll go get Bobby. You watch your idiot friends." She grabs her jacket that Paxton was using as a pillow, and as she walks away, she threads her arms through it and pulls it tight to cover herself.

I scrub a hand across my face and lean back against her car. What in the fuck is so hard?

From the back seat of the car, Hoyt begins singing again.

I mutter a train of curses and reach for my phone to call Lincoln.

"Hey, Forrest," he says.

"I've got your roommate and two other assholes."

"Tell me they didn't...."

"Oh, they did. Paxton is so drunk he's out cold, and Hoyt won't stop singing. Bobby is yet to be seen."

"Mother fuckers," Lincoln growls. "They can't be saved from themselves."

"Are you home? Can I drop them off? I can't bring them home now that my parents are back."

"Yeah, Raegan and I just got here."

"Okay. We'll be there soon."

My thoughts are more restless now than they were on my way

over as Rose's words and silent accusations curse me. Before my thoughts and anger can continue down their merry little path, I hear Bobby's distinct laughter.

"He didn't really blow chunks, did he?" Bobby asks as he and Rose step into view.

"You guys can't do this," Rose tells him. "Not now. Wait a few months until football is over and people aren't watching you under a magnifying glass, then you can do whatever in the hell you want. Tonight was stupid."

"I didn't know they *both* had a drinking problem. After Pax went all *Deadpool* on his cell phone, I figured he needed a night out to breathe."

They stop in front of me. "Hey, Cap," Bobby says, tucking his hands into his pockets. "Sorry about this."

I shake my head. "Did you drive?"

He shakes his head. "We took an Uber."

"Are you sober?"

He nods. "I only had water." He takes a second to look at Hoyt and Paxton. "I can ride with Rose and help carry them inside. Are we taking them home?"

"We'll drop them off at Paxton and Lincoln's."

Bobby barks with laughter. "President's probably going to spray them with the garden hose."

"They deserve it," I say.

"You won't be able to fit in the back. Why don't you ride with Ian? He can take you home. I can help Lincoln get them out," Rose says, going around to the driver's side of her car.

"Yeah, that's not going to happen...." Bobby says quietly.

"Damn right, it's not going to happen," I say. "Bobby, get in the truck."

"That sounds like a better idea," he says in the same soft tone before turning and heading toward my truck.

"So, you're just going to be mad at me and avoid me going forward?" I ask, circling to the front of her car.

Rose's green eyes narrow with another silent stare.

"I knew you had cold feet and this entire set of absurd and asinine rules, but I didn't realize one fucking kiss was going to break all those rules and make you treat me like I'm some fucking stranger."

"*Stranger?*" she cries. She lifts both hands and buries them in her hair. "How do you not see it? You're the only one who doesn't already know that you've gotten into my head. You've crawled under my skin, and it's like I can't get you out, and I hate it. I *hate* that I compare some guy's laugh to yours. I *hate* that I compare some guy's smile to yours. I *hate* that you look angry when I make an objectifying comment about myself, unlike every other asshole who laughs. I kissed you, and I know it was chicken shit for me to turn around and leave, but why couldn't you have stopped me? If you have feelings for Isla, you should have stopped me from kissing you."

My heart beats so loud and fierce I can't hear my own thoughts over Rose telling me I'm under her skin and in her head.

About fucking time.

But that last part has thrown me for one-eighty. "Feelings for Isla?"

"I saw you," she says. "I saw you and Isla kissing."

I shake my head. "No. That was nothing."

She sears me with another glare. "Rule two: never get involved with a guy who's seeing other people. It leads to confusion and betrayal." She reaches for her door handle, and I set my hand on it so she can't wrench it open.

"This isn't a conversation to have out here. Let's drop them off and then we can go to your place or mine and get all of this out."

"I'm done talking. If you haven't noticed, I'm trying to forget about you."

"Well, I'm done letting you." I place my hand on her hip, feeling a gentle shiver run over her skin. "Isla kissed me because she misread the situation. I don't—I've never—had feelings for her. Maybe I could in a world where I hadn't met you. If you hadn't already ruined me."

Rose jerks, her eyes sweeping over my face, trying to read my honesty.

"You scare the hell out of me. Just the sight of you makes me nervous because I never thought I could feel so much for one person. It's like your existence alone defies logic and reason. And I am so damn tired of fighting to stay away from you and respect your damn rules because I'm afraid I'm going to push you farther away. I'm done. I'm here, and I'm going to invade every boundary you've set, and in the end, I'm going to prove I'm good for you. I'm *right* for you." Before she can argue, I lean in and claim her lips. I know it catches her off guard by the way she clutches me for balance. I don't give her time to collect herself. I slant my mouth over hers and kiss her fully.

Kissing Rose outside while my drunken teammates sit in her car while her shirt is soaked from rescuing them was not what I'd planned, but it doesn't stop me from continuing. Her lips are so damn soft, lacking the same assault and aggression from our last kiss. I take another step, closing the gap between us.

I run my hand across her neck and thread my fingers into the back of her hair, brushing the pad of my thumb across her jaw. She releases another quiet gasp that I feel far deeper than my lips, feeding me everything I've been starved for. I slip my tongue into her mouth, and she fists my T-shirt as she runs her tongue along the length of mine. I groan, my other hand gripping her hip tighter, searching for a break in her shirt so I can feel her skin.

Rose hums softly in response as my fingers slide along her waist, and she leans into me fully, her teeth grazing my bottom lip as our caresses become more frantic and desperate. I pull away, ready to drown in the rumors that would follow sleeping with her right here and now because after waiting several months, there's nothing else I want except her. I pull in a ragged breath and lean my forehead against hers.

"You have one week," I tell her.

She pulls away, her eyes bright with lust. "One week until what?"

"To accept that we're dating." I slip my index finger into her belt loop and tug her hips against mine. "One week to finally realize you're mine."

Sparks of fear light in her eyes, and for the first time, I'm not afraid of getting burned—I'm terrified of remaining frozen on the outskirts. I'll gladly learn to feed and tame the flames.

I lean down and sweep my lips against hers. "Follow me. I'll drop Bobby off, and then we'll take them to Lincoln's."

She looks dazed, that edge of panic still present in her bright gaze. "Okay," she finally says.

I start to take a step back so I can grab her door and open it for her, but Rose's hands clench my shirt, and she leans forward, kissing me with a level of urgency and desire that my own body translates and responds to instantly.

A fist hits the window behind us. "Hey! Hey!" Hoyt yells. "She's mine!"

A sly grin tugs at her lips as she takes a step back.

"See?" I say, flipping Hoyt off.

She flashes a smile. "What am I seeing?"

"*Us*," I tell her.

Her smile widens. "I'll follow you." She opens her door and slides into her seat.

I poke my head down so I can see Hoyt. "Don't make me kill you."

He moves to the seat behind Paxton and salutes me. I gently close Rose's door and then circle back to my truck.

Bobby is sporting a full shit-eating grin as I climb into my seat. "You can't be too pissed at us after that," he says, then releases a loud cheer.

Rose

Ian kissed me.

He likes me.

He's *liked* me this entire time.

"You and Cap," Hoyt says from the backseat. "I knew he liked you. He tried to talk a tough game, but he became this uptight pain in the ass whenever you were around."

My cheeks ache from the smile that's been plastered across my face since getting into the car, and somehow Hoyt's assurance only makes my smile widen.

"But if he fucks things up, I'll be here," he says.

I follow Ian to Bobby's and then to Paxton and Lincoln's house. I've been here a couple of dozen times. After all, Arlo lives here as well, along with their roommate Caleb who's on the porch with Lincoln and Raegan as we pull up.

"How bad is it?" Lincoln asks Ian as they both approach my car.

"If he hadn't puked, I'd be suggesting we bring him to the hospital," Ian says.

"*Shit,*" Lincoln says.

Their voices are quiet, and I realize it's likely for Raegan because as she comes closer, they stop talking.

"Is he going to be able to play tomorrow?" Raegan asks, folding her arms over her chest and peeking into the car where the lights are still on from my open door.

Ian looks at Lincoln.

"I don't know if he should," Lincoln says. "He broke his own damn rules and got drunk and broke curfew."

Raegan blows out a long breath. "He needs an intervention."

Lincoln moves closer to her, wrapping his arm around her shoulders and pulling her to his side. He places a gentle kiss on her temple. "He has to make that decision for himself," he tells her. "All we can do is keep being here for him. He has to choose to stop."

She sighs. "What if he doesn't?"

"He will," Lincoln says.

Their honesty makes me feel like an interloper.

Raegan's gaze cuts to me. "Hey, Rose." She takes a few steps closer to me as Ian asks Lincoln where to put Paxton and Hoyt. "Thanks for helping them out."

Her appreciation makes guilt seep into my thoughts. If I hadn't waited so long to check on him or had reached out to Arlo with a simple text, this night wouldn't be ending like this. "I'm sorry I didn't do more."

Raegan scoffs. "What? No. You definitely shouldn't be apologizing." She stands beside me as Ian, Lincoln, and Caleb make a quick plan. "Wow, you..." She lifts her hand to her nose.

I chuckle. "Smell like beer?" I ask. "Yeah, not exactly my first choice of perfumes, either."

"Fun party?"

"No," I say, laughing for what feels like the first time in days. "This was not from fun. This was Paxton's date or hookup or whatever she was."

"No!" Raegan says, splaying a hand across her face. "Oh, Rose. I'm so sorry. Let me grab you a clean shirt so you can change."

I shake my head. "It's okay," I tell her. "I'm heading home after this."

She nods in response and then moves her attention to the three guys carrying Paxton into the house. "I can't believe he did this."

"Hoyt mentioned he broke up with Candace."

Raegan releases a long breath. "I hope it's permanent. She's so toxic."

The guys return a few minutes later without Pax, and as Ian takes the stairs, his eyes find mine, and he smiles.

Raegan bumps her arm against mine. "What was that?"

"What?"

"Oh, don't play coy with me. I've seen that look. I know that smile."

My cheeks protest as my smile returns.

Raegan grins as she wraps her arm around my shoulder. "I'm so on board with this. I used to think he was kind of a jerk, but then I got to know him, and he's seriously one of the best people, and you already know I'm a huge fan of yours." She squeezes me. "And if you guys are keeping it quiet to enjoy the honeymoon phase, I won't tell a soul."

My breaths feel less steady, realizing how many I'll be disappointing and potentially hurting if things don't turn out how they're all hoping.

Hoyt starts singing again, pulling my attention away from the conversation. He's walking toward the house with the guys at his sides.

"Less singing, more walking," Lincoln says.

Raegan laughs, watching as they shuffle him forward.

"You and Lincoln make it look so easy," I admit.

Raegan turns her attention to me. "I had a crush on him for *years*," she admits, shaking her head. "It isn't always easy. In fact, loving someone is really hard. No one tells you that, but it is. It takes a lot of work and patience, and time. It forces you to be vulnerable and weak and also to be stronger than you believe you are." Her lips curve with a gentle smile. "But it's worth it. It's worth the time and effort, and fear. It's worth everything." She turns to me, eyes bright as she bumps her arm against mine. "Plus, they train for stamina. Enjoy the honeymoon phase."

Sex has never made me feel shy, but the thought of Ian and me sleeping together has me feeling more nervous than I've felt—maybe ever.

The guys step down from the porch, and I'm struggling to recall Ian's words. *One week.* Does that mean we're not sleeping together until those seven days are up?

Lincoln places his hands on Raegan's waist and pulls her back against his front. "Thanks, Rose. We owe you."

I shake my head. "It was nothing."

He shakes his head. "It was everything. You guys have a good night."

Raegan smiles at me. "See you guys."

Caleb waves and this moment ends too soon, my uncertainty far too high, and my nerves still strung too tight.

Ian makes plans to meet Lincoln tomorrow, and then he's walking toward me. I trace over his gray sweatpants and red Brighton tee before looking at his face. He's smiling at me, all confidence and strength. He stops, leaving a foot of space between us. "Your house or mine?"

For sex?

For conversation?

What happens in these situations?

What's normal?

My head is spinning as I gently shake my head.

"Your place is closer," he says.

"What are we doing?" I ask.

His smile turns salacious, his eyes bright. "I've got an entire list of ideas," he says, his hand going to his groin, where he adjusts himself. "And I can promise you that we need to be behind closed doors for most of them."

18

ROSE

I drive to my apartment with Ian following in his truck. My heart is pounding so loud and hard in my chest that it's borderline painful. When Ian showed interest in me last year, it was more substantial than a glance at my chest or an innuendo. He had been patient and intentional about our conversations and interactions, making it clear from the start that he was only interested in a relationship—something that terrified me. It took losing him to realize that he was worth the risk, and now I feel equal parts elated and terrified.

I pull into my parking spot, wondering if Arlo and Olivia are still awake, and if so, what will they say? How will they react?

Ian parks beside me and gets out of his truck without delay. I reach for my door and open it before grabbing my purse from under the seat.

"You look nervous," he says.

I laugh, but it sounds almost shaky. "I am," I admit. Not only has it been several months since I've had sex, but every step I take closer to Ian is another rule that I'm choosing to break.

He grins. "Because of your rules or because of us?" He's in my head. I can feel him there.

"Both," I admit.

Ian reaches for me, slipping a lock of my hair behind an ear before resting his palm against my cheek. "That fear means it's real." His multi-toned eyes hold my gaze. "If I'm not what you're thinking about before you go to sleep and when you wake up, we call it quits next Friday. No harm, no foul."

"What happens if we decide to stay together?"

His thumb brushes the length of my cheek as he steps closer, his lips curling with a smile. "I already told you. You're mine."

I tip my face up and lean into him, kissing Ian while my heart continues to drum the new beat.

Mine.

Mine.

Mine.

With every beat, our kiss intensifies and deepens. We're all hands and teeth and tongues, staking claims and promises, only breaking when a car alarm blares beside us.

"We should go inside," I say, trying to catch my breath.

Ian nods, lacing his hand around my waist. I unlock the door and find the apartment dark except for the soft glow of the nightlight beside the door.

"Olivia's been sick," I whisper.

Ian smiles. "I know."

Arlo. The guys talk.

I try to breathe.

Mine.

Mine.

Mine, my heart beats.

Ian closes and locks the door behind us, and then his hand returns to my side, a reassuring squeeze that has me moving toward my bedroom.

I flip on the light, which feels intrusive and invasive, making me squint. "Sorry," I say, flipping it off and turning on the floor lamp in the corner. I kick off my shoes and scoot them under my desk as Ian looks around my space. His gaze passes over the wall of metallic flowers that took Olivia and me an entire weekend to measure and hang and then at the large Victorian-style bed I got this summer when I decided to redo my room, across my dresser and desk, and the large map where pins mark everywhere I want to one day go.

His eyes return to mine. "I'm messy," I admit, excusing the piles of sticky notes and dead batteries, the empty coffee cup on my desk, and the overflowing hamper beside my closet.

Ian grins like I'm sharing something he already knows. Hell, I probably am.

"Can I ask you a question that I don't mean to be inappropriate or rude?" I swallow, feeling my palms itch and sweat.

Why am I so nervous?

I swallow again as Ian's gaze meets mine. He nods.

"I'm really big on safe sex," I tell him. "Like, *really* big on it. Like, take a blood test and physical exam to make sure there's nothing...." I wave my hands in circular motions. "Going on." I swallow again.

Ian grins. "That's a smart rule."

I nod. "I think so."

"I had a physical when I got home from Italy, and they did a full blood workup. I'm clean."

Not going and getting tested and seeing his results is a breach of my rules, but I know Ian, and he's the most trustworthy and respectable guy I know.

"I have the results," he says, reaching for his phone.

"No, it's okay, I...."

He spins his phone to show me the screen. "No. It's a good rule. One you should always keep," he says. "And one we should follow."

I glance at his phone, relieved to leave this rule intact. "I have mine as well," I tell him, reaching for my phone. "They're from May, but I haven't been with anyone since February."

His gaze flashes to mine, bright and victorious and so damn cocky I wish I could take back my words. He takes a step closer to me, and I'm barely holding on to my sanity. He's so close, and all I want him to do is touch me.

"Any other rules?"

I shake my head.

"In that case, I've got a few ... *guidelines*."

Surprise has me lifting my eyebrows. "Guidelines?"

Ian's lips twitch with a smile. "One," he says. "We see each other every day this week. Carve out time. Even if it's only fifteen minutes."

I nod. "I can handle that."

He grins deliciously. "Two." He places his hands on the opening of my jacket and slides the fabric down my arms. "When you start to feel overwhelmed, you have to talk to me."

When I don't respond, he quirks an eyebrow. "I usually talk to Olivia."

He grins. "That's okay, too."

"I have an approved list of people I can talk to, now?"

His grin turns cocky. "She likes me."

"She likes me more."

He laughs, and the sound hits my ears and travels through my entire body like a lightning bolt, making every cell of my body more aware and sensitive. This is the sound I was yearning to hear earlier. I wasn't comparing him with Noah—my senses knew I was with the wrong person.

"Any more guidelines?"

"Just one," he says, setting my jacket on the back of my desk chair. "We're exclusive."

My stomach fills with butterflies that feel far too big for the space. I want to say something sappy about how I've been exclusively his for months without any of the benefits, but I bite back the words and nod once.

"We can slow down. We don't have to have sex tonight," he says, as his blue eyes travel across my face and stop at the top of my stained shirt, ever the gentleman.

I swallow thickly and take a step closer to him so we're toe to toe. "*Have to* is an obligation. I don't feel any obligation. I feel desire. Lust. Anticipation. Longing."

A low rumble emanates from his throat, and he settles his hands on my waist, confident and strong with just enough pinch to reveal his own desperation. "I want you so bad."

And then his lips are on mine, and it feels like I'm breathing straight oxygen as he coaxes my mouth open with his tongue. Desire burns in my belly, and a throbbing between my legs has me shifting closer as he moves his hand under my shirt. I'm trying to pay attention to the pressure of his fingers, the roughness of his calluses, and how delicious they feel against the ticklish skin on my ribs. I am completely rapt by how gentle yet powerfully he handles me, and I want to memorize this touch and save the memory forever. But his kiss grows wild and more fervent with a need I feel through my entire body and far deeper.

I reach for the hem of his shirt and clumsily work on sliding it up. His teeth catch my bottom lip, and he pulls back just long enough to pull off his shirt and discard it on my floor, and then he's kissing me again while the warmth of his skin drowns me in lust.

His kiss is fiercer, harder, and then he pulls back again, eyes dark, breaths heavy as he reaches for my ruined shirt. He pulls it clean off with one move, and then his eyes are studying my breasts, and all I want is to feel his lips on me there.

Ian places his hand over one breast and rubs the pad of his thumb over my nipple. I bite my bottom lips to keep from moaning because this simple touch is already pushing me toward the edge of an orgasm. He presses his lips to mine, running his thumb over my nipple again and again, changing the speed and pressure, making the throbbing between my legs grow stronger.

I trace over his chest, following the taut, warm lines of muscles. He groans beneath my touch, and I kiss him harder, wanting more. I bring my hands to my back and unclasp my bra, and Ian slides the straps down my shoulders and arms, his touch searing my flesh and sending chills up my spine. My bra falls soundlessly as my nipples graze his hot chest. He makes another soft humming sound as he covers my breasts with his hands, skimming his fingertips over my hardened nipples.

He steps closer to me, herding me backward until my mattress hits the back of my thighs. Without a word, his hands fall from my breasts, and he sets one arm behind my shoulders and the other behind my knees and scoops me up to lay me across my ivory comforter. The fabric feels cold against my bare skin, causing me to shiver. Ian stands over me, his eyes greedy as they rake across my body. I've never felt so beautiful. He places a knee on the bed and slowly lowers his mouth to my chest. He gently blows on the already peaked bud and then places his mouth over me, licking and sucking and kissing me as his fingers torturously run over my other nipple. I moan unabashedly and bury my fingers into his hair, never wanting him to stop while also desperate to have him ease the ache between my legs. He licks a path to my other nipple, his fingers gliding over the breast his mouth had been on. My skin is wet, slick from his mouth, allowing his fingers to slide over my nipple with so much ease and pleasure it feels like I could come from this alone.

Ian licks the underside of my breast and then lazily drags his fingers over both nipples and takes the same slow pace with his tongue down my body. My skin is on fire. He reaches the top of my pants and slowly moves his hands along the same tortuous path before releasing the button of my jeans. He lowers the zipper, and my thoughts begin to race. Sex has always been methodical, planned, and choreographed. Foreplay isn't involved, requiring too much time and intimacy, and never has someone undressed me. Ian stands and slides my jeans down my legs, and discards them, leaving me in my fire-engine red underwear. His eyes bore into mine, and the adoration shining in them nearly takes my breath away.

I have no doubt he sees vulnerability in my gaze, which is nearly as terrifying as feeling the emotion.

"Lose your pants, Ian," I command, desperate to see more of him.

He grins and tucks his thumbs into the waistband of his sweatpants. He lowers them slowly, revealing black boxer briefs that he looks so damn good in it's downright sinful.

I hook my fingers into my underwear and lift my hips to tug them off, but Ian grabs my hands, stopping me. "I plan to take my time and enjoy this," he says.

Panic floods my stomach as my vulnerability plants roots as he places a palm on each of my thighs and spreads my legs. My confidence with sex largely rests in the safety of my rules: get tested, no foreplay, one night. They're simple, easy, straightforward, and this is everything but.

"I don't have a lot of experience with foreplay," I admit. Because it doesn't fall into my safe sex category, or maybe because it risks attachments.

His eyes flash with something dark, warm, and borderline possessive, and then he's kissing me, flooding my body with passion and desire and banishing my concerns with each caress of his tongue and stroke of his fingers.

He kisses his way to my ear, then grazes my lobe with his teeth. "I'm going to make you come with my mouth," he tells me.

Before I can catch my breath from our kiss, he puts his mouth on my entrance through my underwear. It feels amazing. Better than I thought. Better than I expected. My entire body feels like it's vibrating. My nails scratch along the bedspread as I tip my head back, feeling the heat of his breath and then the pressure of his tongue. I shiver, and my toes curl. He blows against me, and then his tongue pushes harder, and I spread my legs, wanting more. He obliges, adding a finger that he runs along my seam. When he finally drags my underwear down my legs, I can feel how soaked I am from his mouth and my desire.

"You're so fucking beautiful," he rasps.

I want to kiss him. I want to return to feeling in control and knowing the score and go back to what sex has always been and not risk changing its definition But before I can reach for him, he kisses me between my legs, and without the thin layer of fabric, the sensation is euphoric. I gasp and then moan, clawing at the bedspread until it fists in my hands. Ian runs his tongue along my seam, opening me and licking me again and again, slow and then fast, hard and then gentle. He touches me like he knows my body, understanding every gasp, moan, and shiver.

"Feel that?" he says, running his finger over the epicenter of my sensitivity. I'm panting because it feels so good. "That's me, Rose. I do this to you." He sweeps his tongue over me, and his relentless fingers swirl and trace until I come apart, his mouth still on me. It feels wrong and so damn right as he licks me clean while I tremble and gasp.

Slowly, he licks his way back over my torso, giving my nipples another slow, appreciative visit. His tongue dances across my chest, and I squirm, the feeling so gentle and light it has me realizing for the first time I'm ticklish there.

A husky laugh escapes his lips, and he does it again, making my giggle ring out, adding humor and playfulness, two more things I've never associated with sex. He sucks at the hollow of my neck and then traces my jaw with his tongue. I kiss him, twining my arms around his neck and pulling him closer to me. I taste myself on his tongue as I swallow the rumble of another moan. His hips settle against mine. His skin is hot and smooth and perfect against mine, and for a moment, I want to lie here with him, his weight balancing me so my thoughts can't travel far enough to worry, and I can kiss him until I make sense of everything. Him. Me. The entire universe.

I run my fingers across his shoulders, feeling the stacks of muscles that contract under my touch. He explores my body with his hands, silencing my thoughts as he awakens that same need he'd sated moments ago.

"It's my turn," I tell him.

He shakes his head. "You don't have to."

I grin, feeling almost brazen as desire flows through my body. "I want to."

Hesitancy pinches his blue eyes for a moment, and I use that time to reach down and slip my hand over his erection. He draws in a quick breath through his nose and closes his eyes. "Rose," he groans my name, making me feel more empowered than ever before. He's huge. The ache between my legs grows louder and more persistent. I rub over his length, stroking him gently and then softly like he did to me. "Roll over," I tell him.

Ian does, his shoulders filling much of my queen-sized mattress. I sit on my knees, appreciating the full view of him, his flawless face, strong jaw, straight nose, stacked shoulders, and defined abs. He's perfect. My gaze lowers to his thick erection, and it's equal parts impressive and intimidating. I slip my fingers into the back of his underwear, using the same gentleness he'd shown me. I pause for a second as his full cock is exposed. My heart is beating so fast that I'm starting to feel dizzy as I lower the black material past his ankles and toss it to the floor.

I understand the gist of a blowjob, of course, but as I straddle Ian's legs, my nerves race. "I'm just supposed to bite down, right?" I smile to show I'm teasing, but I'm desperate to break the tension and silence. After all, I talk a big, tough game about sexuality and openly talking about sex, and now is a good time to start walking the walk. Ian's steel eyes widen in alarm. "I'm kidding," I say. "I'm just a little nervous."

Ian chokes out a laugh, his eyes shining with humor and warmth. "Trust me—you don't have anything to be nervous about. You won't do anything wrong ... unless you bite. Grazing is okay, but no chomping."

I bite my teeth, and he releases another laugh, filling me with ease. I draw my hand over his abs. "Walk me through it."

His eyebrows rise with a question.

"Tell me how you like it," I tell him as I slowly lower myself over him. His cock twitches as I get closer, my breath fanning across his sensitive skin.

"Lick my shaft." His voice is hoarse as he tucks his hands behind his head and watches me.

I lean forward, using the tip of my tongue to draw a line up his shaft to his crown. He sucks in a breath, and his cock twitches again. "Like that?"

"Just like that."

I do it again, and he closes his eyes, his jaw growing hard. I use the flat of my tongue, changing the speed and pressure as he had on me, and then cup his balls with my hand. He groans as he lifts his hips off the bed.

"Good?"

Ian's eyes open, burning with desire. "Put me in your mouth."

I take the tip of him, and he threads one hand in my hair. I slowly suck more of him into my mouth, licking him between gentle pulls.

"Fuuuck," Ian groans.

I open my eyes and meet his stare, and his gaze burns into my memories and thoughts. I take more of him in, my jaw already aching due to his girth.

Ian groans, his hand tightening in my hair, and then he shifts. "I don't want to come," he tells me.

I do. I feel powerful and beautiful and sexy by making him feel so damn good. But before I can argue, he hauls me up his body and claims my mouth again. He rolls us, so he's over me. "Do you have any condoms?"

I nod as I open the drawer of my nightstand. Ian reaches inside, grabbing a condom that he rips open with his teeth. He sheaths himself and then lowers his hand to the apex of my legs.

"You're so wet," he says, running his fingers over me, swirling over my clit, then following down to my entrance, where he eases a finger inside me. My breath catches in my throat, and Ian grins. He traces my face and body as though he's also trying to memorize this moment. He pumps his finger, making my thighs clench, and then in one fluid move, he adds a second finger and places his thumb on my clit, massaging me and finger fucking me at the same time. I'm panting, desperate for a release, while also wanting to deny it to carry out this incredible feeling rippling through my body, twisting up my spine, making my bones melt. I can't stop staring at him, the strength in his shoulders and arms, the width of his chest, and the small tattoo along his ribs that I vow to look at more carefully later.

"I need to feel you."

His eyes flash to mine, and he pumps his fingers inside me a couple more times before dragging them over my clit and moving above me so his hips align with mine. His weight is like a blanket, safe and warm and so damn comforting—too comforting. I kiss him again; all desire as my tongue dips into his mouth. He kisses me back, wet and hard, and then he lifts to his elbows, bracing himself as he guides his cock to my entrance. I spread my legs wider to accept his size and tense as he presses inside. His size stretches me, pushing me to the precipice of pain and pleasure.

His steel eyes study me. I nod, encouraging him—wanting him to continue.

"You're huge," I tell him.

He flashes his cocky grin. "All for you."

I close my eyes and force myself to relax as he bottoms out and remains still for a moment, giving me time to adjust to his size. Then his mouth falls against mine, warm and languid, as he skirts his hand over my breast and fingers my nipple. I wrap my arms around his shoulders and shift my hips, wanting to feel him move. He kisses me again and then slowly withdraws before thrusting back inside even slower, allowing me to feel every thick inch of him.

I moan into his mouth, and he hums in response and deepens our kiss before he pulls back and moves, pulling my hips along with his to the edge of the bed. He props my feet on either side of his chest and eases himself even deeper inside me. I feel so damn good. I had no idea sex could feel like this—be like this. I relish in the moment, clutching his hands at my waist. He increases the speed, seeking my pleasure. Then his thumb goes to the ball of nerves at the top of my clit, and my nails scrape across the sheets. It feels like every nerve in my body is aware of the pleasure, and then I'm coming undone, and Ian's thrusts are becoming faster and harder and losing all rhythm and composure as we spiral together.

19

IAN

I study the curve of Rose's spine and the gentle cadence of her breaths. Then I take in her tattoos which appear like artwork across her flawless skin. I awoke early, unease filling my chest. I've been lying here wondering what might happen today, and for the first time in months, I don't try to distract myself with football.

Will Rose wake up and freak out? Will she decide that forgetting her rules isn't worth it? That *I'm* not worth it?

Last night flashes through my thoughts as I close my eyes, recalling how Rose's eyes shined with fear and nerves and then with confidence and strength. It was perfect—she was perfect. My cock hardens at the memory, and I shift away so I don't wake her.

Last night changed everything, and that realization is as exhilarating as it is terrifying. I don't have the time to dedicate to being a good boyfriend like Rose deserves. And we're still early in the season, leaving months of gym time and practices, travel, and analyzing tape.

She and I are both armed with a dozen valid reasons that make our situation seem impossible, difficult at best.

Beside me, Rose stirs, and I open my eyes. She snuggles into the blankets and then rolls over to face me. Her green eyes dance with unspoken words as she looks at me. "Hey," she says softly.

I reach forward, tracing the side of her face with my thumb. "How'd you sleep?"

"Like a baby," she admits. "You?"

I grin. "Like a brick."

She smiles smugly, her foot brushing my leg. "You have a game today."

I nod.

"What's your game-day routine?"

"I carb load in the morning, then study tape and hydrate."

"I'll warn you, Arlo usually gets up around nine, so if you want to...." Her words trail off, but I hear her intention: if I want to change my mind and leave.

I place my hand on the curve of her hip and pull her close. "If I want to, what?"

She runs her tongue over her lips. "This. Us. I just don't want you to feel obligated to offer more. I know you have a lot riding on this year and this season."

I silence her with my mouth, kissing her until her muscles relax.

I slowly lean back and wait until she meets my stare. "The only thing I feel is regret that it took us this long to be together. Obligation is nowhere on my radar."

Rose swallows. "I want to say this will be easy, but the truth is, you're going to be really busy, and so am I, and I've got trust issues long enough that they could stretch across the Pacific." She tucks her bottom lip between her teeth, her eyes dancing between mine.

I splay my hand over her waist. "Why did you make your rules?"

Her lips teeter with a frown. "Inspiration for them happened when I was a senior in high school." She swallows. "This is going to sound so stupid and childish." Her gaze drops, and she starts to roll to her back, but I anchor her in place, forcing her to look at me.

"Try me."

She blows out a long breath. "I dated the same guy for three years. He was a year older, popular, cute, driven...." She shakes her head, and for a moment, I think she's stopped because my jaw is clenched from hearing her describe him. It's stupid to feel jealous over something that happened four years ago, yet I'll be damned if jealousy isn't seeping into my body, wondering why she was willing to invest so much time into him.

"We'd promised to stay virgins until we got married as good girls and boys do." She makes a face, and when I don't react, she swallows again and releases another sigh, this one heavier. "Then, my mom got sick." Her eyes jog to the side, and she presses her lips together as the delicate skin under her eyes reddens. She bites her bottom lip and then releases it along with another long breath. "She got sick, and I started spending all my free time with her, trying to make up for the nights I'd spent sneaking out and going to parties and not realizing she was the coolest person I'd always known." Rose rolls her lips together, and her chin quivers. Aside from last night, this is the farthest she's allowed me into her past. It feels momentous and cruel to encourage her to continue, as the pain in her expression causes a physical ache in my chest.

I tighten my grip on her, and she takes a couple of deep breaths before meeting my gaze. The agony in her eyes sits heavily on my shoulders. "I was admittedly a terrible girlfriend during those months. I didn't want to leave her side, and as she got worse, so did I. I was obsessive, worried if I left, I might not see her again." A tear slips over her lower lid, and she moves to brush it away, but it's quickly replaced by another and then another. "I found out he'd been sleeping around all year."

Anger hits like adrenaline, considering everything she'd already endured. "What a stupid son of a bitch."

She shakes her head and wipes at her face again as she smiles. "I'm glad it happened," she says, sniffing. "It took losing my mom to realize I didn't love him. Not like I thought I did, not like I should have to be promising things like marriage and celibacy. I realized I'd always held this belief in my head that sex equated to love, and I learned those two are rarely mutually exclusive. So, with a chip on my shoulder from being cheated on and the fear of losing someone else ... capped with my parent's divorce...." She shrugs.

"You created your rules."

She presses her lips together and nods. "You scare me, Ian. You scare me down to my core." Her eyes glisten with fresh tears as she bites her bottom lip again.

I shake my head, ready to make pledges and promises and vows about how I won't—*can't*—cause her harm because as much as she thinks I'm under her skin, she's a thousand times deeper beneath mine. "I know that fear, Rose. I felt it all summer," I admit. "I've wanted you since I first saw you. And while it began with curiosity and attraction, those feelings have grown to be so much more—so much greater than fascination and lust. When Isla kissed me, I wanted to like it. I wanted to want her the same way I want you, yet all I felt was anger and disgust with myself for allowing it because I knew she wasn't the one I wanted—will never be the one I want. *You are.*"

Rose's green eyes flair with emotions: compassion, relief, regret, trust, patience—I see them all and understand them like she's saying the words. "I might be a really crappy girlfriend," she says. "I'm impatient and forgetful, and stubborn, and—" Before she can list another thing she perceives as a negative trait, I bring my hand to cup the side of her face and kiss her. She pulls back, laughing gently, the smile rounding her cheeks. "This is important pillow talk. You need to listen. These are vital things to know so you're not blindsided by lust."

It's my turn to laugh. "Then you should probably know that I'm also stubborn, marginally OCD, and occasionally withdrawn."

"I hate movie previews."

"Doesn't everyone hate movie previews?" I ask.

She laughs again, the sound so pure and joyful that it's contagious. "Olivia makes pancakes or waffles every Saturday," she tells me.

"Is that an invitation?"

"It might be."

I've been mindlessly rubbing the length of her arm, and I'm not even sure how long I've been doing it, tracing over the tattooed words that encircle her forearm. I've only caught glimpses of it, realizing it's like a puzzle that starts and ends in multiple spots. With the blankets lowered, I see her full clavicle and see the same delicate script: *"perfection is found in imperfection."* I brush over the ink with my fingers. I'd asked about her tattoos before, and a few, she'd give me a story, and for others, she fell back on snark and sarcasm that left me with a smile and often forgetting my initial question. I gently turn her arm around so I can see the inside where "Love, Mom" is written along the inside of her wrist—the only script that's in a different font.

"How many tattoos do you have?"

She folds her bottom lip over like she's forgotten. "Ten? Maybe fifteen?" She looks down at herself, though she's still mostly covered with blankets. "Oof. I still smell like beer." She lifts her hair to her nose and smells it, her nose wrinkling. "I can't believe you spooned me while I smelled like stale beer all night."

"It was a chore."

She laughs again as I wrap my hand around her bare hip. Lust heats her gaze, but a fist bangs against the door before I can move closer.

"Is that Ian's truck in my parking spot?" Arlo yells through the door.

Rose grabs for her phone to check the time, the swell of her breast becoming visible. "Oh, shit," she says. "It's already past ten."

"It's Saturday," I tell her.

"I know, but I'm supposed to meet Anna, and I'm going to be late. And not just Anna-late but *late* late."

"There's a difference?"

"If you're not fifteen minutes early, my sister thinks you're late," Rose says, flipping off the covers.

"I hear voices," Arlo says from the other side of the door.

"You should probably see someone about that issue," Rose yells back as she stands fully nude, revealing the intricate paths of her tattoos and every inch of her perfect body.

I want to drag her back into bed and watch her come again. I think of her admission, of all the things she hasn't done that I want to experience with her.

"Is Forrest here? You couldn't wait one more day?"

"Arlo, go away!" Rose yells.

"We had bets. Mine starts tomorrow," he says.

Rose's attention snaps to me, accusation and alarm flashing brightly like warning signs.

I lift both hands. "I have no idea what in the hell he's talking about, but I'm about to kill him." I snatch my underwear off the floor and tuck in my erection before grabbing my sweatpants. I have them halfway pulled up before I realize Rose is staring at me.

"I swear, Rose. I didn't make any bets. I wouldn't do that."

She smiles shyly, her teeth catching her bottom lip. "I was just checking you out. I had to see if you were really as big as I remembered," she winks.

My ego inflates along with my chest. "Kostas, don't ruin our friendship. Go away."

Arlo's laughter fades as he moves away from the door.

I turn my attention back to Rose. "What's the verdict?"

"Bigger," she says with a grin. "Now, go kick Arlo's ass and tell him we get half of whatever gambling scheme he's referring to." She points at the bedroom door before turning around.

She makes it two steps before I snag her around the waist and pull her back to my front. She giggles as I band an arm around her waist to keep her from moving. I graze my fingers across her pert nipples, and she turns silent, her muscles relaxing against me. I roll and tease them until she gasps.

"I want to watch you come," I tell her.

"I'm late," she argues.

"Then let's make it worth it."

"You haven't met annoyed Anna, or you wouldn't be suggesting this," she tells me.

I slide her nipple between two knuckles and her back arches. I release my hold on her and slide my hand between her legs. Her heat greets me, already slick. Rose presses her head back, her breasts pushing forward. I dip my finger inside her while continuing to tease her breast.

"Oh, fuck." She draws the words out as I thrust my finger inside her.

"You're so wet."

She turns in my arms, and her breasts graze my chest, impossibly soft and smooth. She slips her arms around my shoulders, unabashed by her nakedness. The faint scent of beer is present, along with the sweet and floral scent of her perfume, but what sticks out the most—what makes my cock twitch—is the scent of *me* on her.

She threads her fingers behind my neck and kisses me as she steps forward, pushing me so that I take a step backward. "We have ten minutes. Otherwise, Anna's going to kill me." Another step toward the bed. She kisses me again, her tongue soft and teasing as she places her hand around my cock, squeezing me.

I moan against her mouth, needing hours rather than minutes.

I spin her to face her bed and press on the top of her spine with enough force to make her lean forward on her palms. My cock stiffens with desire. I run my nose along the nape of her neck, catching her ear between my teeth. I slide my fingers between her legs again, tracing over her slit, so light and gentle she protests with a hard breath as she widens her legs.

I use the same pressure and run along her clit, and she gasps. I press harder, circling over her, rubbing until her muscles begin to tighten, and then I move my other hand to her entrance and slip one finger inside.

She moans, her hips jerking back toward my hand that's fucking her. I circle her clit, tracing along her folds, and then add a second finger. Her back arches, and then she drops to her elbows, panting as I continue exploring her, learning each reaction and moan and gasp and how they correlate with every touch. When I hit the right spot, her breaths become moans.

I press a trail of kisses over her shoulder. "So fucking perfect."

Her breaths grow more ragged, and her hands tangle in the blankets. I feel her clench around my fingers, and a moment later, she bites down on her comforter to stifle her cries as her orgasm rips through her.

She lies still for a few seconds and then rolls to face me. Her green eyes open, soft and lazy. "Tell me you're putting on a condom."

I rub my palm against her thigh. "Tonight," I tell her. "You have to get going."

"That's okay. Let Anna kill me." She reaches for the nightstand.

I chuckle, catching her hand. "Trainers swear that orgasming before a game is a terrible idea."

"I think we should test this theory. Purely for scientific purposes, of course."

I slide my hand along her hip and then higher, addicted to the feel of her skin.

"Tonight." I place a kiss on her collarbone and another on the edge of her shoulder.

"Raegan mentioned we consider not telling people," her voice is hesitant, nervous. "To enjoy spending time together without the mess of other people."

"I don't really give a fuck what anyone else says or thinks. That's why I keep my circle small." I press a kiss on her temple.

"It's not like it would be an easy secret to keep. I mean, Arlo already knows, and he blows at keeping secrets," she says.

A smile tickles the corners of my mouth at how quickly she finds an excuse for us not to be a secret. "And Hoyt knows, too."

She kisses me and then bristles. "Shit. Shit. Anna really is going to kill me." She plants a hard kiss on my mouth. "I have to shower. You need to make sure Paxton is still breathing. I'll see you in ten." She kisses me again and then hurries into the bathroom.

I heave a sigh.

Paxton.

Fuck.

I nab my shirt off the floor and adjust myself again before unlocking Rose's door and bracing myself for Arlo's interrogation.

Cheers greet me as I step into the living room. Thank fuck, I've never had roommates. Arlo does long, exaggerated claps. "About *fucking* time."

Olivia shoves him. "You're supposed to be flipping pancakes," she tells him, handing him a spatula.

"This is newsworthy. We need to stop and record this day," Arlo says, reaching for his phone.

Olivia laughs. "By that, he means we're happy for you. *Both* of you."

"Where's Rose? I need to know if my advice made her finally take the leap. I've been talking you up for *months*." Arlo shakes his head. "And Tyler won the bet. He didn't even want to play, so he had the default week!"

"You set up a wager? You're such an asshole."

Arlo laughs. "Only because I had faith in you." He takes a couple of steps closer to me and wraps me in a side hug. Arlo defies his outward appearance of being a human Hulk by being one of the most affectionate and happy-go-lucky guys I know. He never shies from a hug or a pat on the shoulder, and while it took a little time to get used to, I'm pretty damn certain it's taught me a thing or two and has only reaffirmed my position on not giving a shit about what others think.

Olivia's silent, flipping the pancakes Arlo abandoned. She looks in the direction of Rose's room, her thoughts apparent.

"She's just showering. She's supposed to meet her sister."

Relief floods Olivia's expression, her shoulders falling. "Oh, thank goodness." She sets the spatula down.

"Have you heard from Lincoln this morning?" I ask Arlo.

He shakes his head, eating a strawberry from one of the multiple bowls of fruit. "I'm sure he's with Rae Rae. Why?"

"Because Pax and Hoyt fucked up last night."

Arlo's gaze turns serious. "How bad?"

"Pax was so drunk he blew chunks and passed out."

Arlo winces. "Shit."

I nod. "Hoyt wasn't much better. Rose saw them at a party and got them outside and called me."

Olivia's eyes flash to mine, the hint of a smile before she starts to remove the pancakes. Arlo follows behind her, pouring fresh pools of batter onto the hot griddle.

"I dropped them off at your place last night. Lincoln, Rae, and Caleb were there."

Arlo winces. "Lincoln's going to be pissed. He came home last week, and Pax was drunk, and a million strangers were at the house." He shakes his head as he finishes pouring the pancakes. "Let's hope Coach doesn't find out."

I scrub my hand across my cheek, the sharpness of my stubble reminding me I need to shower and shave. "We have to look out for Pax. He's in way over his head. Maybe we bench him," I say.

"Bench him?" Arlo's eyes grow round as he shifts, folding his arms over his chest. "That could kill the rest of our season."

"Look at Banks," I tell him. "We didn't think he was ready, and now he's starting."

Arlo shakes his head, the news a full confliction of everything we're both comfortable with. Paxton is one hell of a quarterback, but it doesn't negate the fact that he's developed a handful of bad habits that continue to get increasingly more dangerous.

"We need to talk about it," I insist.

Hesitation mars Arlo's brow. "You want the team to decide?"

I shake my head. "I don't give a fuck what most of them have to say."

Arlo settles a hand on Olivia's waist and nods. "We'll call Lincoln after breakfast. Discuss it with him." He kisses the side of Olivia's head, and his shoulders fall as though her presence alone relaxes him.

"Johnston was on the rumor site this morning," Arlo says.

I cringe. He's one of our freshman linebackers—my responsibility. "Bad?"

Arlo nods. "The rumor accused him of getting in a car accident that paralyzed someone."

Every day I hate the rumors a little more, not only because it continues to draw attention away from the game but also because certain rumors like this one have me dreading if there's any truth behind them.

Olivia flips the new round of pancakes as Rose steps out of her room wearing jeans and a hoodie, her hair pulled up in a knot. Stunning perfection.

She hops on one foot as she slips on a shoe. "You're lucky I like your lady so damn much," she tells Arlo. "Otherwise, I'd be plotting revenge."

Arlo chuckles. "She's my free pass."

Rose's gaze lands on mine, and her gaze softens as she smiles. "Sorry to rush off."

I shake my head and slide my shoes on. "I'll walk you to your car."

Rose glances at Olivia, who gives her a gentle smile and nods. "Oh, wait. Coffee." Olivia reaches for a cabinet, withdraws a commuter cup that she fills, and fixes it with half and half and sugar. Next, she grabs a granola bar and a banana and hands all three to Rose.

"Thanks," she says with a sheepish grin.

Olivia shakes her head. "Drive safe. Have fun."

I follow Rose outside. The morning is foggy and cool. She opens her car door and sets her stuff inside before facing me.

I grab the pocket in the front of her sweatshirt and tug her against me. "Are you coming to the game tonight?"

She nods. "I thought I might check out the merchandise."

"My place tonight?"

"Your parents live there."

I nod. "I'm also twenty-two."

"So it's a deal, my place?"

I grin, kissing her again. "Drive safe."

Her hands remain braced against me, though we both know she's late. "I'm sorry to leave. I didn't mean to make you face the firing squad alone." She skates her fingers over my shoulders and weaves her hands behind my neck.

"I don't mind," I tell her honestly.

"I hope you have a good day and a great game."

I kiss her again. "You, too."

This time when she pulls back, she's slow to open her eyes. "I should go."

I again stare at her green eyes, trying to read her thoughts.

She leans forward and kisses me and then takes a step back toward her car. Her hands are the last thing to slip away from my body. "Okay. I'm actually leaving this time."

It takes every ounce of restraint not to ask her to stay. "I'll see you tonight."

She grins. "Sounds like a plan."

Once she's securely in her seat, seat belt on, I close the door. I watch her drive away before heading back into the apartment.

"Grab a plate," Arlo says as he scatters fruit over his pancakes before adding a mountain of scrambled eggs to his plate.

"No. I didn't mean to intrude."

Arlo scoffs. "You're not. Grab some eggs and pancakes. We'll give you some Rose advice."

"Rose advice?"

He nods. "You have insiders. Trust me, take the advice. Rose pulled me aside before I started dating Liv and filled me in on stuff that helped me understand her and not fuck things up." He points to one of the empty chairs at the small dining room table. "Grab some grub and get the inside scoop."

Olivia smiles, handing me a plate with four pancakes. "First off, text her when you go somewhere. Rose worries, but she won't tell you outright. Check in and let her know when you get somewhere. She'll appreciate it."

"And she needs coffee first thing in the morning," Arlo adds.

Olivia nods. "And most importantly, she doesn't realize what a good person and friend she is. Though she's completely wrong, Rose doesn't think she'll make a good girlfriend. So positive encouragement and patience will be your two best assets."

Rose's self-deprecating words replay in my thoughts as I nod. "Can I ask you about her family?"

Olivia flinches. "I've known Rose for almost six years and barely know anything about them. She's closer to Anna now that she's moved back, but Rose and her dad have a very strained relationship."

"Bill's working with my dad on his campaign," I tell them, pouring syrup across my fruit and pancakes.

"Her dad's nice," Olivia says, her face scrunched like she hates admitting the fact. "Even Rose will admit that he's nice." She shrugs. "It's awkward because no matter how kind he is or how many brunches we attend, her feelings don't change, but she won't tell me why."

"She mentioned he was gone for nine years."

Olivia nods. "He moved back just a couple of months before her mom got sick."

Arlo blows out a long breath and reaches for his coffee. "And I thought I was jinxed last year." He takes a drink. "It sucks, but some families just don't get along. My uncle and aunt don't talk to their daughter at all—haven't in years."

Olivia nods. "Son't let that relationship be a reflection of Rose. She's the type of good that gives me hope in humanity." She smiles, though her eyes turn red and glossy with unshed tears. "She's the best. I could give hundreds of examples and stories, but I'm pretty sure you've already figured this out yourself." She collects a bite of her pancake with her fork. "Also, I'll come after you if you screw her over. I've been team Ian for months, so don't make me regret it."

I smile around the bite of my pancake. "Deal."

20

ROSE

I approach Anna like one does a feral cat—slowly and prepared to lose an eye.

"Hey," she says, smiling at me.

"Hey...."

"How are you? Isn't it beautiful this morning?"

I peer at the mist-filled sky, the fog still hanging low and making it feel like time has stuck between day and night. "Beautiful."

She grins. "I got you some Starbucks." She passes me a full venti.

I accept it, my gaze still on her. "You didn't poison it, right?"

She laughs. "Are you ready to go inside, or do you want to sit out here and drink some coffee for a while?"

"Do you know what time it is?"

She turns her wrist. "Ten after eleven."

I stare at her, but all she does is take a drink of her coffee. "Exactly. I'm late,"

She shrugs. "It's not a big deal."

"Who are you, and what have you done with my sister?" I pinch the skin on her forearm.

"Ouch!" She deservedly swats me. "What are you doing? That hurt."

"Just making sure someone wasn't wearing a full Anna costume."

"Can't I just be in a good mood?"

I consider my response for several seconds. "...Yes." I note how her cheeks are rosy, her brown eyes sparkling. "Did you have an orgasm this morning?"

"Rose!" She sounds like my Anna this time.

"You're in a really good mood," I point out. "I thought maybe...."

She shakes her head. "I got my test results back yesterday."

"Test results?" Those two words are like a siren in my memories, armed with unwanted thoughts.

"I was nervous since we've been having such a hard time conceiving." She pulls in a breath. "I was worried that maybe I could have something wrong like...." *Like Mom.* We both know that our chances of having the same cancer as her are only five percent, but that five percent can sometimes feel enormous when fear sticks its head in the mix.

I nod. "And everything's good?"

Her smile isn't as broad, but it's there nonetheless. She nods. "Everything came back great. They said it can take some couples longer to conceive, so I'm trying to be patient."

I have no doubt this is difficult for her because she wants to be a mom so badly and because everything has always come quickly and easily to Anna, a reflection of her time and commitment.

"Did they have any advice?" I ask.

"Have sex every day."

I nearly choke on my sip of coffee. "I bet Kurt isn't hating that advice."

Her cheeks redden. "I'm trying to remind myself that I don't have to control everything—that I *can't* control everything."

"It can be hard, huh?"

"*So* hard!"

I chuckle away my silent innuendos that I know wouldn't be appropriate and take another drink.

Anna sits quietly, nursing her coffee until I nudge her with my elbow. "That's why you have Kurt."

"You're such a pain in the ass."

I laugh again. "I struggle with not having control over things too, sometimes," I admit. "After feeling so powerless and out of control with everything mom went through, it's tough not to want to control things."

"Is that why you don't date?"

"It *was* a contributing factor."

Anna turns so she's fully facing me. "*Was?*"

"I might be kind of, sort of dating Ian."

"Ian Forrest?"

"The one and only."

Anna does a slow blink. "What does *kind of* mean?"

"Are you objecting?"

She blinks in long slow draws. "No. I just ... I'm a little surprised. What made you change your mind?"

"The fact I haven't wanted to kiss another guy in about eight months."

Anna's jaw falls. "It took *eight months* for you to decide?"

"He was in Italy for two of them."

"Still. I can't believe you waited. I can't believe *he* waited. Eight months is a long time."

"First off, neither can I. Secondly, I didn't ask him to wait around for me. It wasn't like I planned this. In fact, I tried to avoid him."

She grins and takes a sip of her coffee. "I like to think when something like that happens, that's Mom putting her touch on things."

"Let's hope that wasn't Mom's touch I was feeling last night."

"Rose!" she objects, but rather than looking angry, she laughs. "You know what I mean. She was helping the timeline, breaking down all of your stubbornness."

"Stubbornness?"

She laughs again. "Need me to say it again?"

"Dating is still kind of terrifying. It fits right into that category of things I can't control. I can't control Ian's feelings for me, or if he gets drafted, or where he moves."

Anna sets her coffee down and wraps her arm around my shoulders. "He's not Christopher."

I scoff as I pull away from her, annoyed that she's bringing him up again, especially now. "I know. He's nothing like Christopher."

Anna's fingers dig into my arm, holding me in place. "I retract my statement, back to neutral ground. I like Ian, and I think it's great you two are dating. He seems like a nice guy, a little on the muscley side ... if you're into that sort of thing, which it seems you are."

I lean into her, a silent laugh tugging at my lips.

"This seems like a place Mom would have loved," Anna says, looking at the doors behind us.

"She did."

"I know I got more time with her, but sometimes I'm a little jealous because you guys were always so close."

Her admission shocks me. "You guys talked about law school and politics constantly."

"Yeah, but she opened up to you. She told you about growing up in Peru and what it was like moving here. With me, it was all about showing a brave face."

"I'm sure it's because she didn't want to hold you back. I feel that way a little with Ian already."

Anna leans her head against mine. "You need to give yourself a little credit." She rotates her wrist to look at her watch. "We're late. We should probably go inside."

"I know this job isn't as exciting as working with presidential candidates, but I'm really glad you're back."

She plants a kiss on my head. "Me too." She smooths her hand over the same spot she kissed, just as Mom used to, and then climbs to her feet and brushes off her pants.

Ian

Lincoln stares at the ceiling while he paces their living room. Arlo is seated on the couch, elbows on his knees, while I sit across from him in the chair. My friendship with Pax wasn't my invitation here this morning. The fact that I'm the captain of the defense was my key, while theirs lies in a brotherhood.

"The site didn't post anything about it," Lincoln says. "For all we know, whoever's behind all this bullshit doesn't even know about last night's party. We need Pax," Lincoln says.

Arlo nods. "I agree."

"To win, we might, but if we continue allowing him to act like this, he's going to take more than just our chances at an undefeated year. He's going to take his own fucking life," I point out.

Arlo leans back. "He's not that bad. I mean, he's overdoing it, yes, but it's not like he's had to go to the hospital or anything."

My gaze flicks from Arlo to Lincoln.

He shakes his head. "I don't know. I hear your concern, but if we take football away from him, it will only shove him farther down this path of self-destruction. Football is the only thing keeping him sober a few nights a week."

"We're enabling him," I point out.

"Between Rae almost dying, and his dad, and fucking Candace— he had one hell of a year last year, and he's still washing off some of the debris," Lincoln says.

"I hear you, and that's why he had a free pass for the better part of last season. *And* the spring. *And* the summer. When does that end? When do we tell him he's no longer struggling but has a problem?"

Lincoln rubs a hand over his head, then lifts his sweatshirt's hood and resumes pacing.

"We can't turn our backs on him," Arlo says. "He's my brother."

"You're not turning your back on him. You're telling him that he means more to us than this game," I tell him. "That his future means more than this game."

Lincoln tugs off his hood, agitation flashing in his eyes. "Rae suggested the same course of action." He pulls in a long breath. "Honestly, we're fucked either way, but as much as I respect your reasoning, I still don't think it's the right decision. If we bench him, he's going to feel betrayed, which will only make shit worse. The NFL is his future, and we'd be taking that away if we don't let him play."

I turn my attention to Arlo, already knowing his vote is against me.

"I respect you, man. You know I do. But Lincoln's right. We let him play, but we give him a tougher curfew and a shorter leash. If anyone can overcome this, it's Pax."

I nod. "I hope you're right."

Lincoln grabs the football set on the coffee table and palms it. "I hope we are, too."

"How's he doing?" I ask.

Lincoln clasps the ball with both hands, the action causing a large clap. "Caleb has a buddy in medical school who brought over an IV and some fluids this morning, so he's feeling better than he should."

"Is that allowed?" Arlo asks.

Lincoln turns a piercing gaze on him. "No. And Rae's pissed. She hightailed it out of here and turned off her damn phone."

Arlo winces and moves his attention to me. "This is why we can't fuck up. If you piss Rose off, Olivia will hate you, and vice versa. Trust me. Been there, done that."

Lincoln slaps the ball again. "We need to get to the stadium. Lock this shit up and shove it into a box until after we beat Oregon."

"You're right." I stand from my seat and flip my baseball hat around.

"This was your version of an intervention?" Pax asks from the doorway. His eyes are on me, hard with accusation. "Just toss me out to dry, huh?"

I scoff. "No. That would have involved leaving your sorry ass on someone's front lawn in your own vomit. You're welcome, by the way."

Paxton sneers. "What happened to protect your teammates?" he asks. "Unity?" He takes another step. "Or does that only happen when your ass is the one on the line? I broke curfew. I had a couple of drinks, so what? That means I lose my position on the team? I've worked my ass off for this every single day."

"This isn't about you breaking the rules," I tell him. "What would have happened to you last night if Rose didn't get you out of there?"

He throws a hand into the air. "I would have slept it off on some-one's couch."

"There are consequences when you act this recklessly," I tell him.

"You don't get to decide that, Ian. Don't act all saintly on me because you were too busy jacking off for some girl who won't give you the time of day."

Lincoln plants a hand on my chest. He's strong and faster than shit, but as a defensive linebacker, I have no doubt I could move past him—or over him. Lincoln's gaze meets mine, and he shakes his head. "He's speaking out of anger. You know that."

I do, but it does little to abate my resentment and hostility.

"Don't be an asshole," Arlo tells Paxton, a hand planted against his chest.

"Ian saved your ass last night," Lincoln says. "And if he were trying to bench you, he'd have gone to Harris, not us."

Paxton remains rigid, jaw flexed. "Fuck you, Ian."

Arlo shoves him. "In Jersey, we call that a missed first shot. Take a walk and cool down."

Paxton doesn't move. I'm sure he's trying to remain strong and show them, me, and hell, maybe even himself that he's still in control.

I stare him down for several seconds, not wanting to back down because I know he'll take it as submission, and the last thing I'm doing is submitting. But I also realize he needs to cool off before discussing the idiocy involved in many of his recent decisions.

"I need to go. I have to meet my team." I take a step back toward the front door.

Lincoln nods, his appreciation for not challenging Paxton apparent. "We'll be right behind you."

I clear the front door and feel the weight of the discussion follow me. It follows me into my truck and into the locker room, where I'm greeted by several members of my teammates preparing for tonight's game. Some stay home until the last minute, but many spend the day here, stretching, going over tape, listening to music, meditating—you see it all.

"Hey! Hey!" Luis says, pulling out one of his earbuds. He stretches his shoulders. A grin spread across his features. "You ready to go Duck hunting?" He tosses a bag of pistachios at me.

"When are you going to tell Alexis you don't like pistachios?"

He scoffs. "Um, never."

I drop my bag and take a seat on the bench, tearing the bag open. "Why?"

"Because we've been together for three years. How am I supposed to bring it up now? *Hey, babe, you know how you get me a good luck gift before every game, and you always include those rancid little green nuts? I pawn them off to Ian every week.*"

I crack open a shell and drop the pistachio into my mouth. "That sounds like a decent start. Let me know how it goes."

He throws a sports drink at me that I catch with a grin. "Some things you can't admit after a certain point. You know what I mean?"

I think about how many things I don't know about Rose—how many things she doesn't know about me. As much as I want to contest his words, I feel the same timer ticking. Like all the important things should have been aired by this point because we went through the friend phase first, or at least something resembling the friend phase.

"Am I talking to myself?" Luis waves a hand in front of my face.

I sit back, cracking open another nut.

"Long night?" he asks.

Images of Rose naked and splayed across her bed immediately flash in my thoughts. I think of my mouth between her legs, my hands on her breasts, her waist, her thighs. The way her lips parted with pleasure and how her gaze went from uncertainty and nerves to trust and confidence. My shoulders straighten. All the energy and thoughts I've allotted to Paxton focus on Rose, igniting my determination for tonight's game. After all, if I finally get Rose to admit that her feelings for me span beyond a single hookup, I'm pretty sure I can do anything.

"Why are you smiling?" Luis asks. "This is the worst one-sided conversation ever."

I shake my head, working to dilute my thoughts of Rose by focusing on the game. "I met up with Rose last night."

Luis's eyes round. "And...."

"We're going to give things a shot."

"That's my boy!" he says, sticking out his fist for me to bump. "I'm going to say it was my hit yesterday during practice that knocked some sense into you."

I throw my head back and chuckle.

His laughter floods mine, causing several of our teammates to glance in our direction with mixed expressions of interest and annoyance. "No better way to celebrate than a win," he says, ignoring all of them.

I wrap up the rest of the pistachios, store them in my bag, and open my locker to change into my uniform.

My mood shifts—I become louder, more animated, more energized. My concerns about Paxton shift to the recesses of my mind, left there even when I note his arrival.

"Let's go," I clap my hands, signaling the defensive team to follow me onto the field. The night air is cold and damp. Everyone has already stretched, but many stretch again before we line up to jog a few lines to get warmed up.

Walker is sucking air as we come to a stop. He's the only senior lineman this year. He will undoubtedly be playing a lot of minutes tonight, as Oregon tends to be a running team with their offensive linemen constantly on the move. "This is your night, Walker," I tell him. "You're going to have four sacks tonight."

"Fuck yes," he says, placing both hands on his head to open his lungs. "It's Duck hunting season."

I grin, slapping a hand to his shoulder before I scan the stands, wondering if Rose might be here already.

Once our warm-up ends, we head back into the locker room, where Coach Harris starts clapping as he chews his gum and paces in front of a giant whiteboard he never uses. "All right. We know they're a running team, so we're going to need our offense to buy some time tonight for our defense, make sure they're getting rested, and have some fresh legs. And Coach Danielson and our defense will stop them from advancing and ensuring we're looking for the holes and collapse on their pocket, forcing them to take the hot routes." He claps again, working to build on the energy.

The defense and offense, two main cogs that play our separate roles on the field with minimal flaws. We're prepared, and Coach Harris uses this time to try and inspire the team, his voice and excitement rising. This is where the energy is born, and when we go out onto the field, the fans raise us even higher. We shift toward the tunnel, and I watch as Paxton heads for the bathrooms for his routine throw-up session that takes place before each game.

Arlo grins as he stands beside me. "I hope you set your TV to record me. I'm going to be tearing up the field tonight."

I laugh, appreciating that he doesn't bring up things with Paxton. I'm in no mood to sort through that shit right now.

As we leave the tunnel, we tap the small Bulldog mascot painted above us, going through the theatrics of fireworks, flags, and cheerleaders celebrating each home game.

The coin toss has our defense taking the field first, and my attention is crisp, focused, and clear, already foreshadowing our win.

21

ROSE

Angry Ian kisses like a king. Victorious Ian kisses like a god.

I close my bedroom door with my foot, and he locks it before kicking off his shoes, all the while, his lips possess mine. My body feels warm and cold as excitement rains across my nerves. I wonder if it will be like this every time. Will I always be nervous and excited, hoping it's as good as the last time? I slip out of my shoes and kick them toward the wall, where one of them hits with a soft *thump*.

Ian grips my waist, his long fingers stretching across my backside, anchoring me in place while he runs his other hand under my shirt, brushing his fingers against my bare skin and making me sigh into his mouth. I grab the hem of his dark shirt, tugging it free over his still-damp hair and dropping it to the floor. Ian's hand climbs higher, gliding across my bra before making a direct line to the clasp that he releases with a quick flick of his fingers. My breasts are heavy with want, and my nipples are peaked and overly sensitive. Ian kisses me deeply, a demand and a warning that leaves me gasping for breath.

"I love your breasts," he says, running his thumbs across each nipple.

Desire pools between my legs. I want to feel him everywhere. Ian reaches for my pants and releases the button before lowering the zipper. His fingers skate down my bare back and slip under the waist of my jeans and underwear, inching them both down so they're low on my hips as he nips at my lips, creating another contrasting sensation.

I love the feeling of his hands on me. I love the feeling of his mouth on me. Every part of me aches for his attention, yet kissing him is so damn addictive and intoxicating that I don't want to stop. Ever.

My bottom lip slips from his teeth, and he lowers to his knees and gently rids my pants and underwear. He places his hands low on my pubic bone, his thumbs at my slit. He spreads me and pulls in a long, deep breath.

Holy Mother of Mary, it's hot.

Before I can find my footing, he runs his tongue over my crease from entrance to clit. Pleasure shoots through me, making my knees tremble. He does it again, this time using the flat of his tongue. A deeper ache starts as he flicks his tongue over me, threatening to beat his last record for getting me to orgasm so quickly. I tip my head forward and open my eyes, discovering his steel gaze already locked on me. He never breaks eye contact as he tilts his head and grazes over my sensitive clit with his teeth. I mewl. I don't even know what I'm saying, if they're sounds or words, definitely pleas as my hands drop to his shoulders, clutching him as I turn boneless and my desire builds.

"You can't come. Not yet," he says, his touch gentler.

A frustrated groan climbs my throat. Desire is making my skin burn and my body ache. I cup my breast, rolling my nipple like he had this morning. Ian growls a low and throaty sound and then licks me again and again and again. I'm uncertain if this is a punishment or a reward. I gently pinch my nipples, imagining it's his teeth, and Ian slides a finger into me. I moan and pinch myself harder, and Ian adds a second finger.

"That feels so good," I tell him as his tongue teases my clit. "I'm going to come."

He stops licking me, but his fingers increase in speed and pressure, curling until they hit just the right spot before relaxing them.

I groan in protest, and he does it again.

"I need to come," I whimper.

"You're going to come. More than once." His voice is husky, matching the desire reflected in his stare.

"Ian," His name starts as a warning and turns into a moan as he thrusts his fingers in me.

He drags them out at a luxuriously slow pace and then thrusts inside of me again. My thighs begin to tremble, and the ache twines with pleasure, creating the most inexplicable and confounding feeling that is so delicious and almost uncomfortable.

"Why did we wait so fucking long?" he asks.

I moan and reach for my other breast, tracing over my sensitive nipples with my fingers.

"That's right," he says. "I want you to touch yourself whenever you think of me." He licks my clit again with one fast pass, and then he withdraws his fingers, leaving me desperate and aching in a way that makes my entire core and stomach clench. He releases his jeans and pulls his pants and underwear to the ground before reaching for my nightstand and withdrawing a condom. He rips it open, slips it over his length, and then leads me to the side of my bed. "Get on your knees," he says.

I follow his instruction, desperate and ready. His fingers massage one globe of my backside, and then his hand trails higher, reaching my breast where he pinches my overly sensitive bud, sending pleasure coursing through me as my hips buck. Then I feel him at my entrance. I look over my shoulder and watch as his eyes close, and his jaw goes slack as he presses his tip inside me. He's huge, almost uncomfortable, and then he slides in a little farther, and pleasure runs through me as he starts to move. His hips rock against mine, our skin slapping and our breaths chasing each others. It feels so good—too good.

His thrusts become harder, driving into me fully until that ache builds back up, and my breaths become pants and then whimpers. I am on the cusp of ecstasy when he reaches his hand around and rubs his middle finger over my clit, and I yell out my orgasm. His teeth sink into the flesh of my shoulder, and then he jerks, finding his own release.

I fall to the mattress, every one of my muscles is weak and sated.

Still inside of me, Ian presses his lips to my spine.

After watching his game and the hours of hits and running, I have no idea how he managed to give me the best orgasm of my life, but Raegan's words about endurance dance across my thoughts.

He slowly pulls out of me and straightens, brushing his hands across my bare skin.

"I'll be right back." He disappears into my bathroom.

I'm so damn comfortable I don't want to move, but I'm sprawled across the middle of the bed, so I lift the blankets and crawl between the sheets.

Ian returns, encircling my waist with his arms. He hauls my back to his front, and his skin feels as warm as the sun, making me sigh with contentment. "I might need a raincheck," I tell him. "I don't think I can have another orgasm again tonight. You wore me out."

I feel his smile tickle my shoulder. "I'll give you a couple of hours to recover."

I fall asleep to him tracing patterns over my skin.

I WAKE up slowly and stretch, my foot hitting a cool spot on my sheets that shouldn't be there.

Last night, after falling asleep, Ian woke me up by drawing lazy circles between my legs. He gave me two more mind-blowing orgasms, one with his mouth and the second with his fingers before he fucked me sideways and found his own climax. This morning I'm sore in the best way possible, but my happy vibe takes a nosedive as I roll over and discover he's gone and the bathroom light is off.

I smell him on my skin as I grab my phone.

Ian: Sorry to leave, but I need to deal with something.

Confusion sits heavy on my clouded thoughts where bliss is trying to celebrate having four orgasms in twenty-four hours.

I roll out of my warm bed, desperate for a distraction. Ignoring the bite of cold, I head into the bathroom and turn the shower to hot and wait until steam appears before getting under the spray.

Did Ian freak out?

Am I overthinking this?

I tip my head back and let the water cascade over my hair, realizing with complete clarity that being a girlfriend is particularly difficult for me because it relies so heavily on trust—something I struggle with.

I finish my shower and take my time blow-drying my hair and picking out my clothes. Ian and I are supposed to be working on his article today. I'd assumed he would stay, and we'd wake up and try out a breakfast spot to call our own—a page out of Arlo and Olivia's playbook, and then we'd get to work on selecting the message he wanted to share.

I check my phone after I finish getting ready, but there's nothing from Ian.

Coffee.

Coffee helps me think.

I step out of my room, and the rich aroma of coffee greets me. Olivia is standing beside the coffeemaker, wearing an unreadable expression that switches to panic as she sees me.

"What?" I ask.

"Is Ian here?" she whispers, her eyes on my opened door.

"No ... why?"

She winces. "He was on the rumor site again this morning."

"When will that site burn? I thought Cooper got a handle on it?"

"Only for a couple of days last week. They've been posting since Thursday."

I grumble. "Don't tell me what it says. I feel like most of these are lies or tiny kernels of the truth that have been blown up."

Olivia doesn't move or object.

The coffee pot makes its final rumble as it finishes percolating and beeps to announce it's ready.

Still, Olivia remains rooted in place.

I reach around her to grab three mugs. "Is it really bad?"

"I don't know," she says. "Maybe?"

I fill two of the cups and then put the pot back on the warmer so Arlo can pour his fresh when he wakes up. "What did it say?"

She flips on her phone and turns it to face me. It's a picture of Ian with another guy, both of them wearing football pads with "*Rumor has it that Paxton Lawson isn't the only guy at Brighton who doesn't know his limits. Ian Forrest is said to have killed his friend and teammate Isaiah Templeton their sophomore year of high school.*"

I look at Olivia and then at my bedroom door. "Ian was gone before I woke up this morning with a message saying he had to deal with something. This must have been what he was referring to."

Olivia winces. "What do you think the truth is? Arlo said Ian suggested benching Paxton for his drinking problem, saying the team needs to give him an ultimatum."

I shake my head. "I have no idea, but this is Ian we're talking about. He's the epitome of responsible. I need to call him."

Olivia nods. "But his family is mega-rich. If he did pay someone off before, they could do it again." I think of the first rumor about Ian that claimed he paid off a girl.

A terrible concoction of emotions and thoughts tangle: doubt, concern, sympathy, accusation, and a dozen more make my stomach feel sour. I send a quick message to Ian, asking him when is a good time for him to meet for the article.

He replies instantly.

Ian: We can do it anytime. Why don't you come to my place? We can take pictures here with my "hobby."

Ian: Come on over whenever you're ready.

Olivia reads his responses over my shoulder. "Why did he put quotation marks around hobby? Are *you* his hobby? Is he planning to take nude photos of you?"

I snicker. "No."

"But it's good that he responded right away. Right?" She looks at me. "Do you still have mace in your purse?" Her brow lowers. "No. What am I saying? This is Ian." She nods. "But, maybe I should go with you."

I hug her. "The article didn't allege him of attacking his friend. I'm going to be okay. Everything's okay. I just need to do the girlfriend thing and talk to him. I've read thirty-five romance novels in the past four months, and if I've learned anything, it's that half of the story climaxes were attributed to misconceptions and miscommunications. I've got this. We know this rumor site has been filled with lies, so I'm going in there with my journalist's hat on and my mind clear."

Olivia nods. "Just send me a couple of updates."

"He's not dangerous."

"Will you just do what I ask?" She sounds flustered.

I grin. "I'll message you when I get there and then every fifteen minutes until I leave."

"Don't make it obvious."

"Beggars can't be choosers," I tease.

Olivia rolls her eyes. "Go figure this out, and then message me."

I take a long gulp of coffee before sliding on a pair of ballet flats at the door. I grab my book bag and camera and shove my keys into my pocket before heading out to my car.

My phone rings as I hit the parking lot. I had thought it might be Ian, but my realtor is a good second.

"Gabriel, tell me everything. What did they say?"

Gabriel laughs. "I love that you answer on the first ring."

"Only for you, baby."

He laughs again. "Can you teach my boyfriend how to talk dirty to me?"

"It's a skill I was born with, that and my winning sense of humor."

"Of course," he says with a chuckle. "Well, I hate to tell you this news, but your offer wasn't accepted. However, I have more places for us to look at, including one that is just a few blocks from downtown."

My shoulders slump with the bad news. "How much did the winners bid?"

"You don't want to know. But I've got more places to show you."

"Maybe we should wait until the market cools down."

"You can think about it. Regardless, I'll be there, wherever you set up shop. I'll follow you to the ends of this earth." Gabriel and I met three years ago while taking a Vinyasa yoga class. We bonded over our shared love for green tea and Chris Hemsworth. He was the first person to sign up for my yoga class when I completed the courses to become an instructor. Using him as my realtor was a simple decision.

"And I love you for that, but I'm going to need more than one student to keep the lights on."

"Rose, people love you. They're drawn to you, babe. Between your tight ass and killer sass, they can't get enough."

"Can we talk all day? I like when you tell me I'm pretty."

He laughs. "I have to let you go because I have a house to show. This couple is even pickier than you. Their number one demand is a window in the master closet."

"Who wants a window in their closet?"

"I don't get paid to ask questions."

"I'll give you a free class if you find out. I want to know if she's planning something dirty that I need to keep in mind for my future wish list."

Gabriel chuckles. "I'll send you some new listings. Let me know what you think."

"Bye."

My disappointment doesn't have much time to grow wings because, without traffic, it only takes me ten minutes to reach Ian's house. Last spring, he invited me over a few times to have dinner and hang out, but he'd been clear that he had no interest in having sex without dating—a respectable rule that would make any girl feel lucky and special, any girl but me at that time. Instead, it led to our messy web of a relationship where both of us wanted more, yet we had no idea how the other felt.

The circular driveway is three cars wide and doesn't lead to the garage, which is likely in the back with a separate driveway entrance. Before I'm out of my car, Ian rounds the house dressed in dark jeans and a black tee that says "Roma" across the front.

"You startled me," I admit.

His grin is unapologetic. "Sorry." He tilts his head and kisses me swiftly. "Come on."

I grab my bags, which Ian takes before leading me across the property. "Thanks for meeting me here," he says, causing my thoughts to stray back to last year and the excuses I'd used then to avoid coming.

"It was either here or you stripping at the library ... which...." I take a moment to mull over the idea. "Probably would have worked in our favor. I bet we could have gained an audience. People might have even done a live feed!"

Ian shakes his head. "You can make that offer to Luis when you interview him tomorrow." We cut through the backyard, where the large swimming pool takes up much of the space—a fire pit, patio, and outdoor grilling area complete the area. The sight sparks a dozen what-ifs about last spring and what would have occurred if I had come. Would we have skinny-dipped in the pool? Would he have grilled something for us to eat? Would I have been able to leave with all the pieces of my heart intact?

But Ian doesn't stop at the lounge chairs or the extended table. Instead, he follows the brick path that leads to a small white pool house.

"Did they kick you out?" I ask.

Another flash of a grin as he opens the door.

And without a second thought about boundaries and rules, I follow him inside.

22

IAN

"Do you want something to drink?" I ask.

Rose's eyes don't leave mine to explore the pool house. With Rose, there's no judgment. No allure about what I could buy her because that's not the type of person she is—and likely because she can afford to buy whatever she wants.

"I'm okay, thanks."

I head to the fridge and pull out a sports drink. I'm drained on Sundays and always dehydrated. Plus, my hands are as restless as my mind, and I need something to hold onto. I open the bottle and take a swig before returning to where she's standing, a faint smile curving her lips. A barrier rests between us, one that I built by leaving her this morning.

"I'm sorry about disappearing," I tell her, running a hand through my hair. My thoughts are on my conversation with Luis and how he can't tell Alexis he doesn't like pistachios because he waited too long to tell her. Only my subject is much larger than pistachios.

Rose shakes her head. "Was everything okay?"

I pull out my phone and open the damn rumor site. "I made the mistake of checking my phone when I woke up this morning, and several people had sent me this." I show her the screen.

She nods. "I saw it. Olivia showed me."

"I was trying to find out if I could get it removed. If Cooper had an email address that I could reach out to." I rake my hand over my hair again, my anger tangling with regret. "It's so fucking stupid."

Rose's gaze is soft and patient but also curious. "Your dad had mentioned his name. When we went to the owl sanctuary, he mentioned you and Isaiah saving an owl."

I nod, only marginally surprised she remembers. "Isaiah was my best friend growing up. He's the whole reason I got into football."

"What happened?"

"High school happened. Girls happened. Parties happened." I lean my head back, gazing at the ceiling as an avalanche of memories threatens to break free. "He was the best goddamn football player at our school. Hell, if he were here, there's no way I'd be the middle linebacker—it would have been Isaiah. Freshman year, he was like a celebrity at school because he blew everyone's mind. He was invited to every party, every bonfire...." I shake my head again. "Isaiah loved it. He hated being home. His mom worked all the time, and his dad constantly rode his ass, so he took every excuse to be gone. But those parties got crazier and crazier. Cops started to show up, one kid nearly drowned, and I lost interest."

I work to swallow the regret that climbs up my throat in the form of bile as I recall his last night. "We'd had a bad game. Everything had gone wrong. I'd invited him over, but he wanted to go party and let off some steam. I offered to go out, but he said he'd call me if he needed a ride. I was so relieved not to go out that I accepted his lie."

Rose places her hand on my knee and scoots closer to me on the couch. "He offered to drive a girl in our class home and on the way, lost control and hit a tree. They both died at the scene."

"Oh, Ian." Rose runs her hand over my back. "I'm so sorry. That's tragic and awful. But you can't blame yourself for not being there. What if you had? What if you were killed too?" She grasps my hand with both of hers.

"I would have insisted on driving."

"You have no idea if he would have listened. He might have left without you. He might have seemed sober. There are too many vari-ables to know."

"When I saw the rumor, I was pissed, and sad, and filled with fucking guilt, realizing someone else believes I failed Isaiah by not showing up that night. And whoever they are had enough conviction to share it with the rumor site."

"We have no idea how they're getting their stories," Rose says, shaking her head. "They're likely making this stuff up by tying coinci-dences to whatever they can find online."

I release a weighted breath. "I wasn't trying to keep this from you. I wanted to tell you. You've been so open about your mom, but then summer came and...."

Rose shakes her head. "You have nothing to apologize for."

I lick my lips as I try to puzzle through everything I want to say. "Luis hates pistachios but Alexis buys them for him for every game. He won't tell her because she's been giving them to him for three years, and he feels like they've passed the window of transparency in their relationship, and if he admits he doesn't like them, she'll feel like he was lying to her. I don't want you to feel like I'm keeping shit from you. I'm an open book, Rose, and I sure as hell don't want you to learn something about me from this damn site."

Rose stares at me for several seconds. "My parents weren't together—living in the same household—for most of my childhood, so most of my dating references are from the past nine months and involve Olivia and Arlo." She pauses. "But they're still learning things about each other because they're still discovering things about them-selves. Their dynamic has changed with football, and I'm sure it will continue to grow and change just like I expect ours will.

"I want to know things about you—I want to know *everything* about you—but if we put a window on this informational period, then we're going to block ourselves from growing both independently and together." Her gaze lifts to mine, a small crease between her eyes as she silently asks for my thoughts.

I lean forward and kiss her like I wanted to when she arrived, without judgment or secrets holding me back.

When I pull back, her eyes are still closed, the corners of her lips curling. She slowly opens her eyes, meeting my stare. Neither of us speaks—we don't have to. Rose and I have always communicated with our eyes, saying things that are far too complex and important for words to spoil. She leans forward and kisses me again and then leans back. "We should start on your article. This entire week is dedicated to the football team."

"I'm probably the worst choice to include in the series," I tell her. "I suck at this shit."

Her green eyes flash with amusement. "Suck at what shit?"

"Interviews. Coach Harris is concerned they'll be a detriment to my career, so he's been trying to make me practice, but I hate answering questions. I'd rather do snakes, mat drills, lines ... anything but interviews."

"Why do you hate them so much?"

"Everything."

Rose laughs, the sound filling the space. She has a great laugh, bold and genuine, but like the smiles that reach her eyes, they're scarce, which only makes receiving them more rewarding.

"It's all posturing," I tell her. "No news source wants to hear about my thoughts for an upcoming game—hell, the fans don't either. They don't want to know that I have concerns or that I'm worried that one of our guys might be unable to stop a play. They want to hear how we're going to win, how we're the best, and how our competitors don't compare to our skill level."

She tilts her head, her plush lips stained a light red and so distracting that I wonder if she notices I'm staring at her mouth instead of her eyes. "I've seen your confidence firsthand, and it's not lacking." She rubs her lips together, and her gaze slides to my mouth and then meets my stare.

My blood warms as my cock hardens. With Rose, it's a single look, a single smile, a single laugh that makes the rest of the world seem dull. "Trust me, it has nothing to do with confidence. I know I'm capable, especially where it counts."

She smirks. "You don't think your confidence translates during interviews?"

"I've been told my confidence is mistaken for arrogance. I know our team is faster and stronger than any team in the league, but I'm not arrogant or naïve enough to believe that outliers couldn't change the outcome of a game. Last year we lost Arlo at the end of the season. Had that occurred halfway through the season, we likely wouldn't have gone undefeated.

"Until I hit the field, my mind is running in a thousand directions, considering any change-ups and potential strengths and weaknesses from their team and ours. Then, once I'm on the field, that's when everything becomes silent, and I can focus. It's like what that woman told us about the owls at the sanctuary, about how they're true predators, and it's impossible to distract them from their prey. I get like that, locked on, and everything becomes about the win."

Her eyes narrow like she's thinking about something, then she sits up a little straighter. "What about after the game? You don't seem to enjoy speaking with the press then, either."

I don't. But I do enjoy hearing that she pays attention to me enough to know this. "As soon as a game is over, there's like a fifteen-minute window where I'm feeling the high of the win, and then my mind starts dissecting the game and where we could have tightened things up and taken advantage of our speed and size."

She moves so she's sitting on her knees, and her hair slides forward. I reach forward and brush my fingers over the strands, tucking them behind her ear. Her pulse flutters against my hand pressed to her neck.

"Let's try to channel those fifteen minutes after the game. I'm going to record our interview again, but just like last time, they're my personal notes, and no one will hear them. Maybe I can help you channel your confidence." She pulls out the small recorder and a couple of pages of notes that she sets on her lap. "So, the theme of this series will be the men behind the jerseys, and we'll have you guys do a photoshoot to offer some of the eye candy that is garnering most of the attention with the other site, and then your interviews—

allowing people into your lives—that will be the icing on the cake that will lure them in."

This seems impossible, though I've argued it isn't. We want to talk about the parts of our lives that make us more human and relatable, and this other site is doing the exact opposite, and people are eating it up and begging for seconds.

"What got you into football?" Rose asks.

"Isaiah," I tell her. "He was obsessed, and I realized in the fifth grade that if I wanted to remain friends, I had to learn to play."

She grins. "And it turned out that you were an all-star player?"

Her compliment has me chuckling. "Not even close. I was terrible for the first couple of years. I grew up with my mom opposing all organized sports, and my dad who never played any sport, and my sister who never roughhoused, and suddenly I was on this field being told to tackle people.

"That was my rude introduction to learning the difference between arrogance and confidence because I was taller and bigger than half the kids out there, but they put me in my place ... *fast*."

This embarrassing trip down memory lane earns me a smile. "But you continued."

I nod. "I continued. Isaiah and I spent our weekends watching football games and running extra practices with kids on our street, and in the offseason, we continued playing every day, even on the rare snow day we'd play."

"When did you first dream of playing in the NFL?"

Her question catches me by surprise and completely off guard, like most interview questions. "Isaiah was always talking about going pro. He had big dreams, but the NFL seemed like a given to him rather than a dream. He was insanely fast and didn't have an ounce of fear, so he'd charge down the field like he was chasing the dogs of hell right back into the flames. I never took it that seriously. I liked to play, and as I got better, I liked it more. And yes, I'm aware of how that blurs that arrogance line."

"As long as you're aware." She tinkers with a small laugh. "You didn't dream of going pro when you were younger?"

I shrug. "I liked school and was decent at it. I always thought I'd grow up to be a guy who wore a suit and worked in an office for nine-to-five as my parents did."

"What changed that?"

I flash a grin. "I learned what confidence was."

"And Coach Harris says you can't be charming."

I chuckle. "He isn't lying."

"You're more charming than you think. You're just quieter than guys like Hoyt and Arlo, who can turn on the charm in a second." She snaps her fingers for emphasis.

"So you're saying I'm uptight and boring?"

"Maybe?" She raises her brows as though daring me to object.

Instead, I release another low chuckle. "I can be," I admit.

She laughs openly, freely. In times like this, when she's fully relaxed, I realize how composed she is so much of the time. "I gave you the perfect stage to talk yourself up, and instead, you called yourself boring."

I shrug. "I'm okay with boring. I like drip coffee, and my favorite pair of sweats is five years old, and I prefer reading books over watching TV, and I'd rather have pizza with a couple of close friends than be at a party with a couple of hundred strangers."

"Those are endearing qualities, not boring ones. But, now the question begs to be asked if you hate parties, why have you been throwing the most notorious parties at Brighton?"

"Those only ran for about six months, and the only reason they became notorious is because I don't have neighbors to bitch to anyone."

"I'm pretty sure it was the stuffed mushrooms," she says.

I grin. "At least we can both agree that it was a variable that can be bought."

"But why host them?"

I stare at her.

Her eyes shift between mine, her discomfort growing as pink stains her cheeks.

"I'd heard you didn't date, and I knew Arlo was starting to spend time with Olivia." I shrug. "I thought under the right circumstances ... you might show up."

"I was your Daisy Buchanan?"

I grin. "Thank fuck, no. She was married and fictional. You, you were always mine, and I was playing with the endgame in mind."

Her gaze dances between mine. "I can't believe you threw parties on the off chance I'd come."

"You left an impression that never faded."

She smiles shyly. "Well, I hate to disappoint you, but I'm actually quite boring."

"The more I learn about you, the more intrigued I am."

Rose smirks before standing so that several feet build between us. "With this article, we can make the meat of it be things you're comfortable sharing, but I think talking about Isaiah and how he inspired you to play could be perfect."

I shake my head. "Do you think it matters? Part of me wants to just say fuck it, and let this asshole keep wasting their time. Eventually, people will tire of reading these insane accusations or realize it's all a bunch of bullshit."

"My mom used to say that about reality TV, and it's still around."

I tip my head back and sigh. "I don't want to drag Isaiah or his family through this again. He killed someone, and his family struggles with that guilt every damn day, just like I do."

"Everyone faces struggles and doubts. You sharing yours will allow readers and fans to connect with you."

"I don't want to invite all of Brighton into my life."

Her gaze softens. "I won't be writing this as a tell-all. I promise. You mentioned your art when we were brainstorming.... I had no idea you were into art."

"I'm going to regret this." I stand, grab my drink, and lead Rose to the spare bedroom. As I open the door, the scents of paint and the paint thinner leak greet us, activating that side of me that loses all sense of time and obligation. My fingers itch to reach for a paintbrush.

"Ian," Rose says, slipping past me to look at one of the three easels with half-finished paintings set upon them. "This is amazing."

"It's for my mom."

"I've seen the Roman Forum," she says. "This is like looking at it in real life. The colors and the shadows and the light ... it's stunning."

"My mom doesn't outright say it, but I know she misses being there."

Rose continues to stare at the picture. "Why do you think they gave it up and moved back?"

"Because politics have always been my dad's dream. He was happy to take the backseat and slow his career when hers accelerated, and now she's doing the same for him. She's putting off her ideal retirement, so my dad can achieve his dreams."

She turns her head to look over her shoulder at me. "That's kind of badass. It makes even cynics like me believe in romance." Her attention shifts to the picture of Deception Pass Bridge I've been working on. "His PR team should lead with that story."

"I'll let them know."

Rose smirks like she knows I'm lying. "I think your paintings would make a great focal point for your interview. You don't have to discuss what inspires you or anything personal. Just make it all about facts—like talking about a football play." She turns to look at the next easel. "When did you start painting?"

I shake my head, trying to recall when I first picked up a paintbrush. "When I was seven, maybe? My sister used to get all of these craft kits from our grandparents that she shoved away in her closet. Do you remember the big ice storm that hit when we were kids that closed schools and the city?"

Rose nods, eyes bright with recognition.

"We were bored, and our parents were going nuts. My mom found all the art kits and pulled them out. She said we had to do all of them before we could do anything else. I chose a painting kit because it was the least girly, and the rest is history."

"Were you good at it right away, or was it like football where you had to learn?" She moves to look at the third easel, which is nearly blank except for the outline of some large pine trees in the distance.

"It just sort of clicked. When I look at something, it's like my mind and fingers know how to replicate it. Sometimes I can't sleep because I need to get an image out and onto a canvas, so I can stop imagining it."

"I bet it's difficult to find the time now."

I expel a sigh through my nose. "That's the thing about art, though. It doesn't matter if I'm the best or if I don't pick up a paintbrush for a month. It's still here."

Rose is silent as she stares pensively at the blank canvas. "Why'd you choose to focus on football rather than art?"

"You've heard the term starving artist, right?"

She snickers. "Yeah, but I already found the answer to that. You just have to paint shirtless and create a couple of live-streaming channels, and people will pay to watch you paint and then buy your art."

"Can I draw stick figures and knock out forty paintings every day?"

"You might need to add some dirty talking to your live feed if you'll charge more than fifty bucks."

"If we add that to the table, the price just went up to three hundred."

Rose flashes a smile. "Own it."

I chuckle and place a hand on the small of her back.

She leans against me. "Are they all landscapes?"

I nod. "Landscapes are more forgiving." I guide her to the art rack that houses multiple pieces and takes up a significant portion of the room. I reach for a canvas I painted of the Pacific Ocean last year after we'd done the beach cleanup, another of Brighton after it had snowed.

"They're incredible," she says. "How long do they take you?"

"This one's taken me six months," I tell her, pointing at the bridge.

"Wow. Okay, stick figures it is."

I chuckle, grabbing her waist and leading her back out to the living room. I close the door and the fumes inside. "Are you hungry? I have a vegetable lasagna I thought we could heat up for lunch."

Surprise, or maybe uncertainty, draws her eyebrows up. I understand her reaction. Things have gone fast between us, but there's an ease about being around her that makes it feel natural and normal, so I push through the whisper of hesitance with humor.

"You won't taste the vegetables. I swear."

She smirks. "Promise?" She follows me into the small kitchen, leaving the island between us.

I pull out the glass dish covered in aluminum foil that Stevie left. "When you interview Banks, be sure to ask him to say aluminum."

"Aluminum?"

I nod.

"Why?"

"Trust me; it's worth it."

Her smirk returns. "That implies he won't like the question."

I shake my head. "He's a good guy, and he likes you because Chloe adores you."

"She seems really nice." Rose takes a seat on one of the tall barstools. "Did you make the lasagna?"

"If I told you yes, would you be impressed?"

Her smile travels to her eyes. "Definitely. I prefer savory over sweet. A man who can cook is definitely sexy."

"I'll let Stevie know," I tell her.

She chuckles. "If it's good, I might even leave him my phone number."

"This is the best lasagna in the world," I tell her. "But Stevie's married and has three children and two Pomeranians that he talks about more than his kids."

"I can exchange stories about Juliet."

"Stevie's not a cat person."

Rose gives me her best shocked expression. "And just like that, the affair's over."

While the oven preheats, I assemble a salad.

"How do you think the rumor site found out about Isaiah?" Rose asks.

I've been questioning this all morning. "I have no idea. I mean, his accident wasn't a secret. It was all over the news, and everyone who went to our school knew. That's where I'm guessing it came from, but I don't know where they're getting any of their information. I mean, they have shit from out of state."

"Do you think it's one person behind the site?"

I lift a shoulder as I add tomatoes to the salad. I know Rose likes them. "I have no idea. Cooper said he's not sure."

Rose releases a quiet sigh. "I hope this series helps. Anna thinks it will, but my dad thinks we should leave it alone."

"He wasn't what I expected."

Rose's eyes dance with amusement. "What did you expect?"

I shrug. "Not him."

"He's a lifetime politician—trust me. You have no idea who my dad is because he changes based on his audience at the drop of a hat. No one knows who he is."

"Is that why you don't get along with him? Because you don't feel like you know him?"

Her brow furrows. I've crossed the threshold of information she's comfortable divulging, but for the first time, she's in my house without a busy campus or a restaurant filled with other diners to change the subject. I push against this barrier. "Because you don't feel like you can trust him?"

Rose licks her lips. "Those play a role." Her discomfort is visible as she glances across the kitchen, avoiding my gaze. "My dad will be a great asset to your father's campaign. I don't want you to think that just because I don't get along with him, it means he's incompetent or anything."

My dad showed me some of his old yearbooks and photo albums last weekend, and my mom found a picture of my dad at her parent's wedding. I have a copy of the picture sitting on my bookshelf. The photos led to stories about their time in college together and the many things Rose's dad accomplished. He fought for voter rights and land use cases before interning for a senator and then working for the president and eventually becoming his Chief of Staff. That's where my dad's general information ended until he returned nearly a decade later, and Rose's mom passed away.

Behind me, the oven beeps as it finishes preheating. I tear off the instructions and put the lasagna into the warmed oven.

"I have a few more questions for our interview," Rose says, reaching for her phone. "These aren't as personal." She sets the recorder on the counter. "Let me know when you're ready."

23

ROSE

"Hey, stranger," Amita says, stopping at the printer, which is still next to my desk in the newsroom. "Haven't seen you in a while."

"I'm still making it a habit to avoid this place," I tell her.

Amita laughs. "I don't blame you."

"How are you?" I ask.

She nods. "I'm currently taking advantage of using the printer because I'm out of ink at my apartment. Don't tell Anthony."

I grin. "Your secret's safe with me."

"What are you working on?"

"More of that personal interest series I've been working on," I tell her.

Amita's eyebrows shoot up her forehead. "Really? I thought you were only publishing a single week's worth?"

"I was, but I'm doing this as a...." The word "favor" balances on my tongue, but it feels wrong because while this series might help the football team and save them from more embarrassment and investigations, that isn't my sole intent. "It's my way to try and correct justice in journalism."

"Color me intrigued."

I shrug. "You remember our discussion about the rumor website that's been posting pictures of the football team?"

She nods.

"Rather than spreading lies and inappropriate pictures like some rag, I'm giving readers what they actually want. Truth in journalism. Real stories. Facts rather than a bunch of bullshit."

Amita winces. "Is either portrayal accurate?"

"Attacking people over their sexual preferences and history is gross and offensive unless it was a violation to someone else."

Amita nods. "I understand, and I get that you're passionate about this. I'd just be careful defending them. What if some of these rumors hold more truth than we realize?"

I shake my head. "Several have been blatant lies. This person or *persons* is publishing these rumors in an attempt to maim and embarrass these guys, and that's tabloid bullshit."

"I blame reality TV," she says.

"There's probably truth in that," I tell her, "Anyway, I'm not hanging my hat on these stories. It's the beginning of the year. I'm going to do this series in an attempt to offer another perspective and then return to writing about sports until Anthony gets bored and gives me national news again." I shoot an accusatory glare at his office.

"Well, I hope that happens. I've missed hearing your voice in the paper." Amita parts with a kind smile, returning to her seat on the opposite side of the room.

I try to resume my focus on the article.

Ian and I have been dating for nine full days, and for me, the girl who hated dating, I'm counting each one of them. I'm kind of glad I didn't date anyone else in college because I have no doubt it would have been a waste of my time. These past nine days have redefined so many of my conceptions—ideas that had already started transforming months ago when Arlo started hanging around us. Even before he began dating Olivia, Arlo had started to change my opinions, and I owe him a large piece of my newly found happiness.

Arlo went from being seemingly allergic to relationships to being fully invested in Olivia. I watched it play out firsthand—from the initial sparks of interest to the reciprocation to the progression of their relationship. I had wondered what made him change his mind, and now I'm wondering if romance books aren't lying. Maybe there really is a single person made for each of us.

These nine days have felt significant, not only because it feels so damn good to be making time for someone and to have that reciprocated but Bree has been working with me at the studio, where she's been making suggestions that are helping me far more than I had anticipated. I also made two new offers on some spaces, and the design duo I met has sent me four of my designs, and I love each of them. My cherry on top has been that between the articles and Cooper's expert computer skills or hacking skills or whatever magic he's been doing, have had fewer people discussing and sharing the rumors.

I glance at a copy of the article published last week about Ian. My thoughts stray to memories of last year. Back when he was a random hot guy in the Statistics study group who was quiet and serious, with a stern disposition that made me often think too much about him, to being the hot guy who threw really great parties who I tried to sneak looks at and understand better, to then being the hot guy who turned out to not only have intelligence in spades but a conscience.

Now, he's the hot guy who gives me mind-blowing orgasms and reads over my shoulder when I find an interesting article that catches my attention so he can discuss them with me.

A drink is placed on my desk, startling me from my wandering thoughts. I look up and find Ian smiling at me.

"What are you doing?" I ask.

"Picking you up to take you to the park cleanup."

My jaw falls. "The park cleanup," I cry, placing both hands on my head. "I completely forgot." I scoot my chair back and start gathering things I need to work on tonight and other things I don't trust to leave here with Anthony as my editor.

"We have plenty of time," he says though the clock says we only have fifteen minutes to make it there on time, and it's almost a fifteen-minute drive from here.

"It's okay. Let me just...." I tap the papers on the desk to straighten them and put them in a file that I close and stack on my laptop.

"That's a lot of papers," he says.

I wince. "I know, don't tell Raegan." She's all about saving the planet and living green, and I probably slaughtered a baby tree with all these printouts.

He laughs. "Need me to get anything?"

I swing my bag over my shoulder and grab the coffee he brought me.

"I think I've got it all." I glance back at my desk and catch Amita's gaze. She's watching me with varied interest or accusation, likely because I didn't mention that the series has become increasingly personal. "Have a good afternoon," I tell her.

"Yeah, you too," she says.

Ian holds the door open for me and links our fingers as I step outside.

It's chilly today, officially feeling like autumn. The leaves are beginning to turn shades of yellow, orange, and brown. We don't get the bright red leaves like DC. Brown leaves litter the lawn, which appears more tired with every cool night.

I step closer to Ian, and he drops my hand and wraps his arm around my shoulders as he draws me to a stop. My heart races and my belly expands with butterflies as he leans close. I tip my head back, drunk on the instant hit of lust and desire that he unleashes. He kisses me softly but thoroughly—thoughts of ditching the park and heading back to my apartment tickle my thoughts.

"Once we're done cleaning the park, we should spend Monday afternoons trying all those restaurants with reviews you like," he says.

"That could be fun. Or, we could spend them naked...."

"Plan B, it is," he says.

I chuckle as we continue toward the parking lot, his arm still wrapped around my shoulders.

"Did you look at the rumor site?"

Ian releases a harsh breath. "I hate that I'm following the damn site," he says. "But I also hate the idea of being blindsided again."

Today's rumor included an old photo of Tyler Banks, with the rumor that he'd slept with a married woman in London and had to move to America because of it. I'd texted Chloe when I saw the story to ensure she was okay, and aside from the bitterness behind another rumor, she said it was hilarious and also wrong.

"I feel bad for Banks, but I'm sure as shit relieved it wasn't Pax," Ian says.

"Don't you think it's weird that he hadn't been on the site again? I know people were taking pictures and videos of him."

"I'm just hoping Pax can figure his shit out before he doesn't get to make a choice."

Isaiah.

I hadn't considered the parallel until this moment, and now it feels so significant that it's impossible not to see it.

"His actions remind you of Isaiah's?"

Ian's steps falter, but he quickly resumes his pace. "Probably more than they should. Pax is older and smarter, and he has a good support system. But, I used to think Isaiah was too smart and driven to let anything come between him and his dreams." He shrugs. Disappointment flashes across his face, but his hand tightens around my shoulder.

"What are you doing tonight?" I ask.

"Practice, and then hopefully, seeing you."

I grin. "I just need to work on my articles."

"I can come over, or you can finally stay at my place and overcome your fear of my parents. They know we're dating."

"I'm all about owning my sexual appetite, but I'd prefer they not actively think I'm sleeping with you until we graduate a couple of levels."

"Graduate? Do I get a hat? A ceremony?"

"A naked one," I tell him.

He laughs and leans in, kissing me. "In that case, we had two ceremonies yesterday."

I elbow him, but he catches my arm, always fast and always antic-ipating. We stop at his truck, and he towers close, forcing me to back up against the passenger door.

"Prepare yourself," he says, taking my coffee and setting it inside the bed of the truck.

"Prepare myself?"

"Take a deep breath or count to five or whatever you need to do to hear a truth bomb."

His steel-colored eyes are intense and focused, with not a hint of nerves like the ones I'm currently swimming in. "I spent two months trying to pretend my feelings for you were purely superficial, another month trying to catch your attention, and then two months working to convince you to date me. I didn't kiss you or touch you during that entire process to prove my level of commitment was beyond how attracted I am to you. I spent the summer trying to forget about you, but your memory followed me all through Italy. We can celebrate whatever arbitrary levels, but they won't matter because nothing is going to change—not my feelings or my desire for you—because you're mine, and I've been yours since the first damn day I saw you."

I lean forward and seal my lips over his as my heart explodes in my chest because it's so full. He sweeps his tongue across my lips, and I tilt my head back and accept him with a soft moan as I thread my arms around his shoulders. His warmth and strength feel so safe and comforting that I lose time and sense as the kiss evolves from urgent to languid and then to possessive as we ravish each other.

"The very last thing I want to do is go work at the park," Ian says, placing his forehead on mine, the cadence of his breaths matching my racing heart.

"I know, but I promised Bree I'd be there."

Ian pulls away slowly, a smile teasing his lips. "Tonight, you're mine." He kisses my temple and reaches for the passenger door to open it for me.

I slide into my seat. Ian hands me my coffee, and the words admit-ting I *am* his nearly slip from my lips.

Ian

Luis laughs at his own joke, which has Logan turning to look at me with an expression that holds too much sarcasm for his age. He flips his red hat around, grabs his rake, and spreads the mulch we've been dumping by the wheelbarrow around the park.

"I saw your game Saturday," he tells me.

I stop raking and stretch my back. "Yeah? Any tips?"

"How do you find the open lanes so fast?" he asks.

"Lots of players have tells. There's a lot that goes into the game besides just training. You have to make sure you know your own team's plays backward and forward, but you also have to learn your competition's. Studying your opponent and getting inside their heads is crucial."

"Why'd you choose to be a linebacker? Why not a quarterback or a receiver?"

I grin. "Because I'm tougher than them."

Logan doesn't laugh at my joke. Instead, he looks at me like I'm wearing on his patience.

I start moving the mulch again with my rake. "I was afraid of getting hit," I tell him. "When I started, I wanted to play safety and stay as far away from the action as possible. Then, I started to learn more and more and realized I was pretty good at anticipating and reading the field. I'd be running upfield to sack someone, which was fine when I was fourteen, and the game was determined by athleticism alone, but as I got older, it made holes on the field, and my coach suggested I try linebacker. I wasn't afraid of getting hit anymore by that time, but I still preferred playing defense. It works to my strengths and is where I enjoy being on the field."

"My dad says you move like a running back."

"I'm not as big as other linebackers, so I have to use speed to my advantage."

"Do you think you could show me sometime?"

I glance across the park to where Rose is with Bree, spreading mulch under the new equipment.

"Yeah, I would make time to do that."

Logan turns to look over his shoulder. "You sure stare at her a lot for not liking her."

I grin. "I never said I don't like her."

"Are you going to tell her or wait for her to file a restraining order?"

Luis dumps another load of mulch. "Catch up. She's his lady."

"That gives me more reason to be a linebacker," Logan says.

I nod. "It's the best motivation I can offer."

24

ROSE

I an moans my name as I explore his body, curious to find a single imperfection, though I know I won't. My fingers brush over the defined cut between his abs and thighs, and his breath catches, causing his cock to twitch against me, and I grin. Being wanted by Ian makes me feel sexier than anything I could have imagined and shockingly self-conscious in equal measure. He slants his mouth over mine, his tongue demanding and slow, causing the ache between my legs to intensify.

I wrap my hand around his length, surprised once again by his size, and he responds by tracing over my opening with his fingers. I moan, or maybe he does, as his fingers press against me with a delectable pressure that sends waves of pleasure through my body. I tighten my fingers around his cock, sliding my hand up and down. Our clothes were discarded as soon as we got home from breakfast, where I found a contender for the title of best mocha in the city. I'm starting to love Tuesdays because neither of us has a morning class, allowing us a few hours to hide from the world and responsibilities.

Ian's phone rings, and I shake my head as I continue kissing him, refusing to share my time. The moment it stops, it starts again.

"No," I whisper. "Ignore it." I kiss him as I stroke his impressive length again.

Ian nods as he kisses me, but another call chases the second.

My first thought is Olivia. She left this morning for a class. Maybe something happened? Before the fear can fully form, my doorbell rings.

I pull away, a cold wave of dread washing over my skin. I look at Ian, and the fears are no longer a trickle. Instead, they're a flood as we both reach for our clothes.

Ian grabs his phone as I pull on a pair of yoga pants and a tank top that was thrown over my desk chair.

I cross the apartment with my heart in my throat. I make a quick glance for Juliet and pull the door open without looking through the eyehole.

Anna is on our doorstep, her hair pulled up into a messy ponytail, wearing a hoodie and sweatpants. Each detail is more concerning than the last—Anna is not a ponytail girl. "What happened?" I ask. "Is it Dad? Is he okay?"

Anna steps inside and closes the door before facing me. "You haven't seen it?"

"Seen what?"

She scrubs her hands over her face. "We have a problem."

"Okay...."

Ian's footsteps draw my attention. He comes toward us, his jaw hard planes of undiluted anger.

"What's going on?" I ask, looking from him to Anna and back again.

"They went after you," Ian says.

"*They?* Who's they?"

"The site. The stupid, fucking rumor site." He draws in a long breath through his nose. "They're going after you because you helped us."

"It doesn't matter," I say. "I don't care what they say about me."

Anna closes her eyes and flinches like my words are painful to hear. "You shouldn't," she says. "You shouldn't give a damn what they're saying." Her chin shakes, and her eyes shimmer with tears that knot my stomach. "But you should be prepared." She pulls out her phone, and I take it before she can unlock it and enter her code.

The site is already pulled up. I stare at my reflection, my face and hair wet, my head angled back, and my mouth open. I remember the bitter, warm beer that had been tossed on me seconds before by Paxton's date. *"Rumor has it, Rose Cartwright is the team's favorite fan for blowjobs."*

Rather than a single image, I have to scroll to see the multiple pictures of me plastered across the site, all from that night. A picture with Paxton that, from the angle it was taken, makes it look like he's touching my breast—another one of my wet shirt and exposed bra, another of me drinking. One picture shows me climbing into the backseat with Hoyt's hand on my arm. Another of me with Bobby, the same night, same shirt, same awful innuendo but this time, I'm looking straight at the camera and smiling along with Bobby like we're posing. Next is a girl on her knees in front of a guy. Another is of a girl with similar dark hair leaning back as a guy touches her breast.

"These aren't even me," I tell them once I scroll to the end.

"It won't matter," Anna says.

I don't know what I expected—if this is better or worse than I'd feared.

"So stupid," I mutter. "Who cares? This isn't the audience they've been building. No one's going to care."

"You know they're going to care," Anna says.

I shrug. "Let them. I'm not going to lower myself to their level." I shake my head. "You're used to big scandals. This is nothing," I assure Anna. "This site has been up for over a month, and they were starting to lose steam. A few people will probably talk, but I'm not worried about it."

Anna looks at Ian like she's hoping he understands her concerns.

"It's on social media," he says. "That was Arlo calling. He said he saw it being posted and flagged it. He called Cooper first to get him working on the site, but if people are already sharing it...."

"It's okay," I say before either of them can say anything else. "It will blow over by lunch." I glance at the clock above the stove. "I have to get ready for my class. I'm sure everything is going to be fine. People always feel way braver on the other side of a keyboard than they do in person."

"You should stay home," Anna says.

"I'm not staying home over this. It will be fine. I'll be fine."

"Rose, if it's on social media, it's not contained. Cooper can't crash the big social media sites or remove posts or tweets."

I shake my head. "You're overreacting. You're used to the entire country wanting to hear gossip. This is just Brighton."

"Just give me one day to get a pulse on things," she says. "I can have my team on this and better understand what we're working against."

"But then they win. These are lies. All of them." I hand Anna her phone.

"Rose, give me one day. Hang out. Order pizza and binge-watch TV."

"I'm not hiding from this."

She releases a frustrated breath. "Why can't you just listen?"

"Because if I stay home, then it means I'm ashamed, and I refuse to lie down and be ashamed over these lies."

Anna presses her lips together. I know she agrees with me and would be going if our roles were reversed. "If you need anything today, call me. I'll keep my phone on me at all times."

"I'll let you know if I get to punch anyone."

She doesn't smile. "Bye, Ian." She gives him a meaningful look that makes me want to roll my eyes.

Ian nods and turns to me as the door closes. "I don't like this."

"I should have seen it coming," I say.

"Are you sure you want to go? I can skip with you."

"No, you can't. You fly out tomorrow morning, and next week, you fly out on Friday. You need to go to class."

He rakes his hand through his hair. "Don't take this on alone. If someone says or does anything, let me know."

I kiss him, but his lips are hard and cold and lack the same passion from earlier.

I PARK on campus and reach for my phone. I didn't have the guts to turn it on while I was still with Ian, knowing that because the site shared my phone number just like they have everyone else's, it's featured, I'd likely have a dozen messages and dick pics.

I power it on and try to think of the worst-case scenarios so my brain can plan accordingly because life has taught me to always prepare for the worst and hope for the best.

> You're a filthy whore.

> I hope you die.

> You're disgusting. I can't believe they'll touch you.

> You're so ugly.

> Die bitch.

Dick pic.

> I hope you kill yourself.

My breath catches, and my face warms. There aren't dozens—but *hundreds* of messages, and rather than finding an array of inappropriate pictures, I skim over threats, names, and angry messages that blaze and brand my thoughts.

Are these people my classmates? Have I met any of them?

I hate considering Anna's advice and ditching. I don't want these lies to make me feel inferior, yet the hurt is already beginning to engulf me.

My phone rings in my hand, startling me from thoughts of hiding out with takeout in my apartment. I glance at the screen and am relieved to see it's Olivia.

"Hey," I answer.

"Where are you?"

"I just got to campus."

She's silent for a minute. "Did you see the rumor site is back up?"

"Posting some of my finest angles. That bra might deserve an award. I didn't realize my cleavage looked *that* good."

"I hate them," she tells me. "I hate them so much."

"Don't waste your energy on hating them. It's like frowning, it takes more muscles than smiling and gives worse wrinkles, and it does that to our souls as well. They're bottom feeders. They don't deserve our thoughts or attention, much less our wrinkles," I say, my bravado finally finding a stepping stone because I believe this. I truly believe they don't deserve my attention or anyone else's.

"They're vile," she says. "I don't have another class for a few hours. We could go get some coffee or a—"

"I have class."

"Which one?"

"Business Analytics."

"Which building?"

"You aren't coming."

"I was just going to sit in and do some homework."

I grin. "I appreciate the offer, but I don't need a bodyguard."

"That's good because while this may come as a surprise, I'm pretty sure I'd lose in a fight to a ten-year-old."

I chuckle. "It's okay. I'm sure most of this is hot air, and like I told Anna, everyone always feels braver and bolder on the other side of their phone or computer."

"Technology definitely makes everyone feel entitled to act like an asshole. But, good news, you're close, and I have a coupon for smoothies. So I'll see you in five."

"Olivia," I object, but she's already hung up.

My phone vibrates with more alerts. More hateful messages.

I silence it and shove it into my bag, recalling how Ian had to get a new number when he was featured on the rumor site.

My body is stiff from nerves as I grab my bag and push open my car door. My vision of "worst" is changing by the second as the messages I'd seen replay in my head.

I'm not a stranger to rumors. While my mom was in the hospital, rumors about me and my family filled the hallways, many of them wrong, several of them cruel. Even during my three years at Brighton, rumors have swirled about me, assumptions about how many guys I've slept with and who I've slept with have been whispered behind my back, marking with me with a scarlet letter that I've primarily ignored by keeping to my small circles of friends.

I cross the road and follow the winding sidewalk with my eyes forward, not daring to look at those I pass.

"I was closer than I thought," Olivia says, smiling triumphantly. She lifts two smoothies, one orange and one pink. "Mango orange or triple berry?"

I accept the orange one. "You know you don't have to go to class with me."

Olivia lifts her brow. "Just like you didn't have to be there to meet Ellen with me," she says, referring to her biological mom. "Just like you didn't have to be there for every fight with my dad, every long conversation about my past and exes and bad days and worse nights. You're my best friend, Rose, and I would be a shitty friend if I weren't here. Ride or die, sink or swim, fly or crash—I will always be at your side."

I reach my free arm around Olivia, pulling her into a tight hug that she reciprocates with a fierceness I feel in my bones and heart and all the way to my soul. There is no doubt that Olivia has been the angel on my shoulder for the past several years.

"Let's get to class," she says with a wink as she pulls back.

I follow her as my heart beats a nervous rhythm.

"I saw an ad for some really cute boots," Olivia says. "We might have to do some shopping this weekend." She takes a drink of her smoothie. "Or we could binge-watch the entire Harry Potter series.

I'm talking all eight movies, with no breaks except a short nap. We'll order all our favorite takeout, so we don't have to get up to cook or clean."

"I don't want to hide from this," I tell her.

As soon as my words leave me, Olivia's phone rings. She silences it. "No one said anything about hiding. We won't be hiding. We'll be telling them we don't care enough to even respond." Her attention turns to her phone, and her steps slow as she reads the messages until she stops, shaking her head in short jerks. "No."

"What?"

Her blue eyes meet mine, sympathy lowering her brow. "They've made more posts."

"About me?"

She swallows. "Yeah."

I blow out a long breath. "Slut-shaming is officially in season."

Olivia's gaze darts to the side as a couple of people pass us. "You're sure you don't want to leave? No one will judge you or think less of you if you want to go home."

"If I go home, I'll just have more time to overthink everything. I need to be here."

Her eyes hold a dozen arguments, but she nods. "Hold your chin high. It makes the assholes uncomfortable."

"I should have worn a mini skirt."

She grins. "We'll save that for tomorrow."

We enter the classroom, and my imagination taunts me with each step. I feel the eyes of my classmates, and it makes me paranoid, questioning if they're staring at me, judging me, or simply glancing in my direction to buy time as the start of class counts down.

Someone coughs. "Skank," they say, coughing again.

"That was original," I say, passing him and continuing to an empty aisle. I sink into a seat, and Olivia sits beside me, her phone out, but her eyes are on me.

"I bet if we save pictures of everyone who acts like an asshole, Cooper could think of a creative way to get some revenge."

I take a sip of my smoothie so I don't fall into the puddle of self-pity that continues to grow wider and deeper with each passing minute.

A few rows in front of us, a guy glances at me. "Hey, I'm friends with the football team. Since I'm associated with the team, why don't you come suck me off?" He sticks a pen in his mouth and makes a show of releasing his belt.

A section of the room falls silent. Others snicker. I don't look to see who's reacting. My gaze is trained on the guy who's hopped onto the bandwagon, humor dancing in his eyes as he looks at me like I'm somehow less than him.

"You're disgusting," Olivia snaps at him. "Sit down and shut up because those friends you claim to have will rip out your intestines if you say another word."

He starts to respond, but our professor steps into the classroom.

"I'll take a rain check, but I'm only good for the BJ. Loose chicks aren't really my thing," he says, loud enough to dare the professor to say something.

He doesn't.

Asshole.

The class crawls by, and no matter how hard I try to fight the feeling of isolation, it surrounds me. When we're dismissed, Olivia grips my hand in hers like she can feel me withdrawing.

"Hey," Arlo says as we step outside.

"Whore," a girl mutters at my back.

"What did you say?" Olivia asks, her shoulders back, voice raised.

"Do I still need to be tested if I double-bag it?" The guy from class stops beside me.

Before I can react, Arlo shoves him with both hands, making the guy stumble several feet. "Get the fuck out of here," Arlo warns, following him several steps before circling back to us.

"You can't do that," I hiss as I place a hand on his back and push him toward the grass. "You just got back onto the field. If you get caught fighting again, you'll be benched."

"Over my dead body," Olivia says. "If my dad tries to bench him for standing up for you, there will be hell to pay."

I reach for my phone to see the new rumors so I can prepare myself. I ignore the multitude of messages, missed calls, and social media alerts and open the rumor site. My rules—my old rules—are posted over a picture of Ian and me making out in the parking lot yesterday. Below it is another picture of me from last year, drinking at a party. *"Rumor has it, Rose Cartwright has had over four-hundred sexual partners."*

"Cooper's doing everything he can to get this down," Arlo tells me.

"It's too late," I tell him. "It's already out."

Arlo shakes his head. "It will be a rough couple of days, but then they'll forget." It's the same hopeful sentiment I'd told Anna.

"Yeah," I say, though I know he's wrong.

25

IAN

I check my messages to see if Arlo caught up with Rose. The team is currently all-hands-on-deck. I know Rose wants to pretend like nothing has changed, but if assholes are willing to mutter comments under their breath and share shit about the team and me, I know the gloves will be off with her.

> Arlo: This is going to be ugly.

I have no doubt Anna is already looking into every legal avenue to get the site taken down. Her determination and concern were evident this morning.

I glance down to see another message.

> Paxton: Where are you?

> Me: About to get out of class. I'm going to meet Rose.

> Paxton: Is she alone?

I scoff

Me: Arlo's with her.

Paxton: We need to talk.

Me: I don't have time today.

Paxton: Five minutes. I'll walk with you to where you're meeting Rose.

I tell him the building I'm in and slide my things into my bag. I haven't managed to pay attention to a single word that's been said and don't have the patience to try any longer. I quietly exit the class and wait the ten minutes it takes for Paxton to arrive.

There's tension between us that neither of us has attempted to address since he woke up and heard my reasons for benching him. It keeps him from standing too close and his gaze downcast.

"I talked to Luis," he says. "I had no idea about your friend Isaiah."

Fucking Luis.

"I know we've got some shit to work through," I tell him. "But I don't have time for this right now. Rose is getting hung out to dry because she helped us."

Paxton nods. "I know," he says. "And it's bullshit. We can do rounds. Make sure someone is with her at all times, so if anyone tries to say anything, we'll be there."

"We already arranged it," I tell him. "Have you looked at your accounts? Have you seen what they're calling her? What they're saying about her?"

His jaw tightens, and he takes a step closer to me. "I fucked up. Those pictures of Rose are my fault." He shakes his head. "And I fucked up with you. I wasn't going to drive, but I understand why you have your concerns."

"Do you think my friend got behind the wheel intending to kill himself and someone else in the process?" I ask. "You can't tell me or anyone what you planned to do while you were fucked up because you don't know. You puked on the grass and then took a goddamn nap in the front yard." I shake my head. "You can have the best of intentions, but the truth of it is that you have no fucking idea what would have happened if Rose didn't call me, and I stand behind what I said because I care more about you being alive and safe than I do about football. I would risk my future to ensure yours."

Pax hugs me. Like Arlo, he doesn't shy away from affection, but right now, every muscle in my body is tense, and it's difficult to accept this moment of understanding between us as another storm brews overhead.

"Cooper's working his ass off to get the site down," Pax assures me.

I nod. "There will be residual effects, though," I tell him. "The rumor mill is working in full force."

"Let the team help. Rae's rallying the girls; they're also ready to help. We'll support her in every way we can. I'm going to talk to my dad and Coach Harris and see if we can get the university to step in. They've been handling this with kid gloves because I think they're enjoying the damn attention it's brought, but going after someone who isn't on the team has to be too low of a blow for even them."

"Let me know what you hear."

He nods. "I know it's too little, too late, but for what it's worth, I'm sorry. I want to be the best quarterback. I want to be the captain the team deserves, and the friend you guys deserve. I will do everything in my power to squash this."

I offer my hand, and he accepts it. "I just want you to focus on overcoming these demons. I know you were dealt with more than your fair share of shit over the past year, but I'm here for you."

Paxton's grip tightens. "Go find your girl. I'll let you know what I find out." He releases my hand.

I nod, turning toward where I know Arlo, Olivia, and Rose are. It takes me ten minutes to find where they're sitting under a white oak tree.

Rose's gaze climbs to meet mine, and she smiles, but I recognize its fictitious qualities. I drop my bag and sit beside her, my hand on her leg.

"Your class isn't over yet," she says.

I kiss the side of her head and thread my arm around her shoulders. She moves to lean against me rather than the hard trunk of the tree. "I shouldn't have left you."

"Yes, you should've. You guys can't babysit me."

"We're not protecting you," Arlo says. "We're protecting the assholes from your mad guns. I've seen you balance on your head and one hand. These fools don't know how tough you are."

Olivia rolls her eyes. "And because we love and care about you, and we don't want you to face this alone."

"I need to change my phone number," Rose says.

I nod. "Let's go. We can do it now."

Olivia is the first to climb to her feet. "Afterward, we can go to the old theater by Arlo's work. Catch a double feature. And they just opened a new ramen place next door."

"I'd argue, but you guys are acing this business of ignoring me." Rose leans forward and stands.

At the store, we wait for her number to be changed, and then Olivia convinces Rose to remove all social media before we fill the middle seat of the old theater I didn't know about. The chairs are uncomfortable, and the cushions are worn, but we ignore those details with popcorn laden with so much butter and salt that my lips burn after the first handful.

Rose sits beside me, but she's quiet, lost in her thoughts.

My phone vibrates against my leg. It's a text from Cooper telling me news I don't want.

I turn to Rose, hating that I can't fix this. "Cooper was able to crash their site, but they got it back up, and they're posting more pictures and bullshit rumors, and he's afraid he's making it worse."

Rose looks at me, resignation dulling her green eyes. "Tell him thanks, but to stop."

"Cooper's smart. I'm sure he can get it."

She shakes her head. "It will only cause worse repercussions for the rest of you." She reaches for a piece of popcorn and places it in her mouth, turning her attention to the trivia playing on the screen.

I'm hoping Paxton's managed to do something and that Anna is plotting something bigger. I consider our flight tomorrow that has us leaving in the morning and not returning until Sunday afternoon. It's against Arizona, one of our biggest rivals, yet the idea of getting onto a plane or stepping onto the field makes me recoil.

Rose looks at me as I shift, moving my knees as restlessness runs through me. She reaches across the armrest that doesn't lift and sets her hand on mine. "You're overthinking it," she says. "There's nothing we can do to stop it. It's been done, and I'm fine—I'm going to be fine. These people who care about the site and the rumors aren't my friends. I don't even know them. Let them think whatever in the hell they want to."

I swallow the need to argue with her.

"I'd rather just pretend it doesn't exist," she says.

I can't ignore the site, though, or the damage it's doing because everything about her pulls my attention, and this site berating her feels like a personal assault.

Her fingers slip between mine, reminding me of how perfectly she fits with me in every way, down to our hands. "I'm going to stay back," I tell her.

"Stay back?"

"This weekend, I'm going to stay with you."

She shakes her head. "You can't. You have a game in Arizona, and your team needs you."

I want to point out that she needs me more and is more important, but I choose to avoid that argument. "They're going early to recruit. I won't be back until Sunday."

Rose is silent as her gaze travels between mine. "I appreciate the sacrifice, but Ian, I don't want you to pay that price. If it's bad tomorrow, I'll just go home. Besides, if you don't go, I won't be able to write you into my article, and I don't know if you've missed this, but I've been leaving Easter eggs and putting you in every article I've written over the past two weeks." Her smile is genuine, but so is my reluctance.

If she notices, she doesn't say anything, turning her attention back to the movie.

ANNA MEETS us outside Rose and Olivia's apartment when we get home from the movies and dinner. "You disconnected your number?"

"I had to," Rose admits. "They posted my phone number."

Anna shakes her head. "How do I not have a key to your apartment? My hands are freezing. I almost considered breaking a window."

"No, you didn't," Rose says, moving around her to unlock the door.

"I might have," Anna responds.

Rose opens the door slowly, checking for their cat before opening it wider for all of us to come inside.

"Hey, Anna," Olivia says. "How are you? Have you met Arlo?" she points at him.

Anna smiles, but it's far from friendly or welcoming. She's clearly here for a purpose. "I think so. At the lake, maybe?"

Arlo nods. "Nice to see you again."

Anna nods and turns her back to Rose. "We need to talk."

Rose toes off her shoes and hangs her purse. "Should I dig in the freezer for the whiskey?"

I expect Anna to reply tritely, but instead, she shrugs. "It's not the worst idea."

I place a hand on Rose's back, drawing Anna's attention. "I'm sorry, Ian, I need to speak with her alone," she says.

"You mind giving me a ride?" Arlo asks. "I need to head to my house and pack."

Anna nods. "That's a good idea," she says, ensuring me that it's the very opposite.

I look at Rose, who offers a playful smirk. "I'll call you," she says, leaning forward. She presses a chaste kiss to my mouth.

Arlo grips my shoulder and opens the door before glancing back at Olivia and ushering me outside.

"This feels like a bad idea," I tell him.

Arlo leads the way to my truck. "Liv's in there. She won't let anything crazy happen."

"You don't think Anna will suggest Rose transfer schools or something insane, right?"

Arlo pulls his head back, the idea surprising him. "No. Definitely not. And if that *is* her suggestion, you know Liv will sink that idea quick."

"Am I blowing this out of proportion?" I ask as we get into the truck. "Because it feels like there's a second shoe waiting to drop."

"I don't know," he tells me. "I wish we had a better understanding of what in the hell this person is even doing. Maybe if we knew their motive, we could figure out why they were going after Rose."

"I'm sure it's revenge," I say. "She's been publishing articles promoting us for the past week and a half."

Arlo shakes his head. "I just hope Coop's able to figure out who this fuckhead is."

I drop Arlo off at his house and decline his offer to go inside. Instead, I head home and busy myself with packing.

It's hours before I hear from Rose. It's a single message.

> Rose: I'm really sorry, but I'm exhausted after today. I hope you have a good trip and enjoy beating Arizona ;) We'll talk when you get home.

> Me: How was your meeting with Anna? Everything okay?

She doesn't reply.

I have half a mind to go by Rose's and make sure everything's okay but hear Arlo's assurances.

My mind is increasingly restless as the hours tick by with no response from Rose.

26

ROSE

I scroll through social media, reading comment after comment of people insulting my name, clothes, hair, teeth, and body— every aspect of my appearance and beyond as people claim they know me and how fake and superficial I am. I click on a few of the people who are posting so I can look through their profiles to see if I recall having met them, but after falling down that rabbit hole a dozen times and realizing I don't know any of them, I've stuck to reading the messages filled with hate and judgment.

I don't know why I'm reading them. It's as though I can't stop like, for some reason, these people I don't know—have never even met— opinions of me matter and somehow influence my self-worth.

I hate it.

And the angrier I become, the more I try to understand why they're wasting their time and energy to throw shade, and then I get stuck in this ugly cycle.

I flip back to the site, slowly skimming over the pictures of me again as I hear the judgment of a few hundred strangers. I stop at the picture of me with Bobby, trying to remember the night and the particular moment captured.

Who had I smiled at?

Why does this feel familiar?

A knock on my bedroom door has me setting my phone down. Olivia opens the door before I can respond, and she doesn't wait for an invite before climbing into bed with me. "You're on the wrong side of your bed."

I don't tell her I'm on this side because it's where Ian's been sleeping, and the sheets still smell deliciously like him.

"Are you hungry?" she asks.

I shake my head.

Olivia tucks her arms around me. "Are you going to tell me what Anna said?"

I shake my head again, my breaths struggling to remain whole.

Her grip around me tightens.

We lie still, neither of us talking for what feels like hours. Both of us have classes, but neither of us mentions the fact.

Eventually, Olivia sits up. "I'll be right back."

Within moments she returns with our leftover ramen reheated. I'm not hungry, and comments so many have made about the size of my thighs and waist only make the food less appealing. I set the bowl on my nightstand. "You should go to class."

Olivia doesn't respond. Instead, she reaches for the remote and turns on the first Harry Potter movie, and then she gets into bed beside me and eats her ramen.

We finish the first two movies before the sun begins to set. "What sounds better, Chinese or pizza?" Olivia asks.

"I'm not hungry," I tell her.

"I know, but you need to eat something."

"You pick."

Olivia turns her attention to Juliet, who has spread across the foot of my bed. "Do you want to go and pick it up? Maybe it will feel good to move around a little."

"I'm not done making a dent in my bed."

"Rose, talk to me." She moves, setting her hand on my knee. "Tell me what's going through your head, so I can help you battle these dragons. Are you worried other people will be as rude and inappropriate as that giant douchebag yesterday?"

"I just need to veg," I tell her. "I'm fine. I'll be fine." I sit up to lean against my headboard. "Let's order Chinese food."

"Lo mein?"

I nod. "Sounds great."

Olivia places the order as I sink back into bed, curling into the blankets and searching for another breath of Ian.

We spend the night eating Chinese food that I mostly move around my plate until I finally give up on it and watching the third Harry Potter movie. We only pause it for a few brief minutes when Arlo calls, and Olivia steps into the living room. Aside from that, we continue to ignore the world.

WHEN MORNING ARRIVES, I shower and search through my closet, debating if it would be better to dress scandalously or conservatively before deciding on jeans and a red top I select because it matches the scarlet letter that's been pinned to my back.

"You look nice," Olivia says between bites of her cereal.

"Thanks."

"Ian texted me," she says.

I start to fix my coffee in a commuter cup.

"He mentioned you haven't called or texted and wanted to make sure everything was okay."

I nod. "I just need a little time."

"From Ian?"

"No," I say. "From my thoughts. You know me. I just need to be around others to help drown out all the white noise."

Her gaze is watchful and patient as she searches over each of my features, likely seeing more than I'd like her to. "Should I tell him you'll call him later?"

"I'm sure he's busy. I know they're recruiting."

"The coaches do that," she says.

I nod as though her words align with my point. "I'll see you later."

"Wait. I'm going with you."

I glance over my shoulder. "No. I'll be fine. I need to get to the newspaper, and the only person who might say anything to me in there is Anthony, and if he does, I've owed him a punch in the nose for several weeks. I'll text you."

"Rose...."

I don't hear the rest of her objection. I hurry out to my car, reassured that she can't follow me to school since she's still in her pajamas.

I park as close to the newspaper as possible. It's early, and I'm hoping it will be buzzing with people who are too busy to notice me. I could go to the library or a coffee shop, but paranoia has led me here, finding comfort in knowing everyone who works on the paper well enough that I'll have no problem laying out if they dare to mention the rumors or the site.

I'm wrong, of course.

It's a freaking ghost town. There are only three people here—two are editors seated in the back, headphones on, noses in their work, and the third is Amita. Her shoulders bounce with surprise as she looks up from her laptop at me.

"Hey," she says, leaning back in her chair. "Sorry." She shakes her head. "You startled me. Apparently, I've discovered my caffeine limit is four cups before eight."

"Four?" I ask, making my way to my desk. "How have you been up long enough to have had four cups of coffee?"

She cracks a smile. "I'm trying to balance too much. I'm sure you know that theme song. You're here early."

I take a drink of my coffee and set it down before reaching for my laptop. "Yeah, I need to tweak an article and submit it to Anthony."

"You've already completed Monday's article?"

I nod. "I have another set in the series I've been doing on the football team."

She cocks her head to one side. "Really?"

"You seem surprised."

"Well, I saw the site yesterday," she says. "I thought after what they wrote about you and your ... *relationship* with the team."

I pull my chin back like I've been slapped. Only I feel the burn far past my skin. I want to defend myself and tell her that I wasn't—that I'm not sleeping with the team, and yet, telling her that only feels like I'm condemning the actions I've been accused of and condoning that slut-shaming is okay under certain circumstances, which it's not.

"Right," I say. "My *relationship* with the team." I slowly draw in a breath. "I don't see why the rumors about me would change what I publish. If anything, it only confirms that these stories need to be written."

I take another drink of coffee and focus on my screen. Stubbornness or maybe fear keeps me glued to my seat. If someone like Amita believes the rumors are true, will everyone? What about the other girls who date guys on the team? Alexis, Vanessa, Chloe, and even Raegan don't know me very well. What if they think I've slept with their boyfriends? It's not as though I have the shiniest reputation.

A wave of heat rolls over me, making my face and body burn. My palms are sweaty, and so is my hairline. The room spins, and my heart is racing so fast, and hard I feel it pound in my fingertips and hear it in my ears. I try to take a breath, but it feels like a car is parked on my chest.

I grab the collar of my shirt and pull it away from my neck though there is a several-inch gap already there. The sensation is overwhelming and reminds me of those months, years ago when my mom was sick, and it felt like life was shoving me down a path I didn't want to be on.

A panic attack.

That's what my therapist had labeled these feelings that used to make me certain I was having a heart attack.

Relax.

Breathe.

I recall the coaching techniques I'd been taught, the ones my therapist began each session with. I start with my feet, relaxing the muscles and climbing to my calves and thighs, my abs and back, my shoulders and arms, all the way to my neck as I take measured breaths. I still don't feel well, but my heart is marginally slower.

I lift my hands and see the discoloration on the desk from the sweat on my palms, and the panic begins a new drum rhythm in my chest. I'm being treated like a pariah because I forgot my rules and looking for the next best time. Everything about these past several months has been uncomfortable and forced, and this only confirms I'm not the girl I've been trying to be. I'm not the pearl-clutching type that guys want to introduce to their parents, or that volunteers to clean parks, or is a role model for kids.

Pop-up clubs, nameless faces, pushing boundaries, freedom —that's me.

I close my laptop, shove my things into my bag, and push my chair back too far. I leave it and head for the door. On the way to my car, I make eye contact with every person I pass, a suggestive smile on my lips.

I peel out of the parking lot, driving too fast and aggressively. I don't know where I'm going until I pull into Chantay's driveway.

I ring the doorbell five times in quick succession, my nerves crawling, itching for a bad decision.

Chantay pulls open the door, squinting. "Rose? What in the hell are you doing?"

"Tell me you have some pot."

She takes a step back, opening the door a bit wider. "It's about damn time. God, where have you been?"

Behind her, a guy in jeans appears, long hair mussed from sleep and things that weren't happening while they slept. "Oh, shit. Sorry," he says, looking from Chantay to me.

"Don't apologize on my behalf," I tell him.

Chantay laughs. "I think your shirt's on the closet door handle."

"Cool," he says. His gaze travels over me, curiosity brightening his gaze. "Do I know you?"

"Nope." I pop the "p" and make myself comfortable on the couch.

Chantay giggles again. "Well, you might."

An hour ago, her words might have felt like a dig, but right now, I don't even care.

The stranger turns toward the hallway that leads to her bedroom while Chantay grabs the tin she stores her weed in. She prepares everything and then hands me a bong and a Zippo.

My thumb slips on my first pull, and Chantay's gaze becomes more critical. It's been a couple of years since I've smoked, and I'm sure she will cackle if I cough and gasp.

I steady myself and flick the lighter. I take a long pull and let the heat sit in my mouth as I close my eyes. I slowly blow the smoke out, light it again, and take another drag. This one makes me cough until my eyes water.

God, it stinks.

I'd forgotten how bad it smells.

Chantay grins. "I'll be right back. I've got the best snacks for this." She disappears into the kitchen and returns with several bags of chips and some gummy bears that she dumps on the couch beside me and then takes the bong and lighter and sits cross-legged on the other side of the couch and lights up. "Oh, yeah," she says, leaning her head back.

The guy exits her room and looks between us. "Can I join you?"

"No," I say before Chantay can respond.

He raises his eyebrows and blinks a couple of times.

"You knew the rules," Chantay tells him as she opens a bag of sour cream and onion chips that make my mouth water.

He looks confused but doesn't object as he makes his way to the door and leaves us in our snack heaven and TV.

"I'm convinced," I tell Chantay, reaching for another chip. "Aliens exist. They have to. It's the only thing that makes sense." My fingers brush the bottom of the bag. "Shit. Where did the chips go?"

Chantay giggles. "We ate them."

"All of them?"

She nods.

I groan. "Those were really good."

"We should go out," she says.

"It's Thursday."

"I wasn't talking about another lame-ass party. I'm over college parties. It's all freshmen acting like a bunch of morons. Let's go to a club or a bar."

"What time is it?"

"I don't know. Nighttime," she says, lifting the curtain behind her. Are you in, or are you going to give me another lame-ass excuse?"

"Let's do it. I just need to get a ride so I can go home and change."

She shakes her head. "My closet is your closet."

We scramble from the couch like we're suddenly under a timer and head into the large walk-in closet in her room. "This one," she says, shoving a hanger at me.

I don't question her. I simply peel off my clothes and slip the cool, black, slinky fabric over my head. It hugs me tight and ends at the top of my thighs. I unhook my bra and toss it to the floor with the rest of my clothes.

"Yes!" she cries. "I'd do you." She shoves a pair of black pumps at me.

"Are these mine?" I ask.

She laughs. "You left them here. I have a corner filled with your shit." She points to a messy pile of clothing.

"That's Olivia's," I say, grabbing the yellow purse.

Chantay rolls her eyes. "Has she been praying every night that it would be found?"

"Why do you have to do that?"

"What?"

"Be rude. Olivia's my friend."

"She makes you boring."

"You're wrong."

Chantay stops. "I'm sorry. You like Olivia, and that's your business. Let's not let this ruin our night. Let's go out and have fun."

I silence my objections with a firm nod. "Let's go." I grab the pile of my things and the clothes I switched out of. "I'm going to put these in my car so I don't forget them again."

When I come back inside, I find Chantay straightening her hair. I pull my makeup bag out of my purse and touch up my eyeliner. Next, I add a heavy hand of dark eyeshadow.

I study my reflection, the heavy makeup, and skimpy dress. In some ways, they feel like my true self, and in another, they feel like a costume.

"A Lyft is on its way," Chantay says, handing me a shot glass. "And Isla is going to meet us at Anarchy and Stilettos. It's ladies' night, and she said it's packed on Thursdays."

I take a final glimpse of myself and then toss the shot back, feeling the sting of the alcohol in my throat as it burns all my reservations.

Chantay cheers and takes my hand, pulling me back out to the living room, where we only have to wait a few minutes before the car arrives.

The club has a line that stretches outside the doors and around the building—all guys. Women are being allowed in first and without a cover charge. The guy at the door stamps our hands, and we head inside, where the darkness, quick tempo, and grinding bodies create the landscape of anonymity.

"Isla's at the bar, waiting for us."

I follow Chantay through the crowd, feeding off the attention of hungry and appreciative gazes.

Isla greets us with a knowing grin. "So many hot guys tonight," she says, passing filled shot glasses to Chantay and me. I'm still feeling a bit light-headed from the drink at Chantay's.

"I'm good."

"What?" Chantay cries.

"It's one shot," Isla says.

"We just had one at her house." I point at Chantay.

Chantay throws back her head dramatically, and Isla laughs. "Rose, where the fuck did you go, and how do I get the old you back?"

I take the stupid shot glass and swallow the gin. "Oh, that's terrible." I cough and sputter.

They cackle.

"Come on," Chantay says, taking my hand. We head out to the

dance floor, where the combination of alcohol and anonymity pump through my veins, making it easier to dance—something that has always made me feel like a giraffe on roller skates. I dance with Chantay, and when Isla rubs her breasts against my back, gaining the attention of several guys, I can't find a single fuck. I don't hate it. I don't like it—I am completely indifferent.

I continue dancing with faceless guys, hot flesh, and grinding bodies until the alcohol fades, and I realize how much my feet ache. The guy I'm dancing with grinds against my thigh and lowers himself, his zipper catching painfully on my skin. I move to cover the scratch with my hand, and my dancing partner misreads the situation, closing his eyes and straightening as his hands settle on my hips. I barely turn in time for his lips to land on my cheek.

I shove at the guy. "It was just a dance," I tell him.

He snickers and backs up as he raises his hands and turns to look for someone else.

Oh, God. What Am I doing?

I look for Chantay and Isla but don't see them nearby. I move toward the bar, craning my neck to see if I can catch sight of them, and finally recognize Chantay making out with a guy near the bathrooms.

"Want another shot?" Isla asks, appearing beside me. "Gin seems to be your drink."

I shake my head. "No. I'm done."

"Are you sure?"

"Yeah. I'm going to leave." I coax my phone out of the small clutch I'd brought.

"Your crown sure fell fast, didn't it?" Isla remarks.

"Excuse me?"

She smiles cruelly. "You went from being on top of the world to...." Her eyes trail over my body, her grimace growing as she returns to my face. "*This*, overnight."

I move around her and struggle to get through the crowd until I hit the exit. I gulp the cool night air as I fumble to ignore all the missed calls and messages and open the app so I can request a ride.

Thankfully, I don't have to wait. A dozen cars are waiting for idiots like me to crawl out of the clubs and bars. The driver looks at the screen on his dash and recites my address back to me.

"Yes," I tell him. I'd bet my inheritance that I'm sober enough to have him drop me off at Chantay's so I can drive myself home, but Ian's story and the loss of Isaiah have me unwilling to take the chance.

I thank the driver as he pulls up to my apartment and slip out of the car. My feet hurt so badly that I'm guessing how many blisters I'll find when I take off my shoes as I stick my key into the door. Before I can turn the handle, the door flies open, and Olivia stares at me, her eyes wide, phone pressed to her ear.

"Where in the hell have you been?" she yells, her Southern accent stronger than usual.

I pry my keys from the lock and slip off my heels. I drop them beside the door as Olivia closes it.

She maims me with another harsh look. "God, you stink. Where have you been? Are you drunk?"

"I need a shower," I tell her.

"I have to go. I'll call you back," she says to whoever she's talking to on the phone. "I love you, too." Arlo. She sets her phone down and follows me into my room.

"You ran out of here this morning, and you haven't answered your phone or replied to a message all day," she accuses. "I went to campus security. I called everyone I know. I thought you were hurt, but instead, you went out and did God knows what!"

I turn around, facing her. "This is me," I tell her. "*This. Is. Me.*" I point at myself. Tears build in my throat, and anger arms a dozen soldiers with bitter words that prepare to fire back at her. I shake my head and disappear into my bathroom, where I close the door and crank on the shower.

27

ROSE

The shower turns cold, and still, I don't move. The chilling water is a welcomed contrast to the hot tears that continue to slip from my eyes as I sit in the middle of my bathtub, still wearing the cheap dress Chantay convinced me to wear.

The door opens, and the shower curtain is pulled back. I don't look up. I know it's Olivia.

"Oh, Rose," she says. The curtain shifts, opening all the way, and then she turns the shower off.

Without warning, she wraps her arms around my shoulders, pulling me toward the edge of the tub. "I'm sorry I yelled," she says, tightening her grip around me. She kisses my damp hair and rubs my bare arm vigorously, trying to warm me. Her grip loosens, and then a towel is draped around my shoulders and secured with another tight hug.

My cries echo in the shower, making my headache become a sharp and relentless pain in my temples.

"Shhh," Olivia whispers, clutching me tighter.

She holds me until my hair and tears dry.

"Come on," she says. "Let's get some warmer clothes on you."

I shiver and tremble as I stand and cringe as I catch sight of myself in the mirror. Chantay's dress is plastered to my body, my eyes are red and swollen, and my cheeks are stained with dark trails of makeup.

Olivia returns from my closet with a pair of sweatpants, a sweatshirt, and underwear that she sets on the bathroom counter.

"I'm a mess," I tell her.

"No, you're not." Olivia grabs a makeup wipe and swipes it across my face, rubbing gently at my cheeks. "It's just makeup," she says.

I change out of the dress and toss it into the tub. It hits the fiberglass with a *thwack*. I quickly cover myself with the warm, dry clothes.

Olivia follows me to my bed, where I lie down, burying my face in the pillow Ian's been using.

Olivia lies beside me on her stomach so we're facing each other. "What happened?"

New tears form and spill over my lids before I can stop them. "I realized I've been changing, or trying to, and this stupid site reminded me of who I am. Who I *really* am."

Olivia stares at me.

"I mean, of course, I haven't been sleeping with the team, but it wasn't all lies. Those were my rules." My eyes close. " I hate that I'm embarrassed. I hate that I feel embarrassed and ashamed when I know I have nothing to regret or feel ashamed of."

Olivia rests a hand on my back and rubs soothing circles across my skin. "You don't. You've done nothing wrong, Rose. Nothing."

"Then why do I feel so bad?"

Olivia shakes her head. "Because everyone else keeps telling you how you should be feeling."

I pull in a breath and try to steady my thoughts, wiping at the tears with my fingertips. "Anna told me she thought the rumors could hurt Ian's dad and the election and might even impact Ian's chances of being drafted." I choke on a sob.

"That's why you haven't called him."

I nod, my eyes still closed. "I keep hoping this will all blow over, and it will just go away."

Olivia curls around me and threads her arm under my neck, pulling me closer so I rest my head on her shoulder.

"I did this. I caused this."

Olivia shifts, holding my face with both of her hands. "Rose Genevieve Cartwright, you listen to me." Her eyes become glassy with tears. "You didn't do anything wrong. You are fierce and beautiful and brilliant, and the fact you chose to have sex does not make you bad or dirty or anything less than perfect."

I close my eyes and shudder.

"And if someone doesn't want to vote for Ian's dad because Ian chose to date a girl who wasn't a virgin, then fuck them," Olivia adds.

"I can't destroy both of their dreams," I tell her.

Olivia shakes her head. "You won't. You can't let Anna scare you into making this decision. You need to talk to Ian."

"I can't," I tell her, my shoulders racking with another cry.

Olivia kisses the top of my head. "He almost got on a plane home today," she tells me. "He's really worried about you."

Her words only cut me deeper. "I don't know how to be a girl-friend," I tell her. "I don't know how to do any of this. It feels like a giant game of pretend."

"No one knows how," she tells me. "No one knows what they're doing."

I want to tell her that she does. That, like Raegan, she makes being an amazing girlfriend look easy, and Arlo seems to know exactly what to do, and my mom knew how to be the best mom ever. I'm the one who trips and stumbles at every path and label, not knowing how to be a good daughter or sister or friend, but especially not a girlfriend. Instead, I tell her all the details of the day, from Amita assuming the rumors were true to smoking with Chantay and our trip to the club.

I expect judgment and a hint of disgust—but Olivia gives neither, offering me the same brand of kindness and patience she always has. And when I'm done unloading my raw feelings, I cry myself to sleep, arms tangled with Olivia.

Ian

"Dude. Sit down," Luis says from his bed.

"I should go."

"You should go to bed, is what you should do."

"She hasn't called or texted me since Tuesday night."

Luis winces. "I know." He does. I've told him at least twice. "Alexis freaked out when we were on the site, too. It feels like a huge invasion of privacy. Especially when it's about sex and being accused of something you haven't even done."

"How do I fix this?"

"You can't," he says. "This isn't a situation that a single person can fix. It's done. It happened. All you can do is be there for her. And if she's like Alexis, she's probably going to be embarrassed and mad for a couple of weeks, and then she might make a list of people she thinks did it, and pretend to be the next Sherlock Holmes. And you should learn from my mistake and be sure to support that shit, too."

"But why is she embarrassed to talk to me? I'm on her side. I don't care about this shit."

Luis shrugs. "I don't know, man. Chicks think differently than us. When that was Hoyt, he was sharing it and didn't care if people were throwing shade." He shrugs. "Then again, there was very little shade being thrown. Hoyt was met with a red carpet, and Rose was met with pitchforks."

I scrub my eyes with the heels of my hands.

Luis sighs. "Olivia said she's home. Why don't you message her? Or go talk to Arlo and see if he's heard anything."

"She's probably pissed at me for leaving. I should have stayed."

Luis sits up. "What would have happened if you'd stayed? Are you going to find everyone who posts something rude and punch them in the face? Would it change the rumors? Do you think Rose would feel better if you skipped out and we lost this game?"

I hit the mattress with my fist. Football has been my life and focus for so long, and right now, I'm struggling to care about the game or our undefeated title. "I'm so damn sick and tired of this fucking website."

"I know. I hear you. They have gone too far.." Luis reaches for his phone. "Listen, man. It's nearly two in the morning. We've got practice in less than six hours. You need to get some sleep and clear your thoughts. We'll get through this weekend, add another win to our record, and then we'll sort this shit out."

I wish I had ignored him and Arlo and gotten on a fucking plane this afternoon. I knew something was wrong before I even left, and now, the regret burns deep in my chest.

I reach for my phone and verify I haven't received anything from Rose before I message Olivia.

> Me: Is she okay?

> Olivia: She fell asleep about twenty minutes ago.

The dots along the bottom of my screen start and stop a dozen times before her next message comes through.

> Olivia: She cares for you so much, but she's worried about how this might impact you and your dad.

> Me: I don't give a shit what other people think.

> Olivia: I know. You guys will need to talk, but she's embarrassed. She might need a couple of days. I'm going to stay home with her all weekend.

Another heavy sigh. I led this war to her doorstep and left when the battle arrived. Guilt floods my chest. How do I apologize for abandoning her now when she needs me most?

> Me: I'm sorry I'm not there. I'm going to look at flights. See how early I can get there tomorrow.

> Olivia: I don't think that's a good idea. I know you want to be here for her and help, but Rose would be so upset with herself if you missed the game on her behalf.

> Olivia: It's sweet, and a grand gesture like that makes me know you care about her, but you have to focus on the game. I'll focus on Rose. Sunday, you can come and slay her dragons.

I sit up and throw on my sweatshirt before reaching for my bag.

"Man, tell me you're not doing this," Luis says. "The team needs you."

"I won't be able to play unless I go and make sure she's okay."

Luis groans. "Coach Danielson is going to be so pissed. What am I supposed to tell him? That you forgot your goddamn tampons back in Washington?"

I shove my feet into my tennis shoes. "We both know if our roles were reversed, you'd be leaving to be with Alexis."

"Yeah, and I also know you'd be telling me I was a moron and chaining me to the bed and telling me about the vow I made to this team."

"Well, now it's my turn to be a moron."

Luis expels a deep breath and shakes his head. "At least be a moron who uses his brain. Look up flights and get something booked. You don't want to spend the damn night in the airport." He punches his pillow and lies down on his side, facing the wall. "Next time, just send flowers. If Rose tells the other girlfriends you flew home just to hug her, we're all going to be paying the price."

"You're so full of shit."

He chuckles quietly. "I've got to pretend I'm still a tough badass. It helps when I'm out on the field."

Rose

I wake up and roll to reach for my phone. It's past nine. Olivia must have turned off my alarm, and I'm grateful. I don't know that I would have been brave or smart enough to have chosen to stay home again. Pride is such a fickle bitch.

The doorbell rings and then rings again and again, and I know without a shadow of a doubt that it's Anna.

Olivia doesn't move. She sleeps through her alarm most days. I flip off the covers and quietly close my bedroom door behind me before quickly checking for Juliet and opening the front door.

"You're so lucky I didn't come over last night!" She barges past me, dropping her heavy purse on our dining room table before turning her angry stare on me. "What in the hell, Rose? You just decided to go AWOL?"

"I didn't go...." Okay, so I did. I totally did. "I messed up," I tell her. "I was just *spiraling*. I had my first panic attack since the summer after mom passed away, and I was just ... losing it."

"Why didn't you call me? I would have come. I would have helped talk you down."

"Because I didn't want to be talked down," I tell her as tears fill my eyes. "I'm pretty sure I had to crash. I'm struggling to know who I am. Am I a fun, crazy, borderline rebellious girl, or am I an adult with a business plan, projections, and budgets who attends potlucks with her boyfriend?" I lift my shoulders. "And yesterday, I felt like I could never be the successful, intelligent version of myself that I keep working toward, and I thought maybe I'd been lying to myself. Maybe I wasn't meant to be anything more than some privileged brat who only knows how to have a good time."

Anna's eyes shimmer with tears. "I hate to tell you this, but those feelings of inadequacy and doubt, they follow you into adulthood." She steps closer to me. "You've always been so good at blocking out the garbage and the negativity, never caring what others thought. I was worried these rumors might hit you, but you were so confident.

So calm. I should have known better. I've seen how people chew someone up and spit them out over less."

I shake my head and move into our tiny kitchen to start the coffee pot. I'm not ready for another cry session, and I don't want to discuss why this felt different—why it still feels different. Plus, I'm feeling the effects of yesterday. My feet and head are both aching. "That's not reassuring."

"People are assholes," she says.

A laugh slips through my lips.

"But for every asshole, there are several genuine, kind, gracious people. Unfortunately, those assholes are sometimes difficult to see past."

"I don't want to mess things up for Ian or his dad."

Anna nods. "I know, and I shouldn't have told you about that. It wasn't fair of me to leave that burden on your shoulders, especially when it was over something you didn't do." She plants her elbow on the bar and drops her chin into her hand. "You didn't actually sleep with four hundred guys, did you?"

"Wouldn't you like to know?"

"I mean, I'm not judging. I'm just curious if that's possible?"

I smirk. "I'm sure it is, but no. Not even close. I don't have an exact headcount, but I didn't have sex for the first time until the end of freshman year at Brighton, and between all of my classes and yoga certification and teaching, it's not like I've had much free time. I slept with a few more guys last year before meeting Ian when Olivia and Arlo were in the early romance stages and were blissfully unaware and shooting all the aphrodisiacs around with their googly eyes. But then I met Ian, and I basically lost interest in all guys except for him."

"You know, if you had slept with four hundred guys, it would still be okay. You still wouldn't deserve to be mistreated and wouldn't owe anyone an explanation. Except for me, of course, because we did that disgusting blood bond back when you turned thirteen and were clearly possessed."

Laughter rolls through me. "*Possessed*," I repeat the word. "It was a tiny cut."

"I had to get a tetanus shot."

"Not my fault you didn't get your booster shot."

Anna scowls.

My smile wears off too quickly, and my thoughts navigate back toward Ian. "I need you to give me the hard facts. If I continue dating Ian, will it jeopardize his future or his dad's election?"

Anna drums her fingers on the counter and pulls in a breath. "Dad filed a court injunction yesterday to remove the site. I'm betting it will be gone before lunch, but we know how things can linger. Someone might bring the rumors up at some point, but I don't believe it will ruin either of their chances. It just might be one of those ugly things that continue to pop up for you, unfortunately."

"So Dad knows?"

Anna nods. "He was livid—at *them*, not *you*. I went over there yesterday, and he was calling in every favor from every contact he knew."

"I bet he was so humiliated to admit I'm his daughter."

Anna shakes her head. "Not even a little. I'm pretty certain he was ready to knock someone out yesterday, including the staff at Brighton and every asshole on social media that shared your picture. You can probably find a hit list on his desk of everyone he plans to call in favors against."

Her words rattle my confidence. Since Anna moved back, I've been seeing her more, but I've essentially taken care of myself for the past three years and change. "You're not blowing smoke up my ass about Ian, are you? You swear I won't jeopardize his future?"

"I'm not lying to you. This is going to be yesterday's news soon enough. I should have had my team learn more and reached out to Dad for his help before I said a word to you, and for that, I'm truly sorry."

The coffee pot does its final strange gurgle and shake and then beeps its glorious sound. I turn from it to Anna. "I could kiss you."

She smiles, but it's sad and forced. "I'm sorry I added to your stress levels. Kurt says I've forgotten how to talk to people, and I'm a little worried he might be right. I'm so used to dealing with crises and talking with others in the same field that I forget that what I say might change in ten minutes or an hour."

"Do you want some coffee?"

She nods, and I quickly fix us both a cup. "Ian called me yesterday." She wraps her hands around the mug I place in front of her. "He seems like a really good guy, and I think he really likes you—the *genuine* type of like."

I stir my coffee.

"This is where you smile again," she tells me.

"I freaked out," I tell her. "I ignored him, didn't call or text him back, and then went and got high, borderline drunk, and nearly kissed a stranger."

Anna closes her eyes and is no doubt counting in her head. "That's okay," she says, though her tone reveals she'd prefer to yell at me right now. "None of those things are illegal." Her eyes are still closed.

"But I'm pretty sure they violate every relationship rule." I dig my fingers into my hair. "I know it was stupid and reckless, especially when I have all this stupid attention on me already...."

Anna nods. "It was really stupid. And reckless but shockingly normal. Trust me, you're not the first, and you won't be the last."

"That's the first time being called normal actually feels good."

Anna snickers.

"How do I even begin to explain any of this to Ian?" I ask, genuinely terrified that he won't understand or forgive me.

Anna frowns. "The same way you're telling me. You be honest and explain you were freaking out, but you may want to mention you were freaking out because you like him so much. That would probably help."

I groan as I rest my forehead against the counter. "I suck at being a girlfriend."

"You made a mistake. I hate to sound cliché, but it happens. And now you learn from it, grow, and move on."

We stay in the kitchen and finish our coffee, and rather than discuss the stupid pictures or my stupid mistakes, we talk about the owl sanctuary and how she'd like me to sign up with her on a project to help the burrowing owls, a project I have no doubt our mom would have loved.

I finally bite the bullet when Anna leaves and turn my phone on. My chest constricts as alert after alert pops up—messages from my dad, Anna, Raegan, Chloe, Olivia, Ian, and more. I start with Ian's and read through the multiple texts he sent that range from asking me how I'm doing to more urgent messages asking me if I'm okay, which provide a timeline for when Olivia started to get concerned. The messages end shortly after eleven when I'd arrived home last night. Clearly, Olivia cleaned up more than one of my messes yesterday.

> Me: I'm really sorry. I know I messed up. If you have time to talk today, please let me know. I'd really like to talk to you. I'm staying home with Olivia and can chat anytime.

I know from Arlo and Ian that when they travel, they're often busy doing things as a team, preparing for the upcoming games as well as team-building exercises, but worry has wormed its way past my thoughts and straight into my heart.

"What should we do today?" Olivia asks as she combs through her wet hair. "We have a couple of movies left. We could get some brunch and hibernate all afternoon, or we could get out and go to Pike's Place Market and walk around a little."

Neither option is appealing, which creates a thought as bitter as yesterday's when I began spiraling. I don't want to hide in the apartment for the rest of the year and constantly fear what others say about me. And I don't want to shut everyone out like I proficiently did after my mom passed away.

"Maybe we head downtown and get brunch. It's nice out."

Olivia brightens at my words.

A knock at the door has me turning to look at Olivia. "Tell me that's not my dad," I say.

She winces. "Want me to check? I can tell him you're in the shower or taking a nap."

"How do I explain this? Something like 'Hi, Dad. I know we never had the birds and the bees talk, but thanks for helping me hide this slut badge...'"

Olivia frowns. "Call yourself a slut again, and I'm going to slap you."

There's another knock on the door.

I straighten my shoulders and unlock the deadbolt before opening it. My breath catches in my throat as guilt hits a new all-time high as Ian stands in front of me, one hand pushing his dark hair back. "Hey," he says softly.

"You're supposed to be in Arizona." All I want to do is kiss him, yet I don't feel like I have that right, not without telling him about yesterday.

Ian shakes his head. "I'm supposed to be here with you. I should never have left. Can I come in?"

I pull the door open wider. "Yeah. Yes. Of course. Please." God, my thoughts feel as unstable as my emotions right now.

"Ian?" Olivia looks as shocked as me, which is even more concerning because if she doesn't know, then Arlo likely doesn't know, either.

He smiles at her, then turns his gaze back to me. It's penetrating and intense as he combs over my features, taking an intel of my thoughts.

"I'm going to do some homework," Olivia says before grabbing Juliet and heading to her room.

"I am so sorry," my words blurt out without explanation or preparedness as Olivia's door clicks shut.

"You scared me," he admits.

"I know. I scared myself a little, too." I rub my fingertips along my forehead. "I have a lot to explain, and I know that, but I don't want you to lose your future for me. You need to get back to Arizona and play."

Ian reaches forward and takes my hand. It feels so good to feel his touch, like the sun warming my skin and heart. "I love football, but it's a game."

I shake my head. "But, it's not. You've worked so hard to get this far. And football has taught you skills and lessons and has brought you friendships that are unparalleled to other experiences. I know this because that's how I feel about yoga. It brings me a sense of serenity and peace and a connection to my mom that makes me feel sane. You can't give that up for me. Not now, not ever."

"It's not about giving it up. It's about making sure it doesn't rule my life to the point I lose you."

I shake my head, tears burning my eyes. "I don't want to be a detriment to you. The website lied, but there was some truth behind the rumor. I did have those rules, and I've slept with other guys. And I hate that there's a chance that my past could define your future. It makes me feel so ashamed, and embarrassed, and angry, and that creates an entire maze of contradicting thoughts and feelings."

Ian shakes his head and moves us over to the couch, where we sit facing each other. "I don't give one fuck about any guy before me. I care about now and the present and the future because *I'm* your future, and you're *my* future. Your decisions, your actions, your mistakes, and your triumphs—they all contributed to making you who you are, and I wouldn't change a single fucking thing, Rose. Not one."

Tears cascade down my cheeks. It's so hard to feel accepted and cared for—though it feels remarkably good. "I messed up yesterday." I proceed to tell Ian my conversation with Amita, my time with Chantay, and dancing with faceless guys, to Isla's comment that ended my night. My chest feels tight, and my cheeks are wet as I look at Ian and wait for his reaction, noticing his jaw is strained, and his eyes are hard.

"I hate that a guy touched you. It makes me feel unhinged to hear someone tried kissing you, but it was dancing, Rose. I don't want to date you so that you'll change who you are. I'm not dating you to strip away your independence. I want you to feel enabled and empowered to keep doing the things you love. And I certainly don't want other people's opinions to change your opinions or your will. I love that you don't give a fuck what people think."

"That's the thing," I tell him, wiping at my cheeks with the back of my hand. "I *do* care. I care what my dad and sister think. I care what Olivia, the team, Chloe, Raegan, and Alexis think. And I *really* care about what you think."

Before my words can settle, Ian's kissing me, his fingers weaving into my hair as his lips trace over mine.

When he pulls away, we're both breathless and as much as it pains me to admit it, I'm so damn glad he's here.

"I hate that this is happening to you. If I hadn't asked for your help—"

I shake my head. "No. This isn't your fault, and it's not my fault. I'm glad I wrote those articles, and the fact that they're going after me only proves we've shaken them." I study the reluctance in his gaze, grateful I can recognize it because our silent conversations have always felt so momentous. Like he understands me so completely and I him. "It brought us together."

He expels a short breath and reaches for my hands again, wrapping them in his larger, warm ones. "That was going to happen, regardless."

My lips curve, enjoying the idea that we would have ended up together eventually. "It sped things along."

He brushes the back of my hand with his thumb. "I should have been more persistent before I left last summer. I knew it scared you when I told you I was going to Italy, I saw it, and I should have given you seven days then."

Laughter tickles my throat. "I don't know that I would have accepted the stipulation."

He grins, but his eyes look remorseful. "I was borderline terrified you weren't going to a couple of weeks ago."

My smile grows, an attempt to reassure him. "Now you're stuck with me." I pull in a deep breath. My cheeks feel dry from having cried, and my head is beginning to ache again, and so is my chest as I consider what I need to do. "We should go get some food, and then I can drop you off at the airport," I tell him.

"I don't want you to face this alone."

I shake my head. "I'm not. Olivia's here, and now that I know I won't sink your future, I care a lot less about these stupid rumors. If people want to assume I'm sleeping with the football team, then who cares?"

"I still hate it."

"The site's been taken down," I tell him.

His eyes widen with surprise. "When? Are you sure it's down?"

I nod. "My dad filed an injunction, and they took it down an hour ago."

His shoulders fall. "Thank fuck. We should have done that from the beginning."

"The rumors will probably continue for a while, but if someone really believes them, then it's a reflection of them, not me, not us."

He kisses me again, building my confidence that is slowly beginning to assemble a new footing.

"Would it be okay if I invite Olivia to go with us?"

Ian nods. "Of course. I'm pretty sure I owe her a lot more than brunch. A kidney might make us even."

I knock on Olivia's door before pushing it open. She's on her bed, Juliet on her lap as she reads a romance book I suggested to her. She lowers the book, her blue eyes filled with questions.

"Rose. Ian's here," she whispers. "This is serious. Like serious, *serious*." She moves Juliet, who protests with a quiet *meow* before curling into a ball. "I hope you kissed the hell out of him. He just hit like the jackpot for brownie points."

"Well, he thinks he owes you a kidney, so you guys are equally enamored with each other."

She grins. "Have I mentioned how glad I am that you pursued your feelings for Ian and were willing to forget about your rules? I'm so damn proud of you. I'm proud of you for being so fearless, and for writing these articles, and for starting your empire. You, Rose Cartwright, are a badass."

I wrap my arms around her and hug her tight. "I wouldn't be without you."

Her arms constrict around my back. "Likewise," she says.

"Are you up for going to brunch with us before I take Ian to the airport?"

She smiles. "You guys should go. I have you all weekend."

I shake my head. "We want you to come—both of us. You're a huge part of my life and always will be. I've appreciated how inclusive you and Arlo have always been with me, and I want to ensure that continues now that Ian's a part of the picture."

Olivia nods. "Yes. Double dates. Vacations. Duplexes ... I'm on board with this."

I laugh, hooking my arm with hers, and find Ian in the living room. He looks so much less tense than when he arrived as he grins at us.

"Raegan suggested a new breakfast place," I tell them. "She said they have the best eggs benedict and french toast."

Ian nods. "That works for me." He looks at Olivia, and my heart melts. Not only does he look like a Roman God that makes me feel heard and seen, but he's also a god in the bedroom, and he cares about Olivia. I consciously drop every last wall and reserve I have toward our relationship, committing fully to him and us.

We spend breakfast laughing and sharing stories, avoiding the rumors and the past couple of days, and I'm so grateful for the reprieve from thoughts and worries as I enjoy my two favorite people. And when it comes time to say goodbye at the airport, it feels both easier and harder, wishing I could go with him and also feeling so much better than I did three hours ago when he arrived.

28

ROSE

Olivia and I sit on the couch and unload our bag of Mexican takeout. Yesterday, after dropping Ian off at the airport, we stopped downtown and walked through Pike's Place, where not a single soul recognized me. I wasn't the girl from the rumor site, and it reminded me this will wash over. Eventually. We ended the day at home with more Harry Potter and pizza.

This morning, we finally went and got my car from Chantay's, and on the way home, we got takeout to eat while we watch the game. Olivia slides my burrito over so it's in front of me on our small coffee table. She sets sides of sour cream, guacamole, and salsa and then reaches for the remote to turn on the game.

"Isn't it early?" I ask.

She shrugs, opening her nachos.

I recheck my phone for the thousandth time. It's becoming a fast habit with Ian being gone.

"It's totally normal," Olivia assures me when disappointment blooms in my chest when I don't see a message from Ian. "I haven't heard from Arlo all day except for the couple of texts he sent before I woke up. Game days away are all about focus and warming up and blah, blah, blah."

I chuckle, reaching for my burrito. I still feel nervous, and I don't know if it's about my impending Monday, or because I'm still in doubt that my dad's injunction will keep the rumor site down, or because I'm still feeling the effects of guilt from Thursday, but there's a heaviness on my chest that makes eating less appealing.

Olivia takes a bite of her nachos. "Oh! This is good queso. Try this."

I take a chip but nearly drop it when I hear Ian's voice on the TV. "What is he...? *What?*" I stare at the TV, seeing Ian with Paxton, their bodies and jerseys marked with black and red paint that my eyes race to read.

Skank

Whore

Slut

Queer

Cheater

Liar

"Joining me tonight are the captains of Brighton University from Seattle, Washington. This is Ian Forrest and Paxton Lawson. Guys, can you tell us about the message you're sharing and why you have these words written all over yourselves and your jerseys?" a woman reporter asks.

Ian places his hands on his hips, and I see "Murderer" written on one forearm and "Whore" on the other. "We're here, standing up to bullying. Someone decided it would be entertaining to post pictures of our team with false and often offensive material for everyone to read online, dragging people's names and people they care about through the mud."

"Rumors. Is that correct?" the reporter asks.

Ian nods. "They're intentionally lying, twisting stories, and fabricating others in an attempt to gain readership. For a while, it was a joke that we accepted, knowing we're in the public's eye, but they've continually crossed every boundary. They're beginning to go after people who aren't on the team, publicly attacking their character. And like most lies, they're more entertaining and addictive than the truth. So we've come out tonight to say enough is enough. We want to apologize to those impacted by the site and let them know we're done standing by. We won't tolerate this any longer." There's a silent threat glittering in his eyes.

Olivia is grinning, clearly in the know about this situation. But before I can ask her how she knew, the reporter asks them how the site has impacted the team.

Paxton leans forward. "It tested us, but ultimately it's brought us closer as a team. We're brothers, and when someone messes with one of us, they're messing with all of us, which extends to our loved ones. Someone wronged our friend recently, and we're done waiting for whoever is behind this to grow a conscience." He lowers his gaze to where 'cheater' and 'queer' are painted on his arms. "These aren't just words—they're weapons, and they're hurting people."

"What a great cause. Thanks for your time." They cut to another reporter, and I turn my attention to Olivia.

"What just happened?"

Olivia raises a brow. "I'm pretty sure Ian just warned whatever asshole is behind the rumor site that he'll disembowel them if they come after you again, in words Anna would approve of."

I chuckle, appreciating her attempt to inject some humor into the situation as tears cloud my vision. The other team members stand together, showing off the rumors we've all been accused of, stopping on Olivia's dad, Coach Harris, who has "Slut" written across his hat.

The camera pans to the cheerleaders, whose arms, legs, and cheeks all have the same ugly words written across them.

I sniffle, brushing a tear as it slides down my cheek, and Olivia hugs me for what has to be the hundredth time this weekend. "We plan to dress up and wear the words on Monday to school, too."

Tears are streaming from my eyes now, even though I'm smiling. "I can't believe you guys."

"We love you," she says. "And we're in this together."

.   .   .

MY PHONE RINGS forty minutes after Brighton wins the game. My heart feels so full and off-kilter that my hands are shaking. "Hey."

"I've been gone a day, and I already miss your voice," Ian says.

"I'm speechless," I admit. "Your interview, the way you guys wore those rumors, that you got the cheerleaders and coaches to do it with you...."

"Your dad got rid of the site. I'm hoping this will get rid of all the rumors."

"Thank you for what you said and did. I wish you were here," I tell him.

"God, I wish I was there."

"What time do you get home tomorrow?"

"Eleven and my only plans are to see you."

"I have brunch at my dad's and will be home around two."

"I can meet you there."

I swallow, unspoken words sitting heavy on my heart that come out in appreciation. "I need to talk to him. But next month, I'm signing you to the guest list."

"I'll be there."

"Thank you, again, for what you did ... for what the entire team did."

"It was a start," he says.

"It meant a lot."

"*You* mean a lot."

The butterflies in my heart flitter and then flutter.

"Goodnight, Rose."

"I'll see you tomorrow."

I lean back against my headboard, feeling the first sense of peace in days.

———

I ALWAYS DREAD BRUNCH SUNDAYS, but I'm dreading it, even more, today as I work at putting the rumors behind me. The site has remained down for nearly forty-eight hours, and this morning, when

I chanced singing on social media, I didn't see a single post about me. Instead, political drama filled my news feeds, giving me another ounce of hope.

"Are you okay?" Olivia asks beside me as I park in my dad's driveway.

"Just hungry."

She looks relieved to hear this—too relieved.

We climb out of the car and head to the front door, where I knock twice before pressing the lever open. He still lives in the same house we moved into shortly after he moved to Washington DC. The house is large, too big for him, yet far less lavish than many of the wealthy who call Seattle home.

"Rose," Dad says, climbing to his feet, a drink in his hand. His gaze is fleeting, making that twinge of shame sharpen.

"Hey, Mr. Cartwright," Olivia says. This is where Dad always corrects her and asks her to call him Bill, but today he doesn't. "How are you?"

Dad says nothing and instead walks over to Olivia and hugs her. "Thank you." His words are soft and gentle, and for reasons I don't want to consider, my eyes sting with fresh tears.

"Olivia, you want to come with me and get the drinks?" Anna asks.

I cut my gaze to my sister, begging and demanding her not to leave me here alone, but she evades my stare. Olivia looks at me, eyebrows drawn with the silent question about whether I'm comfortable with her leaving.

"Please?" My dad says. I don't know if my dad's directing the request to Olivia or me, but Olivia nods in response.

"Sure. I'll just be in the kitchen." She gives me a meaningful look and then turns and follows Anna.

Their footsteps fade as Dad turns to face me. He's wearing jeans and an old hunter-green sweater that zips down partway. He's owned the sweater for years, one of the many articles of clothing that lived in his closet here, waiting for one of his handful of visits each year. Anna and I used to tease him about leaving it unzipped so far because he always wore an old T-shirt beneath it that would have logos and pictures across the front that were always visible. Today, his shirt is solid white, and it's zipped halfway.

"I found out who started the website," he tells me, snapping me out of years past.

I blink several times, completely caught off guard. I expected questions, condemnation, and advice about how my decisions stand to impact my future as well as others.

"You did?"

He nods. "I want to talk to you about whether you want to press charges."

In all my thoughts and considerations about the site and wondering who it might be, revenge hasn't been high on my list, much less legal revenge. "I don't think that's my decision to make alone," I tell him.

He pulls in a short breath. "I can make my recommendations, or you're welcome to speak with my lawyer," he says, reaching for his phone to get the contact information.

"Aren't you mad at me?"

His attention jumps from his phone to me. "Mad?"

"Aren't you upset that I was stupid and reckless and completely fell off the map Thursday?"

His gaze flashes between mine, and he clears his throat. "I was concerned," he says. "When Anna called me and told me no one knew where you were, I was alarmed…" He clears his throat again. "But you've always taken care of yourself, and I know you're clever and resilient and—"

"Don't you want to know where I went and what happened?"

"Of course, but—"

"I push, and I push, and all you do is back up further and further. Why don't you care enough to get mad at me?"

"What would that do?" His voice rises. "If I tell you the sky is blue, you're going to tell me it's light blue, and if I tell you you're too smart to have a single major, you'll drop out of school. I have been patiently waiting, trying to honor your space and time, waiting for you to forgive me, and I'm starting to wonder if you ever will. I wish I could make her come back. I wish I could trade places so you could have your mother, but I can't. I can't do any of that, but I can shoulder your anger, and if that's what you need me to do, I will continue doing that."

I shake my head, tears returning with a vengeance. "I don't want you dead." I close my eyes, an entirely new brand of pain piercing my throat. "God, why would you think that? Why would you say that?"

He pulls his head back like my emotions and anger are misplaced and unjust. "You've hated me since your mom got sick."

"I've been mad at you since you let her go. It's taken me four years and a really shitty week to realize I'm always waiting for someone I care about to tell me I'm not worth the effort and leave just like you did."

He stares at me, but I can't read his expression through the blur of my tears. "Rose." His voice is broken. He raises his hand, resting it in his salt-and-pepper hair as he shakes his head. "What happened between your mother and me...." He shakes his head once more. "It will always be my greatest regret. Time and distance and living two separate lives took a toll on us and our marriage, one we worked to overcome for years. But the more we fought it, the harder it got. I loved your mother, and she loved me. We were a great team and best friends, but we hadn't been in love in many years. I didn't want to get divorced. I was terrified about what that would do for insurance and her treatments, but after all that she did to take care of you girls and me ... not fighting her when she asked for the divorce felt like the least I could do."

"I wanted you to fight it. I wanted you to fight me. I wanted you to be mad every time I got in trouble."

Dad wraps his arms around me, engulfing me. He holds me too tight for the first time in more than a decade, and for the first time in as much time, I don't fight him.

"I'm sorry for everything." His voice shakes, calling on my tears to increase. "I'm sorry I was gone and missed so much, and I'm sorry you've been so afraid, but more than anything, I'm sorry you didn't know how goddamn much I love you."

My heart aches with our admissions.

I don't lie to myself and pretend this will change everything, but I also stop myself from reinforcing walls that have existed between us for years.

I've been telling myself I don't know my dad, convincing myself he's a chameleon who can change hats at the drop of a dime based on company, but the truth is, I knew who he was, I just wasn't sure that he knew who I was or would accept me. Having him here, hugging me after so many hurtful words promised to taint our family name, has hope nestling into my chest, easing that ache.

Ian

I feel like I got hit by a tank truck. My back is sore. My legs are sore. Even my damn fingers are aching as Rose pulls up beside me at her apartment.

I hit the pavement and move toward her, forgetting about the website, the rules, and my discomfort as a smile claims her face. She collides against my chest seconds before her lips crash against mine. When I start to pull away so we can go inside, she curls her fingers into the top of my sweatshirt and tries to hold me in place as her lips press more firmly against mine. It's all the encouragement I need to slide my tongue across the seam of her lips.

She groans softly, her fingers tightening as she tips her head, meeting my demand with a delicious and eager swipe of her tongue that borders on desperation. I kiss her back with fierceness and intent that slays every question and doubt until she's breathless and my cock is straining against my jeans.

"I'm so glad you're here," she says.

I kiss her forehead. "How was brunch?"

"Surprisingly good. Also, a bit enlightening."

"Really?"

Rose nods. "Let's go inside. I'll tell you about it." She unlocks her apartment and slowly opens the door before flipping on the lights. We move into the living room, where we remain standing. I can sense her nervousness as she licks her lips and avoids eye contact with me for several seconds.

"My rules were inspired by my ex and by the loss of my mom, but I don't think I realized until this week and everything that transpired how much my parents' divorce played a part in my rules. When my dad signed the divorce papers, I was so angry with him—I've *been* so angry with him, and I'm still not sure if I'm mad that she got sick or because she died or because I really wanted to believe in happily ever afters and those stupid papers destroyed that for me.

"I know there are no guarantees or certainties, but I want to make a new rule—a rule for us," she says, as I find that place on her hip that feels like it was made for my hand because it fits so damn perfectly. "I want us to promise to fight for each other. No matter how hard it gets or how messy it gets, we fight to be together."

"We fight to *stay* together," I tell her, tugging her toward me as I nod. "I am so fucking in love with you. I have no idea what kind of craziness will come our way, but I know I love you and will always fight to be with you."

Her lips seize the rest of my words, all sense of restraint gone as she presses her chest to mine, fingers tangling in my hair.

"Is Olivia or Arlo going to be here soon?" I ask.

Rose shakes her head. "They went out and won't be home until late."

I claim her lips. We fumble and stumble our way to her bedroom, discarding our clothes along the way.

I run my thumbs over her bare nipples, and when she gasps, I kiss her even harder, loving how she rises to the challenge with a brutal swipe of her tongue and a gentle nip of her teeth. She runs her hand down my chest and follows my hips before grabbing my cock. "Feel how hard I am for you?" I ask her.

She kisses me again, her hand rubbing over my shaft. Her touch feels so good. My hips flex and thrust into her fist.

I moan into her lips and coax her legs apart with my hand,

finding her wet and warm as I slide my fingers over her entrance and circle her clit. "I fell in love with you the second I saw you."

She presses against my hand, another soft groan chasing my admission. "I love you," she says, lifting her chin a little higher, looking me squarely in the eye. "I am so in love with you."

I press my fingers into her and reach for a condom. "I'm so fucking lucky."

Rose takes the condom from me and sinks down to her knees. She cups my balls in her palm. I hiss, already too far gone for her to be touching me like this, and then her lips mouth goes over my tip, and I nearly lose it.

"Slow down," I tell her.

With my cock still in her mouth, she meets my eyes, and I see the humor and challenge in those gorgeous green depths.

"I want to be inside you," I tell her.

She lowers her mouth on my cock, rubbing my balls again. I drop my head back and release a long groan, fighting against my desire to fuck her mouth. She releases me, running her tongue up my shaft, and it feels so damn good I forget my fucking name. All I know is she's mine.

Her lips seal around my cock again, and she bobs her head up and down until I hit the back of her throat, and before she can test my strength any further, I pull out of her mouth, hook my hands under her arms, and drop her back onto the white comforter. I grab the condom from the floor, roll it over my length, and crawl over her.

"Tell me again," I say, positioning myself between her legs.

"I love you," she says. "I love you so much."

I sink into her in one hard thrust, and she moans, her eyes rolling back. I lean down and kiss her before moving, searching for every groan, moan, and gasp like my life depends on it. And when I find that spot that has her thighs trembling and her breaths coming as hard pants, I memorize it as she spirals, and then I lose myself to her entirely.

29

ROSE

"This feels really awkward," I whisper to Olivia as we climb out of my car. The same angry words that had marked the team and cheerleaders are written across our bodies and shirts.

Olivia grins. "We own awkward."

I laugh. "Is that a good thing?"

She laughs as she reaches for her phone. "I need to get a picture so I never forget the day I wrote slut on my forehead." She stops and leans close to me. "Say cheese!"

As I lean in and smile, a memory from the party a few weeks ago when I'd dragged Paxton and Hoyt outside surfaces. I'd gone back inside, angry with Ian, and had found Bobby. We were walking outside together when someone yelled, *'Say cheese!'* and I'd paused mid-step and smiled at the familiar face. That's why the picture was so familiar.

"What's wrong?" Olivia asks.

"I know who sent those pictures of me to the site."

"What?"

I nod. "I have to go."

"I'm coming with you!" Olivia follows me back to my car.

My thoughts repeat that night with increasing clarity as I latch my seat belt.

"Are you going to tell me what's going on? Should I call someone?" Olivia asks.

I shake my head. "The night of that party, I knew nearly no one. That's how I know. I remember stopping to smile and trying to make light of the situation and buy a few minutes because I was mad at Ian."

"Who was it? Do you think they're behind the rumor site?"

I shake my head and drive the fifteen minutes it takes to arrive at the familiar house.

I pull into the driveway and turn off my car, not entirely sure of what I'm about to say or do. Betrayal burns in my chest as I get out of the car and ring the doorbell with five angry jabs.

"Wow. Look at you," Chantay says, opening the front door.

"You helped?"

She has enough sense to act confused.

"You took those pictures of me," I accuse.

Chantay looks from me to Olivia. "It wasn't supposed to become a witch hunt. It was supposed to be a joke, a way to remind you of how much fun we used to have."

"Do you know what people have been calling me? How many people told me to kill myself?"

"You changed," she accuses in a shrill voice.

I nod. "I know, and if you had really been my friend, you would have supported it rather than working so damn hard to punish me for it."

Her brows draw low with anger. "They were ready to burn you at the stake when you showed up at my house, and I was the only one there for you."

"There for me? You're the one who gave them the kindling and passed me a lit match! I came to you asking to get fucked up, and you didn't ask me what was wrong or offer to help. Instead, you led me into the lion's den." I shake my head. "Don't come near me. Don't talk to me ... just don't. We're done. And if you share another picture of me, I will gladly sit back and watch my father's lawyers tear you apart."

"I'd like to see you try."

"Don't push me, Chantay. I'll fucking bite." I turn on my heel.

"Run away, Rose!" she taunts. "Enjoy your boring friends and your boring life."

I reach for my door handle and smile at her. "I plan to."

I duck into my car before she can reply, and Olivia climbs in beside me.

"I feel like we should do something more. Something else to make her pay for what she's done. I can't believe how many lies she posted and was still trying to act like she was your friend. And not to be rude, but I'm shocked she was smart enough to beat Cooper."

"She wasn't," I tell her.

Olivia twists in her seat. "I thought you just said...?"

"She sent the pictures in, but she wasn't the creator of the website."

"How do you know?"

"Because my dad threatened a massive lawsuit with the injunction, and the web hosting company gave him their name."

Her jaw drops. "Do we know who it is?"

I nod and start the car.

"*Rose!*" Olivia cries. "You know who it was?"

"I thought I knew the person, but this experience proved I don't."

"Are you going to tell me who it was?"

"I don't know," I tell her honestly.

Her jaw falls open again, and she shakes her head. "What? I can't believe you know. Why won't you tell me? Why haven't you already told me and Ian and everyone else?"

"Because I'm worried about everyone's reactions and the repercussions."

"*Repercussions?*" She nearly chokes on the word. "Whoever it is *deserves* repercussions. They are the ultimate cyberbully."

I get us back onto the main road that will take us directly to campus. "I know, but after being on the opposite side of this lens, I need to talk to them before making a decision."

Olivia sits in silence, no doubt considering my decision.

"I don't mean to sound hurtful or keep secrets. I was planning to tell you, and not like this." I scoff. "Hell, I tell you everything. But I need to talk to them first," I explain.

"I'll go with you. You don't need to do this alone."

I grin. "I told Ian I love him."

Olivia gives another shocked expression, this one perhaps superior to the last, making me chuckle. "Any other massive secrets you want to lay out there for me?"

"Fresh out, sorry."

I park, but neither of us moves to get out of the car.

"I was never a big fan of Chantay's, but I never thought she would betray you like that. I'm really sorry. I know how hurtful it is when someone breaks your trust, and I hate that she did that to you."

"I knew better. I mean, she never contacted me unless she wanted to drink or party, and I wasn't any better. We were probably a toxic relationship, enabling ourselves and each other to make stupid decisions and bad choices. I just never thought she would stoop to these levels."

"I hope you know I would never do that—I *will* never do that. I'll be here whether you want me or not. You're stuck with me."

I grin. "And you're stuck with me."

"Ready?" she asks.

I consider the last time I went to class, and my stomach lurches, but Arlo's tapping on Olivia's window with his knuckles before I can respond.

"How does he have such stalker powers?" I ask.

Olivia laughs. "I texted him."

Ian appears behind him. They're both wearing their practice jerseys, vicious rumors written across their skin.

"This stuff doesn't stain, right?" I ask, glancing at the red "Slut" written across my forehead.

"God, I hope not," Olivia says. "Arlo and I are supposed to go to my dad's tonight to take a family portrait for their Christmas card."

I smile at the mention of Arlo going with her, but I don't have time to comment because Olivia opens her door.

"Where were you guys?" Arlo asks as I read the word "Murderer" across his arm. They're wearing each other's rumors again, and it's doing something to my heart that makes my altercation with Chantay seem incredibly insignificant.

Olivia turns to look at me over the top of my car.

"I realized who took the pictures and needed to stop by their house," I tell them.

Ian's gaze turns hard. "What? How?"

I shake my head. "That picture of Bobby and me wouldn't leave my thoughts. All the others were candid, but that one, I was smiling and looking at someone, but so much happened that night, and it didn't seem important enough to remember, I guess."

"They created the site?" Arlo asks.

I shake my head. "No. But she submitted the pictures, which might be just as bad."

"Not to throw you under the bus, Rose, but Ian should definitely go with you to talk to *you know who*," Olivia says as Arlo and Ian shoot off a dozen questions. "He's a little tougher than me and maybe a tad more intimidating."

Ian's gaze flickers from Olivia to me. "Talk to who?"

"You sweetened me up for this moment, didn't you?" I ask Olivia.

She grins. "Do you really think I'd let you go alone? I still see this person as a deranged psychopath."

"Who are we talking about?" Ian asks, his voice lower and lacking patience.

"My dad found out who started the rumor site. I was planning to tell you, but I want to talk to them first."

"Why?" Ian asks.

"Because I know what it feels like to make a mistake and because I'm hoping they're going to tell me it wasn't their intention to be so damn hurtful to everyone. And because I don't want them to be treated the same way I was."

"I say let them get a taste of their own medicine," Arlo says.

I turn my attention to Ian. His steel eyes fix on me as his jaw flexes with thought. He slowly nods. "If you want to do this, let's do it together. This person has proven they're untrustworthy."

I want to object and remind them I'm perfectly capable, but I swallow that rebuttal and nod, not because I'm being compliant or afraid, but simply because I understand what it's like to care about someone and want to walk beside them through fire. Ian wants to support me, and I want to let him, and I want to do the same for him.

"Okay."

The four of us cross the street, where I pause at the sight of a stranger who's covered in rumors.

"Do we know him?" I ask.

A grin appears on Ian's face. "A bunch of people are wearing the rumors today. Even several professors. Apparently, we're not the only ones sick and tired of assholes."

"Let's hope it sticks," I say.

As we continue walking, students stare at us and whisper. It's definitely not the majority standing with us today, but I'm okay with that. Ian reminds me that it's not their opinions I need or even care about, and if someone is willing to believe a rumor rather than question it, they're not someone I want in my life.

"We'll see you guys later," I say, turning to Arlo and Olivia.

Olivia glances at Ian. I know how hard it is to trust someone else with the people we love, and I see that indecision in her eyes before she nods at him, entrusting him with my care before turning to me. "Text me and let me know how it goes."

I nod. "I will."

Arlo's hands clench into tight fists. I can tell he wants to come with us too, and while revenge is a factor, I have no doubt my safety is his top concern. "I'm not advising you to hit this asshole, but maybe you mention how hard you *can* hit people...."

I shake my head and grab Ian's hand.

Ian's brow creases when we reach the door, but he follows me inside.

Once again, the newsroom is mostly empty. Anthony being a terrible editor and annoying human, ensures it will be for most of the year, which makes me a little sad, considering it's been a place filled with energy and ideas in years past.

I pull in a breath and slowly approach Amita's desk. She blinks and pulls off her headphones as she swallows thickly. Uncomfortably.

"I've spent the last twenty-four hours trying to understand why someone I respected so much as a journalist and peer would write such awful and absolute shit," I tell her. "What were you trying to gain by hurting the football team? By hurting me?"

Amita slowly shakes her head. "You still don't get it, do you?" Her gaze flicks to Ian at my side. His arms are crossed over his broad chest, and anger rolls off him in waves. "Queer" is visible on his forearm, and I hope she reads it and the hurt intended behind that word is stained to the back of her eyelids like so many of the cruel words have been stained to mine. "Do you know that colleges spend more money on sports than they do on scholarships? That the cost of tuition has skyrocketed in the past decade largely because the budget for sports—for *football*—has gone up by nearly seventy percent? People can barely afford to attend college and then struggle for the next thirty years to pay off their tuition while guys who are good at hitting and running and catching a goddamn ball are glorified as heroes and given a free ride, though few will contribute to our society because they don't even have time to attend classes."

I shake my head, disgusted at her reasoning. "Then write about it. Inform people. Talk about how education is becoming something that only the wealthy can attain and how that continues to perpetuate the wealth gap in our country." I wave an arm at Ian. "What you did is no better than telling a woman she was raped because of what she wore. You villainized them when they aren't the ones at fault."

"And why in the hell would you go after Rose?" Ian asks. "She's not on the team."

Amita keeps her gaze on me. "You weren't supposed to be collateral damage," she says, looking almost remorseful. "You were just missing the point. You were trying to redeem them because they're hot and throw fun parties."

I lean back on my heels, realizing she never respected me half as much as I did her. "You think that's the only reason I cared? If this had been the wrestling team, or the soccer team, or the cheerleading squad, I would have done the same. I told you how immoral and unethical the site was."

"It was to draw a point." Her voice turns hard as her spine straightens. "You saw how fast everyone turned on you," Amita says. "Two hours. That was all it took for you to go viral. I posted about the team for weeks, accusing them of cheating, having affairs, and breaking rules ... I could have posted that they killed babies and drank their blood, and no one would have cared. And then I posted about you having sex with the team, and you became the enemy instantly." She snaps.

I hate that she's right.

"No one connected any of these points," I tell her. "Not even me, and I've been trying to figure out your objective for weeks. But it was lost in your anger and bigotry. You tried to point out a problem, and in turn, you became the problem." I shake my head. "Poetic justice, I guess. Leave the stupid site down. If you try to put it back up again, I'll expose you, and it won't be with rumors. It will be with the truth, which in this case is far uglier."

Amita stares at me, anger burning in her eyes. It looks painfully similar to my anger last week when I wanted to believe what people said about me didn't matter.

"How did you get the pictures and rumors?" Ian asks.

Amita slowly turns to him. "You'd be surprised how many people wanted to see you guys fall from your pedestal. After the first week, people sent dozens of emails daily."

"You lost sight of so much." I turn to leave, and Ian moves with me, his hand on my back. When we get outside, my eyes sting with emotions. I feel sad, hurt, and betrayed but also relieved, grateful, and loved.

"Are you okay?" Ian asks.

I shake my head. "She's a good person. I can't believe she would do this to try and prove a point. A point that no one even saw." I think about her words. "She deserved to be the editor this year, and I don't want to make excuses for her, but I kind of wonder if that played a part in this. Maybe she was hurt. Maybe it's because she didn't have an Olivia to sound every alarm and get mad at her, or a boyfriend willing to give up his dreams, or a dad who had the power to bring it all down?"

Ian gives me a tender smile and brushes my hair behind my shoulder. "She had a chance to stop."

I sigh. "I know. That's what hurts the most." I lace my hands around his neck. "I guess, on the positive side, these rumors brought us together."

He sputters and places his hands on my hips. "Brought us together *sooner*." He draws me closer, lowering his face so his lips are only a whisper apart from mine. "We would have found a way to each other, regardless."

I grin. "I'll take sooner."

His lips seal over mine, restoring my belief in capes and crowns and happily ever afters.

EPILOGUE

"Y ou should be a sexy pirate," I tell Olivia.

She raises a single brow. "I don't want to be a sexy anything. It's cold here on Halloween."

I grin. "How about Davy Jones?"

This time she rolls her eyes. "What are you going to be?"

"I was thinking of getting a gold flapper dress and being Daisy Buchanan." I don't tell her it's inspired by Ian and his purpose for throwing parties last year. While I tell Olivia nearly all of my secrets, there are a few I enjoy keeping.

"I love that idea," Olivia says. "And you could wear tights, so you're not freezing, although it sounds like the Halloween party might be on the smaller side. Rae asked us if we'd like to help. Right now, it's just her and Poppy making plans, and I think they want to keep it low-key to keep an eye on Paxton."

"That's going to be a hurdle."

"Arlo thinks if he and Candace stay broken up this time, Paxton will move forward in a better direction."

"Yeah, but can he? Move on, I mean. Those two don't seem capable of staying apart," I say as I pull up to the park we've been volunteering at.

"We'll see." She opens her car door, and I follow her, pulling my hoodie on. "I can't believe this is our last day working with Beacon Point and Shady Grove Park," she says as we meet on the sidewalk.

"I can't believe we managed to accomplish so much," I say as I look across the chain-link fence that is no longer broken, deformed, and rusted, leading us into the spacious park that looks like an entirely different space than it did when we started. While we can't take full credit for all the work, our group made a big difference and made some wonderfully unusual friendships along the way.

"Rose!" Bree calls my name and waves.

"I can't believe you ever doubted that you wouldn't make an amazing mentor," Olivia tells me as we head to Bree.

I release a heavy breath. "It's weird. I always thought my rules protected me from things I wasn't good at, but in reality, I'm pretty sure they just held me back."

My best friend's smile is kind and sincere as she hooks her arm with mine. "I think this is going to be our best year of college."

I shake my head. "They were all good, and they were all important. It led us here, right?"

"Did you guys see the new stuff?" Bree announces, her voice filled with enthusiasm as she reaches us.

I glance across the park again, disappointed that so many leaves are scattered across the area we worked so hard to clean.

"Someone donated new playground equipment, a disc golf course, and they're putting in a splash pad for kids in the spring. I can't use it because I'm too old, but still, it's pretty awesome," Bree says.

"Seriously?" Olivia's inflection reveals the same doubt I have. "You didn't hear this from one of the guys on the football team, did you? Because one of them might have been joking and—"

"I know better than listen to them," Bree says.

Olivia and I share a smirk.

"Paige announced it." Bree points at Paige and then looks at me. "Your boyfriend did it."

I shake my head. "Ian?"

"Well, I guess his dad did, but I'm sure it's because Ian told him ... or asked him ... or whatever. How rich is he?"

I look at Olivia, who looks just as shocked as I feel.

"Anyway, we're going to have the coolest park in Seattle, and it's in *our* neighborhood." Bree's smile triggers something inside me that makes me want to maul Ian and give him a million kisses.

"Regardless, you're still on the hook to come to my Thursday yoga classes."

She grins. "I've been thinking a lot about how you could make the classes more appealing to kids. We could try doing goat yoga or at least adding some sort of theme, you know? Sports or makeup or something more fun than breathing and silence."

I grin, searching for a sarcastic retort that doesn't seem to want to form.

"Oh, there's Sabrina. I'll be right back," Bree says.

Olivia looks at me again. "You did that."

"Did what?"

"Helped her come out of her shell."

I want to deny it. Similar to Ian's claim about how we would have eventually started dating, I have no doubt Bree would have learned who she was without me, but a small part of me appreciates taking a little stake in possibly helping her find her confidence sooner.

"Two o'clock, boyfriend wonder is on his way over." Olivia smiles and then waves. "I'm going to find Arlo. I'll catch up with you in a few."

I turn in time to see Ian taking his last strides toward me, allowing me to appreciate his confident gait, broad shoulders, and chiseled chest before focusing on his strong jaw, straight nose, and distinctive eyes. His lips come down on mine with a gentle brush. It's a casual and easy kiss, one that is quickly becoming a favorite because of its ease and frequency. I'm discovering there are a lot of wonderful habits and routines I enjoy now with my title of girlfriend.

"How was your morning?" he asks, placing his hand on my waist.

"Anthony offered me to write a piece about climate change today."

Pride shines in his gaze. "What did you say?"

"I didn't give him an answer. I told him I needed some time to think about it."

Ian chuckles. "Making him sweat?"

"He deserves it."

Ian's fingers tighten at my waist.

"How was your day? I heard you and your family made a large donation to help an amazing community."

"It was all my dad," he says. "I simply made the suggestion and pointed out the benefits. I was actually hoping to ask you to volunteer with me again."

"Oh yeah?"

He nods. "Isaiah's mom has an annual street cleanup at the crash sight. It's this weekend, and I'd really like for you to come with me."

I'm honored that he's allowing me into this vulnerable and uncomfortable chapter of his life. "Absolutely." I nod.

His smile is filled with appreciation. "Thank you."

I wrap my arms around his shoulders. "I'm always here for you."

His gaze settles on mine, and I feel that intense connection we've shared since before we even shared words. It feels like we're in a different dimension, another place and time where it's only him and me and us together.

"I love you, Rose. I love you so fucking much." His lips settle on mine again, and I tighten my grip, refusing to ever let go.

Thank you so much for reading Ian and Rose's story!

Please take a moment to leave a review on Amazon or the platform(s) of your choice (goodreads, Barnes and Noble, Bookbub, etc.) Reviews are incredibly helpful and I appreciate them so much!

Additionally, if you'd like to learn more about my books and future releases, be sure to sign up to receive my newsletter where I share exclusive material, giveaways, and more! Sign Up Now!

You can also connect with me:

- Follow me on Amazon
- Email: mariah@mariahdietz.com
- Like my Facebook
- Join my Facebook Reader Group
- Follow me on Tik Tok
- Follow me on Instagram
- Follow me on Bookbub
- Follow me on Goodreads

The Dating Playbook Series is a 7-book series of interconnected standalones (with the exception of Bending and Breaking duet.) See even more of Lincoln and Rae and meet more of Brighton's football team by reading the rest of the series:

Bending the Rules- Falling for your brother's best friend is the very worst of bad ideas, yet, Lincoln Beckett keeps bending every rule I make to stay away from him.

Breaking the Rules- Having a crush on her brother's best friend bent the rules, but what happens when they break them?

Defining the Rules- As Arlo works to recover from his injury, he's faced with an even larger problem when he meets Olivia, the coach's daughter.

Exploring the Rules- Tyler Banks is the billionaire heir of Banks

Resorts and Hotels, and he's met his match with Chloe with this explosive, laugh-out-loud, and outrageously sexy story!

Forgetting the Rules- When rumors about Brighton's football team begin to circulate, middle line-backer Ian Forrest has more to worry about than his reputation in this second-chance romance that will keep you laughing and falling even more in love with the team!

Writing the Rules- Quarterback Paxton Lawson has proposed the biggest lie of the year: fake date his sister's best friend, Poppy Anderson. But what happens when lies begin to feel like the truth?

Missing the Rules- Five years have passed since Lincoln graduated from Brighton. Catch up with him, Raegan, and the rest of the team in this unputdownable conclusion!

ALSO BY MARIAH DIETZ

ACKNOWLEDGMENTS

Thank you so much for reading this book. I can't tell you how much it means to me!

I knew I had to write this book after writing Defining the Rules, but I wasn't ready for it because I wanted to make sure I honored Rose and did her story justice. It took me seven drafts, a lot of walks, many tears, and a lot of good friends to complete this book.

A very special thanks to Ginger Scott, my cheerleader, sprinting buddy, and above all dear friend. You made this book possible.

And a huge thanks to my family, who have shared me with these amazing "people" at Brighton University.

Also, a special thanks to Autumn Gantz for being a constant sounding board and helping me find focus and organization during chaos. You're the best!

ABOUT THE AUTHOR

Mariah Dietz is a USA Today Bestselling Author and self proclaimed nerd. She lives with her husband and sons in North Carolina.

Mariah grew up in a tiny town outside of Portland, Oregon where she spent most of her time immersed in the pages of books that she both read and created.

She has a love for all things that include her family, good coffee, books, traveling, and dark chocolate. She's also been known to laugh at her own jokes.

www.mariahdietz.com
mariah@mariahdietz.com
Subscribe to her newsletter, here

Made in the USA
Middletown, DE
13 September 2023

38215238R10210